I0635988

# An Absence of Angels

## Julie Harris

Copyright © 2011, 2013 Julie Harris

All rights reserved. *An Absence of Angels* is a work of fiction. No part of this book may be reproduced or transmitted in any form or by any means, electronic or mechanical, including photocopying, recording or by any information storage and retrieval system, without prior permission in writing from the publisher.

Excerpt from *All or Nothing At All* by Carmen Willcox, used with permission.

Cover art and design by James at Go On Write.

ISBN-13: 978-0-9873456-5-3
ISBN-10: 0-9873456-5-6

FOR CARMEN, PIA & MICHELLE

# Chapter 1

How he wished his head were full of stone, like the stone beneath his feet, for if it were stone he wouldn't have to listen to that horrible noise.

From the tower window, the little boy stared down into the water, trying hard not to hear the angry, agonized screams. He wanted to be anywhere else—in the courtyard perhaps, watching the farrier, or even the washer-women—but no, his place, so the master had decreed, was in the chateau. One so young could not go with the men.

Christian had gone with the men of course, but Christian was sixteen.

If it wasn't so cold, the boy would have scaled the cliff below, and dived head first into the quick, rocky waters of the river just to get away from that noise. If it wasn't so cold.

"Geoffrey! There you are! Have you not heard my calls!"

How had she found him so quickly? Dare he jump now?

"You were told to wait by the door!"

He dared not look into his aunt's eyes, fearing what he'd see there.

"Come with me, now!"

He nodded—it was all he dared do. Brave warrior, frightened of a woman. Geoffrey de Polignac looked around at his brother's chambers. Should Christian not come back from a skirmish with the Dupuys, should an arrow find his brother an unwilling target, then this would become his chambers and he would then be squire to his uncle, Robert de Polignac. He would not be his aunt's house-boy any longer: the page with no dignity.

Again she called, frantically. Hit me, he whispered. I beg you hit me, don't scream at me. Geoffrey closed the door to his brother's room, for if Christian discovered that his younger brother had been an unwelcome guest there in his absence, hell would have a kinder tongue and fist. Geoffrey climbed each narrow, uneven stair winding forever to the right, and wondered if he should slip, and roll all the way down, landing with a thump in the great hall. Would that be his escape from the sounds of his aunt's sister in childbirth? Could he pretend to break his leg?

"Geoffrey!"

The boy winced. He'd heard the villagers summon their pigs in a friendlier way. He put his ear to the thick wooden door. Had he looked through the keyhole, he would have witnessed the goings-on in that chamber, but the sounds were already enough to dampen any curiosity.

"Yes, Milady?" he called, his eyes closed. Please God, don't let them say I must go in. Why couldn't someone else be here to do this? Why did the mistress send everyone away except for me, Ella, and that horrible old crone from the village?

"Geoffrey, you must help us! You have little hands. Only you can do this!"

Geoffrey felt all blood rush to his feet. He wished he had fallen down the stairs now.

"Milady, please don't ask me to come in. I cannot. I cannot come in."

"Geoffrey, now! Now, or she will die!"

The little boy froze. There would be hell if it was learned that he hadn't obeyed his aunt's command. If not flogged, he would be cast out into the cold, and his future as a brave knight would be over before it had begun. Tears formed in his bright eyes. His hand, flat on the door, was hesitant. It would take all of his strength just to push it open. "Dear God, I've been good. Please don't let her ask this of me," he prayed, his voice a shaking whisper.

"Geoffrey! Now!"

The next scream was unlike any he'd ever heard. It hurt his ears and was far worse than Christian's fists had ever been. With his belly full of bees, the boy pushed on the heavy door.

It creaked open.

He saw many things at once. His aunt's sister, Vianna—the pretty woman who sang so sweetly—was on the wide bed, her knees up. She was still screaming. Marys, his aunt, had her head between the woman's legs. Geoffrey thought he would faint. What was worse? The sight or the sounds?

"Geoffrey, quickly!" Marys grabbed for his arm. The boy squealed and tried to squirm free as she pulled him with great force towards the screaming woman.

It was cold outside, almost snowing, and dark clouds hung low, but the lady Vianna was drenched with sweat and thrashing about so hard that the old crone from the village had barely the strength to hold her down.

"See, Geoffrey? See? This should not be a leg. It should be the head. Do you not see?"

Geoffrey's head was pushed down but he saw absolutely nothing—his eyes were closed tight and his mind was screaming, Oh, God, why have you done this to me? Why?

"Put your hands in and turn it, boy. You must."

The little boy squealed, "No!" He dived for the door but Marys's bloodied hands caught his long, fair hair and she dragged him back to the bed. "Do this, you little runt. If my sister dies, so will you! You will die slowly! A far worse death than any Moor could have dreamed of!"

Anger in her eyes and on her tongue. He had never seen his aunt this way and it was more frightening than any threat of a mere Moor. She shook him, grabbed his face hard. Her nails were claws. The smell of blood was sickening. "You have no courage!"

The little boy felt his heart swell with rage. How dare she say he had no courage!

"Help us, Geoffrey. It is too late to send for the physician. Help us."

Geoffrey shook himself free of her talons and her imploring gaze. He glanced, calm now, at the birthing woman. All was quiet for a heartbeat and peace reigned, then the screaming began again. Nothing was happening that he understood.

"Which way am I to turn it, Milady?"

"Its head must come first."

The boy walked to the end of the bed and looked. He could see the leg, perhaps it was a thigh? He wondered that if he put his hand in there, would he hurt the woman? He touched her leg. The white skin was streaked with blood. Her muscles were rigid. The crone had something in the lady's mouth now to silence the screams. Geoffrey looked over the mountainous belly. The pretty woman's face was almost blue from straining so hard. Then she calmed and stared up at the ceiling, seeing nothing. She breathed as if she had just run most of the way to the abbey and back. How could such small hands hurt her when all she knew was pain? He looked at his mistress.

"Now, Geoffrey!" Marys slapped him on the back of the head.

Geoffrey swallowed, closed his eyes and obeyed. It was hot in there, hot and slippery, and the smell was unlike any he had ever known. What would happen if his master returned now to this?

"Geoffrey, can you turn it?"

His small hands touched a thick cord, then a tiny shoulder and finally, a head. But the baby was caught on something. Is there room in there for my two hands? he wondered, and he eased his left hand in.

"Milady, I'm trying but it seems caught on... caught on... I can't! I fear I will hurt it if I do this!" Wide terrified eyes looked up at his mistress.

"My sister cannot die! The baby matters not!"

How could she say such a thing? Geoffrey wondered, heart racing. Through his hands, he felt the tension within and the hard pulsing of muscles trying to force the thing out. Still it remained caught until his small hands eased it to the right and downwards. Geoffrey withdrew his hands and opened his eyes. There was a great issue of blood and mucus. The screaming continued, although muffled.

Marys thrust him aside so hard that he skidded across the flagstone floor and rolled. He sat up quickly, brushed off the straw and rushes, and tried to see what else was happening. The crone screamed at him to leave. His presence was forgotten immediately.

Geoffrey got to his feet as his aunt said, "Vianna, it is coming, it is coming. One more push, my love, one more push..."

The baby came out onto the bed and lay blue and unmoving. All was silent. The baby was dead. After all of this, it was dead.

"Let me see," the pretty woman cried. Geoffrey's eyes filled with tears. He looked again to the baby on the fouled bedclothes. It was a boy, and the long, thick cord was still attached to its belly, and led back into the dark, deep insides of its mother. Transfixed, Geoffrey was all eyes as something else ejected from the woman's body. There was no other baby in this horrible mess, but the cord was attached to it.

His mistress sank to her knees, howling.

"Milady?"

His aunt didn't hear him for her howling so he spoke louder.

"Milady, there's another. I felt two in there."

Marys wiped her eyes on her sleeve. "Nonsense, boy. There's nothing."

And the screaming began once again. This baby came out head first and slid easily into Marys's hands. A girl, crying from the moment she took her first breath; crying and angry. She was very angry indeed.

Geoffrey saw the way Marys lifted the bloodied child and showed her sister the sight, but the lady Vianna saw it was a girl and turned her face the other way.

It was as if she wanted a boy. Only a boy. He backed out of the bedchambers when he heard the pretty woman say, "I have failed. I have failed you both..."

Geoffrey stumbled down the stairs, those words echoing in his mind. Most of all, he still could not escape the wailing, which was harder now, harder and louder than ever before. This time it was his aunt's anguish. She could not have children of her own. That much already he knew.

At times, in the depths of night, had he not heard his aunt's tears and his uncle's despair at them? Had he not more than once crept to Christian's room to find an answer to his question for if anyone would know, Christian would. Although Geoffrey loved his aunt, he feared her as well, and when she was upset, all close by were in grave peril. So he had crawled into his brother's bed fearing what tomorrow might bring. "What is it now?" Christian had mumbled.

"They argue again, Christian."

"Put your fingers in your ears and a nail in your tongue, fool." Christian had kicked him from his bed.

And as it was just before dawn that time when Geoffrey, wrapped in his rug, went down to the kitchens where Ella was waiting, his cup of milk already on the stool. Often this happened. She, too, must have heard the mistress's howls echoing throughout the castle.

Ella was a tall, thin woman whose age seemed a mystery to all except herself. She was always kind to him and gave him warm milk, and let him speak when no one else would. She had been soaking grain that morning. He remembered it well. "Dry your tears, Geoffrey," she'd said, "For the problems of this house are not yours alone to keep."

Geoffrey had taken up his milk and sat on his stool in the corner of the kitchen. He'd sipped the milk. She had put some honey in it for him. Why did she always pretend she was gruff and uncaring? "This house is my house, too. Why must I not care if someone is distraught?"

Ella had turned to him. "This house is not yours, Geoffrey. Were you born before Christian, this may have been yours one day. But it is not the way and can never be. You will only serve it and if you are unlucky, you will serve it with your very life. You feel too much of the wrong things, child. Harden your heart before all is lost."

The words she had spoken in the past now flew into his mind like a bird straining against the force of the wind. He sat on the stone step, wishing again that the stone beneath him could be his heart, because hearts of stone could never feel pain.

Now it was snowing and a little warmth had settled within the Chateau de Lavoute Polignac.

"Geoffrey!"

Oh God, not again, surely? He closed his eyes, his lip trembled.

"Geoffrey! Find Ella!"

He didn't have to, for Ella had heard the calls and was coming up from the kitchen. She appeared, wiping bread dough from her forearms and fingers. She flicked her rag over her shoulder and ruffled Geoffrey's head as she walked past. He remained on the stairs, morose. "Christian returns," she said as she took the stairs up, lifting her skirts high as she went. "Wash yourself, boy."

9

Geoffrey was on his feet at once. The quickest way to the courtyard was through the kitchens, where he found a pail of cold water by the door. It took immense rubbing with Ella's polishing rag dipped in the water to remove the dried blood from his hands and forearms. Excitement was building. Christian returns, and there was so much to tell him. So much.

And there, at the door, the little boy waited impatiently for sight of his brother on that tall, bay gelding. What a handsome pair they made, his brother and the horse. But first through the gate was the master, followed by four of his knights. Geoffrey knew each's name but they never spoke to him unless it was an order to fetch this, boy, fetch that, boy. And so far he was page to none although every day he lived in hope of being chosen by one; either Louis, Acelin, Raoul or Michel. Michel was by far the friendliest to him, but today Geoffrey felt it was not wise to speak to anyone. Something terrible had happened. He knew it by their faces.

Michel dismounted and nodded to Geoffrey. Words came but died instantly as the stable boy came out to take charge of the horses.

His question, "Where is Christian?" became, "What happened to your arm, Michel?" But Michel walked on by, his left arm a bloodied mess at the elbow. Weren't the sleeves of mail supposed to stop injuries?

"Not now, boy." Michel's face bore witness to a silent pain.

Geoffrey guessed what had happened—there had been another confrontation with the Dupuys over the small stretch of roadway through the woods, north of the village.

"Is my brother dead?" he finally asked of any who would hear, but no one listened. Tears stung at his eyes. No, he thought. No, if my brother is dead they would have brought his body home. Surely it would not be left to rot on Dupuy land? Or perhaps he was captured and he now dies of hunger in a cage suspended from the tallest tree in the valley? My brother is dying as an example to those who would dare...

His thoughts ended abruptly. His heart lifted. Coming through the gate was Christian. "Christian!" he called, happily. "Oh, what a day it has been!"

Christian said nothing. He was not riding his horse, but leading it on foot, and across the saddle lay a body.

Geoffrey ran to meet him, to see who it was draped there, but Christian pushed him aside so hard that the boy tripped over a water trough. And whilst on the ground, Geoffrey saw the downturned, dead face of Henri, his brother's aged teacher. Henri was to be his teacher in only one more year, when, his master said, God willing, he may have grown a little taller and found a little more strength. For how could one so small wield a sword of war which was twice his size?

Besides, it was a favorite and humorous entertainment for the others; for Raoul and Acelin to say, "Boy, put my sword in keeping." Oh, and wouldn't they laugh as the little boy dragged the heavy sword, with its razored edges, across the floor? They would order him to lift it, not drag it, but lift it he could not. He knew that one day he would have one of his own, which he would lift and use with ease. One day.

He'd seen the knights at play, wielding their swords with only one hand yet the weight of Christian's old mail hauberk was enough to crumble Geoffrey's knees. Even his brother laughed, and called him girl for that was how he looked to others. And often the men would grab at his privates to make sure that nothing had in fact, fallen off.

Now what was this? His teacher-to-be, Henri, lay dead? Mortally wounded perhaps? What will become of me now? Geoffrey thought. Who would teach me the ways of manhood as Christian had been taught: the care of horses and how to fight, the most important lessons of all?

Geoffrey wanted to cry at his unanswered questions. What would become of him now?

"Are you deaf, Geoffrey?"

He looked up at Christian who was untying Henri's body.

"What?"

"Ella is calling for you, girl."

"I am not a girl!"

"Girl," Christian repeated. "Pretty, pretty girl." And Henri's body slipped to the ground. Geoffrey was on his feet and prepared to attack because of this newest insult, and he froze at the sight of Henri. How old he looked now that he was dead.

"What happened to Henri?"

"His heart, the old fool." They were only words though, because Geoffrey could see more than just sadness in his brother's eyes. Had Christian been crying? Geoffrey was trying to get a better look at his brother's face when Christian pushed him away again. "Pest! Girl! Go back to the kitchens where you belong, little woman."

Geoffrey's trapped rage exploded. He leapt over Henri, his small hand clamped around his brother's throat, but Christian was too long in the body and arm to be bothered by one so small. He pushed Geoffrey away till he had the boy at arm's length and neither swinging fists nor kicking legs hit anything but air.

"Ah, it snows," Christian said, boredom in his voice, still fending off his brother's futile attack. "We must deliver Henri to his wife now, girl. Help me with his belongings and fetch up the cart. Be a good girl and I will speak to Ella for you." Christian let go. Geoffrey swung once more and split his knuckles on his brother's mailed arm. He held his hand, danced around, moaning, trying not to squeal because anger made it hurt more.

Christian sighed, took up the hand and inspected it. "You'll live," he said. "Fetch up the cart. Do as you're told for once."

Working together, they put Henri's body and all of his belongings from his chambers into the cart. The body would remain at his wife's house in the village until its burial in the abbey graveyard whenever the abbot and the master decreed.

Christian tied his gelding to the back of the cart and got up to drive. He looked down at the fair-haired, beautiful boy whose eyes filled his entire face. "Are you coming or not?" he asked.

Geoffrey, waiting for the offer, leapt into the cart. They drove out of the chateau courtyard and over the narrow drawbridge. As they travelled across the bottomless drop, Christian glanced at his brother. The boy's knuckles were white, his eyes were clamped shut. Once the wheels touched the rough track, the boy was relieved. Christian tried not to laugh. They journeyed up into the hills where the track was narrow and winding and covered on both sides by thick woods. "Does his wife know?" Geoffrey asked.

"Yes, of course she knows. The master sent word."

"Will she be crying?"

"Are you afraid of the tears of a woman now?"

"I am afraid of nothing."

Christian smiled and looked away. He had to or burst into laughter.

Geoffrey wanted to tell his brother what he'd done that day but for a moment dared not. He held tight, hoping Henri didn't bounce out of the cart on the way down the rough slopes. It had been hard enough getting Henri's body into the cart in the first place, he didn't want to do it again. "Do you know where his wife lives?"

"Yes, I have been there many times," Christian said, laughter lighting his eyes.

"Why is it that you go everywhere and I cannot?"

"Your time will come."

That was all Christian ever said. Your time will come.

"What did you want to tell me?"

Geoffrey said nothing for a little while as his mind formed the words to make it sound even more dramatic than it was. But was that possible?

"Tell me, Geoffrey. I am listening."

But Geoffrey could not say a thing. "I... no, I cannot. I am sworn to secrecy for all of my life."

"Secrets? Who with a right mind would trust you with a secret?"

Geoffrey glanced at his brother, saw the smile and decided to ignore it. He held his hand out instead and watched the snowflakes fall everywhere but onto his palm. "Do you never wonder why there is snow?"

"Why would I wonder about that?" Christian asked.

"Do you never wonder what angers our God so much that He takes away the sun and leaves us to shiver?"

Christian, unable to reply and a little taken aback by this sudden outburst, asked, "Why do you think it is, girl?"

"I think it is because He wants us to notice the sun when it finally does shine again."

"Go to a monastery. The life of a monk would suit a fine thinker such as you."

"No."

"No?"

"No. I will be a knight, far better than you and braver, and stronger. And," he added, "Many women will love me."

"You've been dreaming again. A knight you will never be."

Geoffrey finally caught a few snowflakes and licked at his hand. It was no use punching Christian now, he would only hurt his hand again and besides, it was too far to walk back to the chateau in the snow.

"There is something wrong with your head, Geoffrey," Christian said, but even that heralded no reply. The boy was quiet, thinking. Dreaming. That was all the boy ever did—dream.

Soon enough they reached the village and many came out in the light snowfall to stare and wail—already they had heard the news of old Henri's demise.

Geoffrey watched from the cart as Christian sank to one knee and offered his sympathies to Henri's aged wife. And behind Henri's wife, Geoffrey could see a serving girl standing there, wearing little but rags, her dark hair wild and loose, as were her eyes as she feasted upon his brother. Strange looks indeed passed between the two.

Soon enough, Henri's body was taken from the cart by three village men. It was a long, cold while before Christian came out of the house and this time he unhitched his horse and said to Geoffrey, "Go home now and tell the master I have been delayed but I should be home before nightfall."

"But I can't drive back alone."

"Do you not tell me how brave you will be? There is always a time to begin. Go."

Then the serving girl appeared behind Christian as he tied his horse and she put her arms around his waist.

Geoffrey had to drive all the way home, alone.

He had never driven on his own before. His fear of the cliffs became unwarranted because the horse had good feet and he simply looked the other way. Nor did he worry unduly about crossing the drawbridge—he didn't look down.

That night, he ate in the kitchen with Ella.

"You are very quiet this night, Geoffrey."

"Much has happened today to confuse me."

She waited for him to relate his woes as he normally did, but he paddled amid his broth instead and nibbled on his bread thoughtfully.

"Are your thoughts of the birth today?"

Geoffrey looked up quickly. How was it she always knew what tormented his mind? "Did I kill it, Ella?"

"No, Geoffrey. I had to take it away, lay it out for burial. It was already dead. You did not kill it."

"Oh. I thought I had."

"How could these hands kill anything?" she asked and touched his hand just as he was lifting a hunk of bread to his mouth.

"One day, yes, I will."

"You will what, child?"

"I will kill. I shall be known as the... as the... as something. I will be bigger and braver than any knight who went before me."

"Is that not so?"

"That is so."

"I heard you cry today."

Geoffrey looked at her, then to his hands. She let go. He was ashamed now.

"I say, do not be ashamed of your own tears, child. It is the way of God to cleanse all of his little souls."

"I do not like bathing and I do not like crying. Both are things men do not do."

"And witnessing a miracle sometimes will make even the hardest of hearts weep with joy."

What is this nonsense she speaks? Geoffrey wondered. "It was not joy. Surely God would not make miracles such as those so hard to bear? I felt the pain of the Lady Vianna as if it were my own." He stared at his bowl. "And what miracle was it, anyway?"

"The birth of your new mistress."

"My new mistress?"

Ella leaned closer and whispered, "What I am to tell you, you must never say to another living soul, Geoffrey."

He leaned closer, too eager for this secret.

"It was the daughter of your mistress who was born here today and her name is Adelina."

"But the baby came from her sister."

Ella chewed on her lip. "You know about men and women, do you not?"

No, but already he was a master at pretence. He thought of his brother with that serving girl and he had certainly overheard men talking. He always listened eagerly but had no idea what they were talking about.

"The Lady Vianna lay with your uncle and in her he planted his seed and it grew to what you witnessed today. Yes?"

Did it? Geoffrey wondered silently. "Yes, Ella."

"Adelina is your new mistress now."

"How can an infant be my mistress?"

"We must all serve her as we have served the others of his household. You will swear on your honor never to speak of this. Adelina is daughter of the master and mistress, yes?"

"It's a lie."

"It's the only way your uncle can continue his line. It is unfortunate that the boy child did not live."

"I must serve the baby I helped to birth?"

She nodded.

"Christian will, too?"

"All in this house will, and so, too, the entire village. Now, eat. When you are done, take this food to the lady Vianna. But do not eat of it. Should you eat of it, God will punish you severely."

Geoffrey finished his meal, drank his broth and picked up the tray for the lady Vianna. "Please say there will be no more screaming?"

"No, child. It is long over now."

"Good," he said, "I don't like it when people are in pain."

Ella wanted to ruffle his hair, see his smile, catch the twinkle of his sky-drenched eyes and hold him tight, so she could pretend he was her son yet again.

"Ella?"

"Child?"

"Have you had many babies?"

"I have had nine. Only one lived and for a very short time."

Tears welled in his eyes when he heard this news, and she saw his questions forming but said, "Go now, Geoffrey. Go."

"You are the only one who understands me," he said and he walked off, balancing the tray carefully.

Ella's gaze rested on the jar given to her by the master himself only moments after he had arrived home and had seen for himself the new child. 'Speak of this and I shall use your head as a target,' he had said.

A tear filled Ella's good eye.

Geoffrey balanced the tray all the way up the tower stairs, and knocked on the chamber door. The crone let him in. The bed linen was clean now and the woman was bathed, too. He could smell lavender in the air. It was pleasant.

"Milady," he said quietly.

"What is it, boy?" she asked.

"From the kitchen, Milady."

"Come closer, boy. Bring yourself closer to me."

Geoffrey crept closer and put the tray on the bed. The woman was propped on a mountain of cushions and was dressed now in a white nightgown. The crone lingered. "Leave us," the pretty woman said, softly. The crone left although she didn't want to. Geoffrey sensed it. "Come closer, child, beautiful child."

He came closer by one step only. She reached out and touched his hair, so long and fair, and she caught it, curled it around her finger. She looked very tired, very pale, very sick, and she breathed as if it were a terrible chore.

"You have listened to me sing when none other would."

"I like listening to you sing, Milady."

"Today you were here, yes?"

He nodded.

She put her finger under his chin. "Always look into the eyes of a lady, Geoffrey."

She knew his name? His heart lifted.

"For if you look into the eyes of a lady, you will always see the lies there hidden."

He frowned. What did she mean?

"Such a beautiful boy you are."

Geoffrey looked at his feet.

"Had you not been here, I would have died and so would the baby have died."

His face flushed. He didn't want to remember what he'd done, what he'd seen. He wanted to be elsewhere, anywhere but here.

"I can but thank you, child. I thank you with all of my heart. How I thank you." She was silent for a moment, drawing breath, straining for it. "Serve my daughter well, Geoffrey. Promise me you will let no harm come to her. Swear on your life, child. Please."

"I could never harm that baby, Milady. She is yours. And that is why I could never harm her." How he wished he could stop the tears stinging behind his eyes. How he wished he could stop his hands shaking so, even though he had them clasped behind his back, tight.

"It will be our secret. Come closer, child." He came closer still and she reached out, held him close and tight, so tight that her heart was slow and steady against his ear, and he liked it, he did not push to get away. Then she drew him away gently and her tired eyes searched his face with a softness he would never experience again in his life. "Will you now go and tell your uncle that I wish to speak with him? I fear I have not great time left me."

He wasn't sure what she was talking about. "Milady, the master is very busy with his men and he is always angry if he is interrupted."

"Geoffrey, tell Robert that I must now speak with him alone. I fear I am dying. I have not the time left me. Go now. Quickly." She kissed his cheek.

Geoffrey backed away, and his voice shook when he said, "Perhaps if you ate some food, Milady, you would regain your strength?"

"For you alone I shall try to eat."

By the time he'd backed to the door, Vianna was lifting the bowl of broth to her lips. She sipped it. "Tell him, child, that it is urgent and he will come," she whispered, tears in her eyes, tears of pain.

Geoffrey shot from the chambers, a bolt from a crossbow. He was screaming, "Master! Master!" repeatedly as he pelted down the spiral stairs and crashed into Raoul who was still in his hauberk and could not move aside fast enough to avoid the collision. Nor could Raoul save the boy from falling without falling himself, so Geoffrey toppled the rest of the way and thumped to the ground floor, seen now by an army of curious onlookers, each stunned into an amused silence. The boy's nose was bleeding from the impact with Raoul's hard, mailed body. Strong hands lifted him to his feet and inspected the damage done. Raoul saw little except a bleeding nose. He grunted and began climbing the stairs once again.

Everyone sitting at the long, hewn table was laughing. Even Michel. Geoffrey's pride hurt more than his nose and tears blinded his vision.

"Master, come quickly, for the lady Vianna says she is dying."

Robert, a giant of a man whom Geoffrey had learned to avoid at all costs, even though he was his dead father's brother, tiredly rose and excused himself from the gathering. Robert touched Geoffrey's face, turned it this way and that, grunted and handed him a rag to stem the flow of blood. "Calm down, boy, and tell me again."

Geoffrey repeated his statement as best he could from under the rag as he led the way upstairs, too aware of his uncle so close behind, until a large hand came down on his small shoulder.

"Geoffrey, wait."

"Master?" Fear lay in his eyes, and he couldn't look any farther up than his uncle's belt.

"Has the lady Vianna eaten yet?"

"Yes, I think so."

"Good," he said.

Geoffrey walked on, knocked on the chamber door. There was no reply. Robert opened the door as if it were but a feather. He bent low to walk in, and he whispered three words. "Oh, dear God."

Geoffrey strained to look.

The lady Vianna lay across the bed, her head and her long flaming hair touching the floor, her pretty face now ugly, contorted from agony. From her mouth and nose came foaming blood and it dripped to the colorful rug which Michel had brought home from his first eastern campaign.

"Summon your mistress, Geoffrey, but tell her not that her sister is dead. Go, boy. Go and say nothing of what you have done or seen this day. Go."

Geoffrey ran again, calling frantically for the lady Marys.

Geoffrey had never seen a dead person until that bleak November day; then he had seen three in quick succession: a baby, an aged knight, and a beautiful woman.

He was only eight years old, a small boy with a very good memory, who stood shaking on the castle stairs, thinking, my mistress will kill me, just as she promised to kill me. I will die slowly, in more agony than even a Moor could have dreamed of. He stood there, willing now to take whatever fate had to offer.

But his aunt caught her long skirts in her hands and fled by.

Her wailing and her misery had no end.

# Chapter 2

Geoffrey sat in the sun, shielding the precious manuscript with his arms as he tried to read. He had finally captured a few moments of peace until either Michel found him for the afternoon's practise with the quintain, or he was summoned for something trivial by either Ella, the mistress Marys, or that brat, Adelina.

The manuscript, lent to him by abbot Jean of the Benedictines close by, yielded little of great interest to him today, or perhaps it was simply because Geoffrey couldn't concentrate. He could not concentrate in his tower chambers, either, nor could he concentrate in the great hall. Ella talked too much to study in the kitchens, and the brat annoyed him constantly and seemed to find him wherever he tried to hide, so here, finally, Geoffrey had found a little peace. At least, he hoped he had.

The late spring sun was warm, and the writing before him still not enthralling. His mind wandered constantly.

Before long, the brat found him. He didn't know she was there until he was hit on the back of the head by something foul that also splattered onto the manuscript pages. It was horse dung.

Geoffrey took a deep breath, prayed quickly for patience, and closed the book. He set it on the grass, covered it with its red, silken cloth, then he looked out into the distance and waited. The next missile did not hit his head. It covered his back, stained the white linen of his shirt and he could tell by the force applied that it was intended to hurt, too.

"Milady, I beg you, do not do this."

"Or what!" came the dare from perhaps ten, fifteen yards behind him.

"Or you will be very sorry!"

She never was, nor was she ever caught engaged in such unladylike things. What would her mother say if she could see this now? From behind, the girl's laughter was biting. On a good day, Geoffrey could walk away and pretend she was not there, which seemed to work very well—most of the time at least. But on other days his patience was stretched to breaking point. This was one of those days and he knew the brat would not desist her torments, either, until one of them got into trouble and it was never Adelina.

The next projectile splattered against his billowing white sleeve. "I am studying, Milady," he said aloud, then whispered, "I am trying to find the reason why I should not throttle you right now, this very minute."

"You are too stupid to study! Your ugly head is full of rocks!"

Geoffrey closed his eyes, bit his lip so hard that he could taste blood. Ignore her, he thought. It can be the only way. Was there any place in the entire land where this monster would not find him? Soon, he thought, she will bore of this and either go away, or come closer.

Geoffrey heard the grass crunching behind him as she approached cautiously. The little brat was very fast on her feet as she charged and, in one swift movement, coupled with a piercing scream, she rubbed a handful of fresh horse dung into his hair. She shot off, squealing, as she normally did, calling out that he would never catch her, never, daring him to chase her through the garden and into the hundred places she could hide with ease.

Tiredly, Geoffrey rose to his feet and shook the dung from his long, fair hair. He perused the garden, the roses, the hedge-rows. Perhaps today she would know to choose a place untried? There was a new haystack against the stable wall. She was not behind the cart next to the hay, but Geoffrey glimpsed the bright color of her dress as she burrowed into the middle of the haystack. Luck was with him, for Michel appeared through the open gate, and dismounted. His gelding instantly produced a large steaming deposit.

Geoffrey walked to Michel and asked, "Michel, have you not seen our Lady Adelina in your travels?"

Michel noted the stains on Geoffrey's white shirt, tunic and hair, and he hid his smile as Geoffrey reached down to take a good handful of the fresh dung. Michel swept his hood back, scratched his head and said, "Have I seen our Lady Adelina? No, I cannot say I have seen her this day." Michel kicked into the haystack and said, "Is she wanted for another serious crime?"

"Oh, she is wanted true enough."

"Then after you've found our lady, you will move this hay before nightfall. And use the newest, sharpest pitchfork to expedite the matter. But be careful that you do not do yourself an injury."

"Injury?"

Michel reached for the pitchfork, but the girl did not fly squealing from her burrow in the hay. Geoffrey took up the pitchfork which Michel had thrown at his feet. Now both his hands were full. "Where is it to go?" Geoffrey asked as he drove the pitchfork into the edge of the haystack.

Adelina burst out, barefooted, red dress flying, but today she hadn't chosen her escape well. Geoffrey caught her around the waist, turned her upside down and with his other hand, rubbed the hot mess of horse dung into her face. "A present for my lady!"

She coughed, cried, cursed and fought, so he dropped her to the ground. She looked up and snarled at him. She snarled at Michel, too, but he simply stood watching, amused. Geoffrey stood back. "Pooh, you stink. Get away from me."

She charged at him on all fours and sank her teeth into his shin. "Adelina! No! Adelina! Michel, get her off me!"

Michel leaned against the high wall and watched, smiling all the while.

"Help me!' Geoffrey cried.

"What? Can you not defend yourself against a little girl?"

Geoffrey tried to push her away but she bit harder and clung like a wild animal to his leg. He had no choice. He reached down and grabbed a handful of her flaming hair. "I will hurt you! Stop this now!" He tugged, but still her sharp teeth were clamped onto his leg, the grip as fierce as a dog's and just as savage till the melee abruptly ended.

"What is going on!"

Both Geoffrey and Adelina shied from the sound of Robert de Polignac's roar.

"Now see what you have done," Geoffrey mumbled between clenched teeth.

"Adelina, stop biting Geoffrey!"

She did, and covered her head with her hands. Behind in the air, she started crying but it lasted only a moment for tears did not work with her father. "Look what he did to me, Papa! Look what he did!" she cried, indignant.

Robert de Polignac gazed down at his daughter. Her newest dress, painstakingly hand-sewn, was torn, fouled. "Girl, get inside and scrub that... from your face. Now!"

Geoffrey offered his hand to help her to her feet but she spat at him and ran inside to the kitchens, howling, tripping on the long skirts she detested. No doubt as soon as she was out of earshot, the howls would subside. Brat, Geoffrey thought.

"Come with me, Geoffrey. I have news," Robert said and dismounted.

Geoffrey followed Robert into the stables where the master tended to his own horse. This was odd indeed. He was preoccupied, perhaps it was bad news?

"Are you responsible for the mess my daughter is in?" he asked.

"I have no excuses, uncle, except that she aggravates me so. I was trying to study and..."

"Enough."

"Shall I see to your horse?"

"No. I have news as I said. But first, see to that leg of yours. Damned girl. What am I to do?" Robert muttered, more to himself than to Geoffrey, and he made his way into the chateau.

Geoffrey washed his leg with water from the horse's trough. Evidence of the brat's teeth was plainly visible two inches above his right ankle. It was not bleeding hard, but the skin was punctured by five sharp teeth and it stung fiercely. Geoffrey limped over to collect his manuscript and searched the castle for his master.

He was waiting in the great hall, already sitting at the long hewn table, a tankard half drunk already. It was his most potent wine, too. So the news, indeed, was not good.

"Sit, Geoffrey."

Geoffrey sat, put his manuscript onto the table and nervously stroked the silken cloth cover.

"A message has come from Le Puy. I know not whether to believe it. At first I did not, until I was given this. Now I know not what to believe." As he spoke, Robert withdrew a medallion from his undershirt fold and studied it sadly, but as yet he did not pass it to Geoffrey.

"Is it news of Christian?"

Tired eyes turned to him. The nod was barely perceptible. A stone of great weight settled into Geoffrey's belly and lay there, twisting occasionally. Robert put the medal into Geoffrey's palm, and closed the boy's fingers. The master left his hand there longer than necessary but before any more emotion showed, he turned his face away, reached for the tankard and drained it. He leaned back with a huge sigh.

Geoffrey loosed his fingers and turned the medallion over. It almost filled his palm, this medallion that his brother, when but a mere child, had discovered in an old abbey ruin. It depicted Lust as a woman with a snake coiled about her and there was a toad suckling from her breast. Geoffrey remembered the day his brother had first shown it to him. And he remembered, too, the last image he held of his brother, riding out, fully armoured and armed, and his words, Lust will keep me safe!

Christian was never without it. He believed it would always keep him from harm.

Until now, it seemed.

Geoffrey looked at it for a long time without seeing it. His mind was filled with images of his brother's stripped body left to rot somewhere in the south. Killed by Moors. "Where was this found, Uncle?"

"Constantinople, barely a month before the city fell. Or so I was told."

"Do you think he is dead?"

"I don't like what I feel at this moment, Geoffrey, but how, indeed, will we ever know should his body never be returned to us?"

"Did this come to Le Puy by Dupuy hand?"

"It seems so. I understood the amusement in the eyes of the priest."

"If so, then that family of snakes is taunting you again. My brother is not dead. No."

"Geoffrey..."

"No! I would know if he was dead!"

Robert studied his fingernails. The leather on his half-glove was wearing thin.

"No, it is simple. The chain has broken, you see, here? Perhaps it fell off during a battle, and he was unaware of it and..." Geoffrey's voice trailed off because the truth lay in his uncle's eyes and worse, he had lifted his hand for silence.

"How old are you now, Geoffrey?"

"I am seventeen. Almost eighteen." And still nothing but a squire, he thought dejectedly.

Robert refilled his own tankard but did not offer Geoffrey to partake for the afternoon was not yet done and he did not need Geoffrey to be injured by a lance or a sword whilst drunk. "Michel tells me that you are improving daily."

"Would I demonstrate my abilities this afternoon?"

"I have seen for myself," Robert said with a half smile playing on his lips; his smile not hiding in his beard.

"Please, do not judge me on what you saw this day? The Lady Adelina is, well, she torments me, it is true, but she is only a child and I cannot harm her. It is not because I am soft of heart or head, she is just a little girl. I am not soft, uncle, and I don't care who may have told you this, but I say now, I am not... Why did you ask my age?"

Robert sighed.

"Are you considering sending me to search for my brother?" he asked, hope alive in his bright blue eyes. "If you cannot spare Louis or Raoul for this, I will go. I know that their duties here are numerous and they cannot be spared."

Robert was uncomfortable. He shook his head. "No, boy. I cannot send you south. A better and quicker death it would be if I kill you myself. You are not a warrior, Geoffrey. Your mind thinks, yes, I am brave, I am fierce, but your heart... Geoffrey, no. No, you are not a fighting man. It is not in you. And for one such as you, nor should it be. You have other gifts. Knights there are plenty of."

"But it is my brother..."

"All the more reason another should go. Michel has made the journey thrice already."

"Michel is old."

Robert looked into Geoffrey's eyes and silently questioned the statement just made. Again, Geoffrey knew he had said the wrong thing, for Michel was fifteen years younger than the master, which would, if his words were true, make the master more than ancient.

"Michel will make the journey to find your brother and bring him home, alive or not."

Tears stung at Geoffrey's eyes. What was this? Did the master feel Christian was like a lost son? What about me, uncle, what about me? his inner voice pleaded but his mouth remained silent.

"Geoffrey, clear your mind and listen to me."

Geoffrey was still stroking the silken cloth, or so he thought, till he followed Robert's gaze and saw that his fingers were clenched on the soft fabric, tight.

"I have no son, this you know. Since the time Adelina was born, I had hoped that Christian would not marry another until my daughter was of age, for then, Geoffrey, your brother would rightly inherit the estate and I would hand down to him my title. Your brother has always been as a son to me. He thinks as I think, he does as I do." Tears shone in Robert's eyes now as he spoke with affection and love. "I, too, cannot accept that he is dead. Medallion or not. In this way we think alike but only in this way. It pains me that I could not stop him from this Crusade for that is the way of his spirit and it is the way of the Church, and who is to defy the Church and not suffer? No, I cannot accept that he is dead. But I cannot risk your loss, Geoffrey, for you are my last hope."

Now what is he going to say? I am second choice to marry the brat? God, spare me the ordeal and take me now, Geoffrey thought sadly as he stared at the manuscript. He finally asked, "If my brother is dead, who is your choice as husband to Adelina when she is of age?"

Robert sighed. "One of wealth and power."

"Who?"

"The time has yet to come to choose, Geoffrey. And it is not your business who I choose to marry my daughter. Should your brother return, all is well. Michel told me that today you took two geese with one arrow, is this true?"

"Yes, Uncle," Geoffrey said, numbly, trying to look the other way. "We would not be feasting on goose this next meal were we to rely upon the archery prowess of Michel." Anger alone forced the words from his lips. He loved Michel, he admired him. Was Michel not his beloved teacher? "I am also adept at the mace, but I wish the handle was longer."

"And the sword?"

"I can wield it, yes," he admitted, not quite a lie.

"And have you used either the mace, the battle axe or the sword on a man? Have you never been fired upon by the crossbow? Have you never watched the friend beside you hit by such a bolt?"

"The opportunity has not arisen." And it never will, he thought to himself, knowing the master could read that from his mind as well. How many squires were there in the land who had already seen proper battle? Geoffrey was not amid the numbers.

"Geoffrey?"

"Master?"

"Go back to your studies and do not lose the manuscript the abbot Jean has lent you. This chateau, surely the entire land, has not the wealth to replace such a work. Or so I am told."

Geoffrey swallowed and remembered the pages splattered with horse dung. "I am treasuring it, Master, guarding it with my very life."

"Good," Robert said. "Leave me now, boy."

Geoffrey stood up and made to go but Robert reached for his hand. The grip was tight. These are fingers of an artisan, a musician, a doctor, a man of letters. Certainly not those of a warrior, Robert thought dejectedly. "Give my daughter back all that she gives to you, Geoffrey. Spare her nothing."

"I cannot, Master."

"Why is this?"

"I have no wish to hurt her now or evermore."

"You hurt her more by allowing her to willingly pain others and feel none in return. She will not learn civility if this continues."

"But I swore I would..."

"Yes?"

"I was thinking aloud, Master. I shall return to my studies now. And I shall be using the quintain before sunset. With my sword I shall take its head on my first pass. Should you wish to attend and witness this, of course."

"A quintain does not bleed, Geoffrey, and nor does it cry for mercy. Do not forget this," Robert said and indicated the manuscript. "And do not forget that we shall not know the fate of your brother until Michel has returned."

"And should Michel not return?"

"Go."

Geoffrey picked up the manuscript, smoothed out the red silk cloth cover and held it to his chest as he walked with it, but once out of the great hall, he held it under his left arm. The silk slipped off to the floor and he picked it up, threw it over his shoulder. Geoffrey took the stairs to the kitchen two at a time.

In the kitchen, Adelina was sitting on the stool he had once used as a boy, and Ella was busy scrubbing at the girl's face. Adelina poked her tongue at Geoffrey and snarled.

"A lady does not pull faces," Ella said and scrubbed harder with a damp rag.

"Ow, ow!" Adelina retorted, hoping her mother would soon come and save her from this atrocity. Geoffrey stopped, picked up an apple and crunched into it, then snarled at Adelina whilst Ella was not looking. The little girl bared her teeth again. He imitated.

"Scrub harder, Ella. I fear I can almost see a pretty face showing through the filth."

"You will never call me pretty and live!"

Geoffrey smiled. She wanted to be a boy and was assured of it in her mind even though her body was female. And when she bared her teeth again, which made Ella scrub even harder, all Geoffrey wanted to do was laugh: she had one tooth missing from the top. One less sharp fang to assail him with. Hadn't she come to him with the loose tooth? Hadn't he pulled it out for her?

"Stop tormenting your mistress," Ella said.

"Tell her to stop tormenting me."

"She will be a fine lady one day. She will be such a beauty that fine men from all over France will stand in line just to dance, or touch her hand..." As Ella droned on about future impossibilities concerning the brat, Adelina, he noticed, was reaching into the huge bowl which contained Ella's bread dough.

Geoffrey knew what was coming and he said nothing whilst the girl took a handful of dough and brought it up slowly. Ella was too caught in her own fantasy of tomorrows to see what was happening today. Armed only with a squeal and a handful of dough, Adelina thrust both into Ella's face and rubbed the sticky mess in. Released, for Ella was blinded, the child took off, tipping the stool over, squealing again with laughter, but Geoffrey caught her and held her upside down. Apple in mouth, he pretended to drop her into the cauldron of warm water suspended over the pit coals.

Adelina screamed in terror and kicked him in the face for she hated water. But Geoffrey held her there, ignoring her terrors. After all, he was busy doing what the master had decreed, and enjoying it, too.

At that moment, the mistress Marys walked in.

"Geoffrey! Put her down at once!"

Geoffrey closed his eyes and tipped Adelina back to her feet. The girl ran straight to her mother and clung to her middle, burying her face in the mistress's skirts. "What is this on your face? Ella! What is this? It smells like, Mon Dieu, what's happened to you? Is that bread dough? Geoffrey! Will you not answer me!"

Ella tried to save the situation but Geoffrey knew that Marys would listen to no one who dared accuse her daughter of any wrong-doing. "Was I, Milady. I am at fault here. We were at play earlier, a mock battle. Adelina won, of course. As always."

The girl's bright, green eyes peeked out from the comfort of her mother's soft camelot cloth. She heard the lie but could not believe it. "In the course of our battle, we fell, Milady. Adelina fell into horse dung and I did, too, as you can see. Ella, well, she…"

"I fell, Milady. I slipped."

"No harm is done."

Marys knew it was all a lie but she admired the loyalty. She drew Adelina away, a soft finger rubbed at the ingrained filth on that pretty, young face. "Adelina, look at what you have done to your new dress."

"It was Geoffrey!"

"Upstairs now, to your chambers. We will bathe together and you will wash this dress. By yourself."

"But Mama…"

"Upstairs." Marys patted the little girl on the behind as she sulked off. "A mock battle?" Marys asked Geoffrey, glancing towards Ella who was battling to remove the dough from her skin before it dried and adhered like resin. "What are you teaching my daughter?"

"Nothing, Milady. But I fear she has watched me in training since she was but walking. It is only a game, one I am sure we will both come to regret in due course."

"Clean yourself, Ella, then prepare me a bath. As for you, Geoffrey. I will not allow this to continue. Mock battles, indeed. She is not a boy to frolic in, in, horse dung and stable hay."

Geoffrey nodded. What was he to do now? Did she think he was God? For only God could stop the likes of Adelina. She grew worse with age. A demanding babe for sure, a demanding infant whose every whim and cry was attended to instantly and what had she become because of it? Uncontrollable. Her moments of peace, of being human, were exceedingly rare. However, when the infant hurt itself, who did it always stumble to? Under whose nose did it thrust the injured part? Was it really one kiss from the page, Geoffrey, which could take away the pain?

He sighed. Adelina's days of being an infant were long gone. Now there were orders from the master to give back what she had given and Geoffrey knew they were easier decreed than obeyed. For if she again hit him on the back of the head with a lump of wood, how could he take that same lump of wood and do the same to her?

Children of the same age he had often seen in the village and they played without much violence, with some concentration and gaiety. All Adelina knew was how to inflict pain. Perhaps if she had another of her own age to play with? No, that had been tried when she was younger and the child in question was never brought back to the chateau for its mother feared it would lose its very life from Adelina's rough play.

What had he caught her doing when she was but six years old? Adelina, dressed as a boy, had tied another poor child, the daughter of a washer-woman, upside down from the castle keep, using an intricate array of knots, certainly, and she must be secretly commended for that, but had Michel and Geoffrey not come along when they had the child would have strangled to death. Adelina of course could see no wrong in the game.

And she was forever in Geoffrey's chambers, too, drawing his sword across the flagstone, blunting it purposely or stabbing at his bedclothes with his dagger, or dropping the mace on her feet... would this nonsense never end?

Safe now, though. He had some time left to study before the sun fell to late afternoon, so he took the chance whilst Adelina was upstairs, bathing with the mistress, and he found a patch of warm sun, away from the wind, away from the garden, away from, he hoped, everyone. Geoffrey climbed up to the rampart and sat. It was too close to the cliffs here, Adelina would leave him be for she feared heights as much as she feared water.

Geoffrey sat on the narrow ledge, rested his back against the stone wall and breathed deeply of the late spring air. Soon it would be summer and perhaps then he would be invited as a true squire to ride beside his master in the next round of tournaments. But the knowing in his heart told him otherwise, that the master was aging; that tournaments, he often said, were a considerable waste of time and of money better spent elsewhere.

Geoffrey touched the silken cloth over his shoulder and spread it over the manuscript. Abbot Jean from the abbey was helpful and kind, true, and very hopeful as well, but the life of a monk was not for Geoffrey. Why was it that no one else knew this, though? He'd become far too accustomed to others telling him what it was they felt he should be, and he had never forgotten the words which lay unsaid in the lady Vianna's eyes barely moments before she had died.

Serve her well, Geoffrey. Promise me you will let no harm come to her. Swear on your life, child. Please.

For only the lady Vianna was able to see into his soul, to recognise what lay there, hidden, and above all else, she believed in its truth. She believed in him. Yes, a knight he would be. One day.

Perhaps in the next year he would finally grow taller? For even now in the year 1204, at age 17, Geoffrey de Polignac was no taller than a peasant woman whose back was forever bent from carrying wheat sheaves. But he compensated for a lack of height in other ways, by first lifting rocks of different sizes and weights and often Christian would catch him doing so. Geoffrey's mind returned to that very first time.

"What is this?"

"I am strengthening my muscles."

Christian tapped his brother's head. "It is this muscle you should strengthen, girl."

"The brain is not a muscle!" Geoffrey had replied but Christian had walked away, laughing. Laugh he had not when Geoffrey aimed a small stone and it had caught his brother behind the knee and brought him down instantly. Of course Geoffrey, not yet then a squire, had run like the wind itself and had remained in hiding until supper time and by then Christian had forgotten the event. Or so Geoffrey had hoped, but as he'd listened to the battle-talk around the hewn table that night, a glance was thrown by one brother and caught by the other. Christian nodded, smiling.

Now Geoffrey missed that smile so badly that his heart ached to see it again. "Oh, Christian," he whispered as he opened the book. "Where are you?"

# CHAPTER 3

Geoffrey looked up at the bright blue sky. Some said his eyes were the same color, but he noticed it not. All he noticed now was a pain in his heart for he wanted to see his brother again, and it did not matter that he was dead, although he would have preferred him to be alive.

He must have sat there hiding his anguish for so long that all sense of time was as lost as Christian.

A young girl's voice sailed across the afternoon sky, meeting his ears as he sat on the rampart, dreaming. She was singing, and it was music Geoffrey was not familiar with. The lady Vianna he had heard sing when he was but a boy and he remembered it well. She'd sat in her long, flowing dress with its billowing sleeves and intricate lacing. He remembered her best this way, her beautiful, pale face so alive, and the way she'd sat that night with half of her flaming hair about her shoulders, the rest on her head in tight curls. He was entranced by her sweet voice, the way she played the lyre as she sat on the steps to the great hall. Many were there that night who could have heard, too, but the knights heard nothing apart from their own voices raised in battle talk. Geoffrey remembered how he was clipped on the ear for being entranced and not serving Michel's wine; how he had glimpsed, ashamed, at the lady Vianna. And she had smiled.

Geoffrey looked at his hands. How he wished the magic of music lay there, but play he could not, and sing, never. When he tried, dogs howled.

Adelina came into view but she could not see him. She thought she was alone, as he'd thought he was. Geoffrey watched her as she performed a dance amid the flowers, dancing for an unseen audience, just as he'd once battled invisible foes. Some of the sadness lifted from his heart. She was dancing surely but who had taught her? And who had taught her the song she was singing for there was never music in the chateau, none that he had ever heard for many a year at least.

Her performance lasted a long time until she grew tired, and she sat down in the long grass, drawing her knees high and resting her forehead there. After a time, she became aware of another's gaze. She turned and looked up to the rampart.

She rose and danced her way across the grass till she stood below the rampart, looking up. There was no toothy grin today. Her feet were bare, for footwear seemed worse an enemy than water. It was very unlike Adelina to stand there, watching him thoughtfully. He often believed it impossible for her to think of anyone but herself. Yet today, he saw concern in her eyes and wondered if, all along, he had been mistaken.

"No one talks to me, Geoffrey."

Geoffrey said nothing. Adelina pulled a face and looked up into the sky and studied the passing clouds. "Look! There's a horse!" Still, Geoffrey remained silent even though he had seen her horse of clouds. It soon disappeared. "Geoffrey?" she asked in that tone which usually meant, I would like you to do something for me. And if you do not like, then I shall command it.

He looked at her as she climbed up and sat beside him on the rampart, but not too close. Her affections were as transient as the shapes in the clouds above. "Yes, Milady?" He always put a little emphasis on the lady but today she did not notice it, or take offense.

"Mama said I'll have to marry one day when I've grown to be like her, or I come of age whichever comes first."

Geoffrey wished she wouldn't stare at him so. He felt blood heat his face. "It is the way, Adelina," he said and hoped that would satisfy her. But he knew that his hopes were in vain, because she moved a little closer to him.

"But what's it mean? Marry?"

Why is it that always she asks me these things? he wondered. "Well..."

"Look! There's an abbey!"

Geoffrey looked up at the sky again and, sure enough, there was an abbey. He returned his gaze to Adelina. She was watching the clouds with awe but all too soon the abbey disappeared as well. "What's it mean? Married?" she asked again, her gaze fixed on the sky.

"Well, it is when," he hesitated slightly. "It is when a man and a woman become as one in the eyes of God." He finished very quickly.

She thought about the words for a little while, a frown appearing on her face. "Become as one?"

"They... they come together. As one."

"Do you mean they melt into each other when God is watching?"

"What concerns you, Adelina?"

"I do not want to get melted into anyone now or ever."

Geoffrey couldn't hide his smile.

"If I told Mama that she would laugh and say I would change my mind. She said to me today it was a shame that Christian was dead. Is it true? Is Christian dead? Did the Moors kill him?"

"We do not know if he is or not, Milady."

"Then you must be worried. Are you?"

"Some," was all Geoffrey said, lying.

"Mama said something else to me, Geoffrey. It scared me. I know you think I cannot be scared and I am not, not all the time, but this scared me."

"What was this that scared you?"

"She said that Papa hoped one day that Christian would marry me. But he's dead now and I never wanted to marry anyone…" Tears welled in her eyes and Geoffrey patted the ledge close beside him. It was the invitation she'd hoped for. She clambered to him, and sat very close beside him, jiggling her feet in mid-air. The girl could never sit, stand, nor even sleep still. "I can't get married because I would not be Adelina anymore if I do that. Do you see that, Geoffrey?" She put her head against his arm and he raised it so that she could cuddle in. At any moment he expected she would bite, but she drew his arm around her tight. "I am sorry about Christian. I really am. I know you loved him so."

Geoffrey took a deep, shuddering breath and expelled it slowly, then he kissed the top of her head. Adelina buried her face into his chest and there they sat in silence until Geoffrey asked softly, "Who taught you the song you were singing?"

"No one," she said. "I made it up."

"Sing it for me again, Milady, if you please."

"Do you like to hear me sing? No one else does."

"Please, Milady. Sing it again."

She did. At first, her voice was shaking but the sweetness grew and grew until it seemed that he was a boy again, watching the lady Vianna playing her lyre, her sweet voice melting his heart.

Until Michel's calls echoed from the courtyard. "Geoffrey! It is time!"

Time to practise with the quintain. Today Michel was impatient if not angry. "Mama says I cannot watch you anymore. I have to embroider now. I hate sewing."

Geoffrey rose to his feet. "Perhaps it is for the best that you do not watch me. Take yourself inside, Milady, to your sewing. If you think of each brightly-colored stitch as one Moor with a lance through his heart, then perhaps you will not hate it so?"

Adelina brightened. "Perhaps I will pretend that each red stitch is death to the one who killed Christian, and every white stitch will be one for his soul so that he may find his way to heaven without any trouble."

Geoffrey looked down at her. What was this sudden welcome change about? What was she planning now? Why was she being kind? Was she going to push him off the rampart?

"Shall I take this book into your chambers, Geoffrey?" she enquired, her eyes wide, and shining there, curiosity and hope.

"Best you not, Milady, for if it comes to any harm or misfortune, whoever has harmed it is assured of everlasting torment. He would need many, many white stitches to see his soul safe."

"Oh. What is it?" she asked, touching the silk cloth.

"It is a book of God."

"If it is a book of God, why are mortals reading it?"

Geoffrey grinned widely but an answer he could not provide. "If taking the book to my chambers gives you pleasure, then you may. I pray you be careful with it, Milady, and put it on my table, next to my cot if you would." Geoffrey stood, and called his reply to Michel, pretending that only now had he heard the angry summons.

"Geoffrey?"

"Milady?"

"I do not want you to die. Ever. I'd not have a friend left should any harm come to you. I love you, Geoffrey."

"As I love you. Take care with the book."

As he took his afternoon's practise with Michel instructing him, his mind wandered constantly. What is this bond between us? he wondered. Was it born when Adelina was born? Had he not been present that day, would he now feel in his heart the same happy sadness, the same despairing joy whenever their gazes met?

"Stop! Stop! I have seen too much!"

Geoffrey looked down from his horse at Michel who stood by the quintain, suspended from a specially designed frame in the courtyard. Around the horse's feet, chickens pecked and scratched, but came the charge, how they scattered, squawking and flying, and when they squawked and flew, the dogs had some fun as well.

"Where, tell me, is your mind today?"

Where it has always been, Geoffrey moaned to himself. It is away, elsewhere and it refuses to return.

"If you are angry with me, then strike!"

Geoffrey, surprised, took two further looks at his teacher, Michel, who stood, arms stretched to the sides like the Son of God on the Cross. Geoffrey looked away, fearing Michel's mind was twisted now beyond repair. His uncle was sending this lunatic to search for Christian?

"If you are angry with me, I say, strike!"

Geoffrey grew very uncomfortable. "I am not angry with you!

What is this madness?"

"Well, then, if you are not angry with me, who and what is in your thoughts this day? Is it a woman?"

Geoffrey almost choked. "No! It is not a woman!"

"Then what excuse have you! You must concentrate, Geoffrey! Imagine this is the foe!" Michel struck out at the man-shape, stuffed with straw. "Must I say it until the day I die of old age! This is the foe! What is the foe apt to do to you!"

Geoffrey looked at the quintain dispassionately. "It would kill me had it a chance."

"And you are hereby giving it a chance by not thinking!"

"Quintains do not bleed."

"Nor do they scream, but here is where you must begin!"

"Tell me again your instructions?" Geoffrey asked.

"Is it that you are deaf now!"

"What was that you said, Michel?"

Michel threw his arms in the air, surrendering from despair and wasted time. He stepped out of the way, thankfully, for Geoffrey spurred his horse towards the dummy, raised his sword to shoulder height and judged perfectly. The quintain's head flew off into the air. Unfortunately, Geoffrey almost became unseated from the young, headstrong horse. He struggled to regain control and in the struggle, dropped his sword. Thankfully he did drop it, for the horse bolted towards the stone wall and the animal had no intention of stopping. Geoffrey had two choices, collide with the stone wall or propel himself from the stirrups and hurl himself over it.

His full battle armor weighed almost as much as he.

Adelina watched from her chambers window as Geoffrey dived over the wall, flipped mid air and landed on his back, hard, then rolled down the steep slope, through the briars, coming to rest, finally, against a tree. He lay there, immobile. Michel climbed the wall and sat atop it.

She could not hear what was said, but once Geoffrey tried to move, weighed down by his armor, she laughed so hard that she pricked her thumb. She cursed, as she had heard the knights curse so often when they thought none other was about.

And for issuing forth such a loud obscenity, she received a stinging slap on the ear. She was dragged away from the window now that her mother had seen what she had been witnessing.

"You will keep away from him!"

Adelina sat down and changed her thread to another colour, but all the while she hoped that Geoffrey hadn't hurt himself too badly.

That night she was tormented by nightmares, almost the same kind that she'd had after Christian had ridden off to find his fortune whilst fighting the Moors. Adelina lay in her bed whilst the shadows on the walls became terrifying monsters. Everywhere she looked it seemed that she was caught tight in an immense battle. She never slept easily in the darkness and it must have been close to daybreak because her candles were little but melted wax now. The flames flickered and danced and threw monstrous falchions and swords and battle axes across the stone.

She hid under the covers but the images remained, then came the final one, the most horrible. She jumped from her bed and ran across the large room, battled to open her creaking door. It was terribly dark in the corridor and far too early for even Ella to be awake. Further up the stairs, her parents' door was closed tight and it was always bolted from the inside. She peeked the other way as she hung on the edge of her own door. Further down the spiral stairs in the darkness lay the only comfort she knew.

Adelina knew that the squeak of the door would wake him, it normally did. At times, just the crow of an early rooster was enough to rouse Geoffrey. Adelina pushed against his door, one he never locked. But today he was not curled into his covers. She discerned, after a good squint, his silhouette against the small tower window. He did not move, although he knew she was there. He once said she had a smell of her own. It tickled his nose, made him sneeze. But his eyes were bright with amusement when he said it so she need not worry about stinking like a sweating horse in summer or those serfs who worked tirelessly in her father's fields at the bottom of the hill.

"It is very early, Milady," Geoffrey said softly.

"I had a terrible dream."

Geoffrey did not turn but he reached out and silently beckoned her in the darkness. As she padded closer, Adelina saw that he wore only his drawers. She was shivering. His feet were bare too, like hers. His hair askew, as was hers. His cot, too, covers aside. So too it seemed that he could not sleep.

"What was this dream?" he asked as he touched and held to her hand. She, too, looked out into the darkness. For a moment Adelina couldn't speak. She feared he would laugh. But there was no other she could talk to of things like this.

"I dreamed of a battle, Geoffrey. An awful battle. Then there was a procession and I knew it was a body covered so by the cloaks and those flags that are on the wall in the great hall. You know, the ones which hang near the arms of my father?"

"Yes, go on."

"There was stuff, horrible stuff, dripping from the box, Geoffrey. I can still smell it."

He sighed, put his arm around the girl's waist. She sat on his lap.

"I saw myself with my mother. I was older, much older, and I was weeping so, as a peasant weeps for her dead husband." Adelina turned and looked into Geoffrey's eyes. "I have seen that, I have. I have seen them cry."

Now she is watching serfs? he wondered, surprised.

"I think that body was yours." Huge tears welled and only one escaped. Geoffrey wiped it from her face calmly and gently although his heart was dancing. Often when the child dreamed, the events took place. But again, he'd had a bad night of his own.

"Milady, I too could not sleep. My dream was somewhat as yours. I with your mother and I feared that it was you dead. The sadness still hurts me, here." He touched his chest.

"No, it was not me. I shall never die."

"This," Geoffrey said and touched her face, her arm, her hand, "Is but mortal flesh. It ages, it finally dies."

"Yes, but I am not my finger nor am I my face, or my arm. What is me, Adelina, is spirit, so I will never die. You told me this, Geoffrey, and I know it is true." She looked back to the darkness outside. Some color was coming to the edge of the world—what did Geoffrey call that? The horizon, yes—and a new day lay waiting behind that thick bloodstain in the sky. "I woke crying, Geoffrey. I do not know how I can be happy if you are not here."

Geoffrey touched her hair, raked it into order with his fingers. She sat on his knee, very still now, and wished he would never stop for often he had put her to sleep this way.

"How is it you feel now?" he asked.

"Angry. I do not like being a girl."

"I know this already."

"I should have been a boy, for if I was a boy I would fight at your side one day."

"You mean you would fight at my side and not with me?"

Adelina turned to him. "Why is it I do horrible things to you?"

"I am not you to know this. How can I say?" But his thoughts were on Christian's unending torments in years gone. How those years had gone, too. So quickly.

"I saw you today from my window as I sewed. See?" She stuck her thumb into his face and in the dimness Geoffrey saw nothing wrong with it. "I stabbed myself and it hurt."

"You must be more careful, then."

"And you. You will not ride that horse again, will you?"

"The horse is young," he said, wondering what it was exactly that this little girl had witnessed. "It will learn obedience."

"Why do you not ride Jester?"

"He is yours now."

"He has no life. He is as old as... as... Papa."

Again Geoffrey said nothing.

"I had never seen anyone do that before, Geoffrey."

"What, Milady?"

"Leap from a bolting horse and over the wall that way. Did it hurt when you landed on the other side for you rolled a good way."

"Perhaps it hurt as much as your thumb," he said.

"But this is not your thumb, so can you know how much it hurt?"

"That is true," Geoffrey said with a smile. "It seems to me that we shall both live."

The bloodstains spread and faded and blue sky replaced the retreating darkness. Adelina leaned over and saw the bruises on his arms and she peeked at his bare back as well. There was a large, dark bruise across his shoulders, made by the armor when he fell. She'd known by the way he'd fallen that he had lost his wind and when that happened nothing could be done until it returned. She knew this because once she had slipped off that very wall and landed heavily in the briars on the slope below.

"At least you chopped its head off this time. Not its leg."

Geoffrey said nothing. She wasn't inducing him to a fight, or so he hoped. On the rare times like this, when she was amicable, she was good company. She poked at the bruise on his arm and he winced.

"I fear your injuries are worse than mine," she said and rested her head against his chest, grabbed his hands and held them tight around her waist. She did that because when her head was close to his face he always kissed her hair. The only time her father touched her was when she was forced to say, "Goodnight, Papa," whether he had company or not. If he was busy talking he waved her away, but if he was alone he would kiss her forehead and wish her sweet dreams. Her mother never touched her at all unless she was scrubbing dirt from her face or hands. Ella was always busy cooking. Raoul and Louis ignored her, Acelin seemed frightened of her, and once Michel had relieved her fingertip of a shard of wood but he'd stepped away and bowed to her once it was extracted. Geoffrey was her only friend in the entire world.

"Today, when we bathed together, Mama said I cannot be near you anymore."

"Have I done something to displease her?"

"I don't know. She says that soon I will need a girl to help me. She says the washerwoman has a daughter who will want to work here, too. Does she speak of Cateline? And Mama also said, when we were in the bath, that soon, I would grow breasts like hers and when that happens I must be a lady until the day I die. But Geoffrey, I don't want breasts like hers. I won't, will I, Geoffrey? Tell me I won't grow breasts like hers."

"I'm afraid that you will, Milady. God made you so. No mortal's wishes can alter God's will. I am sorry but you will grow into a woman and that will be your lot."

In the early morning light, he looked at her face, noticing for the first time that her child eyes and face were disappearing, fast. Perhaps her journey into womanhood was happening now, at this very minute?

"Mama said my duty is to have babies. But I do not want any of it. I shall run away."

"Milady, you should not talk of these things."

"If everyone had their way, I would never be allowed to speak at all. I tried to talk to Papa of this. I tried to say how I did not want to be a lady, ever, but he said he had much on his mind. And he was very strange. Very strange. He said he knew nothing of women and wished to keep it that way."

"Listen to me." He turned her to him and swept more hair from her eyes. "Ladies were not made by God to fight, and you will be a fine lady one day."

"But I do not…"

"Listen to me."

She was silent.

"There are many men who can fight but there are only a few noble, beautiful ladies as you will be. This I know. So it is much better if you abide the wishes of your mother. There is much ahead for you."

"Do you know what I want to be? What I would be if I had been born a boy?"

Geoffrey yawned and pretended he needed to go back to bed.

"I will tell you anyway. I would be a knight at arms."

Geoffrey coughed. Adelina got off his knee and bunched her hair tight on her head. "See? I would look like a boy if I had less hair. I could pretend. I am fierce, am I not?"

Geoffrey tried hard not to laugh.

"Teach me to fight?"

"I cannot. Ask Michel."

"I asked Michel but he was very shocked and he scuttered away."

"Perhaps he does not know you as I do."

"Why is he frightened of me? Am I already so fierce that I can frighten a knight at arms?" Hope was alive in her eyes now.

"It is not you, Milady. It is what you say, what you do."

"I hate being a girl!"

"Perhaps you should go back to your room now, Milady."

"Why is it you will not teach me to fight?"

"I do not ever wish to harm you."

"But I am strong. I am fearless."

"Are you?" Geoffrey asked.

She didn't like the look in his eyes. She kicked him, hard. "I would not do that, Milady."

"You are not me. I can do what I like."

"Not anymore, Milady. Your father has ordered that I must retaliate, defend myself against your terrors. A good soldier must always obey any command."

"Papa would not say that. This is a lie."

"It is not a lie. You see, Milady, I have orders now that should you hit me, kick me, bite me, or use whatever takes your fancy with whatever is within your reach, I shall do to you in return. Michel has said that my strengths are hidden ones and often surprising." He watched her eyes carefully, expecting a full onslaught.

"You cannot harm me. I am your lady. You cannot."

"But I have permission and my allegiance will always be to your father first. Therefore, if he says I must hit you, I will hit you."

Adelina tested this by punching him on the arm, in the centre of the huge bruise. He winced, and punched her arm in return, matching the force. She grabbed her arm tight and winced but determination shone in her eyes.

"Would you now wish to wake your father and tell him that I have hit you? For you will be in deep trouble, Adelina. You are not supposed to be near me, are you?"

She spat on him. Geoffrey spat back. She ran for his chest, opened it and withdrew his dagger. He watched her step back to him, the way she held the weapon with both hands held high above her head.

"You wish to walk weeping behind my casket, Milady? Weeping with a broken heart and wondering how you could ever be happy because I am no longer here? If this is so, then I suggest that you aim well."

She hesitated, wanting him to continue.

"This is not a toy!" he said, a little too loud. He moved so quickly that she was surprised. Geoffrey grabbed her, squeezed her hands hard to disengage the dagger. It dropped to the floor. "Never do that, Milady. Never, for one day you will choose the wrong party and it will be my dream that has become the reality, not yours! You are the daughter of a nobleman and you will always have enemies."

Momentarily subdued, she said, "Then teach me to fight, Geoffrey. I beg you."

"No. I cannot. I dare not, I would not."

"Then I shall get you."

"And I shall be waiting, Milady."

# Chapter 4

"Adelina!"

She ignored the call and loosed the bolt. It struck the quintain and she smiled; she was not missing many today.

"Adelina!"

The calls were getting closer. Adelina cursed to herself, pushed the crossbow under her bed so that it could not be seen. She ran to the table by the window, picked up her embroidery, and saw, too late, her own hand-made quintain, the one with two cross-bolts protruding through its middle, hanging from the crossbeam high above. She cursed again. Adelina had put it there herself with great difficulty, after devising a series of ropes to first get it up there and secure it in place without it falling each time she used it as a target. It was even harder to take down.

Her mother would not be very pleased with this sight. And Cateline was not here to help her hide her sins. Adelina fumbled for the sword, also under her bed. She stood on a stool and wielded, hard. The quintain fell but the rope remained and she could not jump from the chair high enough to catch it and pull. Again she cursed, softly.

"Adelina! Are you sleeping again?"

"No, Mama. What is it?" she called.

"Make yourself presentable! Michel returns soon with Christian! Word has just arrived!"

Christian returns after all this time? Adelina kicked the quintain under her bed, searched frantically for her comb and dragged it through her long, kinked hair. She patted her face, and looked down at what she wore. The tights she had stolen from Geoffrey's chambers, the shirt she had stolen from her father's laundry. The sleeves of the billowing shirt were rolled to the top of her arms because the fabric was often caught in the crossbow drawback. The only way she could load it was by sitting and using her feet as leverage whilst she drew back with all the strength of her arms and shoulders.

She was barely eight years old when she had seen Christian last, and that was almost seven years ago. She could not meet her future husband wearing a man's clothing, could she.

Hanging behind the screen was a choice of four dresses: the many others were for very best wear, when a lord or count visited and spoke of boring politics and taxes, dues and levies, who was fighting who, all in the name of God. Adelina grabbed a dress at random—a blue one she had not worn for a long time; perhaps the last harvest? She looked at it, patted her behind and wondered if it would fit. She hoped so, it was the only color that she liked.

"Cateline!"

Cateline answered the call almost immediately. She had been scrubbing floors, or so it seemed.

"Milady?" the quiet girl asked.

"Help me with this damned thing."

Cateline put her rag down, wiped her hands on her dark tunic. The lady Adelina lifted the man's shirt over her head, turned her back and sucking in a huge breath, she squeezed herself into the dress. And a squeeze it surely was.

Cateline laced it for her, not brave enough to say that it was far too tight, had she another? There was fire in Adelina's eyes today, so she said nothing except, "Christian returns, Milady."

"Yes, yes, hurry up!"

When the final lace was threaded and secured, Adelina tried to breathe. She looked down. Her breasts were squashed almost flat. She had forgotten the cote. She cursed. "Where is Geoffrey?"

"In the village collecting dues, I think."

Adelina searched for her cloak to wear over the dress. There was a huge, muddy footprint on the hem. She threw it down, angry. Cateline picked up a bodice shawl, silently offering it. Adelina snatched it and put it on. It covered a little, but not much. "Why am I so fat!" Adelina spat.

Again, Cateline dared say nothing except, "Milady?"

"What!"

"The hose?"

"There is no time."

"But Milady, your mother will…"

"Go, Cateline. Now."

Cateline picked up her rag and left her mistress's chambers.

The ridiculous dress was too tight, and too long. Adelina was forever standing on the hem or tripping on it. It served no purpose at all. Adelina adjusted the bodice shawl once again, and dragged the comb through her long hair so it fell in neat waves to the small of her back.

Not bothering with a head covering, except for the gold embroidered headband which only caused her hair to be tousled yet again, Adelina, in bare feet, soon gave up the effort of appearing decent, and burst from her chambers, lifting her skirts high as she ran down the deep, spiral stairs until she came to the great hall.

It was empty except for Ella and the two charboys setting the table for the evening's feast. Adelina did not stop to ponder who the guests would be this time. From the kitchen below came the succulent aroma of pig on a spit. Perhaps it was lamb. Why had no one told her of Christian's homecoming? He had been absent for so long.

"Out of my way, idiot!" She thrust the boy aside as they met on the stairs leading down to the kitchens and the boy had to juggle the platter of fruits. He apologised but by the time he had finished mumbling timidly, Adelina was long gone. She tripped on the final stair and cursed as she lost her balance. She had sense enough to roll, though, and she sprang back to her feet, looking about to see if anyone had witnessed the acrobatic spectacular. Another charboy turning the spits, and the old monk from the abbey who always came to prepare the feasts and aid Ella, had certainly seen. Her curse, too, had been another blasphemous one. The monk went back to stuffing the large, fat goose with bread and herbs and he shook his head and prayed. "Where is my mother?" Adelina demanded.

"In the courtyard, Milady."

"Is Geoffrey back yet?"

"No, Milady."

"Damn! He should be here. And what is that terrible smell!"

"My herbs," the monk said. Gazes met. Adelina pulled a face at him. Again, he said another prayer.

Adelina made her way to the doors and appeared in the afternoon sunlight which was blinding after being so long closeted in her chambers. Her mother was dressed as if she were greeting royalty, wearing that audacious hat which billowed in the wind as she spoke to Gabriel of Lyon, Papa's first knight, and the farrier.

Marys turned to Adelina, and sighed at what she saw: the wind catching the blue skirts, showing no sign of a cote. Nor did she walk as a lady, with flowing steps—she walked like a serf carrying a heavy water bucket. The dress was too tight and it hid far less than it revealed. Marys walked to where her daughter stood, watching the gate expectantly. "Show me your hands."

Adelina held out her hands, palms down. Her fingernails were dirty and chewed badly. Marys tapped the fingers, Adelina turned her hands palm up and sighed. "What is this? Callouses? What have you been doing now?"

Adelina remained silent, looking over her mother's shoulder with ease for she was almost a head taller already.

"How is Christian expected to voluntarily court you if you present yourself this way?"

"It does not matter how I am presented for Papa has already arranged this wedding. I have no choice. You know who it is I would rather marry."

"Enough." Marys took off her velvet cloak and put it around Adelina, fastened it with her own gold and emerald brooch. She studied her daughter's face. "You are too much in the sun," she said, touching the freckles and despairing.

"Here he comes! Papa! Christian has returned!" Adelina's joyous calls were halted, silenced abruptly.

Indeed, it was Christian. She had not seen him for many a year, not since she was playacting at being a boy, when he and Geoffrey would swing her in circles by the feet if no one was watching. It was Christian there, yes, but it was not the handome young knight she'd once recognised. Michel, looking older than ever before, sat astride his horse, and he led Christian's.

Adelina was speechless. She glanced at her mother whose face was white with horror. She also glanced to her father who had only now come down to witness the long-awaited homecoming.

No one spoke for no words could be found by anyone.

Michel dismounted and walked to Christian's horse. He patted Christian's hand and Christian seemed to wake from the touch. He looked down at Michel; he looked at Robert, Marys, the gathering of servants and knight; Ella, and finally Adelina. But he recognised no one.

Marys stepped back, hand over mouth. She turned and ran off, crying. Robert let her go but signalled to Ella to follow, which she did, herself horrified by this sight. Robert stepped toward the two, and took Michel's horse's reins in hand. But he could only watch and listen.

"Christian? We are here now."

Christian's blue eyes scanned the courtyard, the castle itself, and again, all those watching from the ground. He tried to scratch an itch on his cheek but his hand missed, so he rubbed his face on his shoulder.

"Help me, Master," Michel said quietly. "He cannot help himself."

"Adelina, fetch the monk."

Adelina remained frozen.

"Adelina! Fetch up the monk!"

"I will, Milord. I will," the farrier said and ran for the kitchen.

Adelina could only watch as her father and Michel pulled Christian down from the horse. His fingers were locked tight on the pommel though and she watched her father, tears building in his eyes, as he released Christian's fingers, one by one. Michel assisted him to walk and Christian looked about again. His eyes were empty. The vacant gaze fell on Adelina as she stood clasping her mother's cloak tight at her throat.

"Milady, you have certainly grown," Michel said tiredly as he walked the shuffling Christian past. Christian looked back, his hand reaching out to touch. Adelina saw then how the little finger on his hand was missing. She pulled back before he touched.

"He means you no harm, Milady," Michel said. "It is your hair he wishes to touch."

Adelina covered her face with her hand and started running. She ran, tripping occasionally, through the puddles, across the uneven cobblestones until she was out of the gate and across the bridge. Gabriel of Lyon called her back but she did not hear, and if she had, she would not have obeyed.

Her thoughts were wild as she kept running along the narrow, muddy track that was almost hidden by thick woods. On she ran, uphill, until she could no longer draw breath. For half a mile she had run, calling in vain for Geoffrey, but nothing except the birds and the deer heard her calls. Forced now to stop, she leaned against a tree and slid down until she sat on the wet underbrush.

It was no use. She could not run all the way to the village. It was too far. She called for Geoffrey again but her voice would not come, just tears, a river of tears which had no end.

It was then that Jean-Pierre Dupuy, the second born son of her father's enemy, chanced along and heard the whimperings. There was no one about—he had seen Michel Dumont and the halfwit a while before and had been waiting aside the track which encroached upon Dupuy land for Geoffrey de Polignac to appear, driving the cart which bore the village spoils. Henri Dupuy had of course raised the dues on his own villagers at Allegre, and many of the serfs had moved away, to here, Polignac land, escaping what they called the tyranny. And without the serfs working the fields, food was scarce.

But it had been Jean-Pierre's own choice to wait for Geoffrey to return fully loaded, seize the cart and take back what rightfully belonged to the Dupuys.

Jean-Pierre had not expected this, the sound of a woman crying in the woods. He noted the small footprints in the mud and where they led. He dismounted, tethered his horse out of sight and drew his falchion. He stepped carefully through the undergrowth, making barely a sound except for the clinking of metal as he moved.

He glimpsed the cloth of a noblewoman twenty yards ahead. He drew closer, his prey did not know of his presence until he rested the falchion blade on her shoulder. The whimpering instantly ceased.

"Geoffrey?" she asked.

The blade lifted as Jean-Pierre Dupuy rounded the tree. If there was hope in her eyes it soon faded.

Adelina did not recognise the mail hauberk. She looked farther upwards, wiped her eyes for better vision and her heart stilled. A stranger stood before her. On his surcoat was the Dupuy shield, the hawk and dagger, black on red. Her father's enemy. One of many. Resting on his shoulder, a falchion. She knew how sharp a falchion was and what it was designed to do.

"And who are you?" he asked.

Again, she was struck dumb until the point of the falchion caught more than the breath in her throat. Adelina put her legs down. The knight lifted off his helmet with one hand, drew his mail hood back and shook his brown hair loose. He dropped the helmet to the ground at his feet and stepped closer. He kept out of reach of her kick which would do no good anyway for she wore no shoes.

"Your name?"

"Cateline."

The falchion bit into her skin and stung fiercely, and with it, he lifted her chin. Again he asked, "Your name?"

Falchion or not, Adelina turned her head.

Jean-Pierre used the blade to dislodge the brooch which clasped the cloak. The brooch flew into the air and he caught it easily. He studied it. "Marys? Marys de Polignac? No, I think not. You are Adelina, the only child, is that not so?"

Adelina spat on the ground, just missing his leather-booted feet and calves. Her right hand was behind, reaching in the wet for a weapon, and her fingers found rocks too small, but she finally seized upon a stick, and gripped it, tightly. It was green wood, or so it felt, brought down by the storm of last night, no doubt. How much would green wood sting across a bare cheek, especially since he'd slipped his hood from his head? It would be a handsome head, too, if not for the cold, cold eyes staring into her. They were eyes as cold as Geoffrey's were whenever they fought hand to hand amid the fields by the village. Her village. It would never belong to any Dupuy. Never.

"I have heard of your beauty but I never believed one as ugly and useless as your father could produce more than a stillborn newt. Fortune smiles upon me this day. Tell me, how much would your father give for your return? His chateau? His villages, perhaps?"

Adelina said nothing. Geoffrey had taught her the mistake of losing tempers, of letting pride bar the passage of common sense.

"What have we hidden in here, I wonder?" he asked and used the falchion to draw aside the cloak. He made a noise she was not familiar with, but it was one she did not like. Adelina did not care what part of her body his eyes feasted upon. She only wanted him to lift the blade from her throat and move closer so that she could wield the stick and run.

"On your feet," Dupuy ordered.

Adelina stared ahead. Her heart was wildly beating but her mind was calm and the grip on the stick was deathlike. What would she give for a short sword, or even one crossbolt now to drive it into his knee or under his arm.

"On your feet!" He reached down and grabbed her hair. Adelina squealed in pain and anger rose as he pulled her upright. With all her strength, she brought the stick up and swung, hitting him across the cheek, the ear. Once, twice, again and again. The falchion tore across her shoulder. She felt the searing pain, the flow of sudden warmth but she kept hitting until he covered his face and stepped back. Adelina ran. An irate hand seized the cloak and tore it from her shoulders. She tripped on her skirt and caught it up in her good hand and ran again, leaping, twisting through the thicket until she came upon the roadway.

Anger spurred Dupuy on. He was so close that she could hear his angry breathing, but the hauberk restricted him almost as much as the dress restricted her. Then, suddenly, she felt him no more and she turned, tripping again. She was alone on the track. She heard nothing, saw nothing.

Adelina stepped back a way, then turned in a circle. Her shoulder pained horribly, and she looked. There was a long gash from her neck to her armpit and the sleeve of her dress was hanging. She covered the wound with her hand and stumbled on, down the narrow track towards home, each step feeling a mile in length.

She wanted to call out for her father but had not the strength to utter a sound.

Then she heard it, long before she saw it: the thunder of hooves on the ground. Dupuy crested the hill. His horse bore down on her—the knight, the sword. Adelina screamed and dived into the woods to her right, rolling until she was stopped by briars. She felt nothing now. On her feet, running through the thicket again, until, in the distance, she could see the chateau walls. She was screaming for her father. There was no hope of scaling those walls, for the walls were designed to keep out pillagers and keep safe those inside. Her only way in was by the track, across the bridge and through the gate which lay two hundred yards ahead. And there was no sentry. She could not think clearly. Blood dripped from her arm and off her fingertips, down her body to her hips, her leg. She fell and could not rise. The only words echoing in her mind was a promise to God.

She lay on the ground, straining to draw breath, but finding a little strength with each passing heartbeat. She could not walk so she crawled on her hands and knees, climbing the steep, slippery incline, back to the roadway.

Almost at the top and moments from the safety of home, of her father's arms. Joy was rising.

Dupuy was waiting.

"No..." Adelina put her face into the wet grass. She was ready to die. The saddle squeaked, the mail clinked as Dupuy dismounted again. Adelina raised her head, looked up as far as she could. His face bore welts and was bleeding, and so was his ear. But did he hurt as she hurt? No. Amusement lay in his eyes.

My last sight in this world will not be the eyes of a laughing Dupuy, she thought to herself. Adelina turned her head back to the grass and felt her very life slipping away.

Dupuy kicked her over. As he raised his sword to strike, he looked down into her eyes. They were open and no fear lay within. For a moment he must have wondered why there was no fear. Hesitating was his only mistake.

Adelina vaguely heard a familiar sound, a thunk.

Dupuy propped, surprised. He made a strange noise and blood appeared at the side of his mouth. There was another thunking noise and the Dupuy heir, the enemy, fell to his knees, then to his face beside her. All Adelina remembered was his wide, staring eyes and the sound of her father's voice, calling her name.

Robert, crossbow in hand, ran to where his daughter lay.

From the top of the hill, Geoffrey reined the horse into a canter, stopping the laden cart only when he drew aside his uncle. In his arms lay Adelina, limp, dangling, and blood dripping down her arm. To Geoffrey, she looked dead. He leapt from the cart and the crossbow which was once across his lap fell to the roadway.

Geoffrey had fired at the same time as his uncle.

Geoffrey waited outside Adelina's chambers until the door finally opened. Robert, Michel, and the monk appeared.

"How is she?"

"A lot of blood was lost, Geoffrey." the monk said. "I will pray now," he mumbled and walked off down the stairs.

"Michel?"

Michel shrugged and touched Geoffrey's arm. He, too, was away without a word. Robert answered the young man's unvoiced question. "Only stay a short while, Geoffrey. Do not excite her. Then we must talk."

Geoffrey walked into Adelina's chambers. The smell of herbs was pungent, almost foul. Marys sat by the bed, stroking that beautiful mane of hair and a hand in turn. She turned to Geoffrey and away again, quickly. "No one suspected Jean-Pierre Dupuy would be waiting on the roadway."

"I suspect he was waiting for me, Milady. He does so, often."

"She ran off calling for you. Always it is you."

Geoffrey came closer. Adelina lay on her side, a pillow behind her to keep her still. Her eyes were half open, her pain evident: Pain so intense that for a moment, Geoffrey was unable to breathe. Sweat formed in beads on his forehead and he felt ill just to see her this way.

"Geoffrey?" she asked softly.

"I am here."

"Geoffrey?"

He crouched so that she could see his face without having to move her head. She snaked her hand from under the covers and Geoffrey put his hand over her fingers. They were cold. Very cold. Her face was scratched, bruised and so too her hand and arm but that was all he could see. He wished to see no more, for if he did, he would only feel her agonies as his own yet again.

"Michel brought some herbs and ointments and potions from the east," Marys said softly. "He tells me they will stop the bleeding and stave off the fevers. Pray this is so?" she asked.

Geoffrey rested his face against Adelina's bed and kissed her fingers. He did not care that Marys was close by. A tiny smile touched Adelina's face, a smile not unlike the lady Vianna's. Surely Adelina would not die on the very bed in which she was born?

"You must go now, Geoffrey. Robert wishes words with you."

Adelina's grip tightened on Geoffrey's hand. He kissed it again, whispered that he would be back, and he retreated from the room. He took the stairs down to the great hall where tonight's feast was in preparation.

But no one was in a festive mood. On the floor of the great hall lay Dupuy's body, bearing the welts on its face, the torn ear, and two crossbow bolts, one in the breast—Geoffrey's, which had ruptured the mail and then the heart—and the other bolt, Robert's, was in the shoulder and protruding through to the front. Geoffrey looked away. He was sick inside. This had been his first kill. It had not been battle-won.

Michel rose and embraced him. Years had passed since they had seen each other but no joy lay in either's eyes. Michel turned him from the body to the hewn table where Robert sat. Geoffrey gazed down at the feast-to-be. At the very sight of food he usually longed to eat. Not today. "What to do with the body?" he asked.

"I shall send the monk with the body, but Dupuy will avenge this. It is more than a certainty. Jean-Pierre was the son Dupuy treasured

48

most. Sit, Geoffrey."

Robert looked to Michel, who sat opposite. "Your brother has returned," Robert said.

Geoffrey looked up, surprised. "I was not told?"

"He is not, how can I say this?" Michel mumbled. "Geoffrey, he is not who he once was."

"What does that mean?"

"For many years I was gone, this you know. For many years I searched to no avail. In Cyprus I was told, for a price, that one of Christian's looks and bearing had been sold into slavery. I found him in Alexandria. I bought him and although he is here, but he is not whole, Geoffrey."

A dagger in the heart would be a kinder pain, Geoffrey thought. His mouth was dry. Adelina could be dying at this very moment and his brother was not whole? Had the world gone mad? "Where is he?"

Robert nodded to Michel and Michel led the way upstairs to the tower, to a small, bare chambers which was once kept as a storehouse in case of a siege. In it now, a table, a cot and a chair, and sitting on the chair, dressed in a gray tunic, barefooted, and staring at the wall, was his beloved brother, Christian.

Geoffrey's heart leapt in happiness at the sight. Michel put his hand on Geoffrey's shoulder. "I wept when I saw him, Geoffrey. When he was brought to me, I wept."

Michel walked to Christian whose only movement was a blink of one eyelid.

"See here where the hair does not grow? His mind has gone from the strike." Geoffrey saw a scar on the top of his brother's head. "But whose strike and where, we will never know. There is rumour that he fell in Constantinople." Michel picked up Christian's right hand. Geoffrey saw that the little finger was missing. Missing, too, the finger from the other hand. Michel dropped the tunic from Christian's shoulders until it fell to his hips. Gone now the healthy and well-muscled body Geoffrey once envied. Christian was thin now, awfully thin. Across his back, a patchwork of scars from many floggings. There were many scars on his arms, chest and stomach, too. "Stand, Christian."

Christian stood as ordered but kept his stare fastened to the wall. The tunic dropped to the floor. Geoffrey closed his eyes at what he next saw: his beautiful elder brother had also been castrated.

"Slave?" he whispered, voice breaking. "My brother was sold as a slave?"

"He understands nothing, Geoffrey."

"No! It is not true!" He couldn't believe this had happened. Michel pulled the tunic up and fastened it once again. He told Christian he could sit if he wished. Christian sat. There was nothing in the eyes now, no happiness, no sadness. No elation, no despair. There was nothing at all.

Bile rose and found a quick escape. Geoffrey turned his head and vomited on the floor. When done, he pulled from his neck the medallion he had worn for many a year and he threw it from the small window. Then he sank to his knees, put his head on his brother's lap.

For a long time it seemed that Christian was unaware, until, slowly, he moved his right hand. Although it was shaking, he placed it on his brother's head after a great deal of effort, and from his staring eyes rolled a single tear.

"He knows me, Michel! He knows me!"

Michel turned away and closed the door as quietly as he could.

# Chapter 5

Geoffrey finally returned to the great hall, pleased to see that only a few of the guests had arrived. He noticed that Robert's friend, Charles, also a distant relation of Marys's, had traveled from d'Arlempdes and no doubt he would stay more than one night. As he approached, Geoffrey noticed more: That this distant relation, Charles, had brought his new wife, whose name Geoffrey knew not, and a daughter who was, perhaps, the most beautiful thing Geoffrey had ever seen.

She was tall, a hand taller than he, and her hair seemed the colour of night. It was arrayed in an intricate procession of curls framing her pale face, and the mane hung over her shoulders. She wore a glowing red gown and her eyes were almost as dark as her hair.

Geoffrey thought he would faint, but perhaps it was not because of the sight of her. Perhaps it was because he was still unwell.

The girl with the dark hair was standing by his uncle's coat of arms, her hands clasped tight before her as if afraid of the night which lay ahead. She scanned the room as if she hoped that others would soon come and shield her from the gathering. It was then that her gaze turned to Geoffrey who stood motionless on the stairs. He was pleased to note that Dupuy's body had been sent on its way, for that sight he would not wish a lady such as this one to behold. For the moment, only she had seen him and he was conscious of his clothing, too, for he wore only hose and hauberk and neither were his best. He could not turn his back on her now. She smiled, shyly, and Geoffrey turned slowly, making sure that there was no one behind him on the stairs. Perhaps, he thought, she smiles at Acelin, or Raoul? But no, and his heart lifted, for the smile was for him alone.

The wondrous beauty then lowered her gaze, covered her mouth with her hand and lifted her head again, smiling at him, at his action. Geoffrey felt terrible. Such a silent introduction indeed. Her new father—or at least that is what Geoffrey surmised the lord Charles must have been—turned quickly for he had noticed the girl's sudden embarrassment.

"Ah, Geoffrey! Come and join us," he said, and aside to Robert added, "Will he never grow?"

Charles stood as Geoffrey approached and there was a quick embrace, cheeks touched. Charles grabbed Geoffrey's face, turning it one way, then another, before he ran his hand along Geoffrey's cheeks and chin. He sighed, picked up his goblet of wine and said aloud, "Useless! He will grow no more height. Tell me, Geoffrey, do you need a box to stand upon before you mount your steed?"

Robert watched carefully. Usually, Geoffrey was good-natured except when faced with criticism of his lack of height. But Geoffrey surprised his uncle by saying, "A box, yes, filled with the heads of my enemies." He glanced at the lovely girl. She had heard and still her mouth was covered by her hand, except that this time it held a lace handkerchief.

Will no one introduce us? Geoffrey wondered. It seemed not. Talk continued between Charles and Robert, now it was concerned with Michel's travels. Not a word was mentioned of Christian. Geoffrey waited for a pause in the conversation before he said, "Milords, I shall return directly."

Robert nodded. Geoffrey leaped up the stairs and halted as he rounded the curve. He glanced back. What is this feeling? He wondered as he continued on, already disengaging the hauberk and lifting it from his body. In his chambers, he lay the hauberk down. In the corner, covered by cloth, the suit he had worn twice only when accompanying his uncle to tournaments. Normally, on an occasion like this, he wore only hauberk, hose and leather boots strapped from foot to knee. However, the emblem on the hauberk's back and front, of his master's falcon and dragon, was in dire need of new paint for the falcon could not be seen at a distance. Geoffrey took the cover from the suit in the corner. It was by far too heavy and hot as well but he remembered the dark eyes of the girl in the great hall and pondered the decision of comfort against flamboyance. No doubt the others would join the feast in full regalia. Flamboyance won. Before Geoffrey dressed again, he raised his arm and sniffed. His eyes rolled.

How could he get close to such a lady and not have her expire from his very smell?

Michel's chambers were next to Geoffrey's and there was a small door leading directly to Michel's abode. Geoffrey opened it quietly and on all fours, slipped through.

Michel did not hear him. He was busy scrubbing at his face, preparing to wield his blade for he preferred to keep his face shaved, not bearded. It was the itch he found insufferable. Also, Michel did not hear him coming. He was singing quietly to himself. Geoffrey was still crawling along the stone floor when his gaze fell on Michel's dagger. He crawled to it, and hid on the other side of the cot when Michel thought he heard a sound and turned. When Geoffrey again heard the scratching of blade against whiskered cheek, he lifted his head. Michel had returned to his song. A smile lit Geoffrey's face and he stalked as a cat with a mouse.

It was peculiar, because Michel's song told the story of a legendary knight's bravery and skills. Geoffrey's plan was to stealthily rise, seize Michel, hold the dagger to his throat and hear him beg for mercy. So he hoped, because he saw this happening in his mind as he crept evermore forwards. But he came to an abrupt halt when Michel put his keen-edged blade down and said, "Geoffrey, you breathe too loud."

Geoffrey sighed and hung his head, defeated before he began. Could he never win? Michel lifted the lid from a jar, dipped his fingers in it and rubbed the potion into his face.

"What is that?" Geoffrey asked and got to his feet.

"It is a potion that relieves me of the itch." Michel offered Geoffrey some to try. "The Moors have some wondrous medicines and oils and ointments. And this." He threw a lump of an odd substance to Geoffrey, who caught it and smelled it. It had no smell. "It is soap," Michel said. "It cleanses the skin of all foul matters, even dried blood."

Geoffrey stared incredulous at this wondrous little thing. He rubbed it on the back of his hand. The dirt remained.

"It works with water," Michel said. "Try."

Geoffrey dipped his fingers into Michel's bowl and wet his hand, then rubbed the object over his skin. Bubbles appeared. He wiped his hand on his tights. The skin on his hand and wrist, when next he looked, was no longer brown but a wondrous pink.

"It is made from fat and oils. I have given the recipe to Ella. I can only hope she does not serve it to us as food."

"Why?"

"Taste it."

Geoffrey licked it and his face contorted. He wiped his tongue on his bare arm and spat. Nothing would get the taste off his tongue. Michel was smiling. "Take it. I have more."

"Does this..."

"Soap," Michel said as a reminder.

"Soap. Yes, does it take the stink of armpits away?"

Michel smiled once again as Geoffrey scratched his head with fingertips and caught the offending flea. It popped when he beheaded it with his fingernails. Geoffrey scratched at his head again.

"When used often, it also keeps the fleas and lice at bay."

"No," Geoffrey exclaimed. "You joke with me?"

Michel shook his head. Geoffrey studied the soap. A wondrous thing indeed. Michel took Geoffrey by the back of the neck and thrust his head into the deep dish of water, ignoring the protests. He scrubbed at Geoffrey's head so hard that Geoffrey wondered would he not be bald soon. "A wondrous thing indeed," he spluttered as he came up, gasping for air. His dripping head was still itching though, itching more in fact. He touched. Now he would have to drag a comb through it, one of his least favorite leisures.

"The Moors have much to teach us."

"How can you say that?"

"It is true, Geoffrey."

"They have given us nothing but new ways to die!"

Michel studied the young man and shook his head sadly. "Why did you come here?"

"I came to ask had you an oil or ointment which would rid me of a very sour smell."

Michel's eyes smiled and he looked away. "Oh, so a fine lady she must be who awaits you in the great hall."

"You have seen her?"

"In your eyes only, Geoffrey. Yes, I have seen her. I watched as she arrived with the Lord Charles and his entourage. I was told they met two bands of thieves on their journey."

Geoffrey didn't care who they had met, when, where or why. "Do you think she would like me?"

You are far too short to warrant much except amusement, Michel thought, but he saw the hopeful expression in Geoffrey's eyes. "Use the soap and a drop of this. No more than a drop though, Geoffrey."

Geoffrey opened the jar Michel handed to him and he smelled it: Pleasant yet manly. "I thank you," Geoffrey said and retreated to the crawlspace door once again.

"A word of advice although I know you will heed me not."

Geoffrey turned quickly and hit his head against the door sides.

"Be yourself to win the heart of this one, Geoffrey. Be none other than yourself."

"But I should think that if I was myself she would soon fall to sleep when talking with me."

"Would you ride into battle already defeated in your mind?"

"No, but this is not battle."

"Is it not? I have seen the Lady Annette's beauty and youth, Geoffrey, and the other attributes which she is displaying this night, and many will be present, all vying for her attentions. Think of it as a battle if it is her company you seek."

"Would you try to win her affections, too?"

"What would one so young and fair want with one as old as me?" he asked but Geoffrey saw the challenge lurking in Michel's eyes. He also saw the dress which awaited Michel. It was obviously his best.

"The best man shall win." Geoffrey crawled from the room and closed the small door. In his chambers he discovered no water in his washbowl for he had not ordered any. When it came time to wash he waited for warm weather and scrubbed with sand in the river. It was no use calling Cateline to fetch water because she was attending Adelina. Too lazy to fetch it himself, Geoffrey dabbed some of Michel's oil under each armpit before he dressed and finally attached the studded belt to his waist. Then he dragged a comb through his hair. Armed with sword and the dagger he used for eating, Geoffrey took a deep breath and tried to quell his anticipation. He ventured down to the great hall, hesitating for a moment at Adelina's door. He crouched and looked through the keyhole. Sitting by the bed was Cateline.

Geoffrey went in. Cateline stood immediately. "Please, Master, be silent for she sleeps, finally," she whispered. Geoffrey walked to the bed and looked down at Adelina while Cateline studied Geoffrey. Something was different in his appearance and she knew not what it was.

"Has she spoken of what happened?" Geoffrey asked.

"No, Master Geoffrey. She only mentions your name again and again in her sleep. It is as if she cries so because her calling is not answered." Cateline wouldn't look into Geoffrey's eyes.

Geoffrey sighed and looked down at Adelina. In his mind's eye he saw Dupuy again, raising his sword high. Geoffrey glanced at Cateline. "She cries my name often?"

Cateline nodded and studied her feet.

"Summon me should she improve or get worse for I wish to be present either way. Do you understand me, girl?"

"It would be the lady's wish, too, Master Geoffrey."

She did not sit again until Geoffrey had gone, then she sat, looked at her mistress and resumed her sewing. Cateline did not worry unduly about the sweat appearing on her mistress's face and when her mistress called out and kicked the covers off, Cateline simply leant over and covered the nakedness again. The cut was long and deep and when she moved, teardrops of blood appeared under the black ointment. The ointment, Michel had said, would hold the skin together as long as she was kept very still.

Geoffrey appeared again on the bottom stair leading to the great hall. Many were present already and it was not yet fully dark outside. Charboys and servants abounded, filling goblets with rich wines and ales and carrying about the room great platters of fruits and nuts and meats. Geoffrey, of course, was not interested in wines, ales, fruits or anything else. He searched for the Lady Annette but did not see her anywhere. Geoffrey stepped down into the crowd, took an offered goblet of ale and drank it immediately. He took another and held this one in his right hand. Still he could not find the beauty who had caught his gaze and heart only a short while ago. There were many ladies present, some of whom looked upon him with a smile, but his mind was set as it would be before a battle. He would win this Lady Annette tonight.

Raoul in his finery, and with his hair glistening, and also smelling as Geoffrey hoped he smelled, walked to him, sipped on his ale and spoke quietly. "Finish the ale and come with me." Geoffrey obeyed.

On the kitchen stairs, Raoul said very softly, "Trouble is ahead. Word has come from Allegre that Dupuy gathers a force. Before the moon rises he will be here. Help me set the defences proper."

"You expect a siege tonight?"

"I expect blood will flow, yes."

In Geoffrey's time, there had been skirmishes only along the track where Henri Dupuy swore the land was his and Robert swore the same. It was a piece of land ten yards wide by three chain long. The feud had been inherited on both sides. Some said Henri Dupuy was not as his forefather, that he was a reasonable man, but often reason had no place when a son was dead by enemy hand. Geoffrey felt sickness rising. He had not thought of consequences when he loosed that crossbolt—he was saving Adelina. But so, too, had his uncle shot, so guilt if there was any, lay equally between them. Robert had no sons yet Dupuy had two. Now there was one less. His eldest, Baudoin, was as yet unmarried and a knight at arms. What would be, it was often asked, should a Dupuy son and a Polignac daughter wed?

Perhaps it was true that both Henri and Robert were reasonable men. Each's father had met his death in a one-to-one battle over that short piece of roadway. A fair fight, they'd said, but no one had emerged victor. There was not a lot of peace between the families these days, but great amounts of blood no longer stained that short stretch of roadway. Excepting of course today's incident.

This would herald war.

The abbot Jean, who was, in his heart, a peace-loving man, had once given Geoffrey some astonishing wisdom. They had sat together on the hillside enjoying the solitude for however long it lasted, and he had turned to Geoffrey and said, 'Geoffrey, it is this way with the world. What begins as man against man, becomes family against family, then village against village. Before long, it is kingdom against kingdom and for what? For more of this, for more of that? For greed, and the hungers that such greed can never satisfy? Could this not stop by a man extending his hand in friendship to another man once considered his enemy?'

'The world is not like that,' Geoffrey had said. 'Such a world resides in the heart alone. It is not what the eye witnesses.'

'But do you not ponder upon such things?'

Geoffrey had said yes, he often thought of such things but thoughts only they would remain. The abbot Jean was unlike most of his standing. He condemned violence of any kind, regardless of the True Faith's doctrine. Geoffrey was forever amazed that the abbot had not been charged with heresy or excommunicated.

"Are you sure that Dupuy will come this night?"

Raoul nodded.

"Then we shall be ready for him."

Geoffrey turned back to the crowded hall. Still he could see her nowhere.

"The Lady Annette walks in the courtyard alone. Perhaps this is now the time to search her out for her own safety?" Raoul suggested.

"Does nothing pass you by?" Geoffrey asked.

Raoul smiled.

"Are you sure that her name is Annette?"

"Do not look to me with hopeful eyes, boy. I fear you waste precious time. Only moments ago, Gabriel went to the courtyard."

Gabriel? Gabriel?

Raoul did not hide his amusement as Geoffrey darted down the kitchen stairs and Raoul followed at a more leisurely pace. Already his mind was occupied with strategy should Dupuy come with a small force. For a small force of late would be all he could muster at such short notice.

Scaling the three outer walls was nigh impossible because of the angle of the slopes below. A dozen archers on the ramparts could fell fifty men long before any rope ladder could be used. Entry by the gate was also restricted by use of the bridge drawn up and archers placed over the gate. None dared cross for the deep cavern was nigh bottomless and many had fallen to their deaths, their bodies never recovered. The chateau was situated on the side of a mountain and the river's churning waters below was its other defense. A siege tonight would not be favoured. Many nobles and some clergy were inside the great hall, feasting, and unaware of any imminent dangers.

Geoffrey appeared in the courtyard, sight aided by the flaming torches lighting the way for any latecomer.

The moon had not yet risen. Any hope he may have had of securing Lady Annette's attentions were soon shattered. By the farrier's stood Gabriel of Lyon in his war-like finery. Gabriel, tall and handsome, all that Geoffrey was not, leaned against the farrier's wall, his head lowered. He was in deep conversation with the Lady Annette and by the way he stood, Geoffrey knew that the lady dared to make no escape for he stood in such a way that there was no escape. Geoffrey did not know what he felt. Was it anger or disappointment? He had ridden out, prepared for battle and found no one there.

How he wished he had a bow in his hands. He could surely fell him with one well-aimed strike. Gabriel, the newest vassal now in service, had many and varied experiences of battle in the east, in England, Germany, Spain and many places farther afield. Geoffrey did not know him intimately, as Gabriel kept very much to himself, but it was said he had been captured by Saladin himself and admired of courage so great that he had been granted a release. Perhaps, Geoffrey thought, they are confusing Gabriel with Hugo? Gabriel was a mercenary, a wanderer, with no home as such, none that Geoffrey knew of at least, and nor did his loyalties stretch farther than whoever was his current master. When the pay was low or there was little else to do, Gabriel moved on. And he was supposed to be the son of a viscount? A noble himself?

Geoffrey prayed that he would not remain in service here a lengthy time.

Gabriel spoke rarely and his green eyes were forever watchful and trusting of none. No one knew the thoughts in his mind or so it was said. But Geoffrey, as he approached, certainly knew the thoughts in his mind at that moment. He would seduce the Lady Annette and then turn his back on her. His reputation often walked before him and under the spell of his eyes all women were victims. So it was said. Probably by Gabriel himself.

As he drew closer, Geoffrey noticed that Gabriel was busy fondling the precious jewel suspended on a long chain around the beauty's neck. Geoffrey walked by. "Gabriel, a word?"

Gabriel turned, looked at Geoffrey and returned to his conversation with Lady Annette. "Stay," he said. "This won't take long." And he walked to where Geoffrey stood, studying his feet. He quietly told Gabriel what had been told him by Raoul. Gabriel nodded. Geoffrey was about to ask the Lady Annette to accompany him inside when Gabriel said, "Inside, my sweet Annette. I will escort you."

Annette did not even glance at Geoffrey. He watched as Gabriel deliberately dropped to one knee and kissed her hand before escorting her inside, and he looked back at Geoffrey and smiled.

Despairing, Geoffrey took up his crossbow and bolts, and climbed up to the rampart. The villagers were on their way, a small procession bearing torches, and inside the courtyard they waited quietly. Some sharpened aged daggers on flintstone, five archers amongst them seemed restless and fondled their simple hunting bows. Raoul, Acelin, and Michel positioned them and warned for silence as no one inside need know of any danger, real or otherwise until the last possible moment.

The moon rose and, as the night wore on, still there was no sign of Dupuy. Or, for that matter, of Gabriel. He was the only one Geoffrey kept looking for. When he finally appeared, adjusting his hauberk and walking as if he had too much to drink, he climbed up to where Geoffrey was stationed, leaned on the top of the wall and sighed loudly. "There is nothing that equals the taste of some female flesh before a fight."

Geoffrey said nothing as he did not know what female flesh tasted like. Perhaps it was obvious, for he was always being tormented about his innocence in such matters, how he would rather have his head buried in books and philosophies, not breasts or thighs.

Gabriel looked down at the surroundings to the thick woods below. There was nothing yet to be seen on the track and the bridge was raised. Unlike Geoffrey, Gabriel was accustomed to waiting. Gabriel, barely ten years older than Geoffrey, was a commended survivor of many battles. Geoffrey had yet to see one. It wasn't fair.

"There is no difference between a peasant and a noblewoman. They all moan alike."

Geoffrey's mouth was dry.

"But Adelina will be a challenge for me. That beauty longs to be tamed."

"You will leave her be."

Gabriel said nothing to that. "You killed your first today and now we all must pay. This is because of you."

"I had no choice. Adelina was in danger."

"What will you do when I marry her, Sparrow? When all of this is mine?"

Geoffrey closed his eyes. This one is sent to torment me.

Gabriel continued. "By what foul means do you wear the Polignac arms?"

"I bear the name of my father, my uncle."

"It is said you were born bastards. You and your idiot brother."

Anger welled again. Geoffrey knew full well that Gabriel wanted to fight, so he refused to acknowledge Gabriel's presence in the hope he would tire and go away. Gabriel sighed again, reached into one of his folds and withdrew some nuts he had taken from the feast table. "The girl begged for more."

"If she begged for more then perhaps you delivered less than expected."

Gabriel arched an eyebrow and a small smile played in his eyes and on his lips. He was drunk, and Geoffrey wished not for the first time, that he would leave them all in peace. Because peaceful it was before he appeared.

"Tell me, Geoffrey, why is it you use a woman's perfume? Are you hiding something from me? Or can it be what the others say is true? That you don't like... women."

Geoffrey drew his dagger. "Find another station before I cut your lying tongue into pieces. I have killed one man already today and it would be a pleasure to kill you and hold your black heart in my hand for you breed nothing but trouble as easily as you draw breath. Away for your own sake. Away."

Gabriel looked down at Geoffrey and laughed. He could have clamped him under his armpit and broken his neck with ease but the young man was very quick. He had seen the agility for himself many a time. "You are as frightening as your half-wit brother and far less useful." Gabriel went away, staggering, but not to find another station. He retreated back to the castle.

"Where do you go!"

Gabriel did not reply. Geoffrey was silently urged to go into the chambers to see if Adelina was as before, sleeping. If the hand of a Dupuy had tried to kill her once, would another not attempt it again? She was the sole heir. What would become of the estate should she die? Geoffrey jumped down from his post and Raoul intercepted him. "What is it?"

"I must be with Adelina."

"You are needed here."

"No. I must be by her side. What if there is one of murderous intent already in the chateau, and his identity is as yet unknown? She is unguarded, Raoul. I beg you let me go to her."

# CHAPTER 6

She was not 'unguarded'.

Gabriel was in the chambers, with Cateline and it was a sight Geoffrey wished he hadn't seen. The poor girl was partly naked and weeping, her face crushed against the stone wall as Gabriel had his way. "What is this?"

Gabriel laughed at the sound of the indignant voice. "Watch if you must, boy. Learn."

"Enough!"

Gabriel heard the sound of unsheathing metal, felt the sting of blade and turned, slowly. The tip of the young man's sword rested under his ear. Geoffrey reached for Cateline and she took his hand. He pulled her behind him, to safety. "Clothe yourself." Cateline took up her torn tunic and threw it on, weeping still.

"Valiant, boy, but she is of no importance."

Gabriel obviously didn't realise that Geoffrey had known Cateline since she was an infant. Her mother was a washer-woman who'd returned to her duties at the chateau on the very day she gave birth. Gabriel could learn much from a mere peasant's loyalty.

"Don't be foolish. Ask the girl. She'll tell you that we do this often."

Geoffrey, without taking his gaze from Gabriel's face, said, "Is this true, Cate?"

Cateline said nothing, her shame was too great.

"Speak, girl! Speak!"

"It is true, Master Geoffrey. It is true."

"Have you nothing else to say?"

There was silence. He withdrew the sword and Gabriel retreated.

Geoffrey finally took breath. Sweat popped on his forehead and lip, and bees swarmed in his belly as he sheathed his sword and turned to Cateline. She stood weeping quietly, as far from him as possible. "I cannot believe that you would... would... with the likes of him."

"Master Geoffrey, I must obey for he has said, he has said..."

"What has he said?"

Cateline could not look into Geoffrey's eyes. He walked to her, took her face in his hand and forced her to look at him. "What has he said to you, Cate?"

"That should I ever, even once, deny him his needs, he would see to it that no man would waste his time in looking at me."

"Cateline, listen to me. Cateline!"

She tried very hard to look into Geoffrey's eyes.

"He will never touch you again. I swear this on my life. Should he try, call for me immediately."

"But Master, he..."

"Call for me." He put his hand on her shoulder and Cateline pulled away very quickly. "How often does this happen?"

"Almost every day since he came here."

"And you say nothing?"

"He would kill me. If not me, then my family would suffer. He says I am easily replaced."

"Then he does not know us, does he. I suggest that you tend to your mistress now. Thank God she did not see this or she'd have killed Gabriel herself."

"Master." Cateline went to the bed and with shaking hands drew the rag from the oiled water. She squeezed it out and patted Adelina's face and neck with it.

Adelina was mumbling, her hair drenched with sweat, her lips parched. Geoffrey poured water into a goblet, smelled and tasted it before he sat on the bed and lifted her so that she could take it. "Here, my love. Drink slowly."

After she drank, Cateline and Geoffrey laid her down. "Bathe her and clothe her." Geoffrey got off the bed and turned his back. He had seen enough. The black ointment across the shoulder had set like resin but blood still flowed beneath it.

He didn't look back for some time; his gaze rested on the courtyard far below. In the distance, two torches bobbed along the roadway. Only two. "I cannot clothe her, Master Geoffrey. Master Michel said that the wound needs air and is not to be covered."

Below, in the great hall came the echoes of a minstrel's rowdy song.

"Master Geoffrey, I am afraid."

"Of what?"

"I fear that Gabriel will kill you for what you have done and said tonight."

"He can try. I have no fear of him. It is unfortunate that my uncle trusts him with his very life. Perhaps the master's judgment was clouded by that one simple act."

"What?" Cateline asked quietly as she dabbed at her mistress's sweating face.

"Two years ago, as my uncle and Acelin traveled to Lyon, they were set upon by thieves. It is said that from nowhere Gabriel came, aided the fight, and chased them off. He was not seen again until this past harvest moon when he announced himself at this gate. But he shall not remain here long, Cateline. Those like him do not stay in one place forever. Take heart in that. We all must."

"But he says he will marry Adelina. That all this will be his."

"Do not distress yourself over impossibilities, Cate." Geoffrey sat again by Adelina's bed. She slept, although her eyelids danced from the nightmares in her mind. She was very ill and he was sickened to be so close. Geoffrey reached for his lady's hand and he stroked the cold, damp skin tenderly. Gabriel's words that he would take Adelina as his wife were more damaging to Geoffrey's heart than his supposed seduction of Annette had been. Geoffrey would rather die than be forced to watch Adelina marry the likes of Gabriel.

He sighed and stretched his legs. His feet touched something under the bed. Geoffrey looked down. An empty chamber pot, and something resembling a quintain lay under the bed. He reached down and drew the rag-stuffed, human figure out. It bore cross bolts in the center of a painted heart, and around its neck, a rope. Geoffrey raised his gaze to the ceiling and sure enough, there was a severed rope dangling from the crossbeam. Also under the bed he discovered Acelin's missing crossbow. It was one he never used for it had a fault and would, at times least expected, cast the bolt backwards. Acelin had a scar along his neck as proof of the weapon's unpredictability. Where had Adelina got it from?

Geoffrey looked at Cateline. A secret obviously shared. "You knew of this?" She nodded but said nothing, fearing what he would do. "For how long has she toyed with this?"

"Master, I cannot say."

"There will be no secrets, Cateline, or you will find yourself back in the village tending the fields!"

"A while, Master. A full season, perhaps."

Geoffrey couldn't believe she'd not been injured by it. "She has the strength to draw it back this way?" he asked as he strung and drew back using his foot as leverage. Cateline shook her head. Geoffrey, holding the faulted bow with one hand at his shoulder, took imaginary aim at an imaginary Gabriel on the opposite wall.

"No, Master, she sits with it and uses her feet to push while she pulls with her hands."

"She sits?" he squawked, horrified.

"I swore on my life never to tell."

"This bow, girl, has killed two of its users. It almost killed Acelin. It is not used because of its faults."

Geoffrey paced the room before he slammed the bow against the stone wall. It did not break. Had he not wanted it to break it surely would, so he threw it from the window. There was a curse from far below as it nearly hit someone.

"Master, please, do not be loud for there is no pain when she sleeps."

"She has lied to me! All this talk of becoming a lady. Just talk. Talk. She lied to me!"

"Master, I beg you..."

"Why does she do this! Why does she hate me so!"

"She does not hate you." Cateline was shocked that he would even think this. She may have been the serving girl but she was also her mistress's friend, and often they talked and shared many secrets. Had the mistress not said that she would rather be promised to Geoffrey than anyone? Not Christian, no, for Christian, although she remembered him as very handsome, she did not know him as she knew Geoffrey. Geoffrey, she had said, could see into her heart and know what lay there often before she did. Can a boy or a man be a good friend to a girl or a lady? she had once asked but Cateline did not know. No boy or man had ever spoken to her apart from giving her orders. With boy or man she knew not what to do except work or lie with her legs spread for Gabriel when he so desired it. Life had been good before he came to Lavoute Polignac.

"I know of one thing, Master. Our mistress does not hate you. It is you she loves, this I know for she has told me."

"She loves me?" Geoffrey asked, amazed.

"As you love her."

Geoffrey returned to the window. The two visitors were arriving in the courtyard now, Dupuy and his eldest son, Baudoin, and both were still mounted and bearing torches. Robert appeared, surrounded by his armed defenders; Gabriel, Michel, Raoul, Louis and Acelin. Geoffrey longed to be present for he detested hearing news second-hand. Geoffrey watched as Dupuy and his son dismounted and walked towards Robert.

"Bolt the door and allow none entry unless the visitor is Master Robert, Michel, or me. None other."

Cateline bolted the door after Geoffrey departed.

Gabriel walked behind Robert, his current lord. As he walked, he thought it would be best to simply kill the Dupuys now and begone with the politics and lies. He would never welcome an enemy this way. Robert the Foolish trusted too many of the wrong kind. He was too soft and far too reasonable a man and deserved nothing of what he had. Gabriel spat on the floor as they proceeded up from the kitchens. It was not good to invite the enemy into the chateau this way. Baudoin Dupuy was taking too much stock of the interior. Gabriel became very annoyed indeed when Robert led the party directly up into the tower.

This chateau was unlike the many he'd inhabited in his time. It was small, hardly self-contained, and upon the grounds, very few resided except for the farrier and the servants and vassals. It was not strategically placed at all. If the villagers revolted there would be little defense. The villagers, though, would never revolt, for Robert, they said, was a gentle and fair lord, and life in the village was mostly peaceful in such warring times. The Polignac vassals quelled disputes, kept thieves at bay and Robert himself judged on matters of dispute which could not be settled to satisfaction. Great wealth by claiming possession of more land he did not aspire to, unlike the Dupuys, or so it was said. And Robert the Foolish was also a regular visitor to the court of Philippe Augustus. Some said the two were often found in deep conversation, walking alone and unguarded amid the tombs in St. Denis.

Standing on the stairs with his hand on his sword was the sparrow, his pretty feathers still ruffled. Geoffrey moved aside when Robert, not dressed for battle, and the rest of the party, swept by. Gabriel caught Geoffrey's gaze as he passed. His torment had not yet eased for more was yet to come that this little fool knew nothing of. Geoffrey followed the procession up the stairs.

It seemed that before he would believe, Henri Dupuy insisted on seeing Adelina for himself. Baudoin had, as yet, not spoken. He stood taller than his father, was twice as proud and filled with much hatred. All went into Adelina's chambers except Acelin, who stood at the door. Cateline, Geoffrey noted, was shrinking in fear.

"Geoffrey. Come closer."

Geoffrey stepped forward and faced his uncle.

"Relate the events of this day to our good neighbor."

Geoffrey noticed that his uncle was allowing the enemy to get too close to Adelina's bed. Cateline was shaking in terror, because close behind her stood Gabriel.

"I was returning from collecting the dues when I crested the hill a hundred yards from the gate. I saw a horse, a Dupuy horse, untethered in the middle of the road. As I drew the cart closer, I saw Jean-Pierre Dupuy with his sword raised for the kill. I then saw that Adelina was his intended victim. Her clothes were torn, there also much blood, so I raised my crossbow and I loosed a bolt."

"Where was this?" Henri Dupuy asked.

"Barely one hundred yards from our gate."

"Then you must have very good eyes."

"The blood still stains the ground where both your son and my mistress lay."

"On your land."

"This is so."

"Are her wounds mortal?"

Robert nodded to Cateline, who drew back the covers so that only the wound showed. Henri Dupuy moved closer for a better look. The girl was very ill indeed. "Falchion," he said to himself and looked at Baudoin who stood motionless, hatred alive in his eyes. "Robert, I have no words at this time but I do regret what has transpired this day."

"As I," Robert said. "I would invite you to join in our festivities but I know that you are in mourning. Our prayers are with you and your good wife, and you, Baudoin for your loss."

Henri Dupuy looked back at Adelina. "She is very beautiful, Robert. Very beautiful indeed."

Robert simply nodded.

Geoffrey's heart beat fast for Baudoin's gaze was feasting on him, hungry, although Geoffrey knew it was not food he wanted. It was revenge. It was a feeling which Geoffrey knew only too well. He did not lower his gaze, and Baudoin moved only when his father touched his shoulder and beckoned him follow. Baudoin spat and in his dark eyes lay death. Geoffrey again remained calm.

Geoffrey did not move until he saw the Dupuys depart with the body of son and brother, torches and moonlight their only guides. He thought repeatedly, Draw up the bridge. Draw up the bridge. But it remained down.

Michel bade entrance to the room and he crouched by the bed. He put his hand on Adelina's forehead, then touched her hand. "Will she die?" Geoffrey asked.

"I have seen strong men die from less than this, Geoffrey. Only she and God will decide between them." Michel sighed and looked at Cateline, who sat as quietly as she could. Michel saw the marks around her neck, turning into bruises. "What has happened to you?" he asked, but Cateline dared not speak.

"She was set upon by Gabriel. I witnessed it and put an end to it."

Michel, frowning, looked curiously at Geoffrey. "Set upon?" Geoffrey read the eyes well and nodded. "I see. The master must be informed immediately."

"I beg you both no!" Catelina cried to no avail.

"Master Robert will be informed." Michel had decided.

"Fear not, girl, he will never harm you again. Go now to your bed. Michel and I will tend Adelina during the night. You have done enough this day. Go now."

Cateline hesitated.

"Does he frighten you so that you dare not walk about this household alone?" Geoffrey asked and Cateline nodded.

"Then I shall accompany you downstairs."

At her door in the narrow passageway behind the kitchens, Cateline hesitated again. "I beg you not say a word of this to the master, please Master Geoffrey."

"I must. Even Michel thinks it wise that we do."

"But he will kill me. I saw it in his eyes. He will kill me."

"The master would do no such thing, girl. He is a fair, decent man."

"I speak of Gabriel."

"He would not dare harm you now."

Geoffrey was surprised when Cateline put her face against his shoulder and wept. He drew her away and she had a peculiar expression in her eyes. "All will be well, girl. We will be rid of Gabriel soon."

Gabriel waited until Geoffrey had left the serving girl's room before he stepped from the shadows, unnoticed.

Upstairs, a bard was engaging all who would listen with a rowdy song of Saladin, a very long, rhyming verse which it seemed caught more ladies' attentions than any man or boy's. Robert was back in his seat. Beside him, Marys. At her elbow, Lord Charles's wife, and Charles at Robert's. Geoffrey had no inkling of what these festivities were about.

Most of those present were very drunk and noisy. Platters of food constantly appeared from the kitchens. There was music and laughter and no one present guessed the dangers that very night could have brought. Geoffrey ran his fingers through his hair. Although it no longer itched as before, it now felt as soft as a woman's. Damn Michel's soap.

From across the wide, long room he felt the gaze and turned to it. Raóul was speaking with the beautiful Annette. Again, when gazes touched, Geoffrey's heart lifted. Raoul beckoned him and Geoffrey obliged but the bard seized him on his way past and included him in his song. All who were listening laughed. Geoffrey, too, laughed—

there was no other choice.

Raoul put his arm around Geoffrey's shoulders. "Here is the one of whom they sing, this brave young knight, lacking in height, but nevertheless, a beautiful sight."

Geoffrey hoped he wasn't blushing with shame because Annette was giggling quietly. "Raoul, I am pleased you fight better than you pen rhyme."

"My words do not match yours, this I know. Annette," Raoul said and reached for Geoffrey's hand. "This is your future husband, Geoffrey."

The beautiful girl clasped her fingers on Geoffrey's very tightly and Geoffrey, speechless, turned to Raoul. "Surely this is jest?"

"Would I jest?" Raoul took his leave. But why was he laughing so? Geoffrey turned back to Annette. He did not know what to say, or what to do now. He was lost within the depths of her dark eyes.

"Do you not like me?" she asked, surprised.

"It is not that, Milady. I don't understand what's happening. I was told nothing of this."

"Then we shall walk alone, you and I, and I will explain. Come." She took his hand and walked to the main entry doors where a page and a squire waited.

"Milady, it is not wise to venture out at this time."

"Come. I wish to know you better." She tugged on his hand. Geoffrey looked back. Raoul was watching. He lifted his tankard and grinned widely.

The doors then closed and Geoffrey was alone in the darkness with the beautiful girl who had been on his mind for most of the evening. Were he not so frightened, it could have been a dream meeting a waking state with a very fond embrace.

"Oh! Roses," she exclaimed, and ventured off into the moonlit darkness, her hand still clasped on Geoffrey's. "Your uncle and my stepfather are at this moment in deep conversation as to our future."

"But why was I not told? I did not know that Charles had a stepdaughter."

"Geoffrey, you must marry me or I am to spend all my days as a nun. I cannot be a nun. I do not wish my husband to be invisible and unreachable. I need one such as you."

"But Milady, I do not know you."

"Yet you find me beautiful, surely?"

"Well, yes, but..."

"But? But? You do not like me." She let go of his hand and stared at her feet. Geoffrey thought she would cry.

"Please, Milady, do not cry. I am taken aback. I need time to think."

"It is cold out here," she said. "Give me your hands. Warm me. Here." She took his hands and placed them on her breasts. He could feel her heart dancing, or perhaps it was his own. What was this? This did not feel right. He almost objected; he almost withdrew his hands until she slid her cold fingers under his hauberk. Her fingertips were guided by a lot of experience it seemed.

"What are you doing?"

"You don't know?" she asked, amazed.

"Well, yes, I know. Of course I know. Milady, please..."

Annette took hold of him, hard, and looked into his eyes. "You want me. I know it. I feel it."

"Milady, please. Don't. I may not be able to stop." She reached behind her head and pulled at the laces of her dress. She slid it off her shoulders slowly until it reached her hips and from there, after a wiggle, it fell to the grass.

"You want me, Geoffrey. I saw it in your eyes the moment we first looked at each other. Do you remember? For what you felt then, I have felt all evening. Take me now. Quickly. I cannot wait a moment longer."

His body was wild but his face expressionless.

"Take me, Geoffrey. Take me now. Do what you will and I will be yours forever."

But he could only stare, dumbfounded. She took his hands again, and his fingertips covered the soft mounds of flesh, and as in the tales of conquests he had heard so often, he longed, too, to take her breasts into his mouth. And it was easily done because she was taller. Then, she surprised him by suddenly springing at him, and locking her legs around his waist. He was soon smothered and lost balance. They both fell with a clang and a giggle, to the damp, cold grass, Geoffrey cushioning the fall. She was laughing. She sat astride him and fought her way in against the mail, and then settled down on him slowly. Geoffrey's breath caught in his throat from the feeling—one he'd not experienced quite like this before. She began to move up and down, and soon he was aware of nothing else at all. His eyes were closed and a storm was about to break inside him. And when it finally exploded, very quickly, he was able to breathe again.

He opened his eyes, she was still astride him. But she was laughing and shaking her head, giggling his name repeatedly.

Geoffrey heard movement from behind, then beside him. He looked. Raoul and Acelin. Both had large tankards in hand. Raoul offered his to the woman and she tipped her head back. He poured the ale into her mouth. She gulped it down with abandon and it spilled down her body, and onto Geoffrey. Then Raoul seized her hair and it came off in his hand.

The sparkling-eyed whore, no more a noble than Cateline the serving girl, was laughing hard.

Raoul tugged her off Geoffrey's hips, pushed her flat on the grass with his boot. And he took her there.

Someone else came out of the darkness. Gabriel. He and Acelin were very amused and both wished Geoffrey a very happy birthday.

Geoffrey sat up, got to his feet, adjusted his attire and tried to recover what remained of his dignity before he walked quickly back inside to the great hall. He did not stay for the festivities, nor did he go to Adelina's room. He burst into Christian's room, his heart ready to explode from shame and anger and many other feelings he had never experienced before.

His brother was sitting by the window again, staring out at nothing, his only movement the rise and fall of his chest as he breathed. But he made a sound when Geoffrey stood by the window. Geoffrey could have told him what had just transpired but he would rather not, too. It took him some time to settle himself, and wonder if he could ever face his brothers in arms again without seeing the smiles behind their eyes.

Christian made another noise and with difficulty, raised his right hand and pointed to the window. Geoffrey turned. "It is the moon, my brother. It is only the moon."

Christian kept his finger aloft, but Geoffrey noticed, he was also trying to point downwards. His fingers would not work. Geoffrey looked down from the window and his heart almost stood still.

The sentry hung dead over the gate.

The roadway beyond was alive with a swarm of men. Already the bridge was being drawn up, but, Geoffrey knew, far too late.

Christian made another noise. He was trying hard to talk. He tried to stand, too, but Geoffrey pushed him down. "No. You will stay here, brother. Stay here."

Geoffrey immediately went down to make Robert aware of what he'd witnessed. It seemed that he already knew, or perhaps, this had been expected. Robert said calmly, with a twinkle in his eye, "Summon the others."

Geoffrey held back his own enthusiasm as best he could. One third of those present were ladies, the rest, apart from six clergy, were landholders and nobles from Bourbon, Toulouse, and one from as far distant as Aquitaine. Each was accompanied by at least two vassals and all were drinking hard, their hearts stirred by talk of battle after battle. Already there had been one scuffle between a knight from Toulouse and a foreign bowman who was smaller in height than Geoffrey.

Geoffrey ran out to summon the others. Raoul and Gabriel were still in the rose garden, Gabriel was taking his fill of the woman this time. Did this man never stop? "An attack is nigh!"

Gabriel stopped his thrusting and grunting for a second, then continued. Geoffrey kicked his behind, hard. "I do not jest! An attack is nigh!"

Raoul clambered up to the rampart and looked over the wall to the forest below. His drunkenness soon disappeared. He called for his squire to bring his bow, sword, shield, battle axe, but the boy had anticipated his master's needs.

As Raoul was arming himself, a ladder appeared. Gabriel left the woman where she lay, her alabaster skin plainly visible in the moonlight. "Get her inside! We will hold them here!" Gabriel called.

Geoffrey reached down and heaved the woman to her feet. She was screaming for her clothes but there was no time to waste. Geoffrey was ready to hit her when she squirmed from his grip and ran, searching in vain for her clothing. He saw the first intruder appear on the wall and leap down to the rampart. She was little more than a shining target in the darkness. Geoffrey, in the space of a heartbeat, had taken a hard hold on the woman and was dragging her away when he heard the sound of arrow piercing flesh. He felt no pain and although he had hold of her arm, it was she who fell. He dragged her towards the doors, a target himself, until he was defended by Gabriel. The first intruder fell, and the second, third. The doors opened slightly and Geoffrey dragged the whore in. He secured the doors.

Michel was busy herding the ladies and the six clergy up into the tower, and he came down immediately upon seeing another woman. He grabbed one of the cloth covers on the hewn table, food and drink spilled. Michel rolled her to her side, and using his foot for leverage, pulled the arrow from her lower back. She screamed, and finally passed out. Michel covered her with the cloth he had pulled and carried her upstairs to the others.

Moments that felt like an eternity had passed since Geoffrey first saw the sentry hanging dead. Now, the great hall was almost empty except for this inebriated gathering of fighters, all arming themselves.

"Archers!" came the call.

The short foreigner, Geoffrey, and four others stepped forward, and the weapons were handed out by Louis. Geoffrey soon joined the tail of the clinking throng as it proceeded down the stairs and through the kitchens into the courtyard. Geoffrey heard the doors secure behind him.

Several intruders were within the courtyard confines. Although the bridge was drawn up, many were already in by ladders. The noise of the fighting was fierce. Only torchlight and moon aided vision.

The little archer jabbered quickly in a language Geoffrey had never heard before and he pointed to the farrier's, using hand signals so Geoffrey would understand. It was there, along the southern courtyard wall, which held the best position for two archers, as the invaders could be picked off as they scaled the walls and gate and leapt to the rampart. Two others took the northern courtyard wall, the remaining two at the kitchen doors, and did the same. Only those at the kitchen doors though were protected by shields.

Those who did not fall from the volleys of the six archers were taken by Robert's peasants, armed with axes, clubs, knives and hatred.

The battle did not last for hours. It seemed only to endure for a few lengthy minutes. After eight volleys from the six archers, they were defeated, the surprise attack fended off.

Someone was laughing at how they had chosen the wrong night, indeed! Geoffrey did not know whether he meant knight or night. Not that it mattered. His heart beat furiously. He had not emptied his first quiver as yet but as far as he could tell, he had not missed one target either.

The little foreigner, a short distance away, spat a gargle of words again. Geoffrey did not understand until a voice from above his head translated. "He asks where is the leader; where are the knights at arms?" It was Gabriel. The archer mumbled again. "He says there is nothing to be gained by killing serfs who tend sheep better than they fight."

Please God, Geoffrey prayed. I want him to fall now. Fall at my feet with a Dupuy arrow in his black heart. Please God. But Gabriel jumped from the rampart, across to the farrier's rooftop and then to the ground beside Geoffrey.

All was quiet now except for the sounds of the wounded and dying. Those knights who had wanted a fair fight were sorely disappointed. To them it seemed a light relief, as if this had been planned to occur to break the monotony of talk and drinking. Geoffrey was disappointed too. Disappointed that such a senseless event had been instigated in the first place. A call from the gate met all's ears:

"Come! See the cowards run!"

Robert, Gabriel and Geoffrey also took to the rampart beside the gate. On a dark horse, in dark armor painted with the Dupuy hawk, sat a young man none could recognise at a distance. His army was scattering about him, running for their lives. Geoffrey lifted his bow, Robert slapped at his arm. "No. It is Baudoin."

"This is but a taste, do you hear me, you murdering pigs! It is but a taste!"

Gabriel swore and spat to the side. He said quietly, "We have the force at hand to take the Dupuy estate for our own, my lord, if we do it now," and he looked down to the courtyard below, where bored knights stood impatiently wanting more battle. Fair battle.

Geoffrey, too, looked down at the courtyard, but saw only the litter of peasant bodies, some moving, some not. Women were wailing.

How he hated that sound.

"We should take the Dupuys now for their defenses are worn."

"No," Robert said quietly.

"Then let me go after him. We can ransom him."

"No! It is over. Enough bloodshed. I'm thirsty." Robert went back into the chateau, urging the knights, his guests, to follow, and the evening's merriment continued.

Raoul appeared, his left arm hanging useless. He had been hit by a flaming arrow meant for an upstairs window. It not only punctured muscle but burned as well, and pieces of the torn mail were embedded deep in the wound. But he sat quietly and turned his face away, wincing as Louis pulled the arrow out.

And throughout, the short, stocky foreigner still gabbled to Geoffrey, even though Geoffrey was at a loss to understand a word he said. He was followed everywhere by the talented archer, who was always one step behind him as Geoffrey kicked over what he thought was a corpse. He found that the arrow punctured shoulder only. This one had feigned death to escape an axe through his head. He was young, younger than Geoffrey, and his eyes were wide with terror. From the state of his hands and clothing, he had worked the fields all of his life.

Robert now gone, Gabriel climbed down and ambled to Geoffrey and the archer. "How is it you understand the babble this one issues?" Geoffrey asked as they stood over the terrified survivor.

"I spent time in his land. They are wonderful fighters and he has taught me much. Is that not so, Dedwyd?"

The small, stocky man grinned at the sound of his name.

"He is yours?" Geoffrey asked.

"His allegiance is to me." Gabriel slapped the man on the back hard and received another grin. "Now, what is this picture of misfortune?" Gabriel asked as he looked down into the wide eyes. The man could not move. When his bladder emptied, Gabriel's face twisted into a smile, a smile which alarmed Geoffrey because even he knew not its true meaning.

"Who is your cowardly leader that he would not venture into battle with you?" Gabriel asked and drew his sword very slowly. It was bloodied. The man tried to squirm away. "Who is your cowardly leader!"

"Baudoin Dupuy," the man eventually muttered.

Then he begged for mercy. Didn't they all? Gabriel stepped back and turned to Geoffrey. "Finish it, then keep the watch," he ordered and with arm around his little Welsh friend, Gabriel walked off, muttering in the language he knew very well, or so it seemed for the other spoke in return and each laughed.

Geoffrey looked down at the young man, half dead at his feet who begged, "I have children, three children."

"Then I hope you bade them farewell. And they you."

# Chapter 7

The night of festivities and battle gently faded into a bleak nothingness of pre-dawn. None of the guests were injured except for the whore, purchased for the evening for Geoffrey's sake and his colleagues' amusement. Of her wounds she had died during the night. Ten of the villagers had also perished defending their lord and master.

At daybreak would come the task of clearing away the Dupuy dead from the courtyard and the chateau surrounds. But it was not daybreak as yet.

Geoffrey made his way to his chambers as a rooster crowed with the impending dawn. Had he the strength, he would have strangled it. He was tired, exhausted, yet on his way past, he looked into Adelina's room. Marys was asleep, her head resting on her daughter's bed.

He looked in, too, at his brother, who still sat as he had hours before, staring out of the window. Geoffrey went into Christian's chambers, closed the door and said, "We drove them back, brother." Christian made a noise. He already knew.

Geoffrey lay face down on his brother's bed, but his rest was shortlived. Breaking the early morning darkness, Ella's screams. Geoffrey groaned and dragged himself down to the kitchens and the narrow passageway beyond, where two charboys stood, staring open-mouthed at what lay behind Cateline's door.

Ella was still screaming but Geoffrey heard nothing. He pushed the charboys aside and saw, on the narrow palette, what remained of Cateline. He turned away, quickly, and heard his uncle's booming voice echoing: "The noise! The noise!"

Robert, half naked, came in, followed by most of the household. He glanced at Geoffrey but Geoffrey didn't acknowledge his uncle's presence. His head was spinning. When the small crowd parted, Robert saw it, too.

Cateline lay on her bed, naked except for a covering of her own blood. Not one part of her body had been spared, or so it seemed.

Geoffrey pushed out of the room, and he walked immediately into Gabriel who refused to step aside. Was that a smile upon Gabriel's face?

"Will someone stop that screaming!" Robert bellowed, for his head was in danger of splitting. Gabriel used his fist and Ella dropped to the floor and lay there, unmoving. Geoffrey sprang to the attack immediately. Robert and Michel pulled the two apart. "He is responsible! She warned me he would do this!"

Gabriel smiled. "Watch what you say, Geoffrey. Was it not you the last to be seen with her? And she can't speak now. Exactly what would you do to have me out of this employ?" He asked, loud enough for all to hear. Geoffrey fought to shake off Michel's hold.

"Enough! Enough!" Robert said. "I will speak to each of you. Gabriel, with me, now. The rest of you, take this... take this away." Michel and Louis stepped into Cateline's room and began the task of removing the body. Louis, who had seen much in his time, was overcome. This was someone he knew and he could not continue. Michel was left to his own devices and it would have been a solitary job, too, had Geoffrey not aided. He had known the poor creature since she was an infant clinging to his leg whilst he dragged her across the courtyard, enjoying her squeals of delight. But why, he thought, must I remember this now? Not when she poured my wine, or served my food? Michel had a daughter of this one's age, who lived with her mother and two sisters on his benefice on the outskirts of the village. He had been home now for two days but had not the permission granted yet to see his family.

Geoffrey's one thought remained loud and echoing. Who would break this news to Adelina? Please God, let it not be me.

"Out!" Robert roared and the charboys, clearing up from the previous night, scattered at once. Robert sat at the table in the Great Hall and held his head in his hand. "Sit, man, sit. How deep did the intruders come into these walls?"

"Beyond the kitchen doors only, Milord."

"You were there?"

"Defending the stairs to the great hall. Alone."

"And what is this that Geoffrey speaks of?"

"Milord?" Gabriel asked.

"He said you were responsible for the death of Cateline."

"And the sparrow has an imagination," Gabriel said with a soft laugh.

Robert looked up questioning. "Sparrow?"

"Geoffrey, Milord. We call him Sparrow. It seems he would cast the blame for the death of the girl on to me if given the chance. He is jealous of me but for what reason, I cannot say."

Robert studied Gabriel and said nothing for a little while. "You would not lie to me, Gabriel?"

"For what reason would I lie, Milord?"

Robert looked into the bright green eyes and sighed. "Leave me now," Robert said quietly.

Gabriel stood. "If I may?"

Robert lifted his head.

"Is there news of Adelina? I would like to know how she fares."

"She lives."

"If I may?"

"What…"

"Dupuy will not rest until your daughter lies in the ground."

"This was not the doing of Henri, but his son, Baudoin. Send Geoffrey to me, then you shall deal with the dead and they shall be put on that damned roadway which has haunted our families for one hundred years or more."

Gabriel smiled and interjected again. "Milord?" he asked and continued without permission. "Perhaps the feuding between your families can be avoided by the building of a new roadway? Should you build this roadway on your land, perhaps you could also collect a toll from those pilgrims passing through to Le Puy?"

There was silence for some time. Robert rubbed at his aching head, sighed and mumbled, "Perhaps. Bring Geoffrey to me."

Geoffrey, leaning against the kitchen wall, his face white and his hands bloodied, looked up the instant Gabriel appeared on the stairs. His hatred intensified when Gabriel's handsome face creased into what was supposed to be a smile.

Geoffrey was shaking and, like a baby wrenched from its mother, about to cry or so it seemed. Gabriel watched dispassionately as Michel carried the wrapped body out into the courtyard.

Ella was still crying until Gabriel fisted his hand at her and the cries subsided immediately. The scrawny old toad glared at him, it mattered little that the serving girl may have confided her woes to the kitchen maid, for what worth was the toad's word against his? Gabriel was of noble birth and she but a peasant, who, if he had his way, and one day he would, would cast her back to the fields where she belonged. And he would then employ a younger kitchen-maid with a better face and a more pleasing personality.

"Sparrow, your esteemed uncle wishes your devout presence."

Geoffrey washed his hands, then his face, but nothing could take the smell of blood from his skin, nor could words or thoughts relieve his mind of the image of Cateline's dead eyes, staring at him still.

"I warn you, Sparrow, that I have already told the lord how you wish me ill. Ill and away." Gabriel smiled and backed away. "Even though it is I who stretch the hand of friendship only to have it spat upon."

Geoffrey spat on Gabriel's foot in reply. He went into the great hall, kicking aside spilled drinking goblets and tankards, and wasted food, and wondering what was keeping the charboys from their duties.

Robert was sitting alone with his head in his hand and the weight of the world on his shoulders. "You have summoned me, Uncle?"

"Be seated."

Geoffrey cleared a space and sat. He waited for some time for his uncle to speak.

"In seven days, I leave for St Denis to speak with Phillippe."

"Phillippe?"

"The king."

"Oh," Geoffrey said. "That Phillippe."

"I hear that he wishes my holdings as Royal domain. He has already taken some lands further north and appoints baillis to oversee."

"But why?" Geoffrey asked. "Why would the king want our land?"

"Perhaps it is because the hunting here is good. Who knows except God and Phillippe Augustus? Philippe can be reasonable and will hear me, but I cannot lose what is mine. The villages grow, Geoffrey, and will continue to grow. I cannot forsake my people now."

Geoffrey knew better than to ask what else was concerning his uncle, so he remained quiet, although his heart beat fast in a dreaded anticipation.

"You are the youngest son of my half-brother, and my half-brother was a brave and honorable man in his way. But he was a man of letters and extreme kindness which was his downfall. I warned him against taking up arms and he did not listen. Geoffrey, each time I look at you, I see my half-brother. I see Guillame. I have no wish to see you into an early grave, too, and so it is that I have decided." Robert hesitated for a lengthy moment, then quickly he said, "You would do better as a monk. Perhaps a friar. I have spoken at length to the abbot Jean of you."

"But I have no wish to..."

"It has come the time now that I must allot you a benefice. It is a comfortable house and from there you will oversee the workings of my demesne. One eighth of this I grant to you, which is more than enough for your needs unless you marry, of course. But for this in turn, it is my wish that you will study."

"But, uncle..."

Robert held up his hand for silence. "Only experienced knights are of use to me now. I can no longer afford the retainers I once had. All of the landholders whose lands have not been taken, those present here last night, share my position. It is a matter of economics, Geoffrey."

"But, but... this is my home."

"I have made arrangements with Jean, and he feels that the new Franciscan order could be the one for you. But he is willing to train you in Benedictine ways until you choose."

Geoffrey did not care for any Franciscan order. "Have I not proved my worthiness? Have you not said that courage and piety are..."

"Do not argue with me, Geoffrey! I am sending Christian to the abbey, to the infirmary there. He will be well cared for."

"You are ashamed of him."

"He is of no use to himself, let alone to me."

"He has returned from the Crusades an idiot. The one who was to marry your daughter can no longer and you have chosen another, is this not so? Who have you chosen to marry your daughter now?"

"Who I choose and when I choose is not your business."

"Had Christian not been injured, we would not be cast out this way." He stared at his uncle, defying him silently to lie.

"It is a matter of economics!"

Geoffrey rubbed at his face. He could not comprehend because he would not. "Is there nothing I can say or do to change your mind?"

Robert shook his head.

"The foreigner. Dedwyd. He replaces me here? You replace your own blood with foreign?"

"Geoffrey, this is difficult enough!"

Silence reigned a lengthy time.

"I would ask of you one thing only," Geoffrey said softly, his voice shaking.

Robert sighed.

"I ask that my brother lives with me on this benefice. He may not be who he once was, but he is still my brother and I can never shut him away."

"This is lunacy. You cannot possibly care for Christian, study, and oversee the demesne."

"And you should know by now that the word impossible has always been a challenge to any who bears the name Polignac."

"Geoffrey..."

"If my wish is not granted, I will take up arms and wander."

Robert saw the sparkle of truth within Geoffrey's eyes. "You are making a mistake, Geoffrey."

"Then it is mine to live with."

"Michel will see you both settled for your benefice borders his."

Geoffrey rose but Robert was not yet finished. "I have never approved of my vassals conducting private feuds within my walls, Geoffrey. This you know."

Gabriel, he thought. What lies has he told? "Gabriel of Lyon is a treacherous, thieving trouble-maker whose ambition outweighs common sense and decency."

"He is a very experienced soldier. I need him."

"You need one who has sworn his allegiance to three lords before you? I can only pray for the sake of your daughter that one such lord is not Henri Dupuy."

Robert studied Geoffrey carefully. "Geoffrey, in time you will come to see the wisdom of my decision this day."

"Such time could only be measured by eternity."

"Be that as it may, I shall be proven right. Your time will be your own, unless I summon you, and when I summon, you shall make haste. I pray you use this time alone with wisdom, Geoffrey. For now, go. Go and aid the others with clearing the dead, and see to it that the villagers are rewarded for their efforts of last night."

"May I take my leave of Adelina?"

"When all else is done, yes."

Geoffrey could not tell Robert he was making a terrible mistake because if Gabriel of Lyon remained within the walls, he would realise it soon enough. "I cannot leave without telling you that Cateline, the serving girl, feared for her life."

"Why is this?"

"I will only say that Gabriel of Lyon is not what he seems. Anything else would not be believed at this time."

Geoffrey departed, and helped with the task of clearing the dead and dispatching those not yet dead, a task with sickened Geoffrey but seemed to have no effect upon Louis or Henri, nor Michel. It certainly had no effect upon Gabriel for he sang as he worked.

"Speak to the master of what you witnessed last night. I beg you. I speak of Cateline. You saw her distress. It was you who saw the marks on her throat."

"I witnessed nothing," Michel said, as he took up a corpse's feet and Geoffrey took the arms and together they swung it into the dray. But Michel's gaze caught Geoffrey's and something unspoken passed between them.

"You feel as I," Geoffrey said.

"Sparrow, I assure you that Raoul will take care of Adelina in our absence. Gabriel will not harm her. He would dare not."

"No, he would do worse. He is going to marry her."

This was certainly news to Michel. "He told you this?"

"Oh, yes, he told me."

"He goads you, boy. He goads you. It will never happen."

"He is serious. I see it in his eyes."

"He goads you. All know how it is with you and Adelina."

Geoffrey was taken aback. "What do you mean?"

"I am not a fool. I have eyes and I was once young. Disbelieve this if you must but it is true." Michel dragged out a corpse with an arrow in its back. He pulled the arrow out, threw it atop the others, and he and Geoffrey carried the body to the dray. Then it was done.

Michel drove the dray. Geoffrey, Gabriel, Acelin and Louis rode before, beside, and behind it until they arrived on the stretch of roadway that both lords considered their own.

Baudoin Dupuy sat astride his horse and watched impassively as the bodies were unloaded.

"It is not over!" he called.

"Then gather an army with a leader!" Gabriel called in return, smiling. "Or have you not the courage to face a proper battle!" Gabriel spat, turned his horse about and followed the others home.

Geoffrey tried his best to ignore Gabriel. Was there no end to this one's torment? "Sparrow, my little feathered friend, you have been avoiding me."

Geoffrey said nothing.

"I hear the lord has granted you a benefice with a demesne of your own to boot."

"Leave him, Gabriel," Michel said and was ignored.

"Tell me, Sparrow, is this your first? I have fifteen scattered throughout the land with vassals of my own to administer them. Perhaps one day in the near future after I wed Adelina of course this peculiar holding shall be a fief I may grant to some loyal retainer..."

"Enough," Michel warned again, but Gabriel was deaf.

"Perhaps the lord will grant permission of some village serf to marry you. That would be nice. Be sure to choose a woman who is a head taller than you, Geoffrey, unless you want dwarf sons. And be sure that she is ugly as well. For a pretty woman you could never hope to hold and expect her to remain faithful."

Geoffrey said nothing. If he said nothing Gabriel might find no jest and leave him in peace.

"Do not fret, my little feathered friend. I shall take very good care of the lovely lady while you are gone."

"Which lovely lady?" Geoffrey asked, bored. "Already you attempt to steal the heart of my aunt."

"Is this where she was felled?" Gabriel asked as they crested the hill leading down to the chateau gate. The page on lookout had already lowered the bridge for them. Geoffrey said nothing. "It seems that Jean-Pierre Dupuy was unfortunate, indeed." Gabriel turned back and rode to the top of the hill again, his horse danced there. He called, "For even I would have had trouble with such a shot, Sparrow! Perhaps the bolt was guided by the force of love alone?"

"Do not, Geoffrey. Do not."

Geoffrey looked at Michel who was driving the dray across the bridge. Louis and Acelin said nothing. They were not well after the night of merrymaking and fighting, nor had the morning's smell of blood done much to quell each's turning stomach.

"Draw up the bridge," Geoffrey said to the page at the wheel. The boy looked out. Another knight, the lord's new, first vassal was yet to come. "Draw up the bridge!" Geoffrey ordered.

Michel laughed to himself as he drove through the courtyard with the clacking of the wheel echoing behind him.

Gabriel sighed as the bridge drew up and eventually Geoffrey appeared on top of the wall.

"Let it down, Sparrow!"

"What?"

"Let it down!"

"Who goes there?" Geoffrey called, pretending he was both blind and deaf as he walked the narrow ledge on top of the wall, just as he'd done as a child and it was Christian locked out.

"You will make a very good monk, boy, but only if the gospels are full of jest!" Gabriel called as he sat on his horse, close to the bottomless cavern and waited for someone to let the bridge down. If someone ever would.

Geoffrey hastily washed in the stables and went from the courtyard to the kitchens. Ella hung over a cauldron of stew. She was weeping still. Geoffrey walked to her and put his hand on her shoulder. She looked at him. Her nose was swollen and broken, too, her eyes were black due to Gabriel's fist.

"He lies," she said. "What was done to Cateline was not by a farmer's hand. It was by one taught by barbarians…"

"This I know."

"You must tell the master, Geoffrey. You must."

"I have tried, Ella, but it is in his mind now that I am full of envy and jealousy and my words are ignored. Do you have the courage to speak to him?"

Ella looked away and returned to stirring her pot. "What worth is my word?"

"You have served this household for most of your life. I am sure he would hear you."

"And should Gabriel discover I had spoken to the master against him? No. My wish is to live."

Geoffrey sighed. "You know, don't you, that today I must leave," Geoffrey said, not even a question.

"Yes, I know. And I had not believed you would ever go. I do not like these changes. I am too old now to accept these things."

"You will never be old." But he saw the gray in her hair, the lines on her face, her hands.

"You are more of a son to our master than a son would ever have been, but always Christian was his favorite. Now what has he? This, all of this, should have become yours, Geoffrey. Not .. not .. his. I know what he wants."

Gabriel. The poor woman could not even say his name.

"Perhaps you could speak with your mistress?" Geoffrey asked.

Ella made a spitting noise. "Who do you think warms her bed when the master attends to his soulful matters at the abbey? Is it not I she implores to make her bed when Gabriel has left it? Is it not I filled with too many of the secrets of this family? I cannot speak against him for he does what the master can or will not and she will hear of him no wrong. I see and I hear, Geoffrey. So did Cateline. Fortunately, I am neither young nor pretty of face, so it is never me he would want. This fare I serve is my only reason for life. A better cook none can find anywhere and this alone is what keeps me here in the employ of your uncle."

"No, Ella. You are here for more than that reason."

"Geoffrey, hear me well. Cateline carried the child of Gabriel of Lyon. She was mistaken in telling him. I warned her against it but she did not listen. Soon, he will be our master, Geoffrey. I know it. I feel it. I would rather die than see this happen."

Geoffrey patted Ella's shoulder and turned away. Gabriel was watching from the kitchen doors. "Is it not time you departed, Sparrow? Is it not time that you left these gates, never to return?"

"Oh but I will return. You will not win, Gabriel of Lyon."

"And you tweak and flutter as a young bird, featherless and abandoned." Gabriel leapt up the stairs.

Geoffrey put his arms around Ella again. "You will promise me that if I am ever needed, someone will send word?" Ella clung tight and Geoffrey held her for quite some time before he drew her away. "Promise me?" he asked.

She nodded and went back to her work.

Geoffrey took the stairs leading to the great hall slowly, as if it would be for the last time. Charboys who should have been cleaning were imitating the festivities of the night before. Each stopped their game quickly when Geoffrey walked through the hall and climbed the stairs. Soon enough he heard the laughter as their mimicry began once again.

He stood for some time at Adelina's door before he bade entry. Marys was by the bed, sewing. She looked at Geoffrey and away, quickly. His attire was bloodstained although his hands were not. Geoffrey studied Marys and could not believe it possible that she had sinned so knowingly, and openly, with Gabriel.

"She improves," Marys said.

Adelina lay as before, covered to her bare shoulders, her hair flowing across the cushions. Only then did Geoffrey realise how beautiful she was. Why had he never noticed this before? "I have come to take leave of my lady," he said softly, wishing that Marys would see the truth in his eyes and leave them alone for a short time. Because a short time would be all he could endure.

Marys put her sewing to the side. "Geoffrey, I can do nothing to stop the wishes of my husband. I must obey him."

Then you are filled with contradictions, my lady, Geoffrey thought. "I would ask of you one thing only, Milady. In all the time I have lived here I have asked nothing of you."

"Speak."

"I wish to take my leave of Adelina alone."

"She does not hear anyone, Geoffrey."

"She will hear me," he said.

Marys had always found it difficult to ignore the pleading in Geoffrey's beautiful eyes, even though it had been more intense when he was a small boy.

Geoffrey did not sit until Marys had departed the chambers. Nor did she close the door. Geoffrey waited until her footsteps were faint before he closed the heavy door. "You may open your eyes now. Your mother has gone."

Adelina opened her eyes. There was Geoffrey, sitting beside her bed. "You knew I pretended to sleep?" she asked, her voice little but a rasping whisper.

He nodded, face serious, belying what he felt inside. Today, she looked somewhat better, although her lips were parched and cracked. Geoffrey poured some water, raised her a little and offered it. She drank greedily and choked. When she coughed, blood stained the cover. Geoffrey lay her back down. Her eyes, reddened from her choke, now stared through him as if she were plucking the very thoughts from his mind. "Where is Christian?" she asked.

"In his room."

Her eyes glazed as a memory fell like silk from above. "I remember seeing him, Geoffrey. I remember waiting in the courtyard for him to come. I felt great excitement at seeing him again, knowing I was to marry him. But then I saw him. I saw what he had become. I remember thinking, this cannot be, he was to marry me. And I ran. I ran as far and as fast as I could. I had to find you for I thought of no one else. I was in the woods, deep in the woods, catching my breath when he came. He was huge, Geoffrey, so huge. He knew who I was but I had never seen him before. I did not like the look in his eyes, Geoffrey. I did not like the way he stared at me. He did this when I hit him." She put her hand on her shoulder and winced because a simple touch was agony. "I fought him for all I was worth but I had no sword. Had I a sword ... I thought I would die. I hurt him. His anger gave him feet of wings. He caught me again and I looked into his eyes. I was his enemy even though he had never met me. All I wanted was to die and be rid of the hate in his eyes. How could he hate me so if he had never known me?"

Geoffrey stared at his hands. "It was the name you carry which spawned his hatred. It was the name, not you."

"But why?"

"Wars are fought for less."

"But why?"

Geoffrey said nothing. He touched her hand instead.

"Cateline said it was you who saved me."

"I was not alone. Your father was there, too."

"Where is she?" Adelina asked. "Why is Cateline not here? Why will no one tell me where she is?"

Geoffrey looked into her eyes and said softly, "Cateline is dead, my love. It happened last night."

Adelina's face paled further. Geoffrey didn't believe it possible. Tears welled, too. He had to look away.

"How? Did she fall on the stairs? Was it the stairs? So many times I have said, watch your feet, Cateline..."

"It was not from a fall on the stairs, my love."

"Then how?"

"My love, please, I cannot say. Perhaps when you are stronger someone may tell you."

"She died in the battle?"

"You know of what occurred last night?"

"I heard it. I tried to get from my bed but Michel came and I don't remember..."

"Much has happened this past day, my love," Geoffrey said.

"There was a battle and I missed it," she whispered.

"Be thankful that you did."

"But why was there fighting? Were the guests not happy here?"

"No. No, the guests were very happy. There was much merriment."

"Then what? Tell me."

"Jean-Pierre Dupuy, the man who was with you in the woods. He was killed. The attack of last night was ordered by his brother Baudoin. It was a revenge attack."

Adelina did not understand. Her thoughts swam. She was silent for a long time. Eventually she said, "How many lives were lost?"

"There were thirty-two Dupuy dead. Ten of ours. Eleven if a whore is counted."

"And Cateline? She makes twelve?"

Geoffrey's mouth went dry. He could not lie so he simply nodded. He never wanted her to know what had happened to Cateline. She was crying now, crying over her serving girl, crying for her friend.

Adelina squeezed his hand, and Geoffrey allowed her to hold it close to her face. Her tears burned into his skin. He did not know how he would tell her that he had to go, but he knew that the time had come.

"My love, I have come to say farewell."

Her tears almost stopped. Almost.

"Your father has granted me a benefice on the outskirts of the village. It is close to Michel, and is good land, too. I am leaving this day, and I am taking Christian with me."

"I shall come, too."

"You cannot. Your place is here."

"Then I will not allow it. If I cannot come then you cannot go."

"Your father has ordered it."

"I have no fear of my father. I will tell him that it is you I wish for my personal vassal. You alone and therefore, you must stay."

"It is already arranged."

"I shall speak with him, Geoffrey."

Geoffrey knew that once the master had set his mind, nothing would convince him to change it. Nothing. Certainly not a beautiful sixteen year old daughter's pleadings.

"And if this is what I want, would you still speak with him?" Geoffrey asked.

She looked at him, frowning. "How can you say this is what you want when I know by your eyes it is not?"

"Please, my love, make this no harder than it is already. Because I am not here in body does not mean I am not here in spirit with you. You will always be in my thoughts, no matter what it is I do, or where I may be. My door will always be open to you."

"Geoffrey, you cannot go! You cannot leave me!"

"Raoul will be here."

"Raoul? Raoul? He is an ugly, cranky old man who farts!" Tears filled her eyes again and she turned her face away, dismissing him,

"Oh, go away. Go!"

"I am still your friend and servant for all of time."

"I do not want you as a friend or a servant!" she cried, tears spilling.

"And were I not your friend and servant I would have informed your father long ago of your antics!"

"Antics?" she asked and looked at him once again.

"Yes, antics. The quintain, the crossbow which could have killed you. The sword and clothing you have stolen from me. Do you think I did not know? Must I continue?"

"But I am a lady now," she tried, all eyes and innocence which worked on many but never Geoffrey. She soon realised that. "You cannot leave for this is your home."

"What is a home but walls and a roof to keep off the rain? My door is always open to you. Rest now and gain your strength. I will see you again."

"No. I want to see Christian. I wish to talk to him. He is to be my husband. It has been arranged."

"He cannot speak and nor could he be a husband to anyone now. He knows no one."

"I wish to speak to him!"

"Seeing him will distress you."

"He is still the same person who once taunted me. He is simply locked in a chamber of silence. I hold the key."

"You speak madness now." Geoffrey rose. "But if this is your wish, I cannot refuse you. I will bring him to you and then I must leave."

"Do not go! I beg you, do not go!"

"I have no choice," Geoffrey said, voice shaking. He couldn't look at her.

"Send for my father so that I can speak with him?"

"Your father is busy. This I cannot do."

Geoffrey walked to the door and put his hand on it to pull it open. He stopped and closed his eyes when he heard, "What will I have when you are not here?"

He turned back to her. "Adelina, you have told me for too long now, how you ache to prove your courage and bravery."

"This is not facing the enemy with a brave heart, Geoffrey. Without you I have no one. There is no one."

"You are young and beautiful, and before you realise it there will be many seeking your hand."

"No! I want no one but you!"

He had never heard a wailing like it before. It was not of any injury or damaged pride, nor was it born of a temper tantrum. He doubted now that he could hold the injured part and kiss it until the pain disappeared because of his 'special magic'. Geoffrey went back to the bed, sat on it and held her close, barely aware that if he was caught in such an embrace there would be trouble. His heart felt empty. "I will be back, my love. I will."

# Chapter 8

"Stand, brother."

Christian stood. Geoffrey offered his hand, and confusion crossed Christian's dull eyes, until Geoffrey's fingers closed on his. "Come, brother. We have to leave."

Christian grunted and a frown appeared. "Yes, I know how it is you feel, but here we can no longer stay. It is you and I now. Just you and I, as it was in a time long gone. I was a little boy then and you took me by the hand. Now it is I who takes you."

Christian grunted and sat on the cot. He steadfastly refused to move. Geoffrey sighed and crouched. "I know you feel that this chateau is our home, but it is no longer, Christian. Do you hear me? Do you understand me? We have to go. If you do not come with me, Robert will send you to the abbey where you will remain for the rest of your time, locked away in a dark room, smaller than this."

But not a flicker passed Christian's eyes.

Geoffrey sighed. "Is that what you want? Would you not rather come with me, where you will feel the sun on your face once again? You will be able to watch the serfs tend our fields. Your eyes can behold the pretty faces of the girls at work, and who knows, my brother, I may employ one to tend you. You alone. Will that be good?"

Christian turned his head slightly. Was that a smile in his eyes?

Geoffrey's hopes raised. "For you, I will choose the prettiest girl in the entire village."

The noise Christian made this time was one that could not be mistaken.

"Ah, so you wish to choose for yourself?"

Christian looked at his brother. His eyes were moist and full of feeling that he could not express. He blinked, he grunted, but this time the sound was a most agreeable one.

"Stand now. The Lady Adelina wishes your presence. You

remember her as a child, full of mischief and bad temper. She still has the temper and is at times disagreeable, but she will forever be our lady and she wants to see you before we leave."

Christian reached out slowly and touched his brother's hair. Then he pointed, eventually, to the unlit torch suspended in its bracket by the door. For a moment Geoffrey didn't understand. For a moment. "Oh. Yes, that is true. That is her, the one with hair the color of fire and a heart to match."

Christian stood without being asked and Geoffrey rose also. On the way to Adelina's chambers, Christian walked slowly, as a child walks, taking one stair after the other, and Geoffrey, all the while, fought back the sadness that his brother, once so strong, amiable and afraid of nothing, had been reduced to this... this... no word would describe it fairly.

Adelina was alone and dozing when Geoffrey brought his brother into the room. She woke quickly and turned to the door. Was this really the same person she barely remembered from childhood? Was this really the handsome, strong Christian?

"Come closer," she said and drew the covers to her chin. She tried to sit higher in the bed, and Geoffrey, the eternal worrier, helped her to sit up. She could not refuse because it hurt so to move alone.

Christian remained by the door, staring at his feet. Occasionally, his gaze would dart to Adelina, and back to his feet once again. But what he thought, no one would ever know.

"Does he know his name?" she asked of Geoffrey.

"I believe he understands all that is said, and most of what is not said."

"Christian, come closer."

He made a noise and averted his eyes. Terror lingered there. Geoffrey took his hand and pulled him, unwilling, toward Adelina's bed.

"Why is he frightened of me?" she asked.

"He knew that on his return he would be your husband. He is ashamed of himself, of what he has become."

"Sit, Christian. You may sit," she said softly and tried to smile. It would have been easier had she not been aching so badly. Christian shook away Geoffrey's hold and shuffled his way to the stool beside Adelina's bed. There he sat, but his movements were like a puppet's whose strings were in danger of breaking. And so was Adelina's heart just to see him. She could not, although she tried, imagine how it was he felt inside. If it were me this way, she thought, I would want to die. I would find a way to kill myself and end the torture.

Christian kept his gaze lowered, like a serf being spoken to by nobility, and almost as afraid of what the one-sided conversation might bring.

"There is no need for shame. You are here with me now."

Still he stared at his feet.

"What has happened to you?" Adelina asked, voice shaking, eyes stinging.

Geoffrey said nothing. Perhaps Adelina was right when she said that Christian was simply locked in a chamber of silence and she held the key. There was expression in his eyes now. Feeling.

"Christian? I speak to you. When I speak to you, you must look at me."

He looked into her eyes. Frustration appeared on his face, tears formed. His jaw clenched, and, Geoffrey saw, his left hand curled into a fist. "Yes, I know that you understand and can do nothing. Oh, Christian. I can only guess at what it was you have endured. But I want you to know that it is true what the Pope has said, that your true reward comes in heaven."

Geoffrey was taken aback. Adelina speaks of heaven now? What, exactly, he wondered, was damaged by Jean-Pierre Dupuy's falchion?

Christian made another sound, one of sheer despair. A tear rolled. Adelina touched his hand. "I will always be your friend," she said softly, lifting his hand and kissing it. He looked at her again, and his right hand, with effort, reached out slowly and touched her hair. Geoffrey, heart in mouth, could almost see a smile touching his brother's lips: A smile washed by tears he had never seen before.

Adelina looked at Geoffrey. She was almost crying, too. Had he not said that seeing Christian would distress her? When, if ever, would she believe a word he uttered?

"Best now that you leave," she said, voice shaking.

"Come brother, we must go."

Christian, still touching Adelina's hair, did not move. "Christian, we must go."

Geoffrey put his hand on his brother's shoulder and felt him tense immediately. "Come," he said softly. It seemed that Christian did not react favorably to a harsh voice. He let go of Adelina's hair, and tried hard to speak, but nothing would come. Geoffrey guided him to the door, putting his hand on his head to lower him as he went through because he was always bumping his head on the low doors.

"It must be," Geoffrey said, turning back to Adelina, "That Moorish doors are tall ones." He tried very hard to smile. "At times he forgets where he is."

She said nothing. She was resigned now to the knowing that Geoffrey was indeed leaving.

"Goodbye, my lady."

Adelina turned her face into her cushions and Geoffrey closed the door so he would not hear her cries. But Christian was staring at him.

"Yes, I know," Geoffrey said, agreeing with whatever it may have been lurking behind Christian's eyes. He reached out to take Christian's arm but Christian made his sound which Geoffrey had already come to learn meant no. He had a different grunt for yes. "Why is it that you cannot speak and yet we still argue?"

Geoffrey followed him down the spiral stairs, one slow step at a time.

Gabriel waited at the bottom of the spiral, his stocky, happy archer by his side. "Sparrow. Half-wit," he said in greeting.

Geoffrey tried to ignore the smirk lingering on Gabriel's face. "Be not too free with your joy, Gabriel of Lyon, for tomorrow this could well be you and not my brother." To the archer he said, "Goodbye, Dedwyd. You fought well beside me last night. I hold no grudge with you."

Gabriel muttered something to his retainer and the little man's eyes came alive. He blurted something in return, which Gabriel translated. "He wishes you a long, fruitful life. The fool has always been an optimist." Gabriel offered no farewell, nor did Geoffrey. When Geoffrey and Christian had freed the stairwell, Gabriel and Dedwyd ventured up to their chambers.

Michel, Geoffrey knew, was waiting in the courtyard, for he, too, was leaving to spend time with his family. Louis, Acelin, and Raoul waited. Raoul was seated, his arm tied by a bloodied rag. He looked ill.

"Goodbye, Louis." The embrace was a quick, fond one, cheeks touched. Christian was ignored from embarrassment alone. It was more likely that Louis did not know what to say or do. "And you, Acelin, will pay for what you did to me last night."

"But I already have, Geoffrey. She cost us much." There was another embrace, fonder and tighter than Louis's.

"Her cost was greater." To that, Acelin said nothing.

"Serve my uncle well, for I fear trouble lies ahead," Geoffrey said to Raoul, who made to rise. "No, save your strength. You will need all of it and more to keep pace with Adelina. Should you need me, you know where I will be."

"Take good care, Sparrow."

Geoffrey led his brother down to the kitchens. He looked back at Ella. "Mind what was said, for my words were true."

Ella's eyes misted but she wiped her face hard on her sleeve and went back to her work.

Christian shielded his eyes from the sunlight and kept his gaze lowered as he walked past Marys and Robert.

"Geoffrey will never manage," Marys said as she watched Michel and Geoffrey help Christian up into the cart.

"I fear that he will, wife," Robert said as Geoffrey walked back to where they stood.

"Milord," Geoffrey said, not knowing whether he should embrace his uncle or not. Everyone had gathered, everyone excepting Gabriel, Dedwyd, Ella and Adelina. Geoffrey looked up to Adelina's window and for a moment thought he saw her. Or perhaps he needed to. He was taken into an embrace, a tight one.

"God go with you," Robert said.

"Always," Geoffrey replied with a half smile. "And you." For you will need all the divine help available to battle the foe's dagger already embedded in your family's heart. Geoffrey then looked to Marys. Her eyes were wet but her face, as always, remained expressionless. He was not surprised, for she rarely showed emotion of any kind and witnessing it now would only have alarmed them both.

"Times come, Milady, when we must all find our own truths and strengths," Geoffrey said softly. "You have been as a mother to me and I am thankful that it is a good memory I shall take to my grave." Marys embraced him fully for a long time, her eyes clamped shut, her lower lip trembling.

Geoffrey pulled away while he was still able, and walked to the horse, hitched behind the waiting cart; a cart laden with his few possessions. He noticed that there was also food in it; food, dishes, bedclothes and the like. He looked to the kitchen doors. Ella stood there, ladle in hand and tears in her eyes, tears he couldn't see but feel them he surely could. Geoffrey untethered the horse, mounted it and he did not look back as the gate opened and the bridge lowered.

Robert looked down at his wife's face. Tears there. The last time she had cried was the night of Adelina's birth and her sister's death. He said, "Do not cry, Marys. Trust my judgment."

Marys looked up into her husband's eyes. Anger now replaced any sadness. "May the ghost of Guillame haunt you for eternity because of what you have just done. Geoffrey is not like your brother, Robert. Nor has he ever been. Geoffrey has honor and courage, and now he has nothing. Even his pride you have stripped. What becomes of them now? What becomes of them when Philippe Augustus seizes our lands? What becomes of our people?"

"Philippe Augustus will not take our land."

"And you belittle Geoffrey for being such a dreamer? Reach for the stars, Robert. You will have more chance of success in touching the stars than convincing that arrogant pig of a Philippe to leave us in peace."

"I will speak with him."

"I would rather see you forge an allegiance with Dupuy than pay more taxes to Philippe Augustus who steals our lands." Marys walked off.

Robert rubbed at his bearded face, and wondered who had put such notions in his wife's mind. Only then did he notice the servants lingering, and listening. "Back to your duties!" The bellow was obeyed, instantly. Except for the washerwoman, Cateline's mother. Robert stepped toward her but she turned away quickly and fled.

"Milord?" Ella asked as Robert came into the kitchens. He was concerned, deep in troubled thought. He looked at her, and then at what she was preparing for dinner. He walked by the pit where the birds were impaled and slowly roasting over the fire, and from there he took the two stairs up to the serving girl's chambers. It was dark in the passageway, very dark. He came back, lit a torch in the fire and used its light.

Unease had been his constant companion since Geoffrey's words of that morning. It was an unease which grew steadily throughout the day. He knew not exactly what its cause was until he had seen the murdered girl's frightened mother. As he stood, head down, for there was no room to extend to full height, he recalled with clarity Gabriel's words of how he alone defended the stairwell. Robert stood in the cramped passageway leading to Cateline's chambers. Here there was barely room to stand upright let alone wield a sword in here. Now, no trace of blood could he find on the floor or the walls. "Ella!"

She answered the call immediately. "Milord?"

"Have the rushes been changed?"

"This morning."

"Was water thrown on the walls?"

"Yes, Milord. Master Gabriel ordered it."

"You performed this duty?"

"He ordered it of the charboys."

"Bring them to me."

Ella called the boys, and together they faced the master in Cateline's tiny room. They were both shaking from fright, unsure of what it was they had done wrong this time.

"Boys." They looked at each other, eyes wide. "It was a horrible sight indeed, yes? There was much blood in here. And the passageway, too, I would expect."

"Yes, Milord, very much," one said. The other boy remained silent.

"It must have been a fierce battle in this confined space."

"Yes, Milord. Master Gabriel fought very well."

"And with what did he fight and how many intruders were there?"

"He fought with his sword and there were... there were ..." the boy hesitated, trying to remember. "Three? This many." The child held up three fingers.

"That many?" Robert said, surprised. He took his attentions to the smallest boy, who had not yet said a word. "Why is it you do not speak?"

"He has a tongue, but it makes no sound."

Robert looked at him and sighed, and he thought, And if you could speak, little boy, would you say what your friend has said? "Go."

The boys left immediately and Robert emerged from the passageway. Ella was up to her elbows in dough. "How many intruders came beyond the doors?"

Ella, heart beating wildly, said, "Three, Milord."

"And you, too, saw Gabriel fell them?"

"Two on the stairs, yes, Milord," Ella whispered, although her hand shook with rage as she kneaded the dough. She had no choice but to agree because Gabriel had sworn to blind her and throw her from the bridge if she did not obey his order to lie.

Robert seemed satisfied and he soon left.

Ella pummelled at the dough, fully believing it was Gabriel's face, then suddenly she stopped. She thought of the herbs of so long ago, sealed still within that small jar. Ella put the bread into the iron box in the depths of the coals behind the partition, and she felt nothing when chicken fat fell onto the hot surface and exploded on her hand.

She wiped her hands of dough and was soon on her knees, scouring through a multitude of jars, pots and containers until, finally, she saw the jar nestled at the back of the shelf. She drew it out, and used her rag to wipe off sixteen long years of dust. She knew not exactly what poisons it contained, but she knew its effects.

She took Gabriel's brass bowl from the shelf next to the master's.

It was not too late yet to make a very special vegetable and herb broth, Gabriel's favorite of course.

The cottage, on a rise overlooking the village, had been recently whitewashed. The small grounds were fenced by shrubs and although it seemed pleasant, Geoffrey found it difficult to look upon this house knowing he would have to call it home, when home had been the chateau for as long as he could remember.

For as far as the eye could see there was rolling farmland, with fields in use, fields in fallow, fields in use, fields in fallow. Vineyards, rows upon rows of trellis, with scatters of sheep and cattle and goats grazing between. He had come here often in the past, but he had never once considered it might one day be called home.

The village houses sat in a small cluster, the road winding through made its way eventually to Le Puy in the south and a road, which ran past his door, continued directly on up the grassy hill to the abbey.

All of this beautiful countryside, for as far as the eye could see, belonged to his uncle. It was said that one day Geoffrey and his brother would return to make their claim on what had been stolen from them—their father's lands at Langeac, but Geoffrey remembered little of his early days and the one who could have told him most, could no longer speak. Christian was but a boy when their father had taken arms in defense of his holdings and had died for it. So had their mother, eventually. Heracle, who lived in the towering fortress at Polignac, did not want to care for the orphaned boys for they were poorer than peasants. Robert took them in. And what was the inheritance now? A small but rich benefice on the edges of a tiny village, a tiny cottage, blinding white in the sun.

It was much like Michel's. On approaching Michel's house first, Geoffrey heard the welcome. It was like no other. Three daughters ran out, lifting skirts, calling for their father. Michel took the three into his arms, was deafened by their squeals, and his wife appeared, calmly wiping her hands on her apron. Around her feet, two cats slunk. She greeted Michel with a beautiful smile. Geoffrey watched for as long as he could bear before he unloaded Michel's possessions from the cart and as he drove away, his horse tethered behind now, he heard, "I shall send one of my maid servants to cook until you have one in your employ!"

Geoffrey raised his hand in acknowledgement and drove the cart onwards, his horse plodding behind, up the grassy hill toward to his new home. As Geoffrey drew closer, he said quietly, "If I imagine that my life is written as a book, then today I begin a new page." He glanced at Christian, sullen, and a little afraid, beside him. "Perhaps it will be a new book entirely."

# CHAPTER 9

The woman who was sent by Michel refused to look into Geoffrey's eyes. She was short, and far too fat to be a serf. It seemed that life in Michel's employ was very good indeed.

"Do you have a name?" Geoffrey asked as he seated himself.

"Marie," she replied, barely daring to look into her new master's eyes.

"I hope you can cook."

"Yes, Master."

"Then begin," Geoffrey said. "There is wine and tankards," he said, and pointed to the wooden box he had set down himself near the cold fireplace.

Christian had already pulled his chair to the window, had parted the leather curtain and was gazing out at the village. From here, the chateau could not be seen and only God knew what images and thoughts his mind contained.

The woman, who was of middle age, seemed frightened as well as timid, perhaps thinking that she had done something displeasing already. She poured the wine into the wrong tankard but Geoffrey said nothing, for if he did, she would only shake more and spill it. "Are you married?" he asked.

"Yes, Master."

"To?"

"Thierry, the miller."

Geoffrey knew Thierry the miller, somewhat of a thief if his weights were not closely watched but he was the only miller in the village and therefore needed. "You will find me girls who can cook and sew and clean, and you will bring them to me in the morning."

"Yes, Master Geoffrey."

"They must be pleasant on the eye," Geoffrey added, glancing at his brother, and knowing that he sounded like Gabriel.

"Yes, Master Geoffrey. Pleasant on the eye. How many is it you need?"

"One, but we will choose, my brother and I."

Marie glanced at Christian who had done nothing except stare sightlessly from the window. She dared not question.

"You will also tell your husband that a moat is to be dug and filled, therefore I will need many hands to begin this as soon as possible."

"A moat, Master?"

"Yes, are you deaf? This house has no defenses."

Except, of course, the external wooden stairs reaching the living area upstairs. No doubt that could be knocked down if there was an attack. It was not surprising that these people loved Robert, for his protection was all they had. For now though, should Baudoin Dupuy learn that Geoffrey was living in the village in a defenceless house of stone and wood, this new book of his life would be a very short one indeed. And so, a deep and wide moat was very much needed. Geoffrey's first decision was to make this little house into his own fortress as best he could.

He knew by the nervous way that the woman lit the fire and fluttered around, glancing at him strangely, that she thought he was mad. He cared not what anyone thought.

"What will you cook for dinner?" Geoffrey asked as stinging smoke poured into the small house.

"What is your wish, Milord?"

Milord? Geoffrey liked that. "I wish for pheasant, swan and goose with vegetables and fruit," Geoffrey said, watching her carefully.

"Milord, I... I..."

"Have you never prepared pheasant, swan and goose?"

"No, Milord."

"Have you never seen pheasant, swan or goose?"

"I have seen geese in the sky, Milord."

In the sky, indeed. "What is it you cook, then?" Geoffrey asked, needing to know, because his rumbling stomach demanded a reply.

"Stews, Milord, if meat is available. I can make many breads, especially sweet ones. My breads are favored by the entire village. Thierry says that when he becomes a free man he will sell my breads in other towns far to the north and south and... I am sorry, Milord, I have spoken too much."

Geoffrey wasn't listening. I have a woman here who cannot prepare my favorite foods, he thought, rubbing at his eye despondently. "Then see what lies in the container and heat that for my supper," Geoffrey said, disappointed, and turned to his brother who sat staring dead–eyed from the window, his useless fingers clutching the leather drape.

It had taken him a long time to coax Christian into climbing the wooden stairs from the ground to the top floor, and once inside, all Geoffrey had discovered, to his immense disappointment, had been one room, separated in a fashion by a heavy, holed leather curtain. At one end of this charming abode lay a fireplace and a rough table, two chairs with straight backs. On the other end, a solitary bed. Here he would have to sleep at his brother's side until another bed was assembled. The table near the fire was small and heavy; by the wall was a platform seat without back, good only for tumbling off backwards when drunk; two cookpots, spoons, and three trenchers. Until he acquired more, which he would do by stealing them from Ella, Geoffrey could only invite one other person to dine.

Robert had said the house was comfortable. He had lied. This was squalor. There wasn't even a separate chambers for bodily reliefs. Geoffrey decided he would engage someone to build such a room which could empty directly into the moat below. There had to be builders living amongst the villagers.

I have come from a chateau to this, he thought dejectedly, wondering again what it was he had done to displease his uncle. And he had said to Adelina that his door was forever open to her? Vain promises indeed. He could never bring the likes of Adelina into this primitive hut.

Eventually, he received in his bowl a fair amount of a rich, thick stew and hunks of bread which had been baked by Ella's talented hands that very morning.

The woman, Marie, stepped back. Geoffrey looked up at her and knew from her eyes that she wished to return to her family before darkness fell. "Return with your findings in the morn. Remember that they must be pleasant to the eye."

The woman left immediately and Geoffrey went to the window where Christian sat. Soon enough, Geoffrey saw her running. The sun was setting.

Geoffrey took up Christian's bowl and a spoon, broke bread into the stew and said, "It is your favorite, brother. It is time to eat now."

And as Christian opened his mouth like an obedient child, Geoffrey wondered what was being served at the chateau.

Dedwyd walked across the floor on his hands, a dagger between his teeth and a sword at arms balanced on his bare feet. He was naked to the waist.

Gabriel was amused by the sight and sent him on another circuit of the great hall.

Twice around the large meeting hall had been enough for Robert. It seemed that Marys, beside him, was eager for some blood to spill. She was drinking again, heavily. Robert did not like her when she was drinking. If he liked her at all.

"How did you come upon this archer?" Robert asked.

"I bought him," Gabriel said and would offer no more except, "As you bought me, Milord." He looked back at the little man, only now showing signs of weariness. "It is said that his kind can mimic the very landscape."

"Unfortunately, bogs which move, too, at a horse's pace are rare in this land, so his talents are wasted."

"Not in the bogs of England, Milord. This one can teach us much."

"I admire your ambition, Gabriel. I fear it is sadly misplaced. Stop him. Stop this now. He is not here to entertain and I will not allow unnecessary blood spilled. It is a quiet night I anticipate."

Gabriel lifted the sword from Dedwyd's feet, the little man spat the dagger from his clenched teeth. Then he leapt backwards and sprang to his feet. Marys clapped loudly and he bowed to her, a huge grin overtaking his face.

"It seems he is learning some social graces, Milady. When first I met him, when applauded for such a performance, he would strip himself naked and do it again."

Marys pretended to be overcome by embarrassment, but Robert saw the gleam in her dark eyes. Had Dedwyd not been such a gifted archer and foot soldier, Robert would have thought him an idiot. There was no reason he knew of that any man should be so decidedly happy all of the time. The little Welsh archer's constant smile annoyed him greatly.

"And it is about time!"

The charboys arrived with trays bearing bowls of steaming broths. The lord and lady were served first, and they took up their spoons and began immediately, Robert slurping noisily, Marys more graciously.

Ella had made sure that the mute boy took Gabriel's bowl. The little boy, dressed only in drawers, and his body glistening with sweat from the intense heat of the kitchens, put Gabriel's bowl down on the table before him.

Gabriel grabbed the skinny arm, pulled the boy close and inspected every inch of the child with very curious eyes.

Louis and Acelin glanced at each other. Surely he doesn't like little boys, too? each thought.

"I need a page," Gabriel said. "Does this child deserve me?"

"Master, he does not speak," the other boy said.

"But he hears?"

"Yes, Master Gabriel."

"On your knees before me, boy."

The mute boy dropped to his knees.

"To your hands, now."

The boy dropped on all fours.

"Under the table."

Gabriel caught Robert's curious if not enquiring gaze. "Humility is the first lesson, Milord." Gabriel used the little boy's back as a footstool. He took up his tankard, drained it and threw it to the other boy who had put Dedwyd's bowl of broth down.

While his tankard was being filled, Gabriel noticed the shadow appearing and disappearing on the stairs leading down to the kitchens. At any moment, he expected to see the old toad's face peering out: The old toad who looked at him with the hatefilled eyes he had seen countless times upon others' faces—eyes holding wishful promises of death. Slow, slow, death.

Gabriel looked down at the bowl of broth before him and dared not risk it. He pushed it instead to Dedwyd. The archer said nothing as his own bowl was seized. All was food to him and he ate, greedily.

Louis, sitting opposite, said, "Gabriel, the boy you use as a footstool is already in service to me."

Robert sighed. All evening he had sensed the distrust lingering about his three loyal retainers, each of whom had barely spoken a word except when asked. He, too, had found little amusement in watching the foreigner walk on his hands but was that enough to harbor such unease? As far as Robert knew, this boy was, as yet, a page to none.

Gabriel studied Louis intently. "And the other, I presume, is also spoken for?"

Acelin felt the kick from under the table. "Yes. He is mine," he said as he picked up his soup bowl and drained it noisily.

Gabriel directed his question to Raoul. "And yours?"

"Tends my horse in the stable. There are no others for you here, Gabriel."

Gabriel studied the three, but did not take his feet off the mute's back. He rested his gaze upon Louis, who, at this time, seemed his best target. "What will you take for him?"

Half a smile crossed Louis's face. "I would take, let me see, what do you have?" There was silence for a little while as Louis made a great effort to ponder. "I would take your archer."

Dedwyd, unaware that all eyes had turned to him, sat at the table, a frown on his face as his belly rumbled fierce and hot, heralding a raging storm very soon to hit. Sweat was beading on his face. He knew little of the language spoken around him yet, only words here and there made partial sense. Had he felt better he would have been excited over the prospect of a fight developing between Gabriel and Louis for each certainly held the spark of distrust alive in their eyes. Dedwyd though had more pressing things on his mind. How he wished these pressing things were simply on his mind. Suddenly it felt as if a thousand knives were stabbing into his gut and he had to put his face on the table for a moment until the agony passed.

"You want my archer for a mute boy?"

"It seems clear the reason you have chosen the mute."

"And what, pray tell, is this reason for it is not clear to me."

"None hears the screams of a mute boy as he lies on his face, under you in the night."

"Ah, yes indeed, well spoken by one who has experience!"

"Enough," Robert said boredly.

"He lies!' Louis cried, on his feet.

Robert sighed, broke off a hunk of bread and wiped his bowl with it.

"He was with us last night on the northern rampart! He was not as it is said in the kitchens! There were no intruders!"

"And who are you to call me liar when you left your post to drag the wounded Raoul to safety? Did you not hear the cries for assistance coming from the courtyard? Or is it just that Welsh cries, in your ignorance, you do not understand!" Gabriel turned to his retainer. "Is it not so that you called me, Dedwyd?" he asked in the only language the man understood. However there was no reply. Dedwyd leapt to his feet and was away, quickly, so ill that he could not remember where the latrine was.

"It seems that our friend has eaten something which disagrees with his stomach," Gabriel said, smirking. "I will consider your offer of my archer for your page. But I warn you now, if you ever call me a liar again I will cut out your tongue and feed it to the pigs."

Gabriel rose and excused himself from the presence of the lady. He went to check on Dedwyd.

"There will be no feuding in this household," Robert said. Louis nodded and pulled the boy out from under the table. "Nor is it wise that you choose that one as a page."

"Forgive me, Milord, but that is what you said when Michel chose Geoffrey." Louis handed the boy his tankard, which the boy duly filled, and the knight's arm caught him in a fond embrace. "I strongly believe that it is not warfare Gabriel wishes to teach this one."

"Do you wish to be relieved of your duties, here, Louis?"

"No, Milord."

"Then desist this nonsense! All of you! You all act as children!"

Another bellow echoed throughout the chateau. "He is dying!" On hearing it, all leapt to their feet, including Marys.

The Welsh archer was in the passageway, convulsing. Michel, who at times seemed more learned than a physician, was not present, his service at the chateau also no longer required. None knew what to do as the man threw himself about without any acrobatic grace. Marys stood on tiptoe to see what was happening. Blood poured from the little man's mouth and a fetid stench overtook everyone. The little man screamed once, then lay still. But it seemed that he wasn't quite dead.

Gabriel, face white, anger lighting his eyes, turned to Louis. "You may have him at no cost. He is of no further use to me." Gabriel stepped over the little man and within moments the door to his chambers slammed.

"He would just leave him?" Louis asked, although Raoul and Acelin were not surprised. Louis called for the charboys to brings pails of water and he looked directly into Robert's eyes when he asked, "Milord, is it not worth considering an option on Gabriel's stallion should it graze on too much clover and bloat? He casts away his possessions too readily."

"Just tend the archer. And there will be no dice tonight."

Acelin and Louis dragged Dedwyd across the narrow passageway and up into their chambers. The boys attended to the mess on the steps.

The new girl entered Adelina's chambers quietly. "You called, Milady?"

Adelina turned from where she was sitting by the small window. "What was that noise?"

"Noise, Milady?"

"I thought I heard a man screaming."

"It seems that one of the knights became very ill during supper."

"Geoffrey?" she asked, too late realising that Geoffrey was no longer here. "Who was it?"

"You would not know of him, Milady."

"I asked you who!"

"I cannot say his name. It is foreign. He belongs to the Master Gabriel and comes from a land to the north. A place called Wales. He is a very little man."

"And what is your name?"

"Jennet. My father is Thierry, the miller."

"I wish to see this little foreign man at once, Jennet. Help me dress."

Jennet helped Adelina stand slowly and she swayed on her feet. "Jennet is a pretty name. Common, but pretty."

"As is yours, Milady."

Adelina, holding on to the girl's shoulder, looked her in the eye and saw a sparkle there. It was almost enough to make her smile. But Cateline this one would never be. Never. "I shall wear the green dress."

Jennet sorted through the dresses until she found the green one and she helped her new mistress into it, laced it carefully at the back and relieved the lacing a little at each side so that the dress did not pull and cause discomfort. "We thought that you would die from what Dupuy did to you, Milady."

"We? Who is we?"

"Those of us who live in the village," Jennet said and brought out Adelina's shoes.

"No. I am never shod," Adelina said and the girl looked at the soft shoes which were far too small for her new lady's feet anyway. Jennet put them against her own feet. It seemed that they would fit. "You may have them."

Jennet shook her head. "No, Milady. I cannot. I dare not."

"And I say you may have them if these shoes are what you wish for. Do they fit?"

Jennet put them on. She had never felt shoes like it in all of her life. "I thank you, Milady."

"Tend me well or I shall take them back."

"Then, sit, Milady, and I will fix your hair."

Adelina sat by the window and allowed the girl the freedom to comb out a thousand tangles and catch any lice before they scuttled away.

"You are from the village, then?"

"Yes, Milady."

"Is there any news of Geoffrey?" she asked.

"I do not know who Geoffrey is."

"Geoffrey lives in the village now, on a benefice on the outskirts. He is shorter than most men of his age. He is the one who would collect the dues."

"Oh, that one. I believe that my mother attends him this night. Has he a handsome brother who is an idiot?"

"You will never, never speak of Christian as an idiot!"

"I am sorry, Milady."

"I will not abide anyone who speaks ill of either! They are as brothers to me and I love them dearly."

"Milady, I did not mean to upset you. This is my first day and there is much yet I need to learn."

"I am not upset!"

Jennet said nothing. She dared not for some time. "What news is it you wish of Geoffrey?"

"I want to know everything that he does. Every moment of every day."

"Well, Milady, all I know for now, is that my brother Jacques is one of the men who will be digging a moat around the house."

"A moat?"

"Yes, Milady. He has also asked for girls who are fair of face to be employed in his house."

Silence fell until Adelina asked quietly, "Jennet, you would not lie to me?"

"I have no reason to lie to you, Milady. I am very fortunate to be working here."

"Tell me then, and do not lie, for if you lie, I will know."

"Yes, Milady?"

"Am I fair of face?"

"Very much, Milady."

"But he has never ..." Adelina did not voice her thoughts. He has never said so. None had ever said so. "Go now. Go and discover where they have taken this foreigner. Go."

"But your hair..."

"I do not care about my hair! I would not care if I was bald!"

Jennet left quickly and Adelina stood. She was weak still. Half of her longed to remain in bed but the other half fought off such thoughts. The fine cloth of her dress was catching the wound each time she moved. It had not bled for hours now, but nothing would relieve the aching, neither the herbs Michel had left, nor thoughts of Geoffrey. Thoughts of him made her ache more but in a different way. So she prayed to God either to relieve her body of its pain or to fill her mind with other mysteries to unravel. Her only thoughts though had been Geoffrey, Geoffrey, Geoffrey... Already she missed him, so much so that Adelina thought she was going mad.

Thankful that the heavy door was open, she stood in the passageway, unsure of foot and dizzy. Her father's voice in the distance was raised. Her parents were arguing again.

She longed to see her father, to ask him what reason he had to send Geoffrey away so quickly but it was no use. Not now. She would have to catch the right moment to do so.

The air was stale, much-breathed and foul as she ventured downstairs, one step at a time, holding the curved stone for support. Adelina stopped quickly when the door to Louis's chambers opened. Louis was very surprised to see her. He was dressed, leaving. At night?

"Milady, you should not be here."

"And you will not forget who it is you speak to. You cannot tell me where it is I should or should not be."

"I am sorry, Milady. I beg your forgiveness." He was away, quickly. Adelina stepped closer to the door. "Who is in there? Is it the archer? The foreigner?"

Raoul came to the door. "Yes, but we do not know the cause of his sickness. I beg you do not come in."

It was too late. She was already in the chambers. Dedwyd lay on a cot, frothing blood at his mouth. He was feverish, in considerable agony, and mumbling in a very exotic language. "Who is he?" she asked. "Where is he from?"

"He is known as Dedwyd and he hails from a place called Wales. Do not get close. I beg you keep away."

Adelina did not hear Raoul's plea, but when Acelin put his hand on her arm, she pulled out of his grip and defied him with her gaze. He stepped back when she said, "You will never touch me. Never."

She looked down at Dedwyd. "This is not a disease."

Raoul sighed, he knew it was no use arguing with her. Adelina, too ill to be out of her own bed, stepped closer to the cot on which the writhing man lay. She reached down, wincing and touched his face, and struggled to repeat the name as she had heard it. She said it three times in all, all the while her hand touching his forehead. "It is poison," she said quietly.

"Poison?" Raoul repeated.

"Yes. The monk. The one who knows of herbs and ailments and treatments, he once told me of this. What did this poor man eat?"

"He ate as we."

"Raoul, force your fingers into his throat."

Raoul wondered if she, too, was overcome by delirium.

"Do as I say! Have you not sworn on your honor to uphold my every wish?"

"Milady..."

"I have not the strength in me to do it else I would!"

Raoul turned him on his side, held the man still and forced his fingers down the throat until a projectile of blood and vomit issued on the cot and the floor.

"Again, until none remains."

Raoul did as he was told until nothing else would expel.

Adelina stepped to the door and leaned against it, her knees shaking. Raoul, still holding the man, looked up at Adelina. "The monk told you of this?"

"Yes," she said, lying. She had not known whose words were issuing from her mouth. She did not even know why she was in Louis's chambers. And when she said, "Bathe him, keep him warm. Now that most of the poison has been expelled except that which remains in his blood, he may live," she knew not who was speaking. She turned away slowly and climbed the stairs, thankful that her door was ajar for she would not have had the strength to open it.

Acelin ran down to the courtyard and caught Louis only moments before he had crossed the bridge in the darkness. "There is no need to summon Michel!" he called.

Louis looked back. "The little archer is dead?"

"No. No, my friend, it is a miracle."

Adelina lay on her bed, staring up at the crossbeam, at the rope dangling from it, and she wondered how many days it would be before she again had the strength and will to load the crossbow. If, of course, she could find it. It would take many days though to make another quintain. And now that Cateline was dead, who would steal the rags for her and help her make it? Who would hold all of her secrets safely? She had known Cateline all of her life and this new girl, Jennet, although willing to obey any whim at all, was still a stranger.

Tomorrow, she thought, as she closed her eyes, tomorrow, I will visit Geoffrey and watch as his moat is dug...

Geoffrey watched his brother as he slept deeply. Three candles flickered in the breeze and for a time, Geoffrey watched the shapes thrown up against the cobwebs. The first pangs of loneliness were deep and biting. For it was now, after supper, that they would talk—all of them—Michel, Louis, Raoul, Acelin and Robert, while in her corner, supposedly busy with her needlework, Adelina would listen and learn. She only pretended to enjoy her mother's company when her eyes held the truth: she longed for that which she could never have—the opportunity to join men in battle, and to speak freely on whatever subject she wished.

Geoffrey concentrated on the spider working hard at its web. She spun a web about me from the moment of her birth, he thought. Even her first smile was for me. She would not rest or be quieted by any other, not her wet-nurse, not her mother. The sight of her father's beard was enough to warrant many screams of terror and so it was, day or night, with no mind of the hour, that there would come the call: Geoffrey! And I, he thought, I would take the infant carefully in my arms, and I would talk to her and I would walk every inch of the castle until she fell asleep.

Geoffrey felt the sting of tears behind his eyes. He missed Adelina, deeply, and one full day had not yet passed.

# Chapter 10

In the very early morning, Ella could not sleep. Much haunted her mind throughout the night, so much that she scrubbed the entire kitchen until her knees were raw and her fingers bleeding.

It was still dark when Raoul ventured downstairs. Ella heard the footsteps and quickly hid until she knew it was friend, not foe. Her whisper, "Master Raoul?" had frightened him so much that the jug of milk he was lifting to his mouth spilled. It seemed that Raoul's nerves were as ravaged as hers.

"Is there news of the little archer? How is it he fares?"

"He lives."

Ella almost told him of her misdeed. How was she to know that Gabriel would be suspicious? She had taken many pains to ensure his bowl of poisoned broth resembled all else's. Was it, she wondered, its faint, bitter smell? Or did Gabriel have a sixth sense? He was more of a fox with his bright eyes and sweet voice and evil heart...It was too difficult to deceive a master of deception.

"You work late," Raoul said, interrupting her thoughts. "You have been in service here many years, Ella. And you are an obedient servant."

"I try to be."

"I try to be... what is this nonsense, then?"

"Nonsense?"

"Untruths spoken to the master."

"Untruths, Raoul?" she asked, wide eyed, alas too frightened and old to feign innocence.

"Do not play games with me, Ella. I know you."

"I can say nothing."

"You? You can say nothing?" Raoul laughed. How he laughed. "It is said there is a first time for everything. No. I do not believe that you can say nothing. Why did you lie to the very one who feeds you and clothes you and keeps you safe?"

It was true that Raoul, who had been a retainer here for a very long time, almost as long as Ella, knew her too well. He also knew that she would not be in a hurry to disclose any truth. Gossip perhaps but matters of importance? No. He seated himself upon the table and touched his aching arm. "It is not an important matter that a servant was murdered here, for servants are easily replaced. As you know."

He looked directly into Ella's eyes, seeing again fear shining back at him. "But a cook such as you? I do not think you can be replaced as easily. I know all too well that no intruders came within these confines. I am concerned, woman, as, no doubt Geoffrey was concerned, that whoever dispatched Cateline lives here under this roof. I saw what remained of the girl, therefore I know that who is responsible has little respect for neither the living nor the dead. A barbarian affected by some smoking weed has frenzies like that, woman. A barbarian."

Ella said nothing. She dared not.

"Why is it you protect such a monster?"

"I dare say nothing, Raoul. If I do, he will kill me."

"He has a name?"

"I cannot say!" she wailed. And a wail it was, too. He had never in all his days, seen Ella as upset as this.

For a while, Raoul said nothing. "Tell me then, does his very name belie his nature?"

"I beg you say no more. Have I not tried already to rid the place of him?"

"Ah. The broth. I suspected as much," Raoul said with a smile.

"The broth?" Ella asked, innocently.

"With the poison this night. I saw him take the archer's bowl, and Dedwyd, poor clod that he is, lies upstairs now, deciding whether he should live or die. Gabriel is not a fool, woman."

"If you suspect, then so must he. That is what you tell me now."

Raoul nodded. "I suspect this you already know and this is why you cannot sleep."

"What am I to do?"

"Speak to the master of this before it is too late."

"He did not listen to Geoffrey."

"Gabriel goaded the boy tirelessly and easily undermined him. In doing so, Gabriel assured himself of a trustworthy position in this household. A position which should have passed to Geoffrey and none other. A position that was once mine. Once."

"So his torments were designed and not of jest?"

"Proof I have none but still I know it is the case. Those of no use to

Gabriel are simply a waste of his time."

"What am I to do? If I speak, I will surely die."

"And if you do not, you surely will. Perhaps not today, nor tomorrow, but he will have his revenge. How many nights can you last without sleep, woman?"

The silence was thick.

"You cannot dispatch the likes of Gabriel of Lyon. Be assured that God has his own methods of justice. Now fetch me something for this insufferable pain."

Michel had left a potion designed to take away the ache of the head and Ella hoped it would work as well for the relief of Raoul's wounded arm. She poured it carefully into a spoon, as Michel had decreed, and Raoul hesitated. "Is it poison?" he asked.

Never, in all his time, had he seen this strong woman buckle so quickly. She wept, long and loud.

"I jest," he said, taking the spoon. "I jest."

"I find little to laugh about!"

Raoul swallowed the putrid concoction and wiped his face of sweat. "Your own guilt is by far your worst enemy, Ella. Would you feel safer in the tower?"

Ella nodded. She would feel safer anywhere but in her own tomb-like chambers, so close to Cateline's, where screams were readily smothered by the impenetrable stone walls above, below, and to each side.

"Then remain with Adelina this night. I shall speak to the master in the morn and if he will not, then I will make sure that your chambers are secured."

"How can I thank you?"

"Keep me well fed," was all Raoul had to say.

For the rest of the night, Ella sat awake by Adelina's bed. Although she was weary, she dared not close her eyes for a moment. Still she wailed inside that she had poisoned the wrong person. A foolish deed, for the poisoned broth could have been swallowed by anyone at that table. Should Robert ever discover her crime, her punishment would be swift.

She thought of Raoul's words—does his very name belie his nature? Gabriel, with the name of an angel and the soul of the devil. Raoul was right. It was no use attempting to harm that one. He reeked of evil and evil ones were always protected by a cloak of their own darkness. But his own actions, she hoped, would soon have him in his grave. If he did not see her to her own first.

The sun was low in the sky and sleep had barely departed his eyes when Geoffrey saw the procession approaching his house. The miller's wife had been true to her word but why, he wondered, did she bring along every girl and woman in the entire village? He glanced at his brother, who was watching, too. Geoffrey sighed. "Come, brother. There are choices to make."

Geoffrey aided his brother down the stairs. The day was already warm, with no hint of a breeze as yet, nor was there a cloud in the sky.

What a terrible duty, Geoffrey thought as he walked amid the swarm of girls and women of all ages and shapes. His first mistake was to ask the names of those he found pleasant in appearance. After too many replies, no other name would fit in his memory unjumbled.

Geoffrey paid close attention to those who did not stare at Christian. Unfortunately, those who did not stare did not belong to those fair of face. All of them were thin, except for five who were each very fat with child. He soon sent them on their way.

Surely, he thought, looking at this band of hopefuls, it is so that girls were born too pleasant in this village. There were just too many to choose from.

And Christian stood, his gaze on one alone. She was shy and retreating all the while. Geoffrey pulled her out. She stood staring at her bare feet and she would not look at him. Her nervousness was great, almost as great as his. He pointed out those he wished to remain, and the others returned to their homes, some joyous, most not.

Thirteen females remained. "Whoever is chosen will cook, clean, and tend to my brother's every need. Whoever is chosen will reside in this house, so it is that anyone here who is married shall now take their leave." Five walked away. Only five. The final choice was becoming a little easier. Of the eight remaining, Geoffrey watched each in turn as he brought his brother closer. Five shied like horses at a flooding stream, and Geoffrey dismissed them instantly. The first of the remaining three he spoke to, spoke so softly that he barely heard her voice at all. He did not want to spend his time having her repeat everything she said. She said her name was Mirielle, or at least that is what he thought she said. Geoffrey asked to see her hands and he saw that they were encrusted with filth. If she could not keep herself clean, how could she keep his house clean? Her nose ran constantly and he needed no such additions to his food. He dismissed her. He stepped to the next, the shy one. A great beauty she was. He glanced at his brother. Expression lay in Christian's eyes. What was it? Hope? Geoffrey concentrated on the task ahead. "Your name?"

"Agnes, Monsieur." She spoke well for a serf. Too well.

"You are educated?"

"Oui, Monsieur. My father was a man of letters and a bard of renown, once employed by the Viscount D'Abadie of Toulouse for many years."

How can it be, he wondered, that this serf speaks as a noble should? "Where is your father now?"

"Dead, Monsieur. His sagacious words were his undoing. I have no family left now."

"You are able to cook?"

"Oui, Monsieur. I can cook, and clean and I sew very well."

"You fear my brother?" he asked.

Agnes looked at Christian and only compassion showed in her eyes. "Non, Monsieur. I have no fear of your brother."

Geoffrey looked at her hands. They were clean, and her hair, the color of straw, shone in the sun. Although her clothes were little but rags, they were neatly mended and smelled clean as well.

"Agnes," he said to himself, as if repeating it would aid him in remembering it.

"Monsieur?"

"Where is it you live?"

"By the water-mill, monsieur."

"There is no house there."

"Oui, Monsieur. Come the snows I am allowed to sleep in the Dumont house. Beneath, with the animals."

One without family and a house? "You will be in my employ. Go now and fetch up your things. You will begin today."

Agnes nodded and walked immediately to Geoffrey's house.

"I told you to fetch up your things."

"This is all I have, Monsieur." She carried nothing at all except for an aged blanket.

"Upstairs then. Rid the place of its spiders."

Agnes nodded and walked up the stairs. He realised that the third and final girl was still waiting. "You are not needed," he said and she walked off, saddened.

Geoffrey felt very pleased with his choice. He turned to Christian and put his arm around his shoulder. "I see a light in your eyes, brother."

Christian smiled.

"Should her food be equally as pleasing as her face and disposition, we will be fortunate men indeed."

Christian agreed, or at least, Geoffrey hoped he agreed.

"And still it is you who sees the pretty ones first."

Christian turned away and tried to climb the stairs alone.

Ella was scraping bowls into a pail when she heard the clinking of metal on the stairs. She watched the staircase, heart in mouth. Her prayers were not answered.

Gabriel leapt the final five stairs down to the kitchen floor. His eyes were sparkling and alive, full of good humor today.

"Toad," he said, happily.

"Master Gabriel."

"You were not trying to harm me last night, were you?"

"Me, Master Gabriel?"

"Me, Master Gabriel?" he imitated. "Thanks to you I have lost the best archer in Europe."

Lost? she thought. Did the poor little man die during the night? "I do not know what you mean, Master."

Again he imitated her innocence. Why did he think this amusing? "Where is the mute?"

"Drawing water."

"When you address me, you old toad, you will address me in the manner I am accustomed to!" He brought his fist down hard on the table and Ella did not flinch as he expected she would. Truly, she had felt that fist before and had no wish to feel it again, but showing fear to the likes of Gabriel was inviting punishment. He fed on fear.

"Apologies, Master," she said softly and continued scraping her bowls into the pigs' bucket.

"I do not wish to be known as master. You will call me Milord."

"There is but one lord in this household, Master Gabriel, and I am in his employ. As you are." Ella met his gaze without fear. Perhaps it was true that he suspected her of poisoning his food. Suspicion was not enough. Robert had not yet questioned her over the little archer's illness and it seemed that he would not. All morning, she had expected to hear his footsteps on the stairs. He was busy with other matters—perhaps he did not suspect her at all?

"Enjoy the time you have left, toad. For soon you will have none."

Ella ignored him, picked up the pail of swill and took it to the kitchen door. There she called for the charboys and they came to her, each laden with a bucket of fresh water from the well. Such heavy buckets for small boys. "It seems the boys are busy, Master Gabriel. Perhaps you would be so kind as to take this swill to your friends on your way to the gates?"

He could have hit her for what she had just suggested, and the challenge to do so lay in her face, in her icy stare, the set of her jaw. Gabriel laughed and leant against the wall. He studied his fingers for a moment before he said, "Did you see what lay in this pail yesterday morning? No? Let me tell you, toad, how much the pigs enjoy a little unborn human flesh. Perhaps some flesh mature of age would be more to their taste." He took his knife from his belt and cleaned his fingernails with it. When next he looked at the woman, her face was white. The challenge had disappeared from her eyes.

He turned when he heard the voice on the stairs, "Ella, the mistress calls you. She is impatient."

"It seems for now you are safe. For now."

"As you," Ella said.

The new girl, Jennet, came down the stairs, still calling. Her calls ceased upon seeing Gabriel. Ella thrust the swill bucket at him. "Here. Your friends await you. Master."

Gabriel put the bucket down, and with one sweep of his hand, Ella bounced across her long kitchen table amid a clatter of jars and spoons and trenchers and she landed with a thump on the floor. Gabriel turned to Jennet. "Girl, see to this."

Jennet picked up the bucket and Gabriel watched impassively as she quickly crossed the courtyard to the pig pen near the gate, threw the contents of the bucket over the fence and returned. He looked to the mute charboy and said, "Boy, with me."

The little boy obeyed the order. Gabriel put his hand on the child's head and said to the other, "What is his name?"

"I call him Antoine, Master."

"Antoine. The lessons begin."

For two full days, Adelina had remained a prisoner, deemed too ill and weak by the horrendous old monk who could not differentiate between a broken leg and a raging fever. However, her mother believed his every word and not one of her own daughter's. Adelina could not spend one more day on her back. If forced to, she would go insane.

Jennet brought in her breakfast on the third day and was met by the sight of her mistress, out of bed, and full of orders. As she helped her new mistress wash, not a lot was said. It was only until Adelina was dressed, in a man's tunic and hose, that conversation began. Jennet dared say nothing about her mistress's choice of clothing.

"Is there news of Geoffrey?"

"The moat has begun. Unfortunately, they struck rock or so my brother says. Unkindly."

"Did your brother say how Geoffrey and Christian fare?"

"No, Milady, but I shall ask."

"What is their maid-servant like?"

"It seems that the girl in their employ looks something like you, Milady. She was chosen from all of the village girls, it is said, because of her face. She is not from our village, and she lives by the water-mill on her own. Now she lives in the house of the master Geoffrey and tends Christian. It is said. Unkindly."

"Many are jealous."

"My younger sister was overlooked entirely. It is true she is not fair of face but she is a good worker."

"And men choose those fair of face to swell their own pride. Pull up my hair and secure it well. It will be too hot today to have it hanging loose."

Only married women wore their hair up but Jennet dared say nothing.

"I wish it was short. To here." Adelina touched her shoulders, then her ear. "Or here would be better. Do you cut hair or just play with it?"

"I have shorn my brother and father but I could not shear you, Milady," Jennet said as she fiddled with Adelina's beautiful hair. "Your hair is far too beautiful and you would regret it instantly because the curls bring life to your eyes." Jennet combed the thick red hair back and slowly braided it. "What would be if you meet a handsome nobleman who has to wonder if you are girl or boy?"

"Do you say that without hair I would look like a man?"

"Milady, I jest."

"I do not. Answer me."

Jennet studied Adelina carefully. "Perhaps with a grubby face, and provided you did not speak and ..." She paused as she gazed at her mistress's body. "No. I am sorry, Milady, but you are too fair to be mistaken for a boy."

"You are a gossip are you not?"

"Me, Milady?"

"What is said in this room remains spoken to none other. I make that clear now."

"Yes, Milady. I know."

Adelina didn't know whether to believe her or not. Hadn't she just gossiped about Geoffrey's housemaid? "I need rags, girl. Many rags. You will have to steal them from the washer-women and not all at once. If you are caught, I know nothing."

"Can I ask why you would need rags? Is your time of the month close?"

"Dieu! How is it you can speak of such horrors? I need not rags for that. Dieu," she said softly and rolled her eyes. "I wish to make another quintain. Geoffrey burnt my last when he discovered it. He also broke my crossbow by throwing it from the window. I heard it injured a peasant below."

"Milady? What is a quintain? Why would one such as you want with a crossbow?"

"Girl, you are here to serve me, not ask me unceasing questions. If you must know, a quintain is a target which knights use for practise of their warfare."

Jennet's mouth dropped and shock appeared in her eyes. "Milady, why would you want to practise fighting when you should be thinking of marriage and a family?"

"Why would I think of such nonsense?"

"I do. Often. Every girl I know does."

"Dieu! Am I you or every girl you know? Tell me that something more than marriage and family fills your thoughts?"

"What else is there?" Jennet asked, needing to know.

Adelina couldn't answer that because nothing came to mind. Nothing at all. Instead, she asked, "How old are you?"

"Eighteen."

"Are you already in love?"

Jennet smiled and her face took on a strange glow when she said, "His name is Etienne and he does not like it that I am here, for he cannot see me each day. He fears that Lord Robert will not allow our marriage now that I work here."

"Etienne? Is he handsome?"

"Oh, yes, Milady. Very."

"Is he kind to you?"

"Kind, Milady?"

"Is he your friend above all others?"

Confusion clouded Jennet's eyes. "We hope to marry and have many children."

Adelina couldn't understand it. Geoffrey had often attempted to explain love to her; he had once said that when she felt it, she would certainly know what it was. So perhaps it was a strange thing indeed, strange that this girl could think of marrying one who was neither kind nor a close friend. If he was only handsome, what then would be when his face changed with age?

"It is said that you were to marry Christian, your cousin."

"That is true enough."

"Who is it you shall marry now?" Jennet asked.

"No one. Why are you so slow? It does not take this long to pin hair on a head."

"I would rather be here with you than in the kitchens, Milady."

There was silence for a moment. Adelina was warming to this girl and realised it would be a mistake for soon enough she would go and yet another would take her place. Still she asked, "And you wish to marry Etienne even though you do not like kitchens? Cook is all you shall do once you have a husband. All you will do, Jennet, is cook and give birth to screaming babies. Is that what you want?"

"Yes, Milady, very much."

Adelina was nauseated. It was no use talking anymore. This girl would never see sense. Jennet finished securing the waist-length hair to her new mistress's head and Adelina touched it with her right hand only as it hurt too much to lift her left. She rose from her seat and noticed that Jennet wore the shoes, but her dress was the same as she wore yesterday. "Have you no other clothes?"

"No, Milady."

"When my father gives permission for you to marry, come to me and tell me and perhaps I shall give you a dress to wear at your wedding. Perhaps also Étienne can work in the chateau. What does he do?"

"He is a builder, a stonemason and a farmer, Milady. I am very proud of him. He can do anything."

Adelina was becoming bored with the look in Jennet's eyes every time Etienne was mentioned. God, spare me from this love ordeal, she thought. It stops the mind from working as it should. "I shall speak to my father when the time is right. For now, you will help me make another quintain. Cateline would hide the stolen rags in her dress and smuggle them to me."

"Yes, Milady."

"It was easier for Cateline as her mother worked in the laundry and was easily distracted, so you must be inventive."

"Yes, Milady," Jennet said, already wondering how she would steal these rags. First, she had to discover where the laundry was. Already she had been lost three times in the chateau and had to enquire of directions from a boy she later discovered was a mute. Jennet made her way to the door.

"No, I have not finished with you yet."

"Milady?"

Adelina stood by the window, looking down at Louis and Acelin who were having a friendly joust in the courtyard. "Tell me, what is it that you and Etienne do when you are alone?"

"Oh, Milady..." Jennet said, trying not to laugh from embarrassment.

"I want to know."

"It is different for us, Milady."

"I know it is different, for you are a common serf but still I want to know."

"If we are discovered there would be trouble."

"You will not be discovered through me."

When Adelina turned to the serving girl, a deep need shone in her eyes. Jennet looked at her fingers, and down at the shoes she had been given: Shoes she had rarely been without; shoes she was very proud of, shoes that many wanted, so she wore them constantly in case they were stolen. Her new mistress was very generous.

"We wait until dark and all are asleep in his house and mine and I climb from the window and we meet in the vineyard. He works all of the day and I do, too, and we do not see each other as much as we would like to."

"Does he look at you strangely?"

The girl nodded.

"Does he put his arms around you and kiss you?"

"Yes, Milady. And more."

Adelina was silent for a moment. "What is it like?" she asked softly.

"It is… better than the best joy," she said.

Adelina turned back to the window and not for the first time wondered what Christian's touches and kisses would have been like.

"But I am sure that one day you will discover this for yourself. A fine nobleman is waiting for you."

"Leave me. Attend to your duties in the kitchen for the wrath of Ella you have not yet felt. Go! Do as you are told!"

Jennet left wondering what it was she had done to upset her mistress this time.

Adelina stared from the window. The joust was over, they were practising their archery now. If Geoffrey had been here he would have allowed her to loose six or so arrows. But Geoffrey was not here and he would never be here again.

With a sigh she turned away. Geoffrey was still foremost in her mind. Had she known days ago that it would be the last time she would have seen him, she would have made the most of the opportunity she'd had, and she would not have had to ask a serving girl what it was like to be kissed and embraced. She remembered back to the time when Geoffrey had been readying his horse in the stables. She had walked in and asked from boredom alone where it was he was going?

"To the village, my love," he'd said. He always called her that when none other was about, and always with a smile. That day, and many before, too, there had been few smiles. She had watched as he'd saddled his horse, and she had sat atop the rails, rubbing at the horse's head, between its ears where it was always the most welcome.

"I would like to come with you."

"Best you not. I will be gone all of the day. Serf food you would not like and besides, you will become too bored too soon and you will want to return home."

"Why must you go to the village?"

"There is a dispute your father wishes me to settle."

"Why does he not send Gabriel?"

"Gabriel? Ha. He would have all heads for the crime of wasting his time. It is a small matter to us, but grows mountainous by the hour for the two concerned."

"I want to come and witness for myself your diplomacy and judgements."

"I need few distractions, my love. I am sorry, but no. You cannot."

"I am not a distraction. I am your friend."

"I have said no twice, I will say it a hundred times more." He had led his horse into the sunshine and Adelina followed. Their gazes met now, she no longer had to look up into his eyes. "There is a manuscript in my chambers which might interest you and keep boredom at bay. I must go." He had mounted his horse with ease.

"What have I done to you, Geoffrey?" she had asked.

"I do not understand," he'd replied.

"You have no time for me these past weeks."

He had looked down at her with a strangeness of eye she had never seen before. "I cannot talk now, my love. I must go. We shall talk of this later."

Off he had ridden, alone.

She had waited all day for his return and he came home too late for supper and he did not play dice that evening either. He had simply told her father the outcome of the dispute and he walked up to his chambers, tired. He had not even looked at her as he walked past where she sat, attending to a tapestry and listening to silly battle talk. So Adelina had put her tapestry aside, and wished a good night to all. She had walked into Geoffrey's chambers as he was undressing. He did not know she stood at the door until it was too late.

"Adelina! Can you not announce yourself!" He said quickly, angry, and pulled up his hose once more, securing it tightly. Adelina pretended she had not seen what she had seen for he was more embarrassed than she. "Would I do that to you?"

She shrugged, she would not have cared if he had or not. "Why are you so angry with me?"

"You creep up on me too often. I have no privacy here!" He bent forwards and scrubbed madly at his hair. Adelina had looked back to see if anyone was about before she stepped into the room and closed the door. She pulled out the torch from the wall and set it in the bracket by his bed.

"You said we would talk."

"I am very weary, can it wait another day?"

"No, for tomorrow you will find another excuse. Sit and I will flea you. Do as I say or I will order it."

Geoffrey sat on his bed lowered his head and Adelina sat on the stool and searched for fleas and lice, cracking them between her short nails. "Geoffrey," she'd said quietly, "I try so hard to be the lady you would like me to be."

"Then you must try harder."

"It is difficult. I don't have the interests of my mother. I cannot read all day, or write letters, or work on tapestries all of the time. There is nothing for me to do now that I am a lady. I want to ride with you. I miss our games in the woods." She had curled her fingers into his hair softly and Geoffrey had instantly raised his head and looked at her. "I try so hard to be who you want me to be but still you do not notice."

"I have eyes," was all he had dared say.

"Perhaps but do they truly see? You do not notice that this green I wear is the same color as my eyes. Louis did and he also said how pretty I was. He said it so quickly that I am sure he lied."

There was silence in which she had wanted reassurance of her beauty but Geoffrey said nothing.

"You do not notice that my hair is arranged differently now, or that I try not to chew my fingernails. You do not notice that I sit beside you when we dine. You do not notice that I no longer slurp at my soup. There is so much you do not see. Is it because we are no longer friends or is it because another has stolen your affections for me?" she asked and touched his bare arm. Gooseflesh followed her fingertips and Geoffrey shuddered. His eyes were filling with terror.

"I am tired, Adelina. Please, let me sleep?"

"You do not even talk to me now." She put her hands in her lap although she had wanted badly to put her fingers in his hair again, touch his skin, so smooth.

"Do you not see that you are no longer a little girl? I cannot bear being close to you."

"But why? I do not understand."

"Go. Please, go. You are promised to another. I do not like where this might lead." Very strange the look in his eyes had been. His hands tight against his knees were fisting. He turned his face away.

"You will not even look at me now." Her eyes had filled with tears and she rose quickly. I know why it is, she thought to herself. I am ugly. That is why he does not want me as a friend any more. I am ugly. Adelina had run from his room, fighting back tears.

Now those tears were forming again, the memory returned as if it had been yesterday. Adelina wiped her face on her sleeve and walked from her room. She had heard that Raoul had been wounded and she wished to find him, and also there was the little archer she vaguely remembered seeing as he writhed in agony on Louis's bed.

She wound her way down the stairs. The door to Louis's chambers was closed. She knocked on the door and waited. There was no reply. Adelina opened the door and peeked in. The little man with the strange face lay on his side, facing the door. He said something and smiled at her. What a lovely smile he had. He still seemed ill, very ill, and yet he rose above his agonies so easily.

If he could, then she could. Adelina smiled back.

# Chapter 11

It was dark and stuffy in the room. Adelina drew back the heavy curtain and sunlight fell on Dedwyd's face. His eyes sparkled and he spoke again in his exotic babble.

I will have to teach him our language, she thought and stepped to where he lay. He smelled terrible and around his mouth were crusts of blood. His lips were cracked and there was no water. "Who is caring for you?" Adelina asked, uselessly.

Adelina called for Jennet to bring a pitcher, also soap and cloths. The little man lay there and watched her carefully. He asked a question, one she could not comprehend let alone answer.

Adelina sat on the stool by the bed and she took his hand. "You will live," she said. He didn't understand so she squeezed his hand and smiled. A strange little man indeed. His face was round like the moon and his eyes were neither brown nor green. Always he smiled, even when half a frown crossed his face and never before had she seen anyone smile and frown at the same time. Adelina wanted to smile only because he did. Strange indeed. He was looking at her face, her clothes, and especially her hair, in such a way that perhaps he wondered where it had gone when Jennet came in as requested.

First, Adelina poured water for the little man to drink and he did, greedily, and wiped his mouth on his hand. Perhaps what he said next meant thank you?

"Merci," she said.

He tried to say it.

"I am the Lady Adelina, daughter of Robert, your lord and master. This is my serving girl, Jennet."

Dedwyd looked at Jennet but his eyes were only for Adelina. He tried to kiss her hand and Adelina retreated, saying, "No. When you are clean, perhaps."

Adelina sat back and watched as Jennet washed the little man. He did not like this at all. His bedding was also changed, and when the ordeal was finally done, Jennet was dismissed. The little foreigner spoke constantly, as if he wanted something. Adelina turned to the door quickly when she heard Gabriel say:

"He says that he wishes to make for you a garland of stars to match the brilliance of those which shine from your eyes. A loose translation only."

"You understand this babble?"

"Oh, yes. He thinks he is a poet but his uses are more, shall I say, practical. I have seen him fell five men with but one draw of his bow." Gabriel fanned his fingers as if showing her how the arrows spread. Then he pointed to the huge bow and its assortment of quivers against the wall. Wherever Dedwyd was, close by was his weapon. But this little man had no sword, no axe, no mace and he wore no chain mail. Only a very tough leather armor rested against the wall. Her grandfather, it was said, once wore armor like that. Perhaps the little man could afford no other?

"Is he your retainer, Gabriel?"

"Alas, he was, but is no longer. He belongs to Louis now. I am told it was you who saved his life," Gabriel said as he leant against the doorway and studied his fingernails closely. "Not that it matters for he is no longer mine to worry about."

But Gabriel looked at the little man as if he did care, or so Adelina thought. "If I saved his life, I do not remember doing so."

There was silence for a little while. Gabriel said nothing, and Adelina could think of nothing to say, yet still he leant against the doorway, studying his fine hands closely. Geoffrey would do that, too, at times when his mind was filled with questions and he could not find a simple way of expressing the words.

"I hear you were one of many who fought bravely."

"Is there another way to fight?" Gabriel asked and stepped in.

Why, she wondered, does he never call me 'Milady'? "Is it true what he said about my eyes or do you jest?"

Gabriel studied her curiously. "Yes, I believe what he said may be true."

Dedwyd rattled off something else.

"What he wishes to know most of all is why you have been crying."

"Crying? Me? Ha. I do not shed tears. Never. Tell him that if I chanced to, they would be my business only."

Gabriel told him to mind his own affairs and the little man's eyes came alive again.

"Does he sing?" she asked.

Gabriel asked Dedwyd if he sang, and to that he tried to rise from the bed. Adelina shook her head and he lay back, defeated very easily.

"He enjoys showing off to an audience and I have no wish to discover if he can sing or not. I believe he can. Or thinks he can." Gabriel stepped close to where Adelina sat and she looked up at him when he said, "His name, in his language, means 'happy'. Aptly named as a babe, for he is never without a smile on his idiotic face."

"This is not an idiotic face. The light which shines from his soul illuminates the darkness of all who are close-by, friend or foe. Can you not see it or feel it?"

"I feel that you have been too close to Geoffrey too long. All this talk of souls," Gabriel said. "Could he be the reason why you were crying?"

"You, too, can mind your own affairs, Gabriel of Lyon. I wish to teach this little man our language. Do you think he is too old to learn?"

Gabriel, very amused, had to look away quickly. Dedwyd was barely past his twenty-sixth year. Gabriel translated, but the little man was not so amused at what he heard. He said something that Adelina knew could not be turned into her own language without causing some offense, even if she said such things herself at times.

Gabriel said with a smile, "He may learn quickly if his teacher is a fair, young noblewoman who has much time and good intentions but little patience."

"I do not like your sarcasm, Gabriel of Lyon."

"Then I am sure Dedwyd will take notice of every word which passes your lips. I know I do." His smile, a very rare one, seemed almost genuine. Almost.

"I am not one, Gabriel of Lyon, to be duped by simple flattery."

"I am not one to lie when truths are told about the beauty of a young woman. Especially a young woman who does all she can to hide such beauty away under the attire of a page."

Adelina studied Gabriel's handsome face. "You are too free with your tongue."

"Perhaps I listen to you too often?"

Adelina looked away from Gabriel's face. "Tell him to sleep. Tell him that as soon as he is well enough, his lessons will begin."

Gabriel obliged and once again, translated what the little archer said. "He says that he will learn yours only if he can teach you his." Without waiting for a reply, Gabriel departed.

Adelina pulled the covers to the little man's chin, touched his forehead and she heard, as she walked away, "Merci."

She turned back. He was grinning. How many words did he already understand?

As she walked down the stairs further, she wondered how she would begin to teach this foreigner. If she taught him the language, perhaps he may teach her how to use his huge bow, instead of his language? For what good would his tongue do her here? None at all. But oh, how she wanted to use that bow of his. Now that he belonged to Louis, she could order him to, but first he had to understand the words she said.

She came to a quick halt. Her father sat at the long table in the great hall. He was speaking to the abbot Jean. Adelina wanted to speak to her father as well, but knew now was not the time. He would only say no to her request this day, that she knew already, for his face seemed more worried than ever before. His hair was even grayer now and he sat as a man almost defeated. Apparently, the wisdom and solace of the church could not alleviate much today. If it ever did, she thought. She crept by as noiselessly as possible, but he heard her. He always did.

"What are you doing out of bed, girl?"

"I am going to the kitchens, Papa. I am so hungry that I cannot wait until dinner to eat. How are you this day, Abbot?" she asked offhandedly and he replied in the same manner.

"So you are better?" her father asked.

"Much, Papa. Much. Can you not see how fit I am?" Although her arm hurt to lift it, she turned in a circle, almost a dance.

"Your wound bleeds still?"

"No, Papa. I only wear this for it is loose and comfortable."

"And you enjoy your boy-games."

She blushed and lowered her head, and sent him one of her innocent, I have been discovered expressions while she thought Oh Papa, if only you knew half of what it is I do. It is not boy-games, it is warrior games.

"What have you done to your hair?"

She turned around once more to display the huge braid wound tight and pinned to the back of her head.

"Oh," Robert said and waved her away.

Adelina took a very quick leave and as she ventured down the stairs to the kitchens she heard the abbot whisper, "Is she of marriageable age yet?" She stopped immediately, waiting to overhear her father's reply but there was none, so she continued down the stairs, thinking of her plan.

What she intended was to ride off to the village to visit Geoffrey and see this moat for herself—the moat was the only excuse she could find. And should she eat early, her father would not suspect her absence at lunch and no one would know she was gone at all, because she could threaten the stable boys, lie to Ella and be returned long before supper. If any noticed her absence, all she need do was have Jennet lie that she was asleep and weary in her chambers, and not as well as she had thought she was. Yes, she had it all planned. The stable boys were frightened of her, she had beaten up two of the pages already and could argue her way to victory with the squires. She would order the gate open and that would be that.

Ella was stirring a cauldron of stew and it smelled wonderful, so wonderful that Adelina had not known how hungry she was.

"Is it cooked yet?" Adelina asked.

Ella leapt high and covered her heart with her hand. She was frightened so badly that Adelina thought she would drop dead immediately. "Milady, you scared the life from me."

"I am hungry, is it ready?"

"Ready enough. Sit yourself."

Adelina sat on the stool which seemed terribly high when she was small. Ella ladled some stew into her bowl, gave her the spoon engraved with her initials and broke off some bread. Adelina blew on the spoon to cool the food. "Where is Raoul?" she asked.

"I believe he has visited Michel for his arm worsens daily."

"I miss Michel."

"He was away many years, he returned for one night and you say you miss him? How can that be?"

"I have always missed him. Christian, too. Because I do not speak of such things does not mean I do not feel."

"Most of all you miss Geoffrey."

Nothing escaped Ella. Nothing. "I am going to teach the little archer to speak French so that we understand him."

"Very good, Milady."

"He said that my eyes shone like the stars and he would make a garland of stars for me."

"But he does not speak our language."

"Gabriel told me of what he said."

A winter blizzard appeared suddenly in Ella's eyes. She mumbled to herself and banged her pots about angrily. "He speaks to you often?"

"Not often."

"He comes close to you?"

"He does not shout across a distance, of course he comes close. Why do you hate him so?"

"He is a monster."

Adelina thought it was funny.

"I do not jest. Take care, Milady, for he is evil."

"Gabriel of Lyon? Evil?" Adelina laughed, and as she laughed, Gabriel appeared on the stairs. "Monster!" she said and Gabriel looked at her quickly. "It was not I, Gabriel of Lyon, it was Ella."

Ella could do nothing except say, "Our young mistress jests, Milord."

Gabriel, on his way to the courtyard, looked back and said, "Our mistress must find some truths to jest of else it would not be funny, yes?"

Ella looked away quickly and Adelina sat there, eating her dinner and wondering why it was that everything happened when she was ill. Why was it that Ella and the new vassal hated each other so?

"What is happening?" she asked.

"Nothing is happening, Milady." Ella went back to her stew and the charboys brought in four chickens with heads recently lopped. Chicken was Adelina's favorite food, especially when roasted but she could not bear to see them still with feathers, nor could she abide the noises as their insides were pulled out. She finished her stew quickly, left the bowl and ventured out.

The sun was not at noon yet and for spring it was hot with a promise of rain this afternoon perhaps. For a moment she almost decided not to go to the village, for if she came home wet, hell would rain from her father's mouth. But she had a few hours and her father's anger she'd felt many times before. And Geoffrey's face she missed terribly, so she decided to continue with her plans.

Adelina walked to the stables. She told the boy he had not seen her and if he said he had, she would kill him slowly in the dark of the night.

Gabriel attended to his horse's hooves and tried not to laugh at the threat as Adelina chased the boy out. Gabriel wondered what she threatened the gatekeeper with, or did she only time her escapes when the gatekeeper was not at his post and a page was?

"Hold still!" Adelina said impatiently.

Gabriel looked through the rails. There she was, one handed, attempting to saddle Geoffrey's ancient pony. She cursed, too, very adequately indeed. Gabriel dropped his horse's back hoof and leant his elbows on the rail to watch. His horse watched, too.

"Have you not forgotten that ancient hauberk you keep hidden here?" Gabriel asked.

"Dieu!" It was her turn to be frightened half to death. "What are you doing here!" she demanded.

Gabriel climbed through the rails and walked to her. He unsaddled the old pony and smacked it on the nose when it tried to bite him. "You cannot go anywhere unaccompanied today."

"Saddle my horse immediately."

"No. I will not saddle your horse. You are forbidden to leave."

"Do as I say, Gabriel of Lyon."

"No."

"No? You tell me no?" Adelina asked, wide eyed.

"Yes, I tell you no."

Adelina bit back a scream of anger and raised her hand to strike his face but he caught her hand and held tight to her wrist, so tight his fingers were crushing. "Never raise your hand to me."

Adelina kicked him. He flinched and moved so quickly that next she knew she was on her back on the stable floor and Gabriel of Lyon towered above, his arms folded. Her angry, wounded pride was replaced by wonder. "Show me how you did that."

Gabriel laughed and stepped back. He offered his hand and pulled her up. "I am not Geoffrey to obey your every whim. Look at you. What is this supposed to be? A disguise? If so, it is a very poor one."

"It is not a poor one at all providing I wear hauberk and helmet, too."

"That ancient hauberk has not a coif large enough to hide your big mouth. Do you think Baudoin Dupuy would not see that you are the eccentric daughter of his enemy no matter what you wore?"

Adelina could not believe the amount of insults contained in so few words and momentarily, she was speechless with shock.

"I am afraid that you cannot sneak off to see Geoffrey, not today, not tomorrow. Perhaps never again."

How did he know where she was going? He walked back to his horse. Adelina took up the saddle again and heard, "If you touch that saddle I shall drag you in to your father."

"You will try," she dared.

"I will not allow you to do this." Again he stood before her and again she defied him with:

"You, Gabriel of Lyon, take orders from me."

"Not so. I take no order from any little girl who claims she is of noble birth when I know for a fact that this is not the case."

"I will speak to my father of your impertinence!" Adelina stamped her foot.

Gabriel remained unmoved. "If it pleases you. However I know what he will say and who it is he will believe."

She knew by the expression on his face that he would not be moved, so Adelina tried another tactic. "I need to see Geoffrey," she said softly, watching his eyes. He shook his head. That did not work at all. "And you shall take me. You shall be my escort."

"I am not paid to be your escort. Nor will I take you to see the sparrow. He is too busy with his moats and his women to spare you any time."

His words cut deeply. "What do you mean, his women?"

"I mean what I say. His women. Do you not know that he and his idiot brother have two women each? Playthings I hear, easily discarded like the courtesan of the other night."

"Courtesan?"

"More of a whore, I suspect. Geoffrey had his fill sure enough." Gabriel lifted his horse's hoof and picked up the rasp.

"A whore? Geoffrey? No, I cannot believe that."

"Raoul and Louis and Acelin witnessed it, too."

"Is this the one Geoffrey spoke of who died?"

"It matters not now. What is done is done."

Adelina came closer. "Tell me what happened."

"When?"

"The night of the attack."

"Much happened."

"Why will no one tell me what happened to Cateline?"

"It is not fitting for the ears of a child."

"I am not a child! Have you not eyes!"

Gabriel put the hoof down, straightened his back and leant against his horse's long neck. "I have eyes, little girl. I have very good eyes. Why is it you wish to know?"

"She was my friend."

"Then remember her as she was. Your curiosity will only lead to heartbreak."

"I order you to tell me!"

Gabriel mumbled to himself in a language she did not understand and he sighed.

"What did you just say!"

"That your persistence is ridiculous."

"We were babies together, Gabriel. She was my friend." Tears in her eyes now.

Gabriel ran his fingers through his hair. "She was tortured before she was finally dispatched," he said quickly. "Do not venture from these gates alone, as I have no wish to gather up pieces of you." Gabriel took a carrot from his belt and fed it to his horse and he caressed the animal's face and neck as if it were his only friend. "Your ambition to be free of this place is soon realised for your father journeys to Allegre to attempt a truce with the Dupuys. Perhaps an allegiance, and now that you have proved your fitness, I suspect that you will have to accompany your father."

"An allegiance with the Dupuys? What madness is this?"

"Soon enough we shall know."

"You feel as I, Gabriel of Lyon?"

"It matters not what I feel. I do know that your father does nothing without a good reason. Your freedom, as once you knew it, is soon to end. You are of more worth alive. Dead you feed worms only and it is my job to ensure the worms feast on others, not you, your father or your mother. My duty is to keep you alive until the time when I am ordered otherwise and that time shall never be. Unlike Geoffrey, I will not cater to your every whim. Riding alone from this day on, even being alone outside the keep, is forbidden. I have seen the wrath of your father, and I do not wish to experience it. But then," he said softly, "You have not seen nor felt mine, have you, my little, spoilt girl."

"I am your lady and on your honor you have sworn to protect me!"

"Lady? You? You may have to prove it. What I see here before me is a spoilt child, not a fledgling beauty. However, for you, and for now, I will say nothing to your father about this ridiculous plan of yours to escape alone. For now."

"I cannot believe that my father would attempt a truce with the Dupuys after what happened to me."

"There is much needing discussion."

"Is it because of me?"

"More of the king, I suspect."

In Robert's private chambers, a room at the very top of the tower, a room that very few of his closest friends had been permitted entry into, Adelina stood with tears stinging at her eyes but pride alone refused their exit.

She looked a beautiful sight in her finest dress, the one of pale blue with the long train, the one with the edges and flowing sleeves embroidered with gold brocade. She wore a gold brocade head-band studded with gems and to any, she could have seemed a princess. But she stood, slouched against the wall of her father's private chambers; struggling to come to terms with what her father had just said.

Unlike earlier in the day, she now seemed weak and pale. Robert could not decide whether it was anger, pain or betrayal, perhaps all three at once reflecting from her eyes.

"I do not want to go."

"Your wants at this time mean nothing to me, Adelina. You will do as you are told."

"My mother can not approve," she tried, knowing it was futile.

"You will be by my side and you will be pleasant, and you will speak only when you are first spoken to. You will be a lady."

"I cannot look them in the eye, Papa. I will spit on them if I do."

"Gabriel, leave us."

Gabriel nodded to Robert and swept past Adelina without a second glance.

"Stand straight. Be proud that you are a woman."

Adelina tried to obey.

"You were given too much of the wrong freedom and that was my mistake. Now you must do as I command."

Adelina lifted her gaze to the low ceiling of the stuffy room. She was biting her lip, hard.

"There will be an allegiance with the Dupuys."

She glanced at her father. How he was growing old, and with age it seemed that his common sense was dying, too. She said nothing as she looked away once more.

"You will smile and you will be gracious as you have been so taught."

Still, she said nothing.

"Our very future depends on you, Adelina. Our family, the villages. Sit, daughter. Sit and listen carefully to me."

A few moments later, she burst from the chambers, screaming. She pushed Gabriel aside hard enough to unbalance him, and Robert appeared. "Bring her back."

She was fast on her feet though, leaping down the spiral stairs three at a time; leaping hounds dozing on the stairs, hounds that rose and barked and tripped Gabriel. Eventually, in the great hall, he caught her by the arm, and she swung and kicked fiercely. Gabriel twisted her arm until she stopped fighting. She screamed, "I will not! I will not! I will not!" as he dragged her, literally, all the way up the stairs again.

# Chapter 12

Geoffrey was in the hot sun, overseeing the digging of the moat when a welcome visitor came on foot. "Now you know why few places have moats," Michel said, hiding his smile and surveying the mess made. "You have been busy indeed. You do know that now is planting time?"

"They work a mere half a day thrice a week for me. I keep them not from the fields."

"I suppose this moat will make a good ornament at least."

Geoffrey looked at Michel. "You know of something I do not, old friend?"

"Robert attempts an allegiance with Henri Dupuy this day."

"And how is this miracle to occur?"

"The houses will be united by marriage. It is rumor only." Michel spoke on for a while before realising that Geoffrey was neither listening nor present. "Geoffrey?" But Geoffrey was already gone, preparing his horse and calling for his housemaid to come down immediately.

"You can do nothing."

"Perhaps."

"Do not do this."

The new girl, Agnes, came down almost immediately yet Geoffrey was already on his horse, impatient to leave. "Watch that my brother does not venture downstairs alone for he wanders off and will most likely drown in the river. When I shall return I know not. Watch him."

"Yes, Monsieur," Agnes said.

Michel grabbed at Geoffrey's reins. "You can do nothing, Geoffrey. This is foolishness."

"It is my foolishness, Michel. Move aside."

"It is not your concern!" But Michel's final words were not heard by Geoffrey, who was already in a canter and once free of the village, a full gallop. Michel turned to the men, breaking their backs against rock in the shallow, circular ditch. "Finish up here, eat, and tend your fields."

"Go, child. Do not keep your father waiting." Marys kissed her, held her tightly and set her free. Gabriel led her to her horse which was fitted with a side saddle. She looked to her father. "Papa, must I?"

Robert knew she could not ride successfully on such a saddle designed for ladies when she oft rode bareback but he nodded. Yes, she must, and worse, she was forced to allow Gabriel to help her into it. "I would rather walk," she spat.

"But of course you would," he said quietly. She could not mistake the torment lingering in his eyes.

"I shall jump from the bridge when we cross the river."

"Merde," Gabriel whispered as he handed her the reins. "To here, merde." He touched his chin, smiled at her and mounted his own horse. With banners flying, the small procession departed: Louis at the head, Gabriel with his master and young mistress, Acelin at the rear. They were all in their finery, each and every one.

"You shall come to Paris with me," Robert said to Adelina. "I have an audience with the king."

"You go to beg, you mean," Adelina said.

"I go to speak with him."

"Why must I attend? Court is boring. No one speaks with honesty and all pander to others they would rather stab in the heart."

"You have never attended court."

"I have heard of it which is by far enough."

Gabriel walked his horse beside hers and was very amused. "Who are you to laugh!" she spat, hoping that would see an end to it, but, as before, he mouthed merde and touched his chin. "Papa, this knight is a monster!"

Robert said nothing except, "When you accompany me to St Denis, you will remain quiet."

"Papa! Gabriel of Lyon is a torment and I will not abide him one moment longer!"

Robert had too much on his mind to be bothered by a complaining daughter and Gabriel knew it. His smile grew very large and was intensified by the sparkle in his eyes when she said, "Your job is to guard me, not goad me!"

Gabriel drew his sword, a very long sword indeed and he nodded to Adelina and turned his horse about on the narrow track. "We have company. Ah, look. It is feathered company."

Adelina turned as far as she could without unbalancing and her heart lifted. "Geoffrey!" She pulled her horse to a halt and turned back to meet him but Gabriel's horse was across the narrow roadway, refusing Geoffrey's passage.

Robert closed his eyes before he, too, drew about and wondered if this day would ever have an end. "What is this?" he asked, containing his pleasure at seeing Geoffrey again. "Geoffrey, what are you doing here?"

"I am using my time wisely, Milord. You?"

"You were not summoned."

"I am summoned on business to La Chaise-Dieu, and by chance alone we have met. However, as I am now here, I trust you could avail yourself of another bodyguard? I see another is needed."

"Can Geoffrey be my private escort, Papa? Please? Please?" Adelina asked.

Robert mumbled to himself and turned about. Geoffrey grinned at Gabriel who had no choice but to let him pass. "It seems that our beautiful lady wishes my services." Geoffrey allowed his victorious grin to be displayed openly as he walked his horse past Gabriel's. He was met by nothing except a bored stare in return. Geoffrey met Adelina and said nothing of the side saddle. "You look very fair today, my love. Where is it you journey?"

"To Allegre," she said.

"But Allegre is Dupuy land."

"Kidnap me, Geoffrey, now, before it is too late."

"It would be too difficult to hide you. I fear any searcher would know where you were."

"I do not jest. Papa says I may have to marry Baudoin Dupuy. He says that Jean-Pierre acted alone and that Baudoin will obey his father in this union but I have heard that Baudoin ordered the attack on our chateau, Geoffrey, and I cannot marry someone who wanted me dead even though he has never met me." She stopped to draw breath, finally. "It makes no sense. God would never bless such a union so it will be a sin, and a lie, and we shall all go to hell for eternity. Kidnap me now. If you love me as you have always said, you have to."

"I cannot steal you here and now with my friends so close. I wish my heart to expire from age, not from a sword thrust."

"Then it must be that you do not love me. That all these years have been filled with nothing but lies."

"Nonsense and you know it. I can serve you best whilst I am alive, my love. I cannot serve you if I am dead." Geoffrey looked back to Acelin, who grinned at him. "Perhaps the allegiance will not be from marriage but from treaty."

"And perhaps pigs grow wings and fly as fat hawks beyond the very clouds. You do not love me, you have never loved me, it is clear now. May your two women give you nothing but horrible diseases."

Geoffrey had no idea what she spoke of, and this was not unusual when conversing with Adelina on any matter.

"Tell me, my love, is Gabriel of Lyon kind to you?"

"He is a monster."

"He has hurt you?"

"My pride only. All must be his way."

Geoffrey looked away and hid his smile as best he could. "You fare well after your injury?"

"There are times my fingers will not work as I wish but it is a good excuse not to embroider."

"What is it you do with your time now?"

"I think of you. Jennet has said that you build a moat now? That you have struck rock?"

"That is very true."

"And when shall I see your benefice, Geoffrey? When will you invite me to dine with you and your brother?"

"When it is fit for your eyes, my love, and no sooner. A chateau it is not."

"Jennet has said that Christian fares well. That he smiles."

"Yes, at times he smiles."

"So it must be that the door to his chamber has not yet unlocked?"

"I fear it never will be."

"I could come every day."

"Your duties are elsewhere now, my love."

"If Papa hears you calling me 'my love' he will have your head on a stick."

"It is a risk I have always taken."

"Geoffrey, I miss you."

"And I you."

As it was only Acelin riding behind, Geoffrey reached over and caught Adelina's hand and held it tightly. Acelin did not see a thing—if so he pretended otherwise.

"Is it true that your house-maid looks like me?"

This took Geoffrey by surprise. "She is the one who most fitted our needs."

"She was the prettiest of all in the village."

"You have been listening to gossip."

"There is little I do not hear now, Geoffrey, for the very father of my new girl is none other than Thierry, the miller, and she loves to gossip as much as her mother does."

"As you too, it seems."

"Does she look like me?"

"No. You are more fair, by far."

"Why did you never say such things when you lived at the chateau?"

"I knew your head would swell and that hearing it once would not be enough."

"You tease me."

"I speak truths."

"And the other? Tell me of her. Tell me now."

"The other? What other?"

"The other girl. Has she hair as deep as the night and long legs and breasts like watermelons?"

Louis almost broke his neck turning so quickly and Geoffrey wanted to slide off his horse in shame.

"There is no other girl. What would I want with two house-maids?"

"You have one for the work, and one for the bed."

"Where did you hear this nonsense? For nonsense it is. Louis, this is a private conversation!"

Louis took his attentions back to the narrow road but Geoffrey knew that his ears were flapping in the breeze now. "People are unkind at times. Perhaps it was said from jealousy. I have no woman, my love. I have not the time for one and if I did, she would not be a serf but a fine lady with good qualities."

"Like me?"

"Like you, yes," Geoffrey said quietly, hoping no one had heard.

"Why do you journey so far from home?"

"It is .. it is .. to do with my studies."

"You will study at La Chaise-Dieu?"

"Perhaps. I do not know," Geoffrey said, wanting to end the lie quickly. They rode in silence for a way.

"Geoffrey, what am I do to if I must marry this Dupuy?"

"We can hope that the gossip is true. I have heard that his father is an honorable man, as honorable as your father. I have heard that Henri Dupuy does not care for violence which is unwarranted."

"But I shall not be wed to Henri Dupuy."

"Then pray to God that Baudoin is as his father in nature."

"In my heart I know he is not."

"Adelina, listen to me. I do not know the reasons for this, I can only assume that your father makes a sacrifice for the good of all and not the one. Many lives depend on him, my love. Many, as one day, many will depend on you. Some may say that to be born a noble is a gift from God. It is also said that gifts from God come with a heavy price, the heaviest being responsibility for many others."

"But I never wanted to marry. Christian, perhaps, because I knew him and I liked him and we could have been friends, but not like this. I cannot marry a stranger whose brother tried to kill me."

"And if there lies an opportunity to heal old, deep wounds of long standing? If enemies can be united in peace?"

"Come with me, Geoffrey? Be by my side so I will find the strength not to spit on these people?"

"You have much of your own strength as yet untouched. You do not need me to find where within it lies." He took her hand again and squeezed it, tightly. It was safe now to say what was on his mind. "You are so beautiful, my love. Let it not be wasted."

On approaching Allegre, Acelin, behind Geoffrey and Adelina, took his axe from his saddle as a silent warning to any daring do more than spit and curse and yell abuse. Adelina had never experienced hatred in such a measure before, and anxiety, almost panic, showed in her eyes. Geoffrey said, "Look into the eyes of none. None." She tried, but as she walked her horse by a house, if it could be called a house, standing by the open door, she saw a woman with two small children clinging to her knees and a small baby in her arms. They were all crying, and it seemed obvious to Adelina why. They were hungry and terribly thin.

She carried no money, only jewellery, and Geoffrey saw her pull the rings from her fingers. "No. Do not. It will incite robbery."

Adelina looked back at the woman and the babies. "Do they not have any food? Does Dupuy not allot his kitchen scraps? Where is her husband? I see no one in the fields..."

"Adelina, remain very quiet. I beg you."

They passed the church, and within its boundary, numerous, fresh graves. Adelina suddenly knew why the woman stood alone. Precious gems would not bring her husband back. She looked at Geoffrey but he was very watchful now, his hand on his sheathed sword, ready to take the head of anyone who came too close. No one did. They simply stared with despair in their eyes. "Perhaps this union may put food in their bellies," he said, quietly.

Only then did Adelina glimpse a hint of this responsibility Geoffrey spoke of. Only then did she glimpse and feel for herself some of her father's obligation of birth. She wondered how he felt inside, witnessing this, when he could not abide the sight of a thin horse let alone the cries of starving children. That was all she could see, wherever she looked: Poverty, women and children and some old people, hunger the only thing alive in their eyes. Hunger and despair.

Her hands shook. She felt faint. Never had she seen anything like this and never would she want to see it again. "Is it this bad in our villages?" she asked, voice shaking.

"No, my love, but when a woman loses her husband, there is

always much misery until she finds another."

"Can something not be done to ease this misery?"

"If so, I know not what it is. It pains me, too."

Adelina kicked her horse into a canter and joined her father, a sudden move which alarmed both Geoffrey and Gabriel. "Papa, can we not send these poor creatures some food?"

Robert said only, "I see what you see, girl, and I also feel what you feel and it is one of the reasons we are here. But only one. Be quiet now and leave your questions until later."

Adelina could not bear to see these wretches, so many of them, so she kept her head lowered and met none's gaze. Her heart was breaking. Geoffrey, beside her again, was quietly watchful and expectant of a skirmish. If he felt inside what she felt, then nothing appeared on his face or upon anyone else's. But they were soldiers and they had seen far worse indeed.

The party came to a halt at the crossroads. Up the hill lay the Dupuy abode, to the left, the road led to St. Paulien.

The Dupuys lived not in a chateau but a house once a manor, and now a fortress, around which was a battlement wall with towers protruding from each corner. It rested atop a treeless hill and looked directly down on the village. The lands here seemed barren, the grasses dry, vineyards on hillsides unkempt. Few cattle grazed, unshorn sheep wandered with longtailed lambs scattering as the riders made their way towards the imposing, unpleasant house Adelina knew lay within the high walls. I cannot live here, Adelina thought. It will be the death of me, a slow, lingering and painful death of my spirit.

A figure appeared on the battlement, a young man clad entirely in shining black leather, with studs of silver reflecting in the early afternoon sunshine.

There he is, Adelina thought, That is Baudoin. She turned her horse about quickly but Gabriel, crossbow in hand, moved his horse in so close that hers could not move in any direction but forwards.

Robert said, without turning, "Geoffrey, it is best that you leave us now. Your presence will not be wise inside these gates."

"Papa, he must come."

"My love, no. Your father is right. My presence is not conducive to peace at this time. God be with you." Geoffrey turned his horse back to the crossroads. His last sight, before he turned back, was of the small party entering through the lowered gate. "See her safe," he whispered.

# Chapter 13

The gate screamed and clanged shut. The sound was so final that Adelina jumped. She felt the touch to her arm. "Remain quiet, and all will be well, Milady." Adelina looked from Acelin's face down to the people approaching on foot, across the courtyard. They were all men. Then she noticed a woman, dressed totally in black. She stood by the doors of what once had been a very excellent abode. Not a lot of excellence remained, though.

Instead of the clean cobblestones she was so accustomed to, here there was fouled straw everywhere and no trace of a garden, either. There was no beauty anywhere that she could see, although once, long before her time, something beautiful must have existed here.

A strange discomfort overtook her, far worse than what she'd felt in the village, for here she could not explain its origins. Or even what it was.

The one who had stood armed at the battlement wall came down from the rampart. He was tall and very dark-haired. His hair shone in the sun, as black as a midnight sky.

Nothing but wariness surrounded the visitors now.

"Baudoin Dupuy," Robert said, still astride his horse. "I have come in peace to speak with your father on an urgent matter which affects the future of your family and mine."

"My father, at this moment, crawls from his sickbed against the advice of all. You and your followers will not come into my house with weapons. Everyone will disarm themselves. Now."

Robert dismounted and laid all of his arms down, as did Louis, then Acelin, and finally, Gabriel, who did so very reluctantly. Had there been a skirmish it would have been a fair one, for Baudoin Dupuy was surrounded by three of his father's vassals. Baudoin stepped towards Adelina and reached up for her hand. Gabriel stepped in to aid the girl off the horse, but caught the movement of Robert's hand as a deterrent. Adelina looked down at the outstretched hand of the brother of the one who tried to kill her, and she glanced at her father. He nodded. She leaned forwards so that this man could help her down. He did so easily, set her to her feet, and nodded to her before he turned away with, "Follow me."

Adelina saw that the woman who had been watching from the doors no longer remained there.

The party was led up several shallow stairs and into a meeting room of sorts. It was dark and gloomy, decorated with racks of armaments, hauberks and helmets. A coat of arms hung on the wall. Adelina had seen it before, adorning the body of the one who had his sword raised high for the final strike. She shuddered at the sight.

Baudoin turned to Adelina and said, "If you are weary from your journey, you may sit while you wait."

"I would rather stand than..." Gabriel nudged her very quickly. "Than sit for I have been sitting too long." Another nudge. "But I thank you for your offer." She tried to smile sweetly at him but it wasn't very successful. What does he admire, she wondered, that makes him smirk so? Is it my face or the gems in my head-band?

"My father will be with us soon," Baudoin said. "I hope," he added to himself in a whisper.

"How ill is he?" Robert asked.

"It is a sickness of the heart. He is much like a sheep that has willed itself to die."

"May I ask why?"

"Why? His favorite son is dead, is that not reason enough?" Baudoin glanced at Adelina, the cause of it all. She stood, nervously peering about, not liking what she saw, and almost crushed by the three bodyguards. "She will not come to any harm in this house."

The knights did not move and nor did Robert. Some anxious moments were spent until Henri Dupuy appeared, guided downstairs by his wife, the black-robed woman.

"I am honored, Robert, honored and surprised. For what do I owe this visit?" he asked and offered his hand. It was taken, the two embraced, cheeks touched, and each stood back a little way, fearing perhaps that the other had a concealed dagger.

"Words to alleviate the pain of your loss still escape me, Henri. Heloise."

Henri glanced at Adelina and then to his wife, whose face trembled with uncontainable despair. "Heloise, perhaps Adelina wishes for a cool drink?" Henri looked at Adelina enquiringly, almost softly, and she reached for her father's hand. Robert though did not take it. It was she who clung.

"Louis, accompany my daughter."

"I have said that she will come to no harm in this house!"

"My son speaks the truth, Robert."

After a hesitant moment, Robert said, "Go with Lady Dupuy, girl."

Robert squeezed her hand slightly and she walked across the room to where the woman waited at the foot of the stairs. And Robert, flanked by his bodyguards, was led into another room which was better furnished: A round table with eight, carved, high-backed chairs in front of a cold fireplace. On the floor were hides for extra warmth in winter. It was a room used often, the atmosphere not as heavy.

"Before we begin, there is a small matter," Robert said.

"Yes?"

"I offered to fund the funeral of your son, Henri. Why was my offer rejected?"

"It was not intended to offend. Sit, Robert, and tell me how you would have reacted had it been the funeral of your daughter and I had offered so?"

Robert looked into Henri's dull, listless eyes, and said quietly, "I would have taken offence. I am sorry."

"Jean-Pierre was a hot headed fool," Baudoin spat.

"And you are not? Remain silent, boy! Your opinion is not required, and therefore will not be heard!"

Baudoin looked from the window.

"I had planned to visit your estate to apologise for yet another son's actions. Actions that have cost us dearly. Actions for which he has already paid. Be assured of that."

Robert glanced from Henri to Baudoin and said, "I have come this day, with my only child, as proof that I offer you no ill-will. Will you hear me, Henri?"

"Was there a time when I did not hear you, Robert?"

Adelina was handed a pewter goblet and in it was a deep, rich wine. She sipped it, remembering to hold it as she'd been shown, sipping it, not gulping it with her head thrown back and belching loudly afterwards. Geoffrey would be proud of me, she thought.

"How is Marys?" Heloise asked as she sat in her private chambers, which, to Adelina seemed as dim as the rest of the house.

Once, Adelina thought, this woman would have turned many men's heads indeed. "My mother is well, Milady."

"Still she takes her headaches?"

How would this woman know that? she wondered and sipped again on the wine. "Not as often, Milady."

"Tell me of her. How is it she looks now?"

"As she has always, I suppose."

The woman smiled, rather sadly. "Do you know that once we were the best of friends and rarely apart?"

"No, I did not."

"It is true. We were friends, very good friends until we became enemies by marriage, and contact was forbidden. I think of her often."

Adelina almost lied and said, she thinks of you, too, but she remained quiet. This wine was very potent, indeed.

"You are sixteen, are you not?"

"Come the snows I will be."

"You are such a beautiful child."

"I do not think so."

"You are very much like the sister of your mother. Vianna."

This woman had barely glanced at her. She stared the entire time from her window, but what was it she saw?

"My mother has no sisters, nor has she brothers now. Her brothers died at war, and all that was theirs became hers and now it belongs to my father. One day, all will be mine because I have no brothers. And if I wed it will become..."

"Vianna sang like an angel," the woman said to the window. "You are so much like Vianna."

Adelina said nothing, as the name meant nothing.

"When first I saw you from afar, I thought I had seen a ghost. You are the very image of her."

"My mother Marys has no sisters."

"Alive, that is true. Vianna was my friend, too. A beautiful girl who never married. She lived with your parents until her death of a terrible fever on the very day you were born."

Adelina sipped her wine. "My mother rarely speaks to me and nor do I ask much of her. She is a stranger to me and I to her, I suppose. Was this sister younger or older?"

"Younger by five years. Her hair was the color of yours; her eyes, though, were a deeper green. The resemblance is haunting and makes me remember much."

Adelina wondered if she should pour this woman another wine. It seemed that she needed it.

"She sang beautifully and such a dancer she was... Do you sing, child?"

"My mother does not like music except when she has no choice and minstrels are engaged to entertain at large gatherings."

"I asked, do you sing?"

"I do, often, but always where none can hear me, for it is not worth the trouble such things cause. I do not understand how anyone cannot like music. It lifts my heart so."

"I would ask that you relay a message to Marys."

"Yes, Milady?"

"Tell her that I received her letter and her words aided my grief. But tell her I cannot reply." Heloise held up her twisted, painful hands. Adelina had seen this before. Ella suffered from it too, an affliction of the joints.

"Milady? Michel, one of our older knights, returned from his journey abroad, and brought with him many potions from the east. One in particular has helped our kitchen-maid who suffers as you do. Had I known of this, I would have brought a jar of the stuff with me. Had I known the sights I was to see on my way here, I would also have brought food for your people who are starving."

Heloise looked into the girl's eyes and said, "You cannot be the daughter of Marys. I look at you, Adelina, I hear your words, but I see Vianna Dubois. Even her heart you have." Heloise stood with a great deal of effort and stepped to Adelina. She touched her face gently. "What I would have given to have had such a beautiful daughter. Alas, I had no well-meaning sister to aid me."

Is she drunk? Adelina wondered. Drunk or just a lonely woman who was not as old as her face decreed to the world? Perhaps she was mildly deranged from having so few women to talk with, for few, if any, lived here. All the servants she had seen so far were men or boys.

"My mother often says I should have been a boy, Milady."

"Only because she could bear none."

"Perhaps you only wanted a daughter because you could not bear one?"

A smile lit Heloise's eyes. "I carried three daughters but none survived past birth. Three of my sons lived, but only two survived to adulthood. So many children I have buried."

Adelina did not say anything.

"Had I known this visit was nigh..." Heloise said, turning away, distressed.

"If I come again it would be you I will visit of my own free will."

"Vianna," the woman said again and tears rolled. Nothing would stop the tears, the cries. Adelina put her goblet down and embraced the woman tightly, wondering how many years it had been since the woman had felt the affections of another woman. Her heart ached as she felt the gnarled fingers entwining in her long hair. It felt as if Heloise Dupuy would never let go. "I do not understand why Jean-Pierre would want to kill you."

"Geoffrey told me that it was my name alone which spurred his hatred so."

"What are we to do?"

"We can hope that your husband and my father can come to some agreement, for if they do, then perhaps you can visit us, and we can visit you, as then it will be safe to journey without any fear. My father wants peace and unity and free trade between our villages. He says there would be food for labor and soon enough there will be men tending the fields again, not dying senselessly on enemy land. For such enemy land will be a thing of the past. A past best forgotten entirely."

"Oh, your father could charm the rags from the back of a pauper," Heloise said.

"You know him?"

"Oh, yes. I once loved him from a distance. He was so handsome and charming when he was young. Alas, it was my friend he chose. My friend and her sister."

"Does he know that once you had eyes for him?"

"Oh, yes, he knows, but would prefer to forget."

"Your husband knows of this, too?"

"Ah, Henri. He has always had much else on his mind. He is aware of the king's threat to take our lands, child, and now his heart is dying. He has told himself it is the end."

"Can nothing be done?"

"I have been his wife for many years, child, but still he is a stranger to me."

"Perhaps if you shook him and told him that others depended on his strength?"

"Better I shake the battlement wall and tell it to fall. I can say nothing and do less. Always it has been that way and will remain so."

"Then it is true that he is much like my father." Adelina smiled and wished once only to see the woman smile, too. She did, and it disappeared quickly when the door opened and Baudoin came in.

He kicked a chair out of his way, angrily. Far better it would be to walk around it, Adelina thought. She was used to men and their tempers.

"You. Your father is leaving now."

"You will be civil, Baudoin."

"I will be who I am and you will remain quiet!"

"How dare you speak to your mother that way! You have no respect!" She spat at Baudoin, who grabbed her by the arm and spun her to face him.

"And it is a shame that my brother did not cut your throat when he had the chance thereby saving us all this future misery!"

Adelina was ready to fight now, it mattered little that he was a good foot taller, twice her size and swaddled in leather. She would find a way to make him pay for what he had just said. She felt the lady's hand on her shoulder and heard her whisper to come, and as she'd promised all and sundry she would behave as a lady, she followed Heloise Dupuy down the stairs, fighting down her red hot anger. Her long fingernails would come in useful only for scratching out this one's black eyes. Peace, Geoffrey had said. Peace?

Robert saw his daughter stomping down the stairs and he closed his eyes. Now was not the time for one of her tantrums. He prayed to God to keep her quiet at least until they rode from the gate. Quiet she remained, but not for long enough. Baudoin, behind her, gave her a push out of his way and she turned and spat on his boot. "I do not fear you and I did not fear your brother as he aimed his sword at my heart! If it is a fight you want, it is a fight you shall have! Choose your weapon, Dupuy! Now!"

Robert closed his eyes and covered his face with his hand. Henri seemed almost as mortified as Robert when his son picked up a feather and offered it as his weapon of choice.

Gabriel had to look away. He bit his lip hard, endeavoring not to laugh. Robert stepped forward. "Adelina, I should introduce you to your future husband, Baudoin."

He stood with sparks in his eyes and a smirk on his face as he held that silly feather. Reflected in his eyes, Adelina saw her own animosity. He was as happy about this as she, perhaps less so.

"I will never be ordered, or pushed, or shunned by any man who has no respect for the woman who suffered to bear and raise him, for if he has no respect for his mother, he has no respect for himself."

Surprise lit Baudoin's dark eyes. "My wedding present to you will be a gag."

And each, at the same time, turned to their fathers with:

Father, I beg you reconsider this foolishness!

"You will both become acquainted with each other on the journey to Paris. Robert, are you sure you will not stay?"

"No, I must go while there is still light."

Adelina was first out of the door and once in the courtyard, she ordered Gabriel to help her onto her horse the moment Henri ordered Baudoin to do the same. As he aided her up, Gabriel whispered, "I am now the lesser of two evils, I hope?"

Adelina turned her horse immediately and cantered out, alone. Louis rearmed hastily and followed in case some unsuspecting serf tangled with her on the way through the village, for Louis was friend to all, even serfs.

Robert rearmed himself and mounted his horse. He looked down at Henri and apologised for Adelina's behavior. "She will, I hope, see the wisdom in this in time."

"As will he."

With a sigh, Robert said, "Perhaps hope is all we have remaining. Two days at dawn."

"Two days at dawn. We shall be waiting."

Robert rode out, followed by Gabriel and Acelin.

Adelina had galloped through the village and had taken a side track in order to lose Louis, who galloped by, calling for her. Adelina slid off the horse, took off the side saddle and let it fall to the ground. Before long, her father, Acelin, and Gabriel rode by. Adelina waited a few moments more before she climbed on the horse again and took up the reins. She guided the horse back up the steep incline and onto the track. This time, she returned to the village, stopping at the hovel where the woman and babies had stood, crying.

"You!" She called. "The widow! Out! Come out, now!"

The woman appeared, holding her rags together at her chest, her two little boys peeking around the door, faces afraid while the baby was screaming loudly from inside the hovel. "Here!" Adelina pulled off her rings and her jewelled head-band. "Here, for all of you! Sell them, buy yourselves some food and freedom! There is nothing else I can do for you!"

Adelina turned her horse about and cantered off, her anger replaced by tears, tears which refused to stop. And behind her, people scrounged and fought but she did not turn to see, nor did she want to. All she wanted was to ride, and never stop.

Thunder cracked overhead, lightning struck the ground barely twenty feet ahead. The horse shied and stopped and Adelina, still holding the reins, skewered over its head. The animal, rearing, dragged her backwards until she found her feet but it was far too strong and terrified to hold. She was dragged a way further on her stomach till the reins burnt her hands and she released her grip. The horse galloped off toward the village, kicking and rearing still.

Adelina lay in the middle of the narrow track, cursing to herself. Of storms she had no fear; of robbery she had no fear for she had nothing of value left on her person. Adelina slowly got to her feet and inspected the damage. Her very best dress, ruined. Again. It was torn, dirty. Her knees stung fiercely. She lifted her skirts and looked. Grazed and bleeding. Her ankle pained horribly as well. She limped to the side of the track and sat down. Before long, her father would return. Before long.

Thunder cracked and exploded again, and this time, the heavens opened with a blinding ferocity, a cold, hard fury.

If I am fortunate, she thought, God will spare me the ordeal which lies ahead and he will pity me so much that I will be struck by lightning right now.

She sat there calmly waiting but the lightning hit everywhere else.

"I will be struck by lightning. Now."

Still nothing. She sighed and rose to her feet.

Adelina thought she may be a better target for God's compassion if she walked.

# Chapter 14

"Milord, an angel has delivered us. A beautiful angel, dressed as a princess."

A horse without saddle cantered into the village and baulked when it saw the small crowd. Baudoin Dupuy recognized it as the skittish creature Adelina Polignac had ridden. "Where is this angel-princess now?"

No one replied.

Baudoin flinched at the next crack of thunder and noticed that a woman, a widow, had on her head, the gem-studded band that Adelina had been wearing only a short while ago.

"Where is she? Tell me now!"

"She gave us her jewels, Master Baudoin, and said she could do no more to help us, and then she rode off. That way." She pointed toward the road leading to the chateau at Lavoute Polignac.

"Give it all to me. Now. Now, I say!"

The woman took the band off and held it out. Baudoin snatched it and thrust it down his leather armour. Then he saw the ring on her hand. "These jewels must be returned." Reluctantly, the remaining rings were given back. "She wore three. I have only two." The final ring, a huge emerald, was duly handed over.

"Who is she, Milord?"

"She is to be my wife." Baudoin rode off in the pelting rain.

Two hundred yards ahead, he saw Adelina—on foot, soaked to the bone and limping. Baudoin spurred his horse into a canter and reined in beside her. She looked at him, huffed, and kept limping onwards, head down into the roaring wind.

"My people do not need your senseless charity!" Baudoin said as he pulled his horse to a stop in front of her. She tried to walk by it, he would not let her.

"It was not senseless charity!"

"No?" He reached down, took her hand and forced the rings back on. "It is senseless when a peasant attempts to sell a noblewoman's jewels and is hung for highway robbery."

Adelina took off the rings and dropped them on the road. "If those poor people cannot, then you sell them and feed your starving people! What kind of a lord are you!"

"Should I feed myself and family first?"

Adelina looked up at him, curious but still angry.

"It has been five days since I had a proper meal. Yes. Five days have passed and my father grows weaker, and my mother ill and despairing, and what is happening at chateau Lavoute Polignac? Feasting. Feasting while we starve!" Baudoin dismounted and picked up her rings once again. This time he pulled out the neck of her torn and muddied dress and thrust the jewellery down. "Get on behind me. I'll take you home." He mounted his horse and reached down for her hand.

Adelina ignored the gesture. "Why did you not come to my father if you were so hungry? He would have helped."

"Would he have come to me?"

After a pause, she said softly, "No."

"So you have your answer. Now, give me your hand. I have not time to waste and I don't like being wet and cold!"

Adelina relented, and had no choice but to hold on to Baudoin Dupuy as he cantered off down the narrow, slippery track. As his long, greasy hair tickled her nose, she thought, I will get lice from him. Lice and fleas.

"Your gesture, however generous, is appreciated."

"It wasn't for you," she called, wishing that she could simply push him from his horse and steal it and leave him lying in the mud where he belonged. It was no more than a thought, because he was armed and too good of a horseman to be so easily unsaddled. "Why were you riding in this rain?" she asked.

"I am sent to your chateau to collect promised foodstuffs."

"Food? You come to get food? Why was I not told!"

"Who would bother telling a woman anything of importance? Especially one without a brain."

Adelina's right hand fisted and she wanted to punch him on the ear but didn't know him well enough to judge what his reaction might be. He was much larger than she was.

"I am told everything," she lied. "My father is also my friend."

"And were you told that we were to be married?"

"I had hoped lightning would strike me dead to save me from the ordeal!"

"You too?" he asked and pulled the horse to a stop, rising in the stirrups and peering down into the woodland descending from the side of the track. He moved on a little way, then steered the horse down into the woods.

"Where are you going?"

There was no answer. At the bottom of the ravine he spurred the horse up the other side, and told her to hold tight, which she did—there was no other choice. Down another slope and along the gully, fast, and Adelina braced when she saw the log ahead but the horse did not shy, it leapt over it and she squealed with delight.

"You like adventure!"

She squealed again as the horse hurtled down the next slope. Her heart was beating wildly when they reached the track once more and she found with surprise that the chateau gates were barely a hundred yards away. She'd lived here all of her life and hadn't known this shortcut existed.

"Let me down. If you are seen with me, without an escort, there'll be trouble. I don't care whether you live or die but I don't want another war."

Adelina slid down from the horse and the jewellery dropped out of her dress. She picked the rings from the mud, and looked up at Baudoin for a moment before offering them back. "Take these, Dupuy. I have many more."

He shook his head. There was not as much hatred in his eyes now. Adelina wondered why he was staring at her so oddly. When she looked beautiful he saw nothing—after all he was but a man—but now that she was half drowned and muddied, her dress torn and bloodied, he had a very strange look in his eyes. "How old are you?" he asked.

"You dare ask a lady her age?"

"I'd not thought you were a lady, m'selle," he said with a smile. Adelina was forced to admit that smile was engaging, till her common sense returned.

"Why do you stare?"

"I wonder what it is I should call you. Addie, perhaps?"

"You wish for a long, prosperous life?" she asked.

Baudoin laughed and for a moment, so did she.

"I shall walk with you," he said.

"I don't care what you do, Baudoin Dupuy. Best we make that clear now."

"Your ankle pains you badly?" he asked, still walking his horse beside her.

"Nothing pains me badly. Nothing."

Baudoin got off his horse and reins in hand, walked it along the track, with Adelina limping beside him.

"What am I to call you?" she asked.

"Whatever you wish, providing it is not offensive. I don't care for this arrangement, either, so it would be best if we make of it what we can. Addie."

"Addie is not my name. I am your lady Adelina, or I am nothing." When she knew she would be heard, she called loudly for the sentry to lower the gate. Baudoin winced at her high pitched yell. "You know these woods well. Too well it seems," she said as they walked on.

"I played here as a child," he replied. As they drew nearer the narrow bridge, Baudoin said, "On the horse. You limp badly." Before she could protest, Baudoin lifted her into the saddle, took the reins and kept walking.

Raoul, with his arm still wrapped tight, met them on the bridge. He had a crossbow in his good hand and did not like what he was witnessing.

"All is well, Raoul, put down your weapon. Baudoin Dupuy brings me home with goodwill in his heart. Is my father back yet?"

"No. No, and your mother worries for the light fades quickly and the storm will be a bad one."

"They must think I rode off to see Geoffrey. Now Geoffrey will be worried, too."

"What did you do?" Baudoin asked.

"I lost them on the road, purposely. For all I know, they all may have reached Le Puy by now in their search for me. Papa will not be happy."

"You will be beaten?"

"Only with words. Words which hurt more than the back of his hand."

"Leave your arms with me," Raoul said, not wanting Baudoin to get any closer.

"Raoul, this man is to be my husband. Treat him with respect so that he may in turn learn what it is." Adelina stole the reins from Baudoin's hands, spurred the giant horse on, and brought it to a halt at the stable doors. "Tend this creature, feed it well," she said to the stable boy, and walked alone into the chateau.

Her mother was coming down the stairs. Before her ceaseless nagging began, Adelina said calmly, "Mother, all is well. My horse shied in the storm and escaped. That is why I am in such a state."

"Where are the others? Where is your father?"

"Searching for me, no doubt. We have a visitor, Mother. My future husband. Will you please feed him? He is very hungry and has saved me from the storm."

Without waiting to hear another word from Marys, Adelina

limping her way up the stairs, called for Jennet. Marys continued down to the kitchens and there Baudoin stood by the doors, shaking out his hair, cold, shivering. "In, boy. Come in and stand by the fire. Warm yourself."

Baudoin stepped further in where it was warm. "Your daughter was thrown from her horse and I chanced along. When the horse is finally captured, I shall return it. I am not a thief."

"Ella, bring something warm. Some stew. Quickly."

Baudoin sat close by the fire. The warmth would do little good for soon he would have to return home in the rain. He did not object to the bowl of stew, and a second bowl was welcomed.

"You are Heloise's younger son?"

"Oui, Milady."

"And a knight at arms, too?"

He nodded—the food was too good to ruin by polite conversation.

"How goes your mother?"

"Perhaps it would be best to ask your daughter. She spent most of the afternoon in the company of my mother."

Marys knew that she would hear nothing of what occurred until much later, and only then if Robert was inclined to talk after he had his fill of her. Mostly though, all she heard were loud snores immediately after the act and if she withheld her favors he only grew angry and impatient. But wait for news she could not. "Send your mother my regards."

Baudoin looked at Marys as if she were insane.

"We were friends for many a year."

"I shall deliver your message."

"I should see her at the wedding, do you think?" Marys asked, hopefully.

Baudoin's eyes clouded and he said nothing except: "Your cook is excellent. Who is he?" His bowl was empty once again and Marys called for yet another.

"Our cook, Ella, was widowed by a Dupuy sword many years ago."

Baudoin looked up at Marys and said nothing further. Halfway through his third serving, a commotion was heard in the courtyard and Baudoin was on his feet immediately.

Robert came in, a veritable thundercloud, wet and angry. Marys made herself scarce very quickly, as did Ella. Robert glanced at Baudoin and grumbled, "You found Adelina?"

"Yes."

"Where was she?"

"Not far from Allegre, Milord. Her horse had thrown her into a...

into a ravine, which is why you could not find her."

The explanation was enough for Robert. "Then I am glad you chanced upon her." Robert scratched at his wet head and proceeded up the stairs. "You will stay this night. Soon it will be dark."

"But Milord—"

"You will stay. Come with me and do not argue."

Baudoin grabbed his bowl and spoon and took it with him. "May I ask what has birthed this sudden generosity, Lord Robert?"

"No, you may not."

Baudoin followed the older man up the winding stairs. He came to a stop at an open door, and Baudoin looked in. At one time, it had been a store-room of kinds, now it contained a cot.

"I will send someone with dry clothing."

"I am indebted."

Robert's cold gaze met Baudoin's. "I will warn you now, and trust you heed me well."

"Milord?" Baudoin asked, half interested, and still eating.

"If my daughter is mistreated in any way, any way whatsoever, I will have you impaled and gutted and I will perform the deed myself." There was silence until Robert asked, "Do you heed me?"

"Yes. I heed you."

"What my daughter said this day of respect, I taught her."

Baudoin found it difficult to meet this man's gaze. He nodded politely and walked into the small, dark room and turned back when he heard: "We have much to discuss. I will be in the great hall shortly. Join me."

Robert left him on his own. Baudoin could have taken the gesture as a sign of peace, finally, but the notion sat uncomfortably. Peace for the sake of economics, for the sake of saving their lands. He did not like the Polignacs very much, nor their elaborate chateau, but, as he looked out of the window and down to the fields in the distance—the ripe, fertile fields—Baudoin thought that perhaps this union may be fruitful after all. When Robert de Polignac died, all this would become his daughter's, and by law what was the daughter's became the husbands automatically. It was more than enough reason to lay aside old, festering wounds.

He took another mouthful of the delicious stew and thought the cooking was good here, almost as good as the plentiful view. But as he looked out of the small window into the distant lands that would one day be his by marriage, he did not want to think of his true love's reaction when this news reached St. Paulien.

A little boy came in with dry clothing which he put on the bed—hose, boots and a white linen shirt with billowing sleeves. "Do you need to wash, Master?"

Baudoin put his bowl down and lifted his arm, sniffing. "I don't know. Do I?"

The little boy came closer, sniffed too, grinned and retreated, saying, "I shall bring some water now."

Jennet helped peel the ruined dress over her mistress's head and she winced when she saw the grazes and bruises.

Adelina hadn't uttered a word in such a long time. She was torn between her need of sleep and the need to see Geoffrey again. She pulled the rings from her fingers and Jennet, after giving each a good rub on her skirt, put them into the carved silver box with all the other jewels. "Sit, Milady, for if you fall I doubt I would have the strength to lift you."

"Are you saying I am fat?"

"Oh, no, Milady. I am concerned. You look unwell."

Adelina sat and she submitted to the cloth dipped in the warm, fragrant water. Jennet rubbed at her face and body gently, and Adelina's thoughts roamed. With each passing moment, her eyes filled with more tears.

"What ails your heart?"

Adelina looked up at Jennet, hardly aware that she was washing her damp, grubby arms. "Much ails me." Adelina stood when she felt the gentle tug on her hand.

"He is very handsome," Jennet said, eventually. "I told you that a fine nobleman awaited you, but you did not believe me."

"Who is handsome?"

"The one who brought you home in the rain. The one so hungry that he ate three bowls of Ella's stew."

"Do you really think he is handsome?" Adelina asked, surprised.

"Oh, yes, Milady. Very."

Adelina had not noticed, nor really, did she care. After all, Jennet was talking about Baudoin Dupuy, the man she was being forced to marry.

"What will you wear for supper?" Adelina said nothing to the question. "Milady?" Adelina looked at Jennet. Why, Jennet wondered, were her eyes so dead this day? "Perhaps the red one will brighten you."

"I do not care if I wear a cornsack to supper. Should I sit there naked no one would notice."

Jennet tried not to laugh and whispered, "I am sure all would notice if you did that," as she pulled a cote over Adelina's head. It was clean and stiff and abrasive and Adelina pulled a face as it was laced.

"Why was I not born a man!"

"God did not allow it," Jennet said and bade her mistress sit once again to enable her to deal with the wet and dirty hair. "What is his name?" Jennet asked.

"Who?"

"The one who saved you."

Adelina thought, even Jesus Christ cannot save me now. "His name is Baudoin Dupuy. I am being punished for my sins."

"What sins are these, Milady?"

"Being born, I think."

Jennet put the comb and cloth down, and she stepped in front of her mistress. "You can talk to me, Milady. I will tell no one."

"It matters not who you tell. Soon enough all will know. I have to marry him, Jennet. I have to marry the brother of the one who tried to kill me and nothing I can do will stop it. All because when I do marry him, our estates together will reach far, and people will not be hungry, and the king will not take our lands, and an enemy will become an ally by marriage and... I do not know this Baudoin Dupuy."

"When is this wedding to happen?"

"Who am I to know? No one has told me. I am to be a radiant bride and all I want is to run away. I wish I could be like you, Jennet. How I wish I could be like you." Tears flowed now, silent tears. Adelina sat as a statue—a weeping, soundless statue.

Jennet did not know what to say or do, so she went back to attending to her mistress's hair. She said nothing for a little while as she gently drew the comb and the cloth down the length of a section of dirty hair as wide as her hand. Again and again she did this until no dirt remained.

"I did not like Etienne when he first made eyes at me. I found him a nuisance. When we harvested, he would spring out at me hoping to frighten me, and at times he did, and I would chase him away. But he kept coming back."

"Did he ever say he wished you were dead?"

"Oh, no, Milady. He would never say that. Did this man say that to you?"

"He did."

"Perhaps when he sees who you really are, he may change his mind. Beneath your gruff, you are very sweet."

"I am neither gruff nor sweet and he does not like me."

"Do you like him?"

"I don't know."

Jennet settled the clean hair about Adelina's shoulders, the way they both liked it, and chose the red dress for her mistress to wear at dinner. Adelina said neither yes nor no and she stood impassively, wincing when she had to lift her arm, and wincing when she had to put weight on her foot.

Jennet was lacing the dress when Marys came in. "Much better. Such a state you were in."

Adelina turned her face away and wiped her cheeks quickly. Her mother might have known she'd been crying but nothing would ever be said about it. Tears, she'd once said, were a large part of any woman's life, but displaying sadness did no good. Best always to hide it away. Only a queen's tears were acted upon, but often, even a queen wept alone.

"Baudoin tells me you spoke to his mother?"

"Yes, Mama, I did."

"How is it she fares?"

"She seems old and sad and empty and speaks of the past as if there is no future. I know now how it is she must feel."

Marys placed Adelina's hair where she liked it, and not as Jennet had laid it. "She said all this?" Marys asked, still fiddling with her daughter's hair.

"No, I saw it in her eyes and heard it when she spoke. She asked of you, and said that your letter brought her much comfort. But she cannot reply. Her fingers are twisted, Mama. She has the same affliction as Ella. I told her that should I visit again, I would bring her some of the special ointment from the east. Could I?"

"You would have to ask your father. I know not what is happening."

"Is your worth as hers, Mama?"

"What is this?"

"I saw for myself the way Lady Dupuy is treated. I fear the hounds receive more attention than she. Baudoin treats her with contempt. If he cannot love his mother, he cannot love a wife. Yet his wife I am forced to be. He will never love me and I will never love him."

"Love, love, love. What is wrong with you, Adelina? Love has nothing to do with marriage. Nothing. Besides, he is young. With time and patience..."

"Love has everything to do with marriage."

"Adelina..."

"I know, Mama. Our future depends on this union. This is all you will say to me now. Well, Heloise Dupuy spoke more to me in a short time than you have ever spoken to me in all of my life."

"You talk nonsense!"

"Who was Vianna?" Adelina watched the blood drain from her mother's face.

"I don't know what you're talking about."

"I speak of your sister. The one who died the very day I was born.

Is it true I look like her?"

As Adelina spoke, Marys's face paled further and her mouth dropped. She gaped like a fish out of water. She stepped back and turned away, quickly.

"Mama?" Adelina called repeatedly, to no avail. Her mother ran out of the room, howling, and Adelina knew that she would lock herself away, saying she had one of her blinding head pains which required quiet and darkness.

"Find some shoes, Jennet. I must become accustomed to wearing them."

As Jennet searched and brought out shoes, she said, "I was able to steal some rags today. I put them under your bed."

A grateful smile that appeared on Adelina's face but it faded quickly. There was a banging on the door and her father walked in, uninvited. "What was said to your mother?"

"I had questions only. I did not know how upset she would become."

"What questions?"

"Lady Dupuy spoke with tenderness of a Vianna, Mama's sister, that is all. I only asked what she was like and was it true."

"Was what true?"

"That I look like Vianna. That is all."

Vianna. Robert closed his eyes for a moment. "That name is never to be spoken of, do you hear me?"

"Yes, Papa, but..."

"Tonight, you will be civil and charming and sweet. Do you understand?"

Baudoin and Dedwyd stood the moment Adelina walked into the great hall. Gabriel, Louis and Acelin stood as well. Raoul, though, seemed too ill to move a great deal, and her father did not bother. It wasn't until she was seated, beside Baudoin of course, that the knights sat again. Gabriel smiled—as if he knew something she did not.

She studied Baudoin when she thought he wouldn't notice. Jennet was correct in saying he was handsome, but why hadn't she noticed this herself?

She was quiet throughout the meal, unable to eat a great deal because her sadness was too much of a hindrance to her appetite. Her only comforts came from the occasional smiles from Louis and Acelin, and the everpresent one from Dedwyd, who seemed a lot better this night, even if he gazed upon his food with the utmost caution.

Gabriel, sitting at her father's elbow, was very loud, as usual, and the empty chair where her mother sat was a constant reminder of her current sin—a reminder to discover who this mysterious Vianna was.

Adelina, though silent, ate as a lady, sat as a lady, and spoke when spoken to only, which meant that she said nothing at all. Most of the talk was concerned with the journey to Paris the day after next, none of the talk concerned a wedding. Throughout, she took quick, sidelong glances at Baudoin Dupuy and only once did gazes meet. He tried to smile—she tried to pretend she was a lady. Neither effort was very successful.

She could not believe the amount of food this one could consume. Before long, she thought, he will become fat and ugly. When the fruits came, and still he gobbled on, Adelina felt his leg touch hers under the table. It was not a mistaken touch. She looked at him. He was talking to her father, describing his fief and allegiances in a place Adelina had never heard of. When she moved away, his leg moved, too, and touched again. He did this three times in all, until Adelina suddenly knocked her full goblet of wine into his lap and rose, quickly, squealing out her apology and calling for a page to attend to the mess. The wine had tipped on her as well and it was her excuse to leave. She limped off, followed closely by her girl.

"An accident," Baudoin said, as the wine was mopped from his shirt and lap. He held his tankard out for it to be filled and the conversation resumed, although less heartily than before.

Gabriel waited for an appropriate time to elapse before he excused himself from the gathering and made his way upstairs.

He bade entry to Adelina's chambers and the door was opened by the new girl. Gabriel bent to come in but Jennet stepped in his way. "Milady wishes entry from none, Master Gabriel."

Gabriel pushed Jennet out his way and walked to where Adelina sat. She was in her nightgown and her face was swollen from her tears. Gabriel said to Jennet, "Leave us."

"What do you want?" Adelina said to him, her hand raised so Jennet would remain.

"Some words," Gabriel said. "Best for all if you co-operate."

"And I have heard this so often that it plays on my mind constantly and no other thought enters. Leave me alone."

"What I have to say I wish no other to hear. It concerns your wedding to Dupuy and what you may gain."

Adelina wondered what he had to say. Was he offering some kind of escape?

"Send her away."

Adelina dismissed Jennet and Gabriel slammed the door in the girl's face.

"Does my father know you are here?"

"Of course he knows." Gabriel walked to where she sat and his nose tickled from the roses in a vase a little too close for his liking. On the table, too, was a manuscript she pretended to read. "What is this?" he asked.

"Legends of rightful, great deeds."

"Perhaps yours will be written of one day."

Adelina sighed. "Have you, too, come to lecture me on how to be all that I am not?"

"No. I have come to tell you what a knight such as I would do if I were in your position. It would take the courage and fearlessness of a knight at arms to do this, yet I believe now that you have this needed courage."

"Then you believe this alone, Gabriel of Lyon."

"All you need do," he said softly as he crouched in front of her, "Is hear me."

She did not know what lay in Gabriel's eyes but for the first time she was not angered by it. She watched, amazed, as he took her hands between his and raised them to his lips. His kiss was full of a tenderness, an affection that was alien to her. "You must swear on your life never to speak a word of what I am about to say." She nodded and Gabriel smiled. "No, my sweet, you will say it."

"I will say nothing."

Gabriel saw the vulnerable child look into his eyes. It was just what he needed.

"Tell me what it is you would do?" the child asked.

# CHAPTER 15

"No!" Adelina was horrified. "No! I will tell my father!"

She tried to push him away but the grip on her arm was fierce. "I will not go to hell for you, Gabriel of Lyon."

"It is not for me. Think, little girl. Marry Baudoin Dupuy, and when his father dies before the year's end, all to Arlanc will be yours!"

"Only if Baudoin should die would it be mine, and that is only if I do not have a son. I do not know why you are here, saying such terrible things."

"I think only of you. You, and your children."

"But I am not wed yet! What is it you want? Why are you here? You should not be in here."

"All I have done, little one, is seen an opportunity, one which should not be ignored. What is my crime?"

Adelina tried to turn her head so that she would not have to look into his eyes.

"Do not reject me. I am here when others care not to be. I could be in the great hall with the others, but no, I am here, seeking to aid, and if you would allow it, comfort you."

"You? One who thinks only of himself?"

"You judge me too harshly when you do not know me. All day I have been witness to your aching. It seems that I have seen sadness that others choose not to. I feel your confusion. What you think is injustice, this too, I see and I feel. If we do this my way, Adelina, you will gain much."

"What then if Henri Dupuy does not die by year end?" she asked.

"Oh, he will, my sweet. He will. That is a certainty."

What lies behind your eyes, she wondered, frowning. "My father would never allow this. No. My father has honor."

"This way, my way, and all is yours."

"No, Gabriel. Your way, and all will be yours. I am to marry

Baudoin who is the heir as I am the heir. That I understand. I understand that there will be an end to the feuding of a century. I understand that people will not starve. But you ask me to wonder what will be if I am widowed? I do not even know him, I have not wed him, but already you have buried him."

"I think of futures. I think of you. Only you. The time has come." Sadness touched his eyes now, a sadness that Adelina found very curious. "I had hoped I would need not say this, but I have always been fond of you."

"You do not know me."

"But I have. I have known you a very long time. I first saw you with your mother on the streets of Le Puy. You were but a baby, and she carried you with much pride, displaying you to the world as if you were a precious gem. I was young then, it is true, but still I remember attending your baptism with my father. It was a huge celebration. Your father and Heracle laid aside their differences for one day. For you."

"For me?"

"And the festivities lasted well into the night."

"I cannot believe that you were at my baptism. It is lies you tell now."

"I was there. As squire to my father, the Viscount Edouard."

"Your father is a viscount?" she asked, dumfounded. Gabriel continued with his story. Her defences were lowering as he hoped they would.

"Many were present that day to witness the spectacle. You, a newborn miracle that many said could never be. Many had sworn, and some hoped, that Robert would die without an heir. You came as a surprise to many." Gabriel wrapped a lock of her shining hair around his finger. "At the age of twelve as I was then, I would never have believed that one day I would serve you with my life. One so young, so fair." His fingers trailed like feathers over her face, her chin, her long neck and Adelina squirmed a little when he tickled her ear. "If I have pained you in the past, then I am sorry. And if I should pain you in the future, I am also sorry." Gabriel stepped away and said, "But please, speak not of what I have said, for your father wishes you to remain ignorant of what is planned. I have no wish now, or ever, to violate his trust. My respect for him is too deep to squander."

"No. No, I cannot believe that my father would think of such a thing. He is not his brother. You think I do not know of Heracle, but I do. Oh, I do."

"There is so much you can never understand. But one day, little one, all will be yours. Your father and I, we look ahead to the future. Even Geoffrey sees the wisdom of this union."

"How do you know? Do you see through his eyes? Feel what lies in his heart?"

"I know that he is not a fool. Please, consider, before you sleep, that should you ever be widowed and eventually remarry, choose your second husband well. Choose one who would give you all of the freedom you have ever wished for. What do you want, Adelina?"

"What I want can never be and this you know well."

Gabriel smiled as if he knew all too well what lay untouched in her dreams. "I feel that you would have made a fine knight had God not been so unkind to have had you born a woman."

How could this man look into her eyes and know what lay hidden and put it so well into words that she was left speechless?

"Tell me, Adelina, tell me what it is you need." He touched her face again, so kind, so gentle and all the time, Adelina wondered why. "A lucky man Baudoin Dupuy will be. I would give all I have to be him for just one night."

"You flatter me, Gabriel."

"No," he said and moved close again. "No, my sweet lady, I speak truths." He lifted her face and kissed her. How practised he seemed, and she was almost powerless to stop him. For a little while, she did not consider stopping him. There was something in his eyes which she dared not question.

And all came to a sudden halt at the sound of the door opening. Adelina froze. Her one thought, Papa. "Milady, your father is..." Jennet was bending to come in, and whose shock was the greatest, none knew for a terrible moment.

Gabriel snapped, "Can you not announce yourself!" as he departed, quickly.

Jennet was full of silent questions. What was Gabriel doing in here when her mistress's future husband sat with her father in the great hall? Sat innocently unaware that his bride was in another's arms? "Milady, your father is concerned that you did not bid him goodnight."

"Tell him... tell him that I am ill."

"Yes, Milady."

"Tell no one what you have seen here."

Jennet nodded and made to leave.

"No, please, do not go. Not yet. I feel strange, Jennet. I am confused. I don't know what to think or what to do now. He cast a spell upon me. Yes, Gabriel of Lyon cast a spell upon me. What would have been had you not come in?"

Jennet put her arms around her young mistress. "Oh, Milady, it has only now begun for you."

"What? What has begun?"

"So many would want you now. So many. And it is not you that they would want but what it is one day that you shall have. That is what they want," she whispered and held her tighter. "And Gabriel of Lyon is but one of many, Milady." Jennet held her tight for a long time before she guided her mistress to her bed. "One of many who would have their way with you if only they could."

" I wish Geoffrey was here."

"That can never be again."

"He is the only man I will ever trust. There is so much I don't know. So much."

"Then ask me, Milady. I want to be your friend."

It was very late when Jennet made her way quietly through the great hall and down to the kitchen with one candle lighting her way. She took the two steps to her tiny chambers, thinking all the while of her mistress and what had almost happened, of what would have happened had she not walked in.

Jennet opened the door to her room, and as she put her candle down on the only other piece of furniture in her room, apart from her palette, a three-legged table, her thoughts turned to Etienne. Adelina had been curious, as all girls her age were curious, and Jennet had been no different, but speaking so openly about such secret matters had done little except serve her to miss Etienne even more, if it were possible. Jennet was about to undress when she heard a noise behind her in the dimness. She turned quickly, frightened, half hoping it would be Ella but knowing that it wasn't.

It was Gabriel. And Ella had warned her that sooner or later, he would do this. Jennet had prayed to God that he would take his pleasures in someone else. Her prayers, it seemed, had again fallen upon nothingness.

"His name is Etienne, is it not?" he asked and stepped from the darkness, the darkness where it seemed he had been waiting for a very long time.

"Who, Master?" Jennet asked.

"Who, Master?" he imitated. "His name is Etienne and I know where he lives. I know you plan to marry him soon. Remember, girl, that you cannot marry a dead man. For dead he will be if you speak of what you saw this night."

"I saw nothing this night, Master," Jennet said as calmly as she could but her heart was loud in her ears. She tried to step away, to the door, but he would not let her.

"Jennet is your name?" he asked.

She nodded.

"The daughter of the miller. The thief, Thierry. You have two younger sisters, yes?"

"Yes, Master Gabriel."

"I have been watching you. You and this Etienne you want to marry. I know much of you both." He moved even closer, so close that he pressed her hard against the rigid, hot stone wall. "Your eyes see much, and worse, your tongue is loose. I have heard you gossiping with the kitchen toad many times."

Should she scream very loud none would hear. She knew what lay in this nobleman's eyes. He lifted her face with his gloved hand. "If it is true that you love this Etienne, and your sisters, and your thieving father, and your dim-witted mother, then you have no choice but to do what I say or let harm befall them all, one by one."

"Master, I saw nothing. I swear on my life, I saw nothing. I will do anything you wish. Do not harm Etienne, or my family. I will do anything you wish."

"Show me, then, what this boy of yours has seen. This boy and many others if what I have heard is true. Show me."

"Show you, Master?" she asked, relieved because he had stepped away a little.

"Take off your rags."

Momentarily, her heart stilled. Please God, no. Not this. Not with him. When Gabriel looked back, she stood as before, only now she was more confused. And very fearful. He liked that. "Do as I have said. Slowly." Gabriel leaned against the stone wall and watched but still, she did not move. "How old is your youngest sister? Nine? Ten?"

Jennet did as she was told. She had no other choice. Slowly, she lifted her old dress over her head. "Look at me, not at your feet." Gabriel studied her for a very long time, prolonging the torment, prolonging her fear, her shame. "Turn around." Jennet did. Was this all he wanted? To look? She did not think so. "A vast improvement on the last one," he said and she cringed because his voice was so close to her ear. "The last one, Cateline, was fat and ugly but she had her uses. As you will have your uses. On your knees, girl. You know what I want."

The next morning, Adelina watched from her window as Baudoin loaded the cart. Soon she knew she would be called to farewell him. Gabriel was there with the others, all throwing sacks of grain and flour and crates of vegetables into the cart.

Soon enough, she heard the call and she obeyed it. She made her way down the stairs

quietly, across the great hall and down to the kitchen. She stood alone at the huge doors, squinting against the bright sunshine, watching as Baudoin spoke to her father and embraced him, but it was not the fond embrace of friends.

"Again," Baudoin said, "I thank you for your hospitality and generosity. You will be repaid."

Robert nodded.

"Milady," Baudoin said to Marys, then after a nod, he saw Adelina standing by the kitchen doors. Baudoin walked to her.

Adelina found it difficult to look into this man's eyes today but she knew she had to say something. "I have not thanked you for bringing me home, Baudoin."

"I am pleased now that I did. I take your leave, Addie," he said, "And look forward to meeting you again tomorrow." He reached for her hand, kissed it, and she felt nothing at all. He looked up at her with his sparkling, dark eyes and said, "Tomorrow then. I shall remember to keep my distance when a goblet of wine is in your fair hand."

"Be thankful it was not a barrel."

His smile was huge and contagious. He nodded and retreated, leaped into the cart and drove out, his beautiful horse hitched behind. Adelina called, "Remember to take the roadway!"

He raised his hand high and kept driving. When he had driven across the bridge, Robert walked to his daughter. "Take the roadway?" he asked.

"Yes, we came home a different way, Papa. It was a shortcut for the storm was fierce."

"You could have been this pleasant last evening instead of drowning him in wine."

"He was becoming too familiar under the table, Papa."

Robert thought it was amusing—once upon a time he'd been young, too. "It was not a goblet of wine your mother tipped into my lap, Adelina, but an entire bucket of water which she aimed at my head from her window above."

Adelina looked at her mother and then her father, and although she smiled again at the joke she had heard too many times already, she could not imagine her father courting her mother. It was not hard to imagine Jennet and her Etienne, not after all that Jennet had said the night before, but her mother and father doing such things in secret? She was embarrassed by her thoughts and looked to her feet quickly because Gabriel had walked behind her father and had smiled at her as he walked by.

"Why the change of heart, daughter?"

"Last night, I lay in bed thinking of what was to be, and words Geoffrey once said came back to me. He once said that it is far easier flowing with the river of life than it is swimming against its strong currents."

"And do you know who it was who told him that?"

"You," Adelina said with a half smile. Robert put his arms around her and she was squashed in his tight embrace. Adelina waited a good while, and hoped her father would soon tire of this strange show of affection. It was she, though, who had to pull her face from his surcoat, and struggle for freedom.

"Papa, is it now safe to journey alone?"

"You wish to visit Geoffrey."

"I need to tell him what is happening, tell him goodbye. Surely you understand my need?"

"Gabriel shall escort you after lunch then."

"Papa, please, I can go alone. I am soon to be wed. Am I not old enough to go alone? Any danger of traveling alone is now past, you said this yourself last night."

"Until I speak with Philippe Augustus, and until the allegiance is lawful, Gabriel will accompany you."

Adelina looked into her father's eyes and knew he would not be moved. "Yes, Papa."

"Go now to your mother for she wishes to speak with you on matters no man should know of."

"I know already of these things, Papa."

"It is her wish. Go. Away. She is in her chambers, waiting."

Adelina went inside and upstairs to her mother's small sanctuary. She wondered if she were not visiting royalty for such an occasion. Her mother seemed very odd indeed this day.

"Baudoin is handsome and seems pleasant," Marys said uncomfortably as she paced her chambers, decorated with its billowing silks and fragrant roses. "A handsome and pleasant man makes it easier."

Makes what easier? Adelina wondered and noticed her mother was drinking early today but said nothing for she would only deny it as she raised another goblet to her lips.

"Or perhaps you do not notice that he is handsome and pleasant."

"He has interesting eyes and good teeth."

"Is that all you saw?" Marys asked.

"He ruffled me from the beginning, therefore I saw nothing good in him."

"You were pleasant enough this morning."

"I had cause to think and he seems not as bad as I had thought."

"You shall produce beautiful babies together."

Adelina picked up the goblet of wine her mother had put before her. She sipped it.

"What do you know of men and women?"

"I hear that union is bliss."

"Where did you hear that?"

"I cannot remember," she lied, not wanting to get Jennet into trouble for saying things a servant should not.

"All that should come from a union is children. The act is rarely enjoyable. Remember that and you will not be disappointed."

Adelina said nothing and looked at the flowers. That was not what Jennet had told her.

Again her mother paced. "It is against the law of God to enjoy such an unwholesome thing. Keep that in mind at all times."

Be that true, then Adelina knew she would burn in hell for eternity due to her thoughts alone. "Yes, Mama. I will remember that. May I go now?"

"No, you may not. The bleedings stop when one is with child."

Adelina took a large mouthful of wine this time, hoping she would choke on it and be excused from this ordeal.

"When you are a wife, you must never deny your husband."

"Deny him what, Mama?"

"His rights. Such things are important to men."

"Oh," Adelina said. "Yes, of course these things are important." She took another mouthful of wine and wondered what her mother was talking about.

"He is allowed by law to beat you within an inch of your life so always mind your tongue and never say what is on your mind. Always agree. It is the best way. It is less painful that way."

"Does Papa hit you?"

"It is love that binds us. Rarely do I anger him."

Why didn't she answer my question? Adelina wondered. "Do you think that Baudoin Dupuy will raise his hand to me?"

"I did not wish for this to be said, Adelina, but hear it you must. The last time I saw Heloise Dupuy," she said with tears in her eyes, "Her face was swollen and bruised. She had been hit so hard, so often, that she could not draw breath without pain. What does a son learn from his father?"

"Mama, if he hits me I shall hit him back."

"Adelina, no! No, you must not. We are nothing, child, nothing. You were right when you spoke of worth. We are decorations only, decorations which bear children and raise them and that is all we are. Never expect more."

"You tell me that womanhood is a curse when all along you implore me to be a lady?"

"Adelina, you will swallow your pride, and hold your tongue, and let him not touch you until your wedding night for spoiled goods have no worth."

"What do you mean, spoiled?"

Marys sat and reached for her fan. Her face was red and she was sweating. "Let him not take advantage of you."

"Mama, I don't understand."

Marys turned to her beautiful, innocent daughter and said, "Let no man..." She hesitated. "Kiss you, for example. No man except your husband and what he wants, you must do."

There was a great, deep silence.

"Is there anything you wish to ask of me?"

"No, Mama," Adelina said.

"Then leave me. In Paris we shall buy you a wedding gown. You will be a radiant bride."

"Yes, Mama," Adelina said and retreated quietly. Once out of the room, she leaned against the stone and closed her eyes tight. I am spoiled already, she thought. Gabriel kissed me therefore I am spoiled and Baudoin will know. He will know. She ran to the kitchens—what she wanted now was food and any food would suffice. "Ella, when is lunch?"

"A long while yet, child."

"Where is Jennet?"

"In her bed. She is unwell this day."

"Why was I not told?"

Adelina swept past the fire and up into the passageway. She walked into Jennet's room, which was once Cateline's, and there she was in her bed and hiding from the world, it seemed. "What ails you?"

"I am ill," she said, voice shaking as she tried to hide under her covers.

"Oh. I had hoped you would come with me to the village while I visit Geoffrey after lunch this day. Perhaps seeing your mother and sisters again will help? You have not been home for many days now." Adelina touched Jennet's face. There was no fever but her face was pale and fear was alive in her eyes. She seemed very strange indeed. "What is wrong?"

Jennet shook her head and turned her face away.

"Do you vomit?" Adelina said, looking for a bowl or pot on the floor. There was none.

"No, Milady, I do not vomit, although I want to."

"Then, come. Sunshine is needed. Sunshine cures all."

"Please, Milady, I want to die."

"Die? Nonsense. I won't allow it. Why do you sulk?"

Jennet said nothing. "I order you to get out of your bed, Jennet."

"It hurts me to stand."

"Then I shall summon Michel. He knows more of ailments than all the physicians and he is more kind. He will know what is wrong."

"No. No man shall ever touch me or look upon me again." Jennet was crying now and burying herself further into her bed.

Adelina sat on the edge of the bed. "Come. Stop this nonsense. We will sit in the sun and study the rosebuds. I've much more to ask of you. Important things. On your feet." Adelina pulled the covers back and immediately wished that she hadn't. There were many bruises on Jennet's throat, and more were in hiding under her aged nightdress. Adelina took Jennet's hand and forcibly pulled her out of her bed. It was true, she could not stand upright. "What do you try to hide from me? Take off your nightdress, now."

Jennet took the nightdress off but held it against her chin tightly and there was a tug of war which Adelina won. Jennet stood naked before her mistress, trying in vain to hide the bruises and bites which were all over her body. "Who did this to you?"

Jennet shook her head as her tears flowed unchecked.

"Who!"

Again, she shook her head. "It is not important, Milady, it is not important."

"I wish my mother to see this."

"No, no, I beg you."

"Tell me who did this or I shall send for my mother."

"I cannot say. I fear what will happen if I do."

"Who did this!"

"The visitor," Jennet whispered, her eyes closed. "It was the visitor."

"Baudoin Dupuy?"

Jennet looked into Adelina's eyes and could not say yes or no. It was bad enough that she had already lied, had to say what Gabriel of Lyon told her to say else her family would suffer one by one, and bad enough that her mistress would now think she had to marry a monster when it was not so at all.

"Baudoin Dupuy did this to you?"

"Milady, it is nothing. I beg you say nothing. It will not happen again for he was drunk. I am sure that when he is not drunk he is a kind man. A good man. He will be a good husband to you. I know this. I do. I shall dress now and do whatever you ask, but I beg you to say nothing. Please, Milady?"

Too late, Adelina was gone. She went to the kitchen and demanded that Ella find the ointment Michel had left, the one which numbed pain. She returned quickly and alone, much to Jennet's relief, and it was her mistress who rubbed the foul-smelling ointment into the bruises and bites. It angered Adelina that a man was allowed to treat a woman worse than he would a horse. "Why? What sense is there in this?"

"I don't understand. I did as he wanted. I did all he asked."

"To do this to another who is not as strong, does it somehow make him feel more of a man, or does it make him less of an animal?"

"Less than an animal, Milady, but what is it we can do?"

"If we, as women, are not included in the laws of men, Jennet, why should we abide their laws?"

"Milady, it is dangerous to think such things."

"I fear nothing. Ride with me to the village and there you must stay. I will tell my father that I do not want you to attend me any more. Perhaps your sister will be my hand maiden. You say she is a good worker and a good worker I will need when I go to live at Allegre."

"My sister?" Jennet asked, trying not to imagine Gabriel inflicting such horrors on her

little sister.

"I shall give you your freedom to marry Etienne."

"You would live at Allegre, and not here?"

"That is so."

Hope rose. "But Milady, my duty is to you, now and always."

"Even though there is the danger this will happen again when we go to live in the Dupuy house and you must call him master?"

"My duty is always to you."

"Your loyalty surprises me. I would not be as loyal if I were you."

"Yes, you would. I know you. And your caring makes me weep. It is I who should tend you, not you me. You must be an angel."

"Many would disagree with that nonsense." Adelina put the lid back on the jar and handed Jennet her dress, watched her put it on. "Your shoes." Adelina kicked them across the floor. "Now, come. Some sun is needed. Perhaps you can help me teach the little archer our language for we have much time before lunch."

"Yes, Milady."

Adelina took Jennet's hand and held it tight. "What has happened to each of us last night, we must both forget. Yes?" Adelina led her girl out into the sunshine. She called for a page to find the archer and deliver him to the rose garden immediately.

Dedwyd was showing his new master, Louis, how it was possible to loose five arrows at once and have each arrow strike a fatal wound to the quintain. Louis could barely loose one arrow from the huge yew bow successfully.

Dedwyd grabbed the page who appeared calling for him, and set him to stand in front of the quintain. Louis did not like this, for the page was Acelin's, and Acelin would most certainly object should Dedwyd miss and kill the boy. Louis told Dedwyd to stop but the archer did not know the language and continued.

The boy knew to remain very still and still he would have remained had not his knees shook so badly. Within moments, five arrows hit the quintain, one above the child's head, two each by his narrow shoulders.

"What is this?" Adelina asked. Louis turned. Adelina, with her girl close behind, was walking to them. "I need the archer for his lessons."

"But he teaches me, Milady."

"You have time, Louis, I have not. This bow is certainly interesting," she said, taking it from Dedwyd's hands, inspecting it and drawing it back. Dedwyd winced and shook his head. "No? Then show me, you happy little foreigner."

Dedwyd stood behind her, and with his hands over hers, he drew back, aimed for the boy's head and loosed. Adelina was surprised at the little man's strength and accuracy. The arrow parted the child's hair and the boy wet his pants from fright. Adelina walked to the quintain and told the boy to scat. He did, with great speed.

Standing before the quintain now, Adelina held up five fingers at Dedwyd and he grinned, pointed at her and spread his arms to the sides. Adelina stood straight, her arms out.

Louis panicked, tried to stop the nonsense. Aiming at a page was one matter, but aiming at the lord's daughter very much another. "Louis, shut up!" Adelina yelled. "I tire of your squawkings!"

Dedwyd chose six arrows, and smiling at Adelina all the while, licked at each's fletching before loading. He bent to one knee, and Adelina wondered at her wisdom momentarily when he took aim. Yesterday, she had hoped to die, but now, not so. And Louis, brave Louis, closed his eyes and could not look. Beside him, Jennet fainted and there she lay.

Dedwyd loosed, Adelina closed her eyes. Six arrows, almost simultaneously, hit the quintain, a few so close that they missed Adelina's dress by a hair's breadth. She tried to move but could not, for the dress between her legs was impaled to the quintain by an arrow.

The little archer walked to her and silently pulled each arrow out— one above her head, two under each arm, and the one which had holed her dress between her knees. He put the arrows back in his quiver, and put his hands on her arms to lower them, then he stepped back and grinned.

"Teach me," she said. "Show me how you did that."

Louis, heart beating fiercely, grabbed her and steered her away and he smacked the little archer on the side of the head for his foolishness. As he walked by Jennet, he grabbed for her hand, and, pulling her to her feet, dragged her a little way in the process. Adelina, still with a thousand bees in her belly, pulled from Louis's grip and smacked him across the face.

"She is a woman and she deserves respect!"

Louis, touching his face, watched as Adelina took the serving girl in her arms and threw him death stares sharper than the keenest sword.

"Dedwyd! Come!"

The little archer put his weapons down and followed. Some words he did understand and he looked back at Louis, who was still holding his face, and he laughed.

# CHAPTER 16

"What worries you, Monsieur?" Agnes asked quietly as she put his lunch on the table.

"What worries me is beyond my control and worse, none of my business." Geoffrey picked up his spoon and played with his food. His appetite had long since passed. He glanced at his brother, sitting in his favored position by the window, so that he missed nothing happening in the village below.

Agnes sat beside Christian, put his spoon into his hand, closed his fingers on it, then she spoke quietly, so quietly that Geoffrey did not hear her words. She balanced the bowl of soup with her hands while Christian made a mess trying to eat it on his own. Of late, she'd come to serve him double the amount to be assured that he ingested at least half.

"Is your worry because of the visitors of yesterday? The ones who were as angry as the storm?" she asked, glancing at Geoffrey.

"For all I know, she is not found yet."

"That is why you could not sleep?"

"I have known her all of her life. She develops a cough if she is wet by rain. Or at least, she used to," Geoffrey said as he ate a little.

He had not appreciated being wildly accused of providing illegal refuge for Adelina when the news that she was missing hit his heart hard. Perhaps she remained still in the woods and had been there all night long? Adelina, he knew, was stubborn enough to survive the worst weather. The strength of her will alone enough to keep her alive.

And still Geoffrey had heard nothing. Almost a full day of worry had passed and in that day he had forgotten important matters, like his first appointment at the abbey to discuss these lessons he was supposed to undertake.

"I feel she is well."

"I hope your feelings are correct. Mine are too confused to trust."

"Good," Agnes said to Christian. "Very good. Now, try again."

Geoffrey watched. Christian managed to quell the shakings in his hand and aim his hand for his mouth. The spoon clattered against teeth, and the endeavor was a success. Geoffrey was pleased, quietly. Before Agnes came to be a part of the household, Christian moved not, grunted not a lot, nor did he attempt to feed himself. Her presence, it seemed, or the presence of any fair woman perhaps, had inspired his injured mind to at least try. Geoffrey thanked God for this angel who was kind and gentle, who spoke only when spoken to, or offered a few well-placed words when those words were welcome. She attended her duties quietly, too. Her cooking was fair—but not as fair as Ella's—she washed their clothing in the shallows of the river, flead them both without being asked, and tended Christian as if she, all along, had known that the man he used to be still lay beneath, struggling to breathe fresh air once again.

She has more patience than me, Geoffrey thought. He would never have let his brother feed himself—the duration of such a challenge was beyond Geoffrey's forbearance. The mess was great but the results, although slow in coming, were appearing.

He had known that tending his brother alone would be hard and draining on his emotions and he wondered, as he watched Christian with Agnes, did she ever tire of this? If so, she said nothing.

Christian was trying to speak now. Yesterday, after Robert, Gabriel and Acelin had left in the storm, Christian, watching from the window, had tried to say the name, Adelina. So it was true that he understood all that happened, all that was said, and most of what lay unsaid.

Geoffrey looked at Agnes and wondered if it was true that this girl servant resembled Adelina. What had Christian's feelings been for her, anyway? Had he any, he never spoke freely of them before. 'What would have been had you not gone to war, brother?' Geoffrey had asked as they both watched the three ride off into the storm. Geoffrey had put his hand on his brother's head and he had pulled away, angry. 'No, I do not blame you,' Geoffrey had said. 'I have never blamed you.'

"Monsieur? People come."

Geoffrey looked out from the top of the stairs. Four people approached: Gabriel of Lyon, riding beside Adelina on Geoffrey's old pony, Jester. He barely saw the two others, he moved so quickly.

Adelina, from a distance, saw the house where Geoffrey now lived, and there he was, climbing down his stairs, leaping across the bridge. Her heart lifted immediately and she kicked the old pony three times before it would move faster than a walk. Long before Jester had stopped his half-trot, half-canter, Adelina slid from the saddle and ran to Geoffrey. So much was said from both that neither could discern a plain word amid the babble.

Gabriel, bored senseless by this display of sheer affection, walked his horse by, dismounted, crossed the bridge over what seemed to be a moat. He smiled to himself—boys and castles indeed. He led his horse into the shade and there he sat, crossing his feet and closing his eyes. His horse, untethered, stood idly by, lowering its head to graze.

"Show me your house, Geoffrey!"

"Soon. Dedwyd! Come!" Geoffrey called, waving to Dedwyd to join them.

"No, I have told him to stay with Jennet."

"Jennet?"

"She is my girl and you cannot have her. Jennet!" Adelina called. "You may visit your family now!"

"Are you not journeying to Paris on the morrow?"

"I shall worry about that later," she said, and watched Jennet and Dedwyd turn their horses and ride down to the village.

"Is she not accompanying you to Paris?"

"No. I will not allow it." She turned to Geoffrey, and looked into his bright eyes for a moment before she threw her arms around him tight and gave him a mighty squeeze. "Much I have to tell you, but first, where is Christian?"

"Upstairs, my love, but the house is not, well, it is not fit for a lady such as you."

"Nonsense. I have come to see my friends, not judge them by the state of their house."

Geoffrey led Jester across the shallow moat and tethered him beside Gabriel's horse. Gabriel, half sitting, half lying in the shade, pretended to sleep, which suited Geoffrey. Not one word passed between them, not even a greeting.

Adelina climbed the stairs and even she had to lower her head on entry to the house. She did not judge the house, as houses had never interested her anyway. Her eyes gradually adjusted from bright sunlight to interior dimness, and by the window, near the bed, Christian sat with a serving girl whose face Adelina could not yet see. She was holding a bowl on Christian's knees. He stood when he saw her and the girl was quick in taking the bowl away.

"Christian, you look well. Do not stand for me. Sit and continue with what you are doing." Adelina came closer and said, "Girl."

"M'selle."

"Her name is Agnes," Geoffrey said. "As you can see there is no other."

"I am not here to spy on you, Geoffrey."

He did not believe that for a moment. "I have some good wine," he offered.

"Yes. Why not. A big one."

Geoffrey handed her a half tankard. "I have no goblets as yet. As you can see I have much of nothing."

"Then this much of nothing has intensified the sparkle in your eyes. Will you not invite Gabriel in, too?"

"No, he is working. Sit, sit and tell me what I have missed."

"I am your visitor, so you shall tell me your news first."

"There is nothing to tell."

Worse, he meant it. Adelina sighed and looked at her surroundings. A chateau it was not. "This house is… it is… clean and cheerful."

"Then it is Agnes's doing, not mine."

"I see only one bed for three people? Does she sleep squashed in the middle?"

"No, she sleeps on the floor until I find one able to make two beds more. Perhaps three, if I find a woman for my own pleasures."

He was teasing again and Adelina chose to ignore it. "Etienne, who is promised to my girl, is a builder."

"I do not know of him yet."

"Search him out before I take him to Allegre with me."

"Sadness lies in your eyes, my love. What happened yesterday?"

"I cannot tell you here," she said and drank the wine quickly.

"Agnes?"

"Oui, monsieur, I know. Let your brother not wander off alone," Agnes said with a smile. "I will watch your brother while you are away."

Geoffrey took Adelina walking to the top of the hill by the abbey where, he knew, he would eventually spend the rest of his time. But he chose not to think about that now, not while Adelina was with him. Until they were separated, Geoffrey hadn't realised the extent of his affections for her. It was always the way, for he'd felt the same when Christian went off to the crusade.

From the top of the grassy hill they looked down upon the village, and there they were away from others' ears and eyes, or so they thought, but some tending fields were watching, interested. As were a couple of monks wandering in the grounds of the abbey. It wasn't often that the lord's daughter came to the village.

"I have to marry, Geoffrey. I have to marry Baudoin Dupuy."

Geoffrey could find no words at all.

"I thought I would hate him. I had hoped to, and how I tried, but it did not last. I look into his eyes now, and I do not see an enemy. All I see is a man who knows not who I am. He is not pleased by this marriage, he told me so, but yesterday, he saved me from a terrible storm, and as he took me home, he said we must both make the best of this situation."

Geoffrey again said nothing. Of course Dupuy would make the best of the situation, after all, with this marriage, most lands from Le Puy to St. Etienne would be his.

"I like his mother. I think we may be friends. His father is ill, though, very ill. Baudoin says it is a sickness of the heart because his favorite son is dead. They say Henri Dupuy may not live much longer. All that is mine will become my husband's. Do you think that might be why he acts kindly to me now?"

"Perhaps," Geoffrey said. "I am not this Baudoin Dupuy to know."

"They have strange ways. There is only one woman in their entire household, Geoffrey, and that is the lady of the house. She does not even have a woman of her own. I feel that one day I might become as her."

"And how is that?"

"Old and lonely and afraid. She is so unhappy. She asked me of Mama, and Mama asked me of her but each fears what will happen if they speak to the other. They were once very good friends. I wouldn't like that, Geoffrey, having a friend I was forbidden to speak to. Do you know that I would rather live in your house than theirs? At least yours is not gloomy and sad."

She paused for a moment while Geoffrey struggled for something to say. But as he said nothing, she went on. "Papa gave the Dupuys food, you know. Food for themselves and the starving serfs. How long will it be before no one is hungry again?"

"I do not know, my love."

"My heart broke, Geoffrey, when I saw the eyes of those hungry children. I tried to give them my jewels, but Baudoin said it would only bring them misery. Misery and death by hanging."

Baudoin, Baudoin, Geoffrey thought. God, spare me. I cannot take a moment more of this.

"Baudoin says his wedding present to me shall be a gag. Do I talk too much, Geoffrey?"

Geoffrey would have replied but she did not give him the opportunity.

"I should write a book on manners and respect and give it to Baudoin as a wedding present."

Baudoin, Baudoin... Geoffrey closed his eyes.

"The first thing that I shall do when I wed, is to bring some beauty into that house. What do you think?"

"I have not seen this house to know what could be done."

She was quiet for some time. "Geoffrey, what will I do if I am treated the way Heloise Dupuy is treated? Mama says she is beaten by her husband and she fears what a son learns from his father."

Geoffrey lifted her face. "Unless you wish for trouble, never seek it out."

"Speaking my mind and demanding respect is seeking trouble?"

"With some, yes. Yes."

"After the wedding there will be peace on our estates. Your moat will have no use," she said, trying to change the subject. "Geoffrey?"

"Yes, my love?"

"Will you come to my wedding?"

Geoffrey swallowed the rising lump which felt like his heart and he said, "If you want me there, I will come."

Adelina gazed down upon the village and said, "All of my life I thought that if I was to marry, my husband would be a friend, and from that, love might grow. I hoped that if I was ever to marry one I loved, it would be you, Geoffrey. You alone are my friend and you I already love." With that she took hold of his hand. "I always have loved you."

"Nothing will change, no matter who it is you wed, or where it is you reside. Nothing will change. We will always be friends. We will always love each other."

"But I fear I will change."

You have already, Geoffrey thought, and held her close. He kissed the top of her head and swore to remember this moment for the rest of his life. He felt in his heart it would never happen again.

"I have written a poem for you," Geoffrey said softly as he held her close. "I would give it to you now if you promise me faithfully that you will not read it before your wedding day."

Adelina drew away and looked into his eyes. "I promise," she said.

"Whenever there is a time you feel very alone, you will think of it, and it will give you the will to go on."

Adelina wanted it now because her will to go on was already fading.

"You are frightened," Geoffrey said and held her face to his shoulder again. "I see it, I feel it."

"Too much is expected of me, Geoffrey. Too much from too many. I fear I will lose myself. I fear I will become as Heloise Dupuy, and as my mother; sad and alone and bitter and old long before my time. I need to know that you love me, Geoffrey, that you always will. You are the only friend I have ever had."

Geoffrey again was lost for words, for she had said what was in his heart. A sight they must have looked together, embracing like lovers on the hilltop.

"If you were a baron, or a lord, or a count..."

"But I am not. What should have been mine was stolen from me when I was small."

"Can you not take it back? Can you not gather an army and take back what is yours by birth?"

"And with what do I gather an army? I have no rank. No title. I have nothing, Adelina. Nothing."

She said nothing to that. Geoffrey had nothing. She, in line for so much, and he, nothing. It should not have been this way. "Will you still be my closest friend when I am wed?"

"We will always be friends."

"What shall you do, Geoffrey when I am not here?"

Mourn your loss, he thought. "I would study, fulfil the wishes of my uncle and become a monk, I suppose. Perhaps a wandering friar, a teacher, a minstrel, a poet... I don't know. These things are not yet settled in my mind. Tell me, why is it you limp?"

"I was thrown from a horse during the storm."

"Your father came here expecting to find you with me. You ran away, yes?"

"Only you and Baudoin know that I ran away. He found me, took me home."

"How was he before he was told he must marry you?"

"Civil."

"How is he to you now that he knows what he gains?"

"How should he be?"

"It would depend on which face you show him."

"You know me too well," she said and sat on the grass, pulled some and chewed on it. Geoffrey sat, too, and drew his knees high.

"I was worried about you. I did not sleep last night."

"I thought of consequences when it was too late. Papa was not angry, which makes me think that Baudoin lied to save me from his anger. Baudoin asked me what trouble lay ahead. Do you think he likes me, Geoffrey?"

Geoffrey looked at her as she sat beside him in the long grass, chewing thoughtfully. He studied her, the long hair shining golden red in the sun, her deep emerald eyes alive with thoughts of what he knew not. She was so beautiful. "Who could not like you?" was all Geoffrey could say.

"I do think he lied to spare me the back of my father's hand."

I have lied for you, too, many times, Geoffrey wanted to say but did not. "Then all is not hopeless, it seems. Perhaps you will grow to love him," he said quietly, almost choking on those last words. "And he you," he added quickly.

Adelina lay back and lifted one knee. Geoffrey looked away, and rubbed at his hair. "He is not what he seems, though. Inside, his heart is black and cruel."

Geoffrey looked at her again, surprised.

"I have decided, Geoffrey, that I will marry him but only if I must, as it will be for the good of all if I do, but he will never touch me."

Geoffrey was secretly pleased but remained silent.

"Do you think that would hurt him, repay him for all the hurt he has caused others? Do you think?"

"What would hurt him?"

"Having a wife who will not allow him near."

"Adelina, when you were little, you were mystified by fire until the time I let you touch the flame. You say Heloise is treated badly, yet here you are, telling me what kind of marriage you intend when it can only result in pain for you and all those around you. Either marry him or do not. There are no half measures for one such as you who loves to play with fire."

"Even though he is cruel?"

"Inspire no cruelty and you will find none."

"Who said that?" she asked.

"A very wise man."

"You have been reading again. You have been reading things about the spirit which make no sense to the body."

"No. They are the words of your father."

"It is a lie."

"How so?"

"Cateline never hurt a soul in her life yet she died horribly."

"Who told you this?"

"Gabriel. And Jennet, my Jennet, she inspires no cruelty but she finds it. The villagers of Allegre are starving, are you saying that they asked to be hungry?"

"No, but..."

"But nothing. You will only recite more profound words I have not the power to make sense of."

"How is this then? Some in the east say that we live more than once. That the bad we do follows us through each life until we right it."

"If that is so, then I have sinned a thousand times. You?"

"Two thousand," Geoffrey said with a smile.

"You speak of such things at the abbey?"

"I have no wish to burn! Michel told me. We have long talks on such things."

"Michel is a dreamer as you are. I cannot be bothered with other lives I do not remember. I have enough worry with this one."

"And I say again, inspire good and keep love in your heart and nothing but good can come. For if it is true that the bad follows us through each life, then it must be that good does as well, for without one, there can be no other. Life, you see, is..."

"Pleasant thoughts, Geoffrey, but they are silly ones." She rolled to her side and propped on elbow, facing him. "When shall you take your vows and become this monk that everyone except you wishes you to be?"

"I don't know."

"I don't want you to lock yourself away and chant and pray and give your life to God. A fine lady awaits you, Geoffrey. I know this in my heart."

"Then she must be very special for I have nothing to offer her."

"You alone are a great treasure."

"You talk nonsense again." Geoffrey stood and reached down to take her hand, but she lay in the grass, looking up at him.

"Geoffrey?" she asked in that tone he knew so very well, and he sighed, waiting, wondering what she would ask of him now. Was not attending her wedding enough torture?

"Geoffrey, is it wrong to kiss one not your husband? Or wife?"

Geoffrey studied the sky for a moment and again, his head was itching. So that, too, he attended to. "There are many different kisses. Or so I hear," he added, trying not to picture in his mind the 'Lady' Annette. "Can you not ask your mother these things?"

"Mama? She would faint. You do not know, do you, Geoffrey."

"Adelina, why do you torment me with questions I can never answer?"

"You are the only one I trust. Tell me, is it wrong?" Adelina reached up for his hand, their fingers locked and Geoffrey pulled her to her feet. She was close enough now to kiss him the way that Gabriel had kissed her, but fear was there in his eyes again. She recognized it now. He was afraid. "Find me this poem, Geoffrey," Adelina said. "I feel I need to read it, now."

"No, you made a promise to me."

"But you said whenever I felt alone, your words would give me the will I need to go on." Tears filled her eyes and Geoffrey couldn't help himself. As he'd done before, many times over, he put his arms around her and tried to pretend that she was still a little girl. But she was not. She certainly was not. It was no use asking who had kissed her. Her talk would only continue of Baudoin Dupuy. Geoffrey enjoyed the moment he had with her, alone, because he knew that it would never come again.

"Best we return. I dare not leave Christian too long alone."

Hand in hand, they walked down the hill, slowly. "Your girl seems kind."

"We would be hopeless without her."

"I wish I could be your girl, Geoffrey. I wish I could swap my noble finery for the rags of your Agnes. I do."

"You have much more important things to do with your life, Adelina. How often must I say it before you hear me? You were born a noble and this can never change."

There was a call in the distance and both turned to it. A lone knight was riding up the hill toward them. "Is that Louis?" Adelina asked.

"It seems so."

"What can he want?"

Soon enough, she knew. "Milady!" Came the call. "Come quickly, you must come!"

"What is it? What is wrong?"

From Michel's house, she saw Michel emerge and he saddled his horse with haste.

"Quickly, there is no time to lose."

"Louis! What is wrong?"

Louis reached down for Adelina's hand. "Raoul is dying," he said. "He begs you to come. Now. Quickly."

Louis pulled her up behind him on the horse.

# Chapter 17

"His blood is poisoned," Michel said the moment Adelina walked into the dark chambers. She immediately went to the window and pulled at the leather curtain until light entered.

"He is not dead yet. Let him see the light. With you and the monk, all is darkness, darkness. Is there no place for light, for sun?"

Robert and Marys said nothing. They stood together, looking down at the dying knight who had served them both faithfully for many years.

Adelina sat on the narrow bed and took Raoul's hand. He was unaware of where he was, or that all of the household had gathered. Poor Raoul, she thought. The flaming arrow took its slow time in finding its target. "Why was I not told he was so ill?" Adelina asked.

"I had thought he would live," Michel said quietly. The monk with him stopped his praying and nodded in agreement. "Nothing can be done."

Someone else was praying quietly, too, and Ella was weeping. Louis's face was pale but he stood tall and allowed no emotion to show, as did Robert, whose arm was around his wife's shoulders.

"Raoul?" Adelina whispered. As she touched the hands already folded on his chest, Raoul's dull eyes opened. What he saw, she did not know, but he tried to speak. It was Michel who leaned close and only Michel who understood the soft gurgles.

"He says that all are here but Geoffrey."

"Not so," came the voice from behind the crowd at the door. Geoffrey pushed his way through and kneeling by Raoul's bed, he too touched the hands. Raoul closed his eyes, then opened them once more. He looked, in his final moment of clarity, at the people near him: Robert and Marys, Louis, Acelin, Dedwyd and Gabriel, the servants, charboys and pages, and in particular, Ella. He said something again to Michel. It was all too much for Robert. He departed, quickly.

Then Raoul fixed his gaze on Geoffrey and Adelina.

One moment later, there was a sigh and he was gone. There was a strange, deep silence until Michel put his ear to his friend's heart and shook his head. He walked from the room quickly and took Ella's hand. Michel said to her, "He did not like to see you cry and that is what he said to me. She is not to cry for me."

But that only made Ella howl even louder.

"Come," Geoffrey said to Adelina, and led her from the room, past Raoul's friends whose duty was now clear. Whether death came on the battlefield, by error, by disease or old age, a knight's colleagues always tended the remains. It was no place for a woman, not even a wife.

Adelina walked down the stairs with Geoffrey and saw her father standing alone in the great hall. She had seen this before, the way he stood when his grief was so great, leaning against the cold fireplace, supporting his weight by outstretched arms while his head was low. Nothing could relieve his deep sadness, which seemed almost too heavy to carry. Adelina didn't know whether to approach him or not. But Robert, who knew she was there, turned his head anyway. "How goes it, Geoffrey?" he asked quietly, his voice low.

"All is well."

"And Christian?"

"He improves. He seems content."

"Good," Robert said with a sigh. "Good."

"Do you wish another escort for the journey to Paris, Milord?"

"No. Your offer is appreciated though."

Geoffrey did not know what else to say. Had he half hoped, like an opportunist, that he would fill Raoul's vacancy? It was only a half hope, he should not have even considered such a thing. Raoul had been his uncle's first retainer (until Gabriel chanced along); a good warrior, an excellent horseman, not boisterous or full of his own importance. Raoul was almost Robert's age and much had they in common or so it seemed. Raoul had been a friend long before Robert had married. And of all times to die, he would choose the eve of a long journey to a most important meeting with the king.

"I take my leave, Milord," Geoffrey said.

Robert nodded and Geoffrey walked away. Adelina did not. "Papa?"

Robert looked under his arm at his daughter, whose eyes were red from quiet tears. "I thought you would be with Geoffrey, escorting him home, perhaps? Keeping him from danger?"

"Papa, must we still journey to Paris?"

"Yes. We must."

"But Papa..."

"I said yes!"

Adelina retreated quickly and for half a moment, Robert wished he had not bellowed. But he had. He wanted to find a place where none at all would find him, and there, gain his thoughts and his courage to go on. But he was tired, a little ill and aching now. Too many wanted so much when little it was he could give. Nothing had gone as he had planned. Nothing.

He was about to summon Gabriel when he realized that Gabriel was already seated at the table and patiently waiting. "Your timing is always impeccable, Gabriel."

Gabriel remained silent except to say, "I thought it best to leave those who knew him to tend him."

"It should be me," Robert said and Gabriel watched him carefully. "But I cannot. I cannot."

"I am told he was your friend of many years."

"That is so."

"Not a pleasant task," Gabriel said and sighed. "Will you delay your journey?" he asked.

"No. I cannot." Robert sat and leaned back in his huge chair. "Henri Dupuy is soon to die," Robert said. "Do you agree?"

"From what I saw of him, yes, I would agree."

"Baudoin tells me of his personal allegiance to Philippe Augustus."

"Yes, I know this already. What plays on my mind is the unanswered question of what will become of Adelina should she marry and Baudoin die."

"All would be hers unless she is graced with an heir."

"You know, of course, that the holdings of my father extends south to Moulins?"

"It is our land Philippe wants. Not yours."

"If I may? What is the reason the king wants this land?"

"I would guess... good hunting," Robert said without any emotion at all.

"Then I have the utmost faith that you will change his mind on this matter."

"I would, too, did I not feel that the door to life closes slowly on me."

"But you are still young."

"Flatter me not, Gabriel."

"It is observation, not flattery, Milord."

"It is my wish that should I die before Henri Dupuy, you will care for my wife, and administer the estates peacefully in cooperation with the Dupuys."

"Milord, these things are normally discussed on a deathbed," Gabriel said.

"I ask this of you now, Gabriel. My wife speaks highly of you."

So she should, Gabriel thought. "As I speak highly of her, Milord."

"It is settled then."

"Verbally, when many others would vie for my position here, Milord? Perhaps these wishes, when written in your hand and accompanied by your seal, shall undoubtedly prove themselves irrevocable?"

"You are sharper than I thought." Robert rose and found his parchment, his seal, ink and quills, but before he sat, said, "One thing plays uneasily on my mind, Gabriel and it concerns you."

"Milord?"

"Is it true that you wield a sword well in confined spaces?"

"I learnt the art at an early age, Milord. I fought with Philippe Augustus during the lengthy siege of Chateau Gaillard. I was young then, barely twenty and very agile, even though my size is the same now as it was then. I was one of the first to gain entry through the open latrine window, and the citadel was thus taken. Gaillard had many passageways darker and smaller than yours, Milord, and thirty-six fell to my sword alone."

"So it must be that you, too, have an allegiance to Philippe."

Gabriel smiled. "I was honored by him, as were many others who fought beside me, and I was granted lands for my service."

"You did not tell me this."

"I have learnt to keep my victories to myself."

"And if I were to war against Philippe?"

God forbid the notion, Gabriel thought but said, "I would stand by your side to the death. If I may? What you plan now, for your daughter, I can only admire. You must despair at not having a son as heir for none of this would be necessary were it the case."

"I have always despaired, Gabriel, but my daughter is a joy to me."

"As she is to all who know her. Could it be, Milord, that Raoul fought death until her face he had seen one last time?"

Robert nodded. "It could be. He was fond of her, too."

"Are not we all? Is there anything more?"

"No."

"Then I shall leave you in peace."

"Care for my family, Gabriel if the need arises."

"You need not have asked. Already it is done," Gabriel said as he watched Robert's flowery hand spread easily across the parchment. "And should your daughter become a timely and wealthy widow, Milord?"

Robert looked up. "If I no longer live, then all would be dependant upon you, Gabriel. I will speak with her on this matter but I can give you no guarantees."

Gabriel needed no guarantees. Whatever he wanted, he acquired, by fair means or foul, it mattered little. He left the great hall a very happy man indeed.

That night after supper, Gabriel visited Adelina's room. She was alone and she welcomed him with a sad smile. He walked to where she sat by the window.

"Thoughts of Raoul?" he asked.

"I have never known a time when he was not here."

"Even if you ignored his presence?"

She did not answer that. "I have been close to death, Gabriel, and I felt nothing. There was a calmness only, as if it were inevitable, but for some reason the angels intervened and I was spared. Is it true what Geoffrey says, that each of us has an angel watching over us?"

"Of such angels I know nothing. I am not responsible for my name, Milady."

"I watched Raoul today and I felt the same calmness descending, and like me, he did not fight it. But there was no angel to save him." Tears formed in her eyes. "This afternoon, and this evening, I felt him behind me. He is here now, can you not feel him?"

"No. I think it is your wish that he was here which makes you feel him so strongly. He is gone, little one. He will never come back."

"I know," she said quietly, wiping her eyes and looking out of the window. "I could say nothing to comfort my father. Nothing would come. He was so sad... Why are you here? Have you come to tease me again? To cast another spell?"

"That was not my intention to begin with, my love."

"Do not call me that. Only one man can ever call me that."

"And how was your meeting with Geoffrey today?" Gabriel asked.

"Good, but sad."

"So it seems."

"Are you accompanying us tomorrow?" she asked.

"Yes, I am."

"Do you think I will speak with the king?"

"I do not know. Perhaps, if time allows. He is a busy man with much on his mind always."

"I hear he is funny of face and laughs when others do not."

Gabriel said nothing.

"Already I have forgotten what to say should he speak to me."

"Worry of such things when it is time and not before. Good night, little one," he said and kissed her forehead. "Sleep well, for tomorrow a long journey lies ahead."

"Good night, Gabriel."

He turned at the door and said, "Will you be as kind to me when I am dying?" he asked.

Adelina turned and looked at him. There was a very strange softness in his eyes now. "I would think that one such as you could never die."

"A good thought if not an absurd one." He closed the door quietly.

"What is this?" Robert asked as he looked down upon his daughter. Her hair was braided and pinned to her head, and she wore yet again, man's attire.

"It is a long way to Paris, Papa, and I wish to ride on a horse and not in the carriage because it makes me ill. This you know."

Robert sighed. When will these esquire games ever cease? At her side she even wore Geoffrey's first sword. Had she access to a crossbow no doubt she would thrust that on her saddle as well.

"I promise to be a lady again the day before we reach Paris. I do. Really, I do."

Best he allow it than have long days of continual whining. "You will not ride bare-back, girl."

Her smile lifted his heart and he waved her away quickly, before she threw more requests at him, requests she knew would be allowed. Robert was pleased that he had not a half dozen like her for one was certainly enough.

At first the journey was an adventure. Adelina had been told that she had visited Paris before, but she was so young at the time that memory of it was dim. Her mother's though was not and for once Marys was pleased that her daughter was not in the carriage with her but outside in the fresh, warm May air, and playing for the last time her childhood games. Soon her childhood would be over.

Marys had hoped, vainly, that Heloise would make the tiresome journey as well. It had been too long since they had spoken and embraced each other and it seemed that they weren't to meet until the wedding now, for at the crossroads, Baudoin and Henri waited with their three knights. There was no sign of Heloise. So now the prospect of purchasing a wedding gown would be very dim indeed. Marys did not look forward to taking Adelina with her, Adelina who had no interest in anything the least feminine. There would be argument after argument unless Robert accompanied them, and that was unlikely for he knew as much of fashions as Adelina and cared less. Perhaps it would be a wasted journey entirely, for if

Philippe did not see reason, there would be no marriage at all. If the king took the lands, there would be nothing for anyone to gain.

Philippe Augustus was tiring, it was said, of feuding nobility. He wanted unity in the land and two enemies of long standing now united by marriage he would consider most favorable. Or so Robert hoped. Marys did not know, though, for Robert told her nothing. She could only surmise.

Marys thought of her own wedding: an arranged one. With all of her brothers dead, her fortune was great until the vows. She had eventually succumbed to Robert's courting and charm. Although what little romance that existed had long since died, they cared for each other still. She was fortunate that Robert was a decent man at heart. But no amount of wealth made one happy.

Marys glanced at her daughter, and wondered what was wrong with her. Poor Baudoin was trying hard to entice her to talk. I hope he has humor, Marys thought. He will surely need all he has and more if he is to wed my daughter.

Baudoin, from the outset, had chosen to ride with Adelina. "What is this?" he asked.

"What is what?" she replied, her nose in the air.

"You, in squire's clothing, riding with us and not with your mother. You look ridiculous. My father cannot understand you at all."

"I don't care what your father may think, or you for that matter. Why I dress this way is my business. Do I ask of yours?"

She was a strange one for sure, or was it that Baudoin was not accustomed to females like her, if females like her existed. Happier by far was he in the arms of his love, the one who resided in St. Paulien. "Perhaps the weather will remain kind to us?" he tried.

"Baudoin Dupuy, if you cannot find any words of intelligence to utter, remain silent. You are so tedious!"

"Oh, and you are not?"

"I am not the one making dull conversation. Do I care what the weather will be? If it rains, it rains. If it does not, it does not."

There was quiet for a long way. "Why is it you always dress in black?" she asked.

"I like it," he said, surprised she had spoken to him first.

"Do you think the color makes you appear fierce? If so, you lie to yourself."

"Perhaps you would rather I dressed as a jester?"

"I would not rather you in any way at all."

He frowned for a moment, wondering what she meant. "Why do you carry a sword? Can you use it? Are not our bodyguards enough for you?"

"If robbers appeared now from all directions..."

"Your sword alone would save us all. Does it have magical properties?"

"Why are you so dull?"

"You are the only one who thinks so. Adelina, be assured that if robbers appeared now, they would see me in black, a sight far too fierce, and they would turn tail and flee."

"Is it enjoyable, this dream world in which you have lived all of your life?" Adelina asked.

"It is as enjoyable as yours must be," Baudoin said.

"You think I am a girl and therefore I cannot fight. Well, one day you shall see how I fight."

"I do not enjoy watching a beautiful girl spilling her own blood."

"I cannot believe that I have to marry you! You are a monster!"

"My love does not think so," he said and scratched at his face.

"I cannot believe that you have a love. Has she sight and sense? Who is she?"

"The one I had hoped to spend my lifetime with. My love is to me what Geoffrey is to you."

"Then we do have something in common. But you are still a monster. I know about you, Baudoin Dupuy, and should you ever come near me, I will kill you."

"With that old sword?" he asked, laughing.

"I do not jest!"

Again there was silence for a way. "Tell me about this love of yours. What is her name?"

"Why would you wish to know? Your only wish is to kill me."

"I am curious, it is a long journey and I am very bored. What does she look like?"

"Fair enough, reserved. My love speaks well and not often, and..." He struggled for something else to say. "My love wants many children."

"Dieu, another one," Adelina said. "She would have to be old and blind and brainless to find one such as you attractive," Adelina said, looking upon his very handsome face and meeting his curious gaze. It was she who looked away quickly. His eyes were too bright.

Again she wondered if such a monster could exist within him, because he had been, so far at least, gentlemanly under much strain, and although his eyes teased her a little when he thought none other noticed, he seemed that awful word, that word which she hated more than any other: Nice. How could one so nice inflict such horrors upon a simple serving girl? He did not drink to excess, and even when he did, it seemed his disposition became happier and he tended to sing a lot. Surely Jennet had been mistaken?

As the journey progressed, Adelina became confused because the man riding beside her all the way, and chatting constantly to her, did not seem the monster Jennet had depicted.

And worse, it was very difficult not to like him.

On passing through St. Paulien, it was Baudoin who pointed out his love's house. Adelina thought that if this woman were half as beautiful as her house, then it was no wonder that he was not happy about this marriage.

"Tell me the name of your love, Baudoin Dupuy for you know mine."

"My love is called Eleanor."

As the journey slowly continued, conversation came a little easier. It was on the fifth day when the party neared Bourges, that Baudoin asked again why she persisted in disguising herself as a man when one so fair should be proud to display herself to the world.

"I wear these clothes because they are more comfortable when riding. I can prove it by allowing you to wear one of my dresses if you wish."

"Thank you, but no. You would be more comfortable in the carriage with your mother. In there, your skin would not burn from the sun." He reached over and tapped her nose.

"I refuse to ride with her. All she will speak of is the wedding."

"Is that not foremost on your mind?"

"God forbid!" Adelina cried. "Do I seem one to pander to feminine nonsense?"

"Perhaps if you gave yourself the opportunity you would enjoy such things."

For the next few miles, Adelina chose to ride with Gabriel. At least his conversation was far more interesting.

"I am not my brother, Adelina," Baudoin said softly when the travellers stopped in Orleans and she sat next to him in the inn.

"I know you are not your brother. For some things I am thankful." She sipped on her cool drink politely, but all she wanted was to devour a huge meal as quickly as possible before her mother saw her. She dreamed too much now of Ella's cakes and buns, covered and filled with their thick custards and creams and topped with fruits and nuts. But of course, her mother, after seeing what she ate at Montlucon, forbid her such delicacies now, saying she would get too fat, too quickly.

Gabriel had made it worse by saying it best she walk to the altar, not flounder. And her father had been no help at all, for all he had done was choke from laughter.

And now, in the dim Orleans inn, Baudoin sat beside her, nibbling on his cake. He made a great show of licking cream from his fingers, too, and demanding another two cakes be brought immediately.

He must have known she was hungry and pitied her, because he surprised her when he whispered into her ear, so close that she tingled, "Here, quickly, while your mother is distracted."

Adelina seized the cake, lowered her head and gobbled it down, wiping her mouth on her sleeve before she rose. To anyone else it would have seemed she had dropped her spoon on the floor. Baudoin patted his mouth and sighed and whispered aside to her, "Well done, Adelina. Very well done indeed."

"Such things take years of practise, Baudoin," she said and smiled at her mother ever so politely.

"This time tomorrow," Baudoin said as he studied the one remaining cake, "We shall arrive in Paris. The day after, we shall be in the abbey of St. Denis. Will you be by my side, Adelina, as a friend?" he asked.

Adelina looked at him, smiled and nodded, but her attention was on the cake balanced on his fingertips.

"And will you hold my hand as if we were very good friends?" he asked, taking her hand under the table. He squeezed it, held it for a moment longer than he should have.

Adelina did not pull away. She smiled softly and sweetly, and thought, You fool. You should not trust me. "Mama? Baudoin wants to know if I am allowed to eat this cake?"

"I suppose one cannot do any further harm."

Adelina took the cake from his fingers. "I cannot be bribed so easily," she said.

# Chapter 18

Above all else, he liked her.

Baudoin had, of course, seen this beauty approaching him before: had he not played childhood games in the woods near the enemy's chateau, killing in his mind, all who resided inside? Now and then whilst hidden in the woods he had seen the little girl dressed in boy's clothes up high on the rampart, fearlessly sword fighting an invisible enemy with a stick. He had known of her for a very long time, perhaps all of his life, yet he had seen her, the young woman, for the first time a short while after his brother's body was delivered home. Anger had prevented clear vision. That night, the worst night of his life, he had seen for himself the damage done by his brother's hand, but of her he had seen nothing. His thoughts were on avenging the death, proving to his father that he was as good, if not better, than his brother. But pain for all ensued.

Now this little girl who played upon the rampart was coming down the stairs of the guest house. Such a sight as this had never before stilled his heart or made him smile. In fact, Baudoin was looking forward to the wedding.

Oh, that Marys, such a nag. Best he give his mother in law the gag. You will do this, you will do that, you will not do such and such, and if so and so should speak, what is it you will say? On and on, would she never be quiet?

Adelina cursed softly and saw Baudoin sitting, patiently waiting, half a smile on his lips again. Save me, save me, her eyes pleaded and she pulled away from her mother who was busy arranging curls to suit herself again. The green camelot Adelina wore was almost as deep as her eyes, which were sparkling from impatience alone. Should she walk into sunshine now, he knew that he would have to turn his head away from the shine of her hair. Hair he longed so often to touch but dared not for she kicked hard, with or without shoes.

"Come, come. You take too long and we cannot be late!" Robert, who had not slept, was already out of the door.

Baudoin stepped to Adelina and offered his hand. "We are not in the abbey yet," she snapped. Her mother, close behind, was still nagging and fiddling.

"You did not tell me you served in the king's army," she said, looking at his attire—the radiant blue of the king's uniform.

"You did not ask me."

"Do you keep everything to yourself unless asked?"

"Yes, I am like you."

As he helped her into the carriage, she noticed Gabriel, also patiently waiting. He, too, wore the blue uniform and like Baudoin, the Crusader's emblem was emblazoned on the topcoat—the huge white cross. Gabriel was not staying in the guest house with them. He had chosen other accommodation whilst in Paris, his sister's house, he'd said, not far from the city.

If Baudoin and Gabriel were not called to arms, which they were not, then Adelina knew the reason why they wore such a uniform, probably at her father's request. It would help

Philippe agree to her father's plea that the lands not be seized.

For the short journey to the abbey, she was not aware of her mother's promptings which had not ceased since last night. Adelina prayed for a miracle instead, a miracle which would save both her father's lands and herself from a marriage she did not want.

She took little notice of her surroundings, or of the noisy colorful crowd which swallowed her once she was inside the abbey gates.

Robert and Marys walked into the abbey, Henri Dupuy beside her father, and behind them, Baudoin held Adelina's hand. He was aware of the heads which turned constantly in appreciation of her beauty, but Adelina was not, and as they took their seats behind their elders he turned to her. "The fright in your eyes detracts from your beauty, Addie."

"Addie is not my name."

But still they held hands for she feared what would happen should she let go; or if her father was called and she had none other to look upon, none other familiar at least. The seats were harder than the rocks by the Loire where she and Geoffrey had often gone to talk and ponder.

The crowd was crushing and breathing up all of the air on this hot day. Uncertainty grew to despair. They seemed to wait forever in this gloomy place with arches so high. "If something does not happen soon I shall scream fire," she whispered.

Baudoin squeezed her hand. "All will commence soon. I hope. A long day it will be. I feel it."

She squirmed in her seat, and wished she could take off her shoes which were becoming tighter by the moment. On the other side of the abbey, an aged noblewoman fainted and when she fell she took two others to the floor with her, two poor innocents who floundered to escape from under her great weight. It took two men to carry her out. Adelina thought the spectacle funny until she realised she could do that too and escape. "I feel so ill," she tried.

"As I do. Should I faint, would you carry me out?" Baudoin asked, which ended her escape bid immediately. He is like Geoffrey, he can see what is in my mind, she thought. Her hand was sweating, she wished he would let go. She thought she knew why he would not though, for she was seated on the very end of a middle row and could be halfway to the doors before he realized it. Run, she certainly could.

Then, finally, someone appeared and the doors to the abbey were closed tight. All hushed. A bishop appeared in his sacred, gold-trimmed finery and Adelina leaned close to Baudoin and said, "I passed beggars on the streets, Baudoin. Look at this man of God in his finery. It is a disgrace. At least I threw the paupers some..."

Baudoin shushed her. Surely she would not say such things so loud throughout this long day?

After the prayer there was silence, and Philippe Augustus, the king, took his throne. Everyone stood again until he impatiently waved them to sit. From a distance, Adelina had to crane her neck and squint to see his face. To her, he did not look like a fierce warrior king at all. His face was fat and were it not for his nose, it would appear squashed. From a distance she could not tell if it was true that he had only one eye.

The king looked at all those gathered before him without any joy at all. Adelina wondered if he wished that he, too, were elsewhere. Life, Geoffrey had once said, is full of chores which cannot be ignored. For the king, holding court was one such chore. Or so it seemed. She squirmed again, and Baudoin asked in a whisper what was wrong. "The seat is hard."

"You sit on a horse long enough without complaint," he said softly. "Be quiet."

"Never tell me what to do."

Baudoin rolled his eyes and sighed.

The session began and as it droned on, endlessly, the heat grew fierce, more ladies fainted, and Adelina wondered just where on the list her father's business lay. She was almost overtaken completely by the sleep she had missed the night before, and she woke with a start three times in all, for her face was resting against Baudoin's shoulder each time. But she woke properly when there was a huge commotion at the doors. She was grateful for the interruption and turned with the assembled crowd, all curious.

There was a peasant boy fighting his way in, and with him, a horde of children. "I will speak with the king!" he demanded but the soldiers at the doors would not let him by. His business it seemed was not listed. He was so young that his voice had not yet broken but his demands reached Philippe's ears.

"What is this?" the king asked.

"I must speak with you for I am sent by God!"

A murmur passed over the gathered crowd. Ladies stopped their fanning momentarily, then resumed again. There had been a lot of people of late claiming to have heard the voice of God, or claiming to work miracles and this boy was no different.

Philippe sighed and said, "Let him through," and beckoned the boy closer. The boy, dressed as a peasant and barefooted, with a roll of parchment in his hand, walked the length of the abbey alone, oblivious to the faces staring at him. He dropped to his knees and rose again. Philippe looked down on him, half amused. "Sent by God, you say?"

"I am Etienne; Stephen of Cloyes, a shepherd, and I would have you bless my mission."

"Cloyes? Is that near Chartres?"

"Where I am from is of no importance, but where I go is." The boy turned to the people, studied them, as they studied him, and some talked behind their hands at this waste of their precious time. Adelina leant all the way to her right and there she had a perfect view of this Stephen, the arrogant shepherd boy who no doubt believed he was chosen by God, or that one day he would become a saint.

"I had a vision, and in my hand, I have a letter from God Himself!"

The entire abbey hushed. Philippe looked down at the boy and studied him carefully. The only movement from the king was a steady blink, and the occasional arch from his already permanently surprised brows. "Let me see this letter."

The boy handed the parchment roll over. "The Lord came and spoke unto me."

As Philippe read he asked, "And what were you doing when this happened, if I may ask one so blessed?"

The letter was passed to the bishop, who read it and did not smile. The boy did not smile either. He was perhaps a little angered at the king's condescending tone. He was not ashamed of his duties for the Lord himself was but a carpenter before he became a shepherd of men. "I was tending my sheep when the Lord came unto me and he said to me, 'Stephen, do this I command you. Take back what is yours. Take back Jerusalem!'"

He said it so convincingly that the murmur from the crowd became very loud.

Philippe, though, grew uncomfortable. Who was this child to think he could take Jerusalem when France, England and Germany, could not? "And tell me, boy, for I am very interested. How will you accomplish this? How is it you will take back Jerusalem?"

"I am to gather the innocents around me, children like myself. Already I have a large number of followers. I am told that with my army of innocents, we shall reclaim the Holy Land, the place of milk and honey that thousands of Crusaders have failed to reclaim for Christendom. We will succeed."

"With an army of children?" Philippe asked, staring at this boy now as if he thought he were insane.

"A mere token of my numbers are with me." Stephen whistled and more children, so many of them, from six years old to sixteen, flooded into the already-crowded abbey. Some wore colors of nobility, but most were peasants, barefooted and looking hungry, yet all bore the determined eagerness of Stephen's in their young eyes.

A heavy weight settled on the king. What arrogance made these children think they would succeed when his army could not, when even the Lionheart's towers had failed to gain entry into Jerusalem? Did this child not know the amount of Christian blood already spilled on eastern sands? No, and nor, it seemed, did he care. The Lord had spoken and that was all he needed to fire his heart to action.

"How did the Lord say you would arrive at the Holy Land?"

"He showed me in a vision, how the seas would dry up and upon its bottom, shall we all walk."

"You will walk to Jerusalem when the sea dries up." It seemed that Philippe was talking to himself now.

"It will be a miracle just for us, we, the true children of God."

The bishop whispered something into Philippe's ear and Philippe nodded. "Yes, I now that, but I cannot," he said in return. "I cannot sanction this." The bishop whispered again, and the king was silent for a moment. To Stephen and the gathered children, he said, "You have no arms, no food, and worse, you have no idea."

"We believe, and that is enough. I have come to ask your blessing for it is the Oriflamme which we shall carry."

Again, the bishop whispered and Philippe was becoming very annoyed with him. He said something which no one heard but the bishop stepped back, very quickly. "Stephen, shepherd boy from Cloyes. All I will say to you is," and everyone waited while the king sighed and remained thoughtful. "You have my admiration for this quest, which be assured, I feel is little but a dream. A dream of good intent, yes, but a dream it is nonetheless. For your own sake, let it remain a dream. I say to you now, disperse your army of innocents and lead them all safely home, for some I am sure are in need of their mothers." Philippe said this because behind Stephen stood a ragged girl of no more than thirteen years and on her shoulder a small child slept. "Take them home, boy, and go back to your sheep. That is where your duty truly lies."

But Stephen stood before the king, still arrogant and proud.

"I tell you, be good children and go home, now."

"We shall return home when we have reclaimed the Holy Land with your blessing or without. God has ordered this of me and I cannot disobey. Do we have your blessing?"

"No."

Stephen stared at the king for a few moments before he bowed and departed.

There were a few noisy seconds in which the king and the bishop again traded words not to the other's liking, or so it seemed. And eventually, when the children had left, the court's business continued.

Adelina sat for a moment, trying to think of an excuse to leave but nothing came. "I must attend personal matters," she said to Baudoin, and she rose and departed quickly.

After a few words to the guard at the door, the sun was on her face once more and fresh air was filling her lungs. Her heart lifted for Stephen had not yet gone. He was at the abbey gates, preaching, and even more children surrounded him now. As she drew closer, Adelina heard:

"The seas shall dry up as they did when Moses led the Israelites from Egypt. God will deliver Jerusalem into our hands. Did not Christ say that we must be as little children to enter the Kingdom of Heaven? Yes, he did and he spoke to me. The Holy City will open its gates to us and only us! Trust in God, and follow me and I will lead us to victory for the power of the Holy Spirit is ours!"

A strange feeling overtook Adelina as she stood not far from Stephen, as children of all sorts, ages and classes asked questions of him. The questions she did not hear. In her mind she saw again that Dupuy sword lifting and she remembered her own promise to God. Is this the reason why she had always wanted to bear arms and fight but God had kept her inner guessings secret until now? At last, a Crusade for Adelina. No more waving goodbye to her father and his knights. She was not yet sixteen, and some of the littler ones would need her. And she admired their leader, Stephen; she admired his way with words, his sincerity and conviction. She would accomplish what Christian had not, what her father when young, had not. And Michel, and poor Raoul, and Louis, and Acelin, too. Yes, she thought. Yes, this is for me. I will join this Crusade of Children.

She reached out and touched Stephen's arm and he turned. "I heard you speak, boy. I want to join your army of innocents."

"You are a noble."

"I am a child of God, like you. This Crusade has been my lifelong dream. Only today when I heard you speak did it come alive within me." Stephen embraced her with a smile. "May I read this letter from

God himself?" Stephen gave her the roll and watched her eyes as she read. "My hair prickles," she said as she handed it back. "One of the vassals belonging to my father knows much of illness and I have learnt much from him. You would need one such as I."

"Although God will see us safe from harm, I believe what you say."

"I have a problem, though. I am to be married if all goes well with my father's business in court this day. I will not be allowed to join you."

"Then steal yourself away in the dead of night like so many of these children have done. Tell your parents not where you go. God will see you home safely once the Holy City is ours."

"Where and when shall we meet then?"

"We will gather in Vendome at the end of June."

"That is near Orleans. I am from Lavoute Polignac, near Le Puy in the south, near the mountains."

"Then meet us in Marseilles. I will see you then. What is your name?"

"Adelina de Polignac."

"I am Stephen of Cloyes. Like Jesus, I, too, am a shepherd of souls." Stephen took back his parchment. "Are there many children in your villages?"

"There are some. If today, our business is successful, there will be more villages under the control of my father."

"Good. In these times of hardship I have found that most parents let their children go with blessings."

"Mine will not. I am the only heir."

"Bring many children with you, Adelina de Polignac, and the Holy City will be ours."

Children surrounded Stephen again and Adelina knew she had to return to the abbey and be by Baudoin's side. When she turned, Gabriel was on the steps, talking to one of the king's soldiers and watching her as well. Adelina visited the latrine which was her excuse to escape initially, but not the reason.

"Adelina," Gabriel said when she came out. "Your family business is soon to be heard." He took her hand. "Why were you talking to that stupid boy?" he asked.

"Who I speak to is none of your affair, Gabriel of Lyon."

"Do not condone it, Adelina. Their Crusade will end in death and misery."

Gabriel led her back into the abbey, to her place beside her future husband.

It went of course as she expected. No doubt her father, who had served Philippe faithfully and personally knew him, plus the two who had already served in the king's army, helped to sway the decision. Philippe wanted it all over with quickly, her father was on the bottom of the agenda for that reason, too, no doubt. After court had ended, the invitation was extended to Robert and his family and followers to attend supper with the king.

The goblets were of gold, not silver or pewter; the chairs were of finest tapestry and many servants were waiting on the king and his visitors, attending to their every whim.

Adelina watched Philippe and sometimes he looked at her, too, and she wondered if he would rather be alone or in his bed for he looked tired and constantly sniffed from a cold.

The king seemed pleased to see Robert and Gabriel, too. It was as if Gabriel's face was familiar but the name escaped him. Gabriel reminded him gently of the chateau Gaillard siege, very much a personal victory for Philippe. Henri, Baudoin and Adelina were eventually introduced, and all Philippe had to say was, as he looked directly into Adelina's eyes:

"It is good that two lords no longer hold hatred and endeavor to cease their warring. It seems lately that children are to be the saviors of us all. What are your thoughts on this crusade of children, little girl?"

Adelina glanced at Baudoin who knew how she felt at being called little girl, but she held to his hand and said softly, whilst looking directly into the king's funny little eyes, only one of which, it was true, held sight, and they were eyes she would not trust for a moment, "If ideals and much faith win battles, then Stephen shall return victorious and you will look foolish indeed for not blessing his mission."

Philippe took her words with good humor and Robert was able to breathe once more. "We would all claim victories if faith and ideals were weapons. Are you training her for politics, Robert?"

Robert looked at his only daughter with pride. She had kept her promises of politeness, of femininity and best of all she had remained silent unless spoken to.

The next night, Adelina awaited the opportunity to speak in private with her father. It seemed that she would wait forever. Even here in Paris too many people demanded his time. Must I make an appointment to see my own papa now? she wondered. It was a surprise when Robert excused himself from the gathering and took his daughter's hand. "Let us away from here. I need to speak with you, too."

He had never done this before. Was it because of the good day he'd had? Outside in the street, the night air was cool, and passers by infrequent because of the lateness of hour. Even those who did pass by did not look at them. In the city, very few were friendly to strangers.

Her father, who had said he wanted to speak, could not find words for quite some time. Words were his best friends; words had always served him well. All they did was walk in silence and Adelina wondered if Gabriel had told her father of her talk with Stephen, the shepherd boy. But the only person who had asked her opinion of Stephen was the king.

"Your mother tells me the dress is a beautiful one."

"Yes, Papa, I suppose it is."

Robert sighed. What was wrong with her? Any other girl about to be married would be happy, anticipating the wedding with much fervor.

"I do not trust that man."

"What man?" Robert asked.

"Your friend, the king."

"I would not say he is my friend. Of true friends, I have very few."

"But you have taken up arms for him and with him more than once."

"In these matters, we sometimes have no choice."

"He is getting old, Papa."

"He is not old yet."

"What will happen when he dies and his son reigns? What will happen if Prince Louis is worse than his father?"

"He wants for France what belongs to France."

"And should his son be like his father and over-rule all of the barons and lords of France and replace them with his own officials... these, these... what are they called?"

"Baillis."

"What then, Papa? By then, our estates will be one and governed as one, and we will have no choice but to give it all to the king or suffer. I do not trust him. He speaks with his mouth but his eyes hold other, unspoken words. We will lose our lands. If not now, then in the years soon to come."

"Worry of that when it happens and not before. You shall always be surrounded by men able to make decisions."

I do not need men to help me make decisions! she wanted to say, but instead, she said softly, "You worry of it now."

"My worries are not yours," Robert said and walked on toward the bridge. "Baudoin is more than I expected. You seem comfortable in his company, which is good, although Henri knows not what to make of you."

"I do not care for Henri at all."

"Why is this? You have barely spoken a word to him."

"He beats his wife. I do not care for him or for the laws, made by men, for men, which allow such things to happen."

"There is much in this world I, too, do not care for, Adelina."

Robert put his arm around her shoulders and on they walked. Once on the bridge, Robert leant on it and studied the dirty waters below. "I do this for you. My hopes for you once rested with Christian."

"I know this."

"I do not, have never liked, second choices."

"Well, Papa, I would much rather marry the one you have sent away for it is he who should have been first. It is he who has been more of a son to you. Always he was overlooked."

"I know what it is you feel for Geoffrey but he is not able to administer estates or battle to retain what is his."

"He is not a coward! I shall never have it said that Geoffrey is a coward!"

"You and Geoffrey can never be."

"That is because he is not what you think he should be! You do not see who he really is for he reminds you too much of your dead brother."

"I do not allow my equals to speak to me in that tone. You should know better."

"I am not your equal. I am your daughter."

"You will marry Baudoin and the marriage will be what you would choose to make it."

"You married for love."

"No. I married for gain. Love, if there is such a thing, came much later."

"Mama says differently."

"What is between your mother and me is our business and none others'. Part of your wedding agreement is that, should ill befall me and I die..."

"Papa!"

Robert continued, regardless. "Should ill befall me and I die, your voice shall be heard equally with Baudoin's. Henri had some disagreement with this but Baudoin had not."

"How could he not? Should you die, he has much to gain. Much indeed."

"You have intelligence and strength, Adelina, but remember always, it is never wise to make quick decisions based on feelings, on emotion. As you grow older you shall find wisdom. So, for the time we remain alive, Henri and I will manage the affairs of our estates in cooperation. Unfortunately, we must now pay minimal dues to the king, and should war banners fly, all of our able men will report at once to Philippe's ranks."

"Then I pray war banners will not fly. Papa, why must we pay him dues? Our lands are not so productive that we can grace the king's table or add to his treasury. I had hoped we could first see to the serfs who are hungry, for if their bellies are full, they are content to work harder in the fields to produce more food. Everything depends on the fields and our fields are not like those I saw on the journey here."

"There is more on my mind than hungry serfs. If there is ever war, Adelina, you will administer the estates."

"Alone?" she asked, surprised.

"As I said, it is part of the wedding agreement that you be included in all administrative affairs. You, girl, are all I have."

"Is this all that has ever concerned you, Papa? The lands, the villages, the estate?"

"I am concerned with you. You, and your children, and your grandchildren. I urge you to give Baudoin a son as soon as possible after the wedding."

Tell me you love me, Papa, she silently pleaded.

"Did you hear me, Adelina?"

"Yes." She wondered how quickly she could scale the bridge and leap into the water but her father took her arm, turned her towards him and touched her face.

"Do this I ask without complaint and never forget your true name for my line ends here, with you. On the day you were born, I looked down upon your brother and my heart broke."

My brother?

"You are the hope of my father now, and of his father, and of his, but always, you will be my daughter."

"I have a brother?"

Robert was very surprised that she did not know. "You had a brother. There were two babies. He was born dead and you were not."

Tears of pure anger filled her eyes. She wanted to scream aloud: scream and cry and curse because she had never been told this. What else had she never been told? But she didn't cry or scream or curse. "Mama never said I had a brother," she said, her voice shaking.

"Then for me, keep this to yourself. Your birth was hard enough on her. It seems that she has not told you and for this she must have reasons."

"Is that why she does not like me? Because the one that lived should not have?"

"Never think that way, Adelina. It only leads to misery."

"But it is the truth. I see it in your eyes."

Robert said nothing. He tried to touch her again but she moved away.

"Where is my brother buried?"

"Where all else are. He lies with my brother, my cousin and..."

"Why am I told this now when all of my life I have wondered why there is a huge, dead place in my heart? Why did you never tell me I had a brother? Is the memory that I lived and he did not too painful for everyone except me?"

"Adelina! I said no more of this!"

"I need to know!"

He would not allow a grown man to speak to him that way yet he stood there, unmoving, gazing down on his distressed daughter and wondering why he was so weak where she was concerned. "I wish you had both lived," Robert said with tears in his eyes. "But God willed it differently. There is nothing I could have done then and there is nothing I can do now. You shall never, never speak of this with your mother. Skeletons are best left in the ground, girl. Just do your tired old father proud. Make him proud and give him a grandson before he dies. That is all I want, now. A grandson."

Together they stared down into the murky water once again. Tell me you have always loved me, Papa? she needed to ask, but the words would not come.

"Come, girl. It gets late and cold. An early start we have."

As they walked back to the guest house, Adelina broke the silence with, "Papa, when is the wedding to be?"

"On your birthday."

Good, she thought. I will be well on my way to reclaim the Holy Land by then. She took her father's hand as they walked.

"I love you, Papa," she said but he said nothing in return. She thought she saw him smile and for a moment the grip on her hand tightened, but the words he never expressed. It was as if he could not.

"Adelina, ride the way home with your mother. Stop this boyish nonsense. For me." Then he kissed her and held her tight. Still, she needed to hear the words that he loved her. Throughout the walk back to the guest house she felt that hearing those words were more important than breathing in the very air.

Adelina walked upstairs to her room, alone, after wishing all who still remained awake a good night. She closed the door. On the ornate table under the window was her wedding gown, neatly folded and wrapped in cloth. She had no wish to see it again, it only brought back reminders of the long, hot, tortuous day with her mother.

From one seamstress to another they'd plodded. Her mother knew the streets well and seemed to glory in what to Adelina was nothing but a frightful chore. Each dress had seemed the same. Some had trains very long and to her, dangerous, some were very white, some were dirty white. She spent too long dressing and undressing and bit her lip so that she wouldn't hit out at the assortment of women cooing and telling her how beautiful a bride she would be.

One place in particular—the place where the dress was chosen for a sum that could have bought six months food for the entire estate—was visited often by royalty from all over Europe, but most important visitors here were the first and second wives of the king. There were mirrors in the elaborate viewing room where wealthy brides would step out and show their mothers and fathers or whoever else was paying for the gown, a view of the splendor-to-be. Adelina had sat where countless princesses and countesses had most likely sat, her feet and fingers jiggling impatiently whilst her mother took on her Paris accent and transformed into the Lady yet again.

Gabriel had stood a long way back and he seemed bored by it all. He had been sent in her father's place. It seemed that the choice of wedding dress was to be decided by him and Marys. Her father must have sensed the horrors of the day ahead and shied at the prospect. Baudoin had not come, and nor had Henri, and for that Adelina was pleased. She had wanted Jennet and none else with her, for at least Jennet was truthful.

Her mother, after showing Gabriel, had decided upon a silk dress with a train far too long. Its neck was high, its sleeves tight and many chains and brocades of gold and silver were arranged around the waist. It was a glowing white and once put against Adelina, it seemed that every spot on her face sang as loud as a drunken jester. "Mama, it is too white. It is too long. It is too heavy."

Her mother was determined she would put it on.

Adelina had, to her horror, liked one plain dress with beautiful billowing sleeves and deep pink roses on the neck. It was not special enough, or so her mother decreed, and Gabriel was of no assistance at all.

With a heavy heart, she was subjected again to strangers undressing her and dressing her and fiddling with her hair. But at last, she stepped out and the room hushed. "Stand tall," her mother had said and Adelina stood tall. She knew by the expression in Gabriel's eyes that this was indeed the dress. It pinched tight at her waist, fell in volumes over her hips. The mirror was brought to her and Adelina looked at herself, not knowing for a moment who it was looking back. She turned one way and then the other, wondering where her belly had gone. She touched. It was still there but it looked so small. Sorcery, she thought.

"I would like roses here," she said and touched the neck. "Pink roses because the white makes me look ill and fragile."

Marys looked at the woman who had handmade the gown and she nodded. Already her girls had made plenty of pink roses, and the dress would be ready to collect by sunset.

"I would also like to wear silk roses around my head. Pink and white ones. And instead of all this gold and silver, I would wear tassels of silk, pink and white, and plaited. And make sure that the price is lowered accordingly."

Adelina walked back into the room which was curtained and the women ran after her once more and aided her out of the dress, talking to her all the while about how radiant she would be in November; how spring would come very early for even sleeping birds would see her and sing with all their hearts... Adelina glared at the women and said, "I do not even want to be married!" They immediately quietened.

She longed for something to eat, some real food, something which lasted; then she would go back to the guest house, put on her hose and tunic, braid her hair so it would not tangle and comfort would be hers once again.

Even this was not to be. Her mother dragged her along to the inn for lunch, where her father, Henri, Baudoin and all of the knights except Gabriel, were waiting.

Baudoin had wanted to speak with her during a meal that would not have filled the belly of a hungry rabbit and she answered his questions in single words.

Had she enjoyed being in court? No. Had she liked the king? No. Did she think that one day Notre Dame would be magnificent? No. She preferred the abbey at Le Puy for God was closer on top of a hill in a place she loved. Did she like Paris? No, she hated Paris. All she wanted was to get home. To her home. Lavoute Polignac.

Then he asked, "Adelina, what have I done?"

She turned to him, angry. "You have done much of nothing."

Baudoin admitted defeat and joined Robert's and Henri's conversation without being heard. What a terrible day he had had, and it was getting worse by the moment.

Adelina noticed that Baudoin was being ignored, for again the conversation between their fathers was about politics and what each believed. Henri was as one-eyed as Robert, but it seemed that on a few issues they agreed. Is Baudoin little but an ornament, as I am? she wondered.

Her mother was busy nibbling and sipping at her drink, and excluded too. But she was accustomed to it.

Adelina had looked at Baudoin and he had caught her gaze. The sad disappointment in his dark eyes was quickly covered by, it seemed, affection. Forced affection. Adelina, whose hand rested on the table, lowered it to her leg and then she touched his leg. Caution more than surprise came alive in his eyes and he quickly pushed his goblet of wine away. She smacked his leg, his brows arched. She smacked his leg again, loud enough for her father to hear and still talking, Robert glanced at his daughter and future son in law who were, it seemed, playing secret games under the table. He hid his smile and said nothing about it.

On the way back to the guest house, she walked with Baudoin. "You do not hold my hand this day. Why not?"

"I do not want my fingers broken," he replied.

"I seem that fierce?" she asked.

Baudoin stopped walking and turned to her. She looked up into his face. Ahead, the others walked on, unaware they had stopped. Around them people strayed. "Father says the dress you chose was very expensive."

"Not as expensive as it could have been. I did not choose it, my mother did as everything else she chooses for me. Even the way I should wear my hair she chooses when all I want is to shear it off."

"Your parents are too extravagant."

"I am not my parents."

"Adelina, I am concerned."

"For what?"

"I am concerned that all this you are used to... You have seen my house. We are not wealthy."

"Baudoin Dupuy, you do not know me at all."

"I am concerned that you will become as your mother, demanding the best of everything."

"And I fear I will become as your mother, hidden away as an embarrassment and left to rot."

"That is not so!"

"That is what I see!"

"I love my mother."

"It does not appear that way to me."

"There is so much you do not know, yet you judge us so quickly. You say I am a monster when you do not know me and will not even hear me. I do not know how your mood will be from one moment to the next. You are nothing but a spoiled child, Adelina de Polignac. That is what you are." He walked off.

"You throw your upsets at me to make yourself feel better. I tell you, Baudoin Dupuy, the day shall come when we shall both be heard." Baudoin stopped walking and looked back at her. "It is not our time yet. Our fathers are too loud and they both enjoy the sound of their own voices. All we need do is wait." Adelina had walked to where he stood but they did not hold hands. They hastened pace to gain on the others ahead.

"Do not shear off your hair."

"It is my hair to do with as I will."

"Please, do not shear off your hair."

Why had he said that and looked at her so oddly? She wondered again as she took off the heavy dress she had been forced to wear all day long. Adelina washed and slipped her nightgown on. She wished Jennet were here to do this as she sat on the bed and took up her comb. Her hair had been loose all day in the wind and it was knotted badly. It was a long, time-consuming process, combing it out, and she was pleased for the interruption when the soft knock was heard on her door. Thinking it was her mother who usually came at this time, she said, "Come."

It was not her mother. It was Baudoin. He closed the door and her heart leapt for his face was strange. Had he been drinking hard? Would he now do to her what he had done to Jennet?

"I could not sleep," he said and walked to her, sat on her bed. He didn't seem drunk nor could she smell it. "Adelina, these things you say."

"What things?"

"One moment you are a friend, the next a foe. Is it me?"

"Yes, it is you."

"I do not understand what it is I have done."

"Yes, you do. It is the pain and suffering you have inflicted on those defenceless ones around you."

"You blame me for the hunger in our village? I do all I can."

"Do you not know that they think and they feel as we do?"

"They are serfs."

"I have seen for myself your own brutality."

"The day my brother was killed, I admit I did a foolish thing. I have paid for that, I am still paying. All my life I shall pay. Can you not forgive?"

"Do not look so innocent. I know what your hands can do."

"That was my brother! It was not me! You speak in riddles."

"I speak truths. Remember that when my girl comes with me after the wedding. Remember that she is my girl and my girl alone. She will be wed by then, her husband is a builder and he shall come as well. Etienne is a big man and afraid of nothing."

Baudoin had no idea what she was talking about.

"Jennet is my handmaiden and I love her dearly even if she is a serf, and I will protect her. You have not seen me fight, but I, too, fear no one."

"What tales have you been told of me?" he asked, taking the comb from her fingers.

"Tales? They are truths. I know they are truths. I know why it is you dress in black, Baudoin Dupuy. It is because it matches the color of your heart."

Confusion became despair. "Must I be tormented all of my days for what my grandfather did? Your grandfather was equally responsible but do I torment you over it? No. I do not!"

"What did your grandfather do?"

"He could not attack the Polignac fortress, so he attacked the chateau at Lavoute and tried to take it as his own. He failed so he tore your villages down, burned the houses, the fields, killed hundreds. Hundreds. But your grandfather did the same to us. But this, our union, it puts an end to the feuding. When will you stop hating me?"

"You talk nonsense. It is not for the past I hate you."

"Then what?"

"I have promised on my life I would not say!"

Baudoin moved closer and very gently put the comb through her hair. "Whatever this tale is, Addie, I am innocent."

She said nothing. Had he not been sitting so close, she would have wished him away. Far away. But he was more gentle than even Jennet when it came to combing out her hair. Occasionally his fingers touched her neck and sent shivers down her spine.

"I beg you not to shear this. Never."

"It seems you have done this before. You have had many women. I can tell."

"You listen to tales again."

"I am not your Eleanor. You should remember that."

"As I am not Geoffrey."

Adelina turned quickly and snatched the comb back. "You will never speak his name. Never. Go. Go now before we are both in trouble."

Baudoin stood slowly. "Tell me what it is I am supposed to have done."

Adelina looked the other way. Baudoin left the room, more confused now than when he had entered. He would do a lot for some peace of mind, but he would never beg.

# Chapter 19

For several days on the return journey, the carriage was filled with Adelina's dark silences which only served to feed Marys's guilt moment by unending moment. To see her back on her horse, dressed in her hose and tunic, and riding behind her father was neither disappointing nor elating. Her daughter had always been a stranger to her and would remain so for all of Marys's time.

Adelina would not be drawn into conversation on any subject fearing, it seemed, that her mother would turn it eventually to marriage. It was futile speaking to Adelina as an equal. She did not want to be a woman, had fought against her gender since infancy. Such a pretty girl, but the unseen, impenetrable fortress she had built around herself was mightier than Heracle's at Polignac. He would, as Robert's elder brother, be invited to the wedding but the brothers had not spoken since Guillaime's death at Langeac so long ago.

Heracle would not attend of course, but the invitation had to be extended. Nor would he, when the news arrived, bless the union of Polignac and Dupuy for whatever reasons it was nigh.

It was an horrendous journey home. Robert took ill at Nevers. The food he'd eaten had not been the cause, as all else ate the same—as pitiful as it was. He'd tossed and turned all night long in the narrow bed beside Marys and woke too often, his breathing strained, his skin cold and damp. He complained of strange aches which sapped at his strength.

At breakfast, well before dawn, even Adelina had stared at him, concern in her eyes. Too often Marys had asked if he was still unwell and too often he replied in his gruff way that he was fine. But there was an odd color to his eyes, his skin was paling daily and when he spoke, he took too many breaths. Occasionally his face would contort as if he was seized by an unspeakable pain and more than once she looked from the carriage to see him hunched forward in his saddle, in agony.

For a full day from Nevers he rode silently in the carriage with his wife and kept a strong hold on her hand as well.

It was Baudoin who wanted to send to Vichy for a doctor, for he too was concerned. Marys was very upset that Gabriel had chosen this shorter route for the return journey. She did not feel safe at all. Few villages were passed through, decent food was very scarce and too highly priced and always Robert had in his eyes that look of an animal sensing danger as yet unseen. The tracks were rough, some almost impassable.

South from Thiers would be Dupuy land, and the guarantee of safe passage through it came from Henri Dupuy himself, although Baudoin was uncertain from the outset. Momentarily, Robert considered asking Baudoin for his thoughts but Gabriel entered the conversation. He knew many of the Auverne byways and tracks and soon enough they would be home two days earlier than planned.

Gabriel had not expected Robert to grant permission for Adelina to ride out of the carriage and told his master that perhaps it was not for the best, to which Adelina responded, "Gabriel, are you expecting robbers? If so, I shall be as ready as any man here to deal with them." But even Baudoin was on alert, as Acelin was; Acelin, who had to negotiate the carriage along the narrow, inhospitable tracks.

"Speak to me, husband," Marys said to Robert the night they finally reached Thiers, as he paced the earth floor of the squalid little inn, the roof of which leaked miserably. "Tell me what ails you."

Robert turned to her then, his face almost frightening in the candlelight. "I do not know what ails me. It has been with me since Paris."

"Since Paris? Robert, there were doctors there!"

"No better than the idiot at Vichy who would not have known a wart from a woman giving birth."

"I have been watching you. I am concerned for this pain you try to hide. You pale, you do not eat. You do not sleep."

"I cannot sleep." He did not say he feared it.

"Then let me help you," Marys said and got out of bed. She walked to him, stood close, shivering because she was naked. She touched his long, thick set body with practised, knowing hands. "You have not taken me for many months, Robert."

He pushed her hands away and turned his back on her.

"Tell me what is wrong that I may make it right?"

"I cannot. It is simple. I cannot."

He had been this way since Christian's return. Nothing she had attempted and nothing she had said made any difference. "You are aging long before your time. I look at you now and all I see is Heracle."

Robert turned to her, more confused than angry. "You dare

compare me with him?"

"I did not know your father," she said. "How can I compare you to a dead man? One I never knew? One you refused me to meet?"

"Too many worries," he said. "That is all."

"Then lie with me, I beg you. Close your eyes. Pretend I am Vianna. You know that has always worked for you. I need you, Robert. Pretend I am my sister."

"Leave me, woman. Just leave me." He slapped at her wandering hands again.

Marys stepped back. "You take your daughter walking. You speak of God knows what to her for most of these long, tedious days, and what do you give me, Robert? What have you ever given me!"

"You are well provided for."

"Clothes and jewels and foods and wines are nothing. It is you I need but you I have never had! Only in halves. Who has your heart, Robert? Do you even have one?" Marys lay back in bed and rolled to her side, away from him. Of course he said nothing, his wise and comforting words were always set aside for others, those who did not know him as she did.

And now she could not sleep either. Marys reached for her nightgown and slipped it on. With her hair down, she opened the door to the squalid, tiny room.

"Who are you going to?" Robert asked. "Gabriel again?"

But the door slammed and gave him a reply.

Over the soft, falling rain, he heard Gabriel's voice: "Milady? Why do you weep?"

But he heard nothing else, so quiet were the words. Robert looked down to the corner of the small room where Adelina slept deeply. He sat on the narrow bed he was to share with his wife and eventually he lay on it, and rolled to his side. The inn may have been constructed of stone but the walls were thin to ears that should not have heard. He listened to each noise, and thud, and squeak as he sank into a very welcome darkness.

"Did you sleep well?" Baudoin asked.

"A bed of stone would have been more comfortable. You?"

"Nails, perhaps. I shall be pleased to get home. I am worrying for my mother."

Adelina regarded Baudoin with surprise, for his words were sincere. "What is wrong with your mother?"

"No one knows. But she is ill. Doctors come with their leeches and leave again and she is worse. I do not know what it is, Addie, but today I feel death is nigh somewhere. These feelings I have had all my life. Rarely do they lie to me."

She regarded him strangely for a moment. At times he seemed so much like her. "Your mother cannot die. I do not know her yet. But what I do know of her, I like. She is more of a mother than ... it does not matter."

Marys was walking to the carriage, alone. She looked brighter today, almost happy. And she gave Gabriel a beautiful smile.

"Where is Papa?"

"He comes soon."

"How is he this day?"

Marys said nothing and climbed into the carriage with Gabriel's help. Adelina went back to saddling her horse. "It will rain all day," she said and Baudoin too looked up at the low, boiling clouds.

"Best then that you ride with your mother."

"Best you not give me orders, Baudoin Dupuy, for wed or not, I shall never obey."

"That was not an order. It was a suggestion. You take ill when wet, I am told."

Adelina whispered into his ear before he mounted, "I would rather take ill than be tormented by woman-talk day in and day out."

"Come then," Baudoin said. "We shall scout ahead."

Adelina mounted her horse and was about to turn it and join Baudoin when she heard Gabriel call out:

"Do not ride off with him alone!"

Adelina rode off, anyway. "You worry too much, Gabriel. We are now safe on Dupuy land. And it will soon be my land as well. Best I see it now before I am wed and everything is denied me."

"What is wrong?" Marys asked.

"There is nothing wrong," Gabriel lied. "I will see what is keeping the master." He kissed her hand, looked into her eyes and winked at her mischievously.

"How long has Gabriel of Lyon been in your employ?" Baudoin asked.

"I don't know. I haven't taken notice. One or two seasons, perhaps. He is a lord himself, you know. He once saved the life of my father and came to know him that way. You do not like him, do you."

"It is not for me to like or dislike any in your employ."

"Many do not like him. None of my father's vassals do. Perhaps they are jealous, you think?"

"It seems that you like him."

"He treats me not as a child."

"Your mother seems smitten, too."

"My mother?" Adelina repeated, surprised.

"I saw your mother with him last night. I heard them."

"So? Often she talks with him."

"I think he performs more than his obligatory duties."

"What do you mean?"

"I heard them last night. It went on for half the night. Squeaks and groans and gasps. It was very distracting."

"Squeaks and groans and gasps?" Adelina repeated.

"Is it that you are deaf? You repeat almost everything I say."

"What you say sometimes surprises me. Why would there be squeaks and groans and gasps?"

"Do you know anything of the world?"

"Yes, but squeaks and groans and gasps between my mother and Gabriel? If you assume what I believe you assume, it cannot be. She is old and ugly."

"Your mother? I do not think so."

"You look upon my mother that way?"

"No. But much can be overlooked by one who has much to gain. What did Gabriel say when we rode out?"

"That we must not ride alone."

"Where did he stay whilst in Paris?"

"With his sister, I believe."

"Adelina, something is wrong." Baudoin pulled his horse to a stop and it paced, impatient. Hers by now was very tired and would not go beyond a plodding walk. Even its ears it was too tired to raise.

Baudoin scanned the hillsides, and he even looked down into the ravines below where the river ran wildly.

"Baudoin? What is it?"

He glanced at her and turned his horse about. "Best we ride with the others. Gabriel speaks truths. I cannot protect you alone. Not here. Not now."

"We can wait here. My horse is tired, poor thing."

"Not here, no. The woods have eyes. Can you not feel them?"

"But I am ready for anything," she said, touching the sword which lay in its scabbard and banged constantly against her left knee.

Baudoin grabbed her reins and turned her horse about, smacked its rear hard. "Go back!"

She had no time to argue. The horse cantered off down the steep slope, the one it had groaned with each step to climb. Close behind was Baudoin.

The party was only a few minutes behind, and this day, Robert was feeling well enough to ride again with Henri Dupuy. Acelin was boredly driving the carriage and beside him, Gabriel. The Dupuy knights rode behind.

Robert looked up when he saw his daughter cantering towards him, Baudoin close behind.

"What is it?"

"Baudoin says the woods have eyes."

Henri Dupuy sighed and sent two of his two knights to forward scout.

"Adelina, ride with your mother."

"But Papa…"

"Do as I say!"

"Papa, no! I know what to do if there is a skirmish with robbers!"

Robert raised his hand and struck, and Adelina fell on her behind in the mud. Then he was off his horse, pulling her to her feet and ready to hit her again if she tried to argue. But the shock of being hit by her father was enough to silence her into submission. He had never hit her before, not even when she was a child and deserved it. One of his huge bellows, or an icy stare had always been enough. He pushed her into the carriage and secured the doors tight.

Adelina glanced at her mother who turned her face the other way. The journey continued, eventually, and Adelina kept her hand on her face. It still stung and no doubt had left a reminder there.

"Perhaps you will now learn never to question your father."

The climb was rough and slow and so steep that Marys had to hold tight. Then they were almost at the highest point and the carriage came to a stop. Was Acelin resting the horses? There was much talk outside. Adelina tried to open the door and could not.

"Do not question, we shall be told nothing."

"But I feel now what Baudoin felt this morning, Mama."

She watched horrified as her mother began to take off her jewelery—rings, bracelets and a necklace that had belonged to her grandmother and one day would belong to Adelina. "Mama, what are you doing?"

Marys said nothing. She kept her jewelery shielded by her hands, in her lap. In her eyes there was nothing. Nothing at all. They could not see out now because the wooden windows were secured tight. Down another slope they went, and this time it was Adelina holding tight in case she slid on to the floor.

Then she heard it. The calls, the yelling, the battle cries, the brakes coming on to the carriage, rough, jerking. It was an attack, the robbery that Baudoin had sensed earlier. Sounds of bolts pelted through the air and ended with thuds. More calls, more cries, sword against sword. Bolts hit the wood of the carriage, splitting it, allowing slivers of daylight in. Then someone outside was using an axe against the carriage. Adelina grabbed her mother and they huddled together on the floor of the carriage. Marys said nothing except a repetitive prayer in a fearful whisper.

The axe stopped its onslaught, more bolts flew.

After a short while, the cries subsided, and there was silence. It was very loud. And then the carriage door was pulled open and Gabriel stood there. In his hand a bloodied sword. He was breathless.

Adelina pushed him out of her way and did not hear what he had to say. It was raining again, hard, but she did not feel it. On the track lay Acelin, poor Acelin, a target for four crossbow bolts and probably the first of them all to fall. She stepped over him in the mud. She could not find her father anywhere. "Papa! Papa!" she called but heard no reply.

To her left, the mountainside, to her right, the steep drop to the river below, but the fog was thickening and she could see little. Still she called for her father.

"Adelina!" It was Baudoin, and she ran to the sound. He was crouched by his father who lay in mud, a bolt protruding from his hip. Further down the track lay a scatter of bodies, bodies she did not recognise because of the thickness of the fog but all of the knights, except for poor Acelin, were alive.

"Where is my father!"

"Help her find Robert," Henri Dupuy said above his own agony. "I will live."

Adelina, calling wildly, again heard her voice return amid the silence.

For some lengthy minutes, no one could find Robert de Polignac until there was a call from afar and below, a call that all able followed. One of the Dupuy knights, Antoine, was making his slippery way down the embankment towards the river where a lame, saddled horse was seen. Beside the horse, on the ground, Robert de Polignac.

"Papa!" Adelina screamed.

Baudoin was not quick enough to stop the girl and he had to run, as she was running, and slipping and sliding and rolling down to the river.

"Papa, no. No!" She did not know where to look, or what to do. He was still alive, but barely, and he could not talk. An arrow was in his throat, and two crossbolts protruded from his body. Each had shattered his chain mail. His beard was bloodied, his eyes were open, and one knee was raised from where he had attempted to get up. He tried to say something to his daughter but no words emerged. Around him was a gathering but his daughter's tears were his last sight.

"Papa, no! No!"

She threw herself on to her father's body and it took both Antoine and Gabriel to lift her off. She fought like a wild cat until she had no strength left and she collapsed weakly into Gabriel's arms.

He looked up the steep embankment to the mountain track. High up on the roadway stood Marys, alone, her hand covering her mouth.

Gabriel whispered to himself and ignored Baudoin Dupuy who repeatedly ordered, "Give her to me! Give her to me!"

# Chapter 20

Geoffrey woke with a choked scream. It was another terrible dream. Once awake, though, he was almost clear of mind, except for Adelina's face, still lingering in his mind's eye, still haunting him. Even in his nightmares he could hear her calling his name.

Something had become of her, something had happened to her, that much he knew. Nothing could relieve the naggings within or the strangeness which had been with him since the previous dawn, and now it was nearing dawn of the following day.

Geoffrey sat up and ran his fingers through his hair, across his face. He rose from his new bed and lit a candle from the firecoals, took the roll of parchment from his chest and he unsealed it carefully, without a sound. He did not want to wake the others.

It was true that he had painstakingly written a poem for her, a full year ago now. The words had come when, one day in the dim past, he had watched from his tower window, the young beauty below as she wandered through her mother's roses, touching, smelling, and no doubt, singing as she always did when she thought none could hear. If any heard, there was always trouble.

Will Baudoin Dupuy allow song within his house? Geoffrey wondered. If he will, then my love, my life, may find some happiness. Some.

Geoffrey looked to his brother, nestled close and naked against the serving girl. She too was asleep in his embrace. The life of a monk I may as well lead, Geoffrey thought. Not much is left for me now.

He looked down at the words he had written for Adelina and he whispered those words to himself as he read. But they did not rhyme and she liked rhymes. Geoffrey rubbed at his face again and let the parchment roll itself up. He resealed it, tapped it against his hand. He hadn't the time to give it to her on the last day he had seen her. Not that she would understand, not that she would care. She was no longer a child, and was promised to another now. It was futile. For a moment, Geoffrey almost held the roll to the candleflame, but destroying words of the heart would not help him love her less, nor would it rid his mind of her face, her eyes. Her face it had been which roused him from sleep so quickly: her words, Geoffrey, Geoffrey… What had happened? Three weeks gone with no news was far too long a time.

Geoffrey put the roll back in its place and sat by the fire. He did not know that Agnes was watching him as he teased the coals with a poker, much as a bored child would poke at a dead insect. But he was very aware of Agnes easing out from his brother's useless embrace. She was light of foot, yet the floorboards creaked and Geoffrey did not look as she sank to her knees beside his chair. She said nothing as she pulled her rags around her tight. The night was hot, why was she cold? Geoffrey looked down at her. She was perhaps his age, but with women as ageless as her, it was difficult to tell. Sometimes, especially when she was laughing, she seemed very young, and at other times, as when Christian had decided that trying to regain a little of what he once had was futile, Agnes seemed very old. Perhaps she was as Geoffrey, neither nor, yet far beyond the stage now where she should have been wed. She should have been married and a mother many times over by now.

"Again, you cannot sleep," she said softly.

Geoffrey continued poking at the firecoals. The lights there seemed as dead as he felt inside.

"Will you worry yourself into the ground because of the lady Adelina?" she asked.

"I have always worried of her."

"Why?"

"I do not know why, girl. Perhaps it is because of an ancient promise. A promise I made when I was a child. The very day she was born. And each day since I have kept this promise."

"To who?"

"If I said, it would not be a promise, would it."

"Even Christian whispers her name."

"They were to be wed so that the lands would remain in the Polignac name."

Agnes reached up and put her hand on Geoffrey's knee. His heart beat quickly, unexpectedly, because of her sudden, warm touch. "You carry the Polignac name also."

"But I am not worthy of it. Or so it seems."

"No. You are more than worthy. This is what I believe."

"Agnes, it matters not what you believe. My fate is sealed."

There was silence for a while. "Today, will you visit the abbot?"

"Today has not yet come."

The night's darkness was slowly fading though. Perhaps he had not noticed. "Monsieur, why did you choose me to work in your household?"

"The reasons are best known by me alone."

"I am pleased that you did."

"As I am, girl. You serve us well."

"I can serve you in many ways, Monsieur," she added softly and rested her face against his knee. Geoffrey sighed and touched her hair. It was not as long as Adelina's, and paler too, and she had the same heart-shaped face, but that was where the similarities ended. Geoffrey liked her but she was far too close. He wanted to move away but her face was on his knee now and she was looking up at him. "I remember the first day I saw you. You were quelling a dispute peacefully."

Geoffrey did not remember seeing her, and which dispute would it have been, and where?

"When I saw you, I remember thinking that one day we would meet and then I would see not from a distance, the sparkle I knew lay in your eyes. I have been here, safe and warm and fed for many weeks now but I have not seen your eyes sparkle. All I feel is your unending sadness. It is as if you are lost and cannot be found."

She sighed and Geoffrey hoped that was all she would say. He was very uncomfortable.

"I, too, have felt as you feel now, lost and unable to be found again. But I promise you that you will find your way again. Happiness will come. It did for me."

"How is it you were lost, girl?" Geoffrey asked, his voice no more than a whisper.

"I was there when my father was killed."

"And how was this?"

"He was beheaded by a drunken knight who took offence at my father's song. I had nothing, then. I had no one. We used to travel, my father and I. We traveled all over the land, and suddenly I was alone. I prayed to God to help me and I wondered for a long time what I had done so wrong that made God hate me so. Then, I came here, to this place. I followed pilgrims on their way to Le Puy, but here it was I stayed. The people were kind but none as kind as you. Kindness seems not to exist in our world now. Others are jealous of my place here and wish me ill. Others would give much to be where I am now and this is the price I pay. But the price is not great at all, for now I have a home. I am indebted to you, Geoffrey."

The warm hand on his knee was moving and caressing. Geoffrey was transfixed by fear, for he knew very well where this encounter was leading. He had been laughed at once and swore he would never be laughed at again but his body would not obey his mind's command to remain impassive.

"I see in your eyes how much you love the lady Adelina. I feel how your heart breaks as you can never have her." Agnes rose to her knees. She took the poker from his hand and put it down and played her fingers against his skin as if he were a jeweled harp. She touched his face, too, but Geoffrey did nothing except look at her curiously. "If other things occupy your thoughts, then perhaps the sparkle which the lady took with her will return to your eyes."

She loosed the drawstring of her nightdress and it fell off one shoulder. Geoffrey touched. She was warm and soft and so very thin. He loosed the string further and Agnes did not catch the nightdress when it fell. She stepped out of it and Geoffrey stared at the length of her before he reached out and again, touched.

Agnes lay down at his feet in front of the fire and reached up for him. There was a moment's hesitation in which Geoffrey looked to his brother's bed. Christian was still facing the wall and deeply asleep.

There was no one here now who was likely to laugh.

"Come," she said. "Lie with me. Now, while it is not a sin in the eyes of God."

Geoffrey stepped out of his drawers and lay on the hard floor beside Agnes. He raised on elbow and touched her again, from ear to shoulder, breast and belly, thigh and upturned knee. Still very unsure, he lowered his head and kissed her mouth and soon enough, no thoughts or sadness remained. Nor was there any shame or laughter, or dull, aching pains which lasted indefinitely. There was only a heady aftertaste, like a warm, rich wine on a cold night. He was warm inside, warm and happy, and filled with strange emotion as she lay quietly in his arms, asleep against his body. He kissed her hair as she slept and he whispered a name. But it was not Agnes's name he uttered.

As the sun appeared, Geoffrey finally fell asleep.

And Christian was watching.

"We are nearly home," Baudoin said. Adelina said nothing in return. She had said nothing for one day and one night. Her lips were closed tight and it seemed that she would never speak again.

Her mother rode accompanied by Henri who lay wrapped in a blanket within the carriage, too gravely injured to ride. Each hour the party stopped, if only to see that Henri Dupuy still lived.

Baudoin rode one-handed, leading Adelina's horse with his other. Antoine rode ahead to alert Heloise and the doctor at Allegre. Barely a word had passed since Gabriel had thrust Adelina into his arms, the day before. She had only cried the once yet Marys had done little but weep for a very long time.

Although she said nothing, Baudoin knew Adelina blamed him for the ambush. And ambush it had been, not a robbery, although it appeared as one. It seemed to Baudoin that the three targets had been chosen ones. First to fall was Acelin, driving the carriage. Then Henri, then Robert as he spurred out, sword high to attack one fleeing robber. Crossbolts and arrows flew around Baudoin, not into him, and there must have been excellent archers amid the attacking party, for Antoine and Baudoin rode in front of Robert and Henri yet were missed. Had he not beheaded the one with axe attacking the carriage, Baudoin knew Adelina would be dead as well.

Adelina and her mother.

Or perhaps, as he considered it further, just the mother.

For in reality, the girl was too valuable to kill.

Again, he glanced back at Gabriel of Lyon. He was riding behind with Francois, seemingly unperturbed as he one-handed, led the horse which carried his lord's wrapped body. A body already beginning to rot in the sweltering heat.

"Adelina?"

Adelina turned her head and expressionless eyes only half saw Baudoin Dupuy. "We are nearly home now." He expected she would say, your home is not my home but she nodded, vaguely. "I must tend my father first and when he is comfortable and has received attention for his wound, I will escort you and your mother home."

"I will escort the women to their home."

Baudoin looked back at Gabriel again. "She is my woman, Gabriel of Lyon. My responsibility begins now."

"I said I would escort them home. There is no allegiance yet, Dupuy. I have it in writing that I am now in charge of all Polignac affairs. All. You understand?"

"This is idiocy," Baudoin said.

Adelina, it seemed, had been wrenched from her misery by Gabriel's news. "When was this arranged?" she asked.

"Before we departed for St. Denis. Your father sensed his own mortality after standing over the deathbed of that knight..." Gabriel seemed to fight for a name.

"Raoul," Adelina said. "His name was Raoul." With a heavy heart, she remembered her father's words as they stood on the bridge, both looking down into the murky waters. Should I die...

"Convenient, Gabriel of Lyon. It seems very convenient indeed. I take it that Lady Polignac knows of this, too?"

"Of course she knows."

"And the remaining Polignac vassals?"

"As I said, it is none of your affair. The allegiance is not lawful yet and will not be until November. If it will be at all. As I said, and as I will keep saying, I am now in charge."

"You would go against the wishes of your dead master?"

Gabriel said nothing and only God Himself knew what lay behind the man's eyes as he rode in silence until Adelina said, "Baudoin shall take me home."

"You will come with me."

"Baudoin will take me home. All you need do is attend my mother. It is she who needs you, Gabriel. Only she. I will never submit to any man's authority now that my father is dead."

Her gaze met Gabriel's and neither's wavered. And Baudoin hoped that her nature would soon change for the better, for he knew, how he knew, the length of time a woman of her ways would last in the Dupuy house.

At Allegre, she did not even wish her mother goodbye. Nor did she say she would soon be home. Since Robert's death, not one word had passed between the two.

She had sat upon a horse at these imposing gates once before, but this time there was no fear felt. Nothing at all was felt. If was as if her heart had been torn out and replaced by a cold rock the size of her fist. The gates duly opened and the procession entered. Adelina did not look for the woman in black lingering by the doors for she knew there would not be one. For almost three weeks, Heloise had been alone in her dim house with an aged knight and servants only as protectors and company. Adelina again saw herself aged and standing by a window, alone. She turned her attentions to her horse's head until she felt the tap on her thigh. She looked down. It was Baudoin silently offering to help her down. Adelina moved in the saddle and slid off but her knees did not hold her upright. Baudoin's strong hands stopped her from falling. She was shaking still as he guided her into the house, calling for boys to water the animals.

Once inside, she watched as Baudoin took his wounded father in his arms and upstairs. Soon, the doctor from Allegre would arrive. The big, gloomy house echoed with gloomier voices and Adelina leaned against the wall and stared at her shoes for a long while. Then came silence, punctured only by one long, fierce bellow of pain. A man's pain.

Then an aged knight came down the stairs and saw her standing alone but he swept by, without a word. The silence echoed, how it echoed, until Antoine and the doctor came into the house. And they, too, knew not that she stood there. She had come to know each of these Dupuy knights except for the father who would not even look at her, or be drawn into conversation with her. Now he was dying, too. Or so it seemed. What will be? she wondered, afraid. What will be? Her tears burned at her eyes but she refused to allow them exit for crying was what a woman would do and crying served no purpose whatever.

She seemed to stand for so long that her legs ached. No one came and offered her a chair and there was none to be seen but she dared not venture off to find one in this gloomy house, alone. She was frightened of what may have lay in the darkness. So she sat on the floor and it was not enough. Weary, she lay down, and for the first time in many hours, she slept almost immediately.

It was the sound of knees cracking which roused her from a needed dreamless sleep. She woke quickly, muscles aching. It was not Baudoin, but Francois, the aged knight who had accompanied them such a long way. In his hand, a tray, and on it, a trencher with meat, and a bowl of soup, a hunk of bread, and half an apple. It was late, now. Very late. She wondered how long it had been since she first closed her eyes.

"I cannot eat, Francois. I cannot."

He smiled as if he knew it was a lie. "Try, Milady."

Adelina sat up and leaned her head against the wall, took one look at the food and shook her head. Francois put the tray on the floor and folded his hands as he crouched. "We have beds here, Milady."

Adelina stared at the soup but could not eat. "I thank you for this, but I cannot. Where is Baudoin? Has he forgotten his promise to take me home?"

"He tends his mother."

"She is ill?"

Francois nodded. "She has been for all our time absent, it seems."

"May I see her, Francois?"

Francois reached for her hand and he led her upstairs and down the dark passageway, past many rooms until he stopped and knocked upon the door of Heloise's chambers.

"How is Henri?" Adelina asked.

"The doctor still does not know."

"The doctor knows little. May I see your master before I leave?"

"I am not the one to ask," he said and knocked again. Down the passageway came a boy, lighting the torches. It was very late indeed. Baudoin had forgotten her, that much she knew.

It was Baudoin who opened the door of his mother's room. Adelina saw immediately that his eyes were very red. Had he been crying? A man? Crying? "Lady Adelina wishes to see our lady," Francois said.

Baudoin turned his face away quickly and stepped aside. Adelina said nothing. Heloise lay in her bed, her face was turned to the wall, and on the covers of the bed lay a book. Baudoin had been reading to her. Adelina stepped to the bed. "Milady?"

Heloise turned to the sound of the young voice and her face brightened at once. "You have come. You said you would."

Baudoin quickly left the chambers and Francois followed him.

"I knew you would come back. They said you were dead, but I

knew you could not be. Sit, Vianna. Sit."

She calls me that name again, Adelina thought, but did not protest. Tonight, the lady looked very strange indeed. Adelina sat on the edge of the bed and Heloise reached for her hand, touching her fingers, then holding tightly. So close, she smelled of rotten apples.

"Why did you not bring Marys?"

"She has gone home to Lavoute Polignac with Gabriel."

"Gabriel? Do I know him?"

"No, Milady. You do not."

"Then how long has Marys lived at Lavoute Polignac?"

"Lady Dupuy?"

"Vianna, what is this nonsense? Why do you call me lady?"

She has lost her mind. She thinks I am my mother's sister again.

"Sing for me, Vianna. Sing for me, take away the pain."

"I cannot, Lady Dupuy. I cannot sing. My songs have long since died," Adelina said, tears burning once again.

"Your songs shall never die. Sing me the song that Robert loved."

Adelina thought she was strong until this woman mentioned her father's name. "Do I know it?" was all she could think of to ask, her voice shaking.

"Yes, of course you know it. It is the one where she waits for her lover to come home. She stands by the window, waiting. You know it. It is yours. You said it is Robert's favorite. How were the words? Yes, I remember." A strange glow came upon Heloise's eyes as she whispered: I wait within these castle walls, my fine gown spread out on my window seat, my silver needle rises and falls on my coloured silks with stitches neat... There is more. You know it. It is yours. You wrote it for Robert, can you not remember it now?"

"But that was so long ago, Milady. So long ago that I do not remember it all." Help me, Adelina's mind screamed silently. I cannot bear another moment of this.

"Yes. It was. It was very long ago." Heloise fell silent and studied Adelina closely, her old knotted, misshapen fingers touching Adelina's face, and she did not pull away. "Why have you never grown old?" she asked.

"But I am not old," Adelina said. "Milady, I am not Vianna. I am Adelina. Robert is... Robert was my father."

"I want... I need..." Heloise sighed and agony hit her eyes and remained there for a long time.

"What ails you, Milady?" Adelina asked, unable to contain those acid tears and when the agony passed, Heloise did not recognise Adelina at all.

"Where is Jean-Pierre? Who are you? Where is my son? Where is

Jean-Pierre?"

Adelina got off the bed quickly and ran to the door because Heloise was calling now, impatiently, for her dead son. But it was Baudoin who answered his mother's calls. "Yes, mother, I am here." To Adelina at the door, he said in a whisper, "When she settles we must talk. It is too late to take you home now. Here you must stay till morning."

"But I have no escort, no chaperone."

"I am to be your husband, or have you forgotten?"

From her bed, Heloise still called for Jean-Pierre. Adelina could not take any more, so she walked out and the door closed behind her. She heard Baudoin say again, "Yes, Mother, I am here. I am here."

Francois came down the passageway. He was so tired. In his hand, a chair for her. He put it down and she sat on it, weary, upset. Francois did not walk away though. He stood beside her for a little while and they both listened to the agonised cries of the lady from her room. Adelina wiped at her eyes tiredly as she tried to hold back more tears. Francois' knees objected again when he crouched and he said softly, "Milady, your father was a fair man. A good man. Once, I knew him well, but it was a long time ago. In time your pain will ease. I assure you, it will." And he reached for her hand. At the touch, the tears came unchecked.

Until now, all sympathies were for Marys. Until now. Francois held her hand tightly, then his arm went around her for that was all she seemed—a little girl. He only let go when Baudoin came from his mother's room and closed the door. She was still calling for Jean-Pierre.

"Come," Baudoin said. "I do not know how it is with you, but I am tired and weary and I am also hungry. Come with me, Addie. Then we may both be able to sleep."

Baudoin walked her off down the passageway and took one of the torches from the wall as he went. "It is good that you cry," he said softly, wanting to himself but knowing he could never, unless he took himself out into the woods where none could see or hear and then let forth. "What did Francois say to upset you?"

"I can never be upset by kindness and truth."

Baudoin led her into the kitchen and he roused the cook, an ancient old man who studied Adelina with great interest. "He has not the talents of your Ella, but his food keeps us alive." And it was here, in the small kitchen, where she finally ate.

"How is your father?" she asked as she dipped her bread into her soup.

"If his will was stronger he may live."

"Your mother?"

"Some agonizing affliction of the body that has also touched her mind, now. I should not have gone to Paris at all. I should have remained here."

"And what is it you could have done for her had you stayed?"

"That is not the point."

There was silence for a short while.

"What will we do now, Baudoin?"

He looked into her eyes and shook his head. "I do not know. They say bury the dead and continue living. Is that not what your father would have wanted us to do?"

"I do not know. Papa could never farewell those he loved. He said nothing, of course, but ... it is not important now."

Adelina noticed that Baudoin's hand shook a little as he lifted the wooden spoon to his mouth. In her house, the spoons were of silver.

"I am sorry."

Baudoin looked up, very surprised.

"I am sorry if I have upset you in the past. I do not know why I act as I do. I am sorry that I am not your Eleanor. I am sorry that this has to be when I know that it is not me you want. But be this way it must, for it is the wish of our fathers. And if I have anything of my father in me, then I will always uphold his wishes for he was more right than wrong. Always."

"Why are you apologizing for things beyond your control?"

"I needed you to hear me. It seems you can listen to the voice of a woman. Most men do not."

He thought about that and smiled, and then it faded. "Gabriel of Lyon worries me. I don't know what he plans."

"Be assured that Gabriel thinks only of Gabriel. All else matter not unless they are of use."

"It seems so."

"It is so. I need to talk with your father, Baudoin. I cannot have him die without telling him that I am not a monster or a spoiled child. I am not his enemy."

"And if he will not hear you?"

"I am used to not being heard. I am a woman," she said, her eyes stinging yet again.

Baudoin regarded her strangely. Very strangely. Then he put his spoon down and he reached across the table and he took both her hands in his. "Then we shall do what we must. Addie," he added softly and tried hard to smile. As she did, in return.

# CHAPTER 21

"You will sleep here," Baudoin said as he opened the door to a very dusty room, a huge bedchamber much like the one her parents shared. But this bedchambers had not been used for a long time. It was not especially gloomy, but nor was it welcoming. There was a wash bowl laid out and someone had attempted to rid the room of dust in such a hurry that failure was certain. On the bed lay a nightdress, one of Lady Dupuy's, far too big.

Adelina's clothing had traveled home with her mother.

"My chamber door is not locked," Baudoin said and stepped from the room, pointing down the passageway. Then he looked back at Adelina. He hesitated for a moment. "My mother is dying," he said, his eyes expressionless.

"I smelled it on her skin," Adelina said. "She reeks of death."

"She thinks I am Jean-Pierre."

"She thinks I am the sister of my mother who died when I was born."

"She knows not what she says. It is best that you take little notice, because all you will be, if you listen to what she says, is hurt. It has been that way for some years. She worsens daily now. The doctor today said it is only a matter of time. I say this to you, because I shall not have the time to visit you or court you as necessary. It is not that I would neglect such duties but time is my enemy. Much is required of me here, and I cannot be here and there and everywhere else at once." He tried to smile.

Mother and Jennet are right, Adelina thought. He is very handsome. Very.

"But I will visit when I am able. There is much to be planned. With the wedding, I mean." Baudoin almost touched her face but he hesitated again and rubbed his neck instead. "We should depart at dawn. Sleep well."

He closed the door.

There was only one torch for light. No candles were seen anywhere. Adelina opened the door quickly. "Baudoin!"

He looked back as he walked toward his room.

"I cannot sleep in the dark. I need candles or someone with me."

"We cannot afford to use candles unnecessarily in this house."

"But I cannot sleep without some light."

Baudoin walked back to her. "What lies in the darkness which is not there in the light of day?"

"All manner of evils. My mind plays tricks, tricks which seem very real."

"Addie, we have no spare candles and we cannot sleep in the same room. Not yet."

A child's eyes looked up at him. A child's eyes glowing from the face of a woman. Baudoin relented. "I suppose I can sit here until you sleep if that will help."

"And if I wake suddenly in darkness and none is here?"

"You will not wake. The day has been a long, tiring one. I will sit till you sleep. I need my sleep, too."

He came in and closed the door, turning his back while she took off the tunic and hose and threw his mother's nightdress over her head. "Is it true that you hate only my name?" she asked as she washed her face of the day's sweat with the cold water.

"I do not know if ever it was hate now that I have come to know you."

"But you will not take me to your father."

"There has been much sadness already. I have no wish to burden you with more." He heard the bed squeak and turned. She was watching him from under the covers. Baudoin made himself comfortable in the chair.

"If your father would see beyond my face and my name, he may think as you do."

"My father sees what he wishes to see and nothing else. It is not wise and nor is it important that all must like you when the one who should already does." His smile was warm, so very warm. Adelina longed to touch him, to hold his hand again but he sat at a distance, his arms folded. She cuddled further down into the soft bed and sighed. It was much better than hers at the chateau.

"Do you like music, Baudoin Dupuy?"

"Some, Adelina de Polignac."

She smiled to herself. Whenever she called him by his full name, he did the same to her. "I sing, you know. The sister of my mother, Vianna, used to sing, too. Or so I am told. I am not allowed song in my house. Is song allowed in this house?"

"Is it allowed? Yes. I think so. The servants sometimes sing and their heads remain intact."

"Oh, it is not that bad at my house," she growled.

"Well, I like song," he said. "But not sad ones."

"More notice is taken of sad songs. Sad songs touch the heart more than happy ones do."

"Sleep now. You chatter too much," he said, yawning and rubbing his face. Adelina yawned, too, closed her eyes and was, finally, peaceful and quiet.

Baudoin watched her for a short time but he thought of nothing and was so tired that he felt even less. He rose, his leather squeaked. She did not wake as he knew she would not. But sleep he had little of, between his father's calls and his mother's cries.

In the morning, Adelina found Baudoin in the courtyard. Her horse was saddled and looked as eager as she did for another journey. She scratched the horse's nose as Baudoin greeted her: he too, was still weary.

"Have you changed your mind about my visit to your father before I go?"

"No. I have not."

"Best we leave then."

"Have you eaten?"

"I shall wait until I get home."

"You do not like our food."

"I shall wait until I get home."

As they rode, together, alone, through Allegre, Adelina noticed that some fields were being worked by men and women while very small children played with sticks in the dirt. And as they passed, there was not the hatred, the outbursts as there had been once before, but silence. An awesome silence. "I misjudged you."

"How so?" Baudoin asked.

"I had thought that you would keep the food for yourselves."

"It was distributed fairly."

"Gabriel would never have allowed such a thing."

"Yes, I know. Gabriel would have attacked us at our weakest to ensure victory."

Adelina watched the children at play, especially two boys too small as yet to carry harvest sheaves. They were fighting with sticks, wielding imaginary broadswords. "I used to do that. The boys are lucky to have each other. I had none except friends no other could see."

"Yes, I know."

She turned to him. "How is it you know?"

"I would hide in the woods and watch you on the rampart. I would be planning my own attacks. I saw you fall from the wall once. I was going to come along and finish you but I galloped home instead the moment I saw your father."

"Such a story."

"It is true. Your father saw me hiding, and asked was I lost. I ran off, terrified. I had listened to too many tales of the savagery of your family."

"But my family are not savages."

"Nor is mine."

She was too tired to argue. "Soon there will be no fighting. No hunger."

"No hunger providing it rains here when it is needed the most."

"For the crops?"

"Yes, for the crops."

They rested awhile at the place where Baudoin had first saved her from the raging storm. And they sat together, too, on the grass by the roadside, but he kept a good distance away.

"You seem not hurried to get home."

"I go home to death, Baudoin. Funerals. I do not like them. I do not know how I will be. My father and Acelin... I once thought they would never die."

"Tarrying does not make the ordeal go away."

"Will you come?"

"Yes, if Gabriel of Lyon allows Dupuy presence. I fear he will not. He still sees me as the enemy and always will."

"I will make him allow it."

"He does not take orders from you, Adelina. He is the master of Lavoute Polignac now."

"No. All is mine now. I am his master."

"I wish you well, then. I know I am right."

They climbed back onto their horses and continued the ride but he did not gallop off along his short cut. He took the road this time. They crossed the river near Vialette. Home was very close now but hidden in the mountains. On they rode, in silence. Baudoin did not speak of the weather, nor she of anything for it seemed that no conversation was needed. Adelina was very comfortable in Baudoin's company and he in hers.

And once upon the damned stretch of roadway, three chain long, Baudoin stopped his horse and sighed. "Had my brother any brains at all, none of this would have happened."

"But happen, it has."

Over the rise and beyond, the chateau gates. The bridge was up. It looked no different but it was a sight Adelina had longed many weeks to see. She called to the sentry to lower the bridge and glanced at Baudoin as they waited.

"It is all mine now," she said. "Yet it feels no different. As if it still belongs to my father; as if nothing has changed."

Baudoin said nothing. To him, it seemed that she was thinking aloud again.

"These walls will remain long after I am gone. Geoffrey says things of the earth we never own. We simply borrow them for the time we are alive. We borrow and fight and steal for things which remain long after we have all died. Does that make sense to you, Baudoin?"

Again, he said nothing, but he nodded.

"Always though, this will belong to the Polignacs. The name may change but always the Polignac heart will beat here. Strong and undying."

Baudoin sighed. He allowed Adelina to ride across the bridge first and listened to the excited calls of boy and servant alike—Milady is back! Milady is back!

Ella appeared from her kitchen wiping her hands as she ran towards Adelina. She was howling again, howling as she prepared the funeral feast no doubt. Adelina slid off the horse and embraced the old kitchen maid tightly. Baudoin looked away and hoped she did not treat the servants at Allegre in the same way.

Louis appeared, his face lined with misery and behind him, Dedwyd, who, too, seemed sullen yet silently happy to see her home, safe and well.

This is all who remain now? Adelina thought as she embraced Louis. There is only this man left from the many who used to belong here. "Where does my father lie?" she asked.

"In the great hall, Milady."

"And the funeral?"

"Tomorrow."

Adelina turned to Baudoin and said, "Will you not stay a little while?"

"No, I must go back. I have told you why."

"Goodbye, then, Baudoin. I shall see you again one day."

"Adelina," he said and nodded and turned his horse about. Louis ordered the bridge raised once Dupuy had crossed it, and he took Adelina's arm as she attempted to go into the chateau.

"Milady," he said. "It is not a sight I recommend for you."

"Sight?"

"Your father."

"Louis, I was there when he breathed his last. He died in my arms.

He is my father and you cannot stop me. Where is my mother?"

"In her chambers, I believe."

"Gabriel?"

"I do not know. Somewhere."

"Find him."

"Milady?" he asked, still he had not let go of her arm.

"What," she demanded, trying to shake off his hand.

"I must leave this place."

"What?" Huge green eyes stared at him in disbelief.

"I have been dismissed. Gabriel sends soon for vassals more to his liking. I am dismissed. Tomorrow, I must depart."

"To where?"

"I do not know as yet."

"No. This cannot be. You will go nowhere. Your place is here. This is your place, Louis!"

"It is ordered of the new master. Gabriel."

"I am the master now."

"Milady…"

"I said, I am the master now and you will go nowhere!" She pushed Louis out of her way and walked into the kitchen where Ella wept as she worked, and up the stairs Adelina went. But she came to a sudden halt in the great hall.

Her father lay in his best of dress, his battle armor, his hands were folded, his eyes closed and covered with two gold coins. She stood, numbly, the only sound the beat of her heart. Adelina put her hand over her face for the smell was abominable. Incense burned which made it worse. Far worse. The casket was surrounded by lit candles, and freshly cut lavender was piled on the floor.

In that box lay her father but it was not the man she knew and loved. It seemed that this body was nothing but a shell. All who passed by would have dropped to their knees and howled at the sight but she did not. She felt instead a touch on her shoulder and she turned but no one was there. From the corner of her eye she saw someone on the stairs.

"Geoffrey?"

She walked across the huge hall but whoever it was had gone up the winding stairs before her. She followed, catching only a glimpse of cloak or topcoat, perhaps. Up she went quickly, past the knights' chambers, past hers, up still past her mother's closed door, to the very top. To her father's room—the room which was his and his alone. But no one was here. No one. Where had the person gone who had been leading her this far? Who had touched her? Adelina opened the door to her father's retreat.

She did not see the paintings of her father's ancestors on the walls, nor did she see his books, or his ancient armors, nor did she see his beautiful gilded chair. She saw her mother instead, with her dress unlaced and hanging to her hips. Behind her was Gabriel, almost naked, too. Both were making terrible noises and he was sweating and groaning.

She'd seen this before. Farm animals did this.

She stood in the doorway, staring for quite some time, and unseen. Then Gabriel turned her mother to him, kissed her. He lifted her on to Robert's table, clearing it with one hand. Her father's treasures and keepsakes clattered to the floor. And Marys moaned and laughed and moaned. Old, hanging breasts in Gabriel's hands, in his mouth, too. Such a noise it was, joyful, happy, until he climbed on top of her mother and began his thrusting again.

Adelina, sickened, put her hand to her mouth and closed the door as quietly as she could. She was shaking as she went down the stairs slowly, numb again. Past her father's casket, she floated, still numb. She did not see Ella, huddled over her food. Adelina went to the stables, saddled her horse, called to the sentry to lower the bridge, which he did.

And she was gone.

Agnes rarely left him alone for any length of time but today she had to fetch water from the river. When she had said, "Now, you will sit and you will not go anywhere, oui?" to him as if he were a child, he had only looked up into her eyes and away again, slowly. Where once she imagined affection present there in his bright eyes, nothing was there today. Nothing at all. "What is wrong?" Agnes had asked. He turned his head away.

"Christian?"

He was angry with her. "What have I done?" she had asked. But he was not talking today. As much as he did talk of course, but she had been here long enough to know what he wanted, and when, and sometimes even why. They were in fact, good friends who kept each other warm at night. She found his body a comfort, but of course, it wasn't as comforting as Geoffrey's had been. But that could and would never be again. It should not have happened, but she had no thoughts of shoulds and should nots the morning she had touched him and loved him so. She could not stop herself because he, too, was despairing then. And how well she knew what it was to love someone and it was not returned.

Agnes picked up the pail of water from the river and heaved it all the way up the hill towards the house. She stopped walking suddenly. Something felt wrong. It was a sense of foreboding and very, very strong.

And it quickly disappeared because galloping towards her, the Lady Adelina. She was soon off her horse. "Geoffrey! Where is Geoffrey!"

"Lady Adelina, he is not here."

"Where is he!" she cried, her voice full of despair.

"He is in the abbey, Milady."

Adelina was soon on her horse again, not hearing Agnes's calls that Geoffrey could not be spoken to. She kicked her horse into a canter toward the abbey.

No one answered her frantic bangings on the doors though, not for a long time. Adelina punched so hard that her knuckles bled. But eventually the doors opened and an old monk stood there, very surprised. "Lady Adelina?"

"Where is Geoffrey?"

"Who?"

"Geoffrey de Polignac! Where is he!"

The door closed in her face. Adelina again pounded upon it until she had no strength left. She turned away moments before it again opened. She looked back. Abbot Jean stood there. Abbot Jean who had never liked her, nor she him. He hated anyone who was female and it showed in his eyes and in his voice. He had always found her very distasteful and even now she did not regret having put rat droppings into his tankard, or placing dead frogs on his chair. Frogs that smelled and squashed when he sat on them unknowingly.

"You cannot see Geoffrey," was all he said.

"I must. My father is dead. Things have happened, terrible things. I must see Geoffrey. I need to know what it is he would do."

"I know that your father is dead. It is I who prepares his funeral."

"Please, Abbot Jean. Please let me see Geoffrey? Just this once?"

"His name is no longer Geoffrey de Polignac. His name is now Brother Christophe."

"No. No, his name is Geoffrey!"

"His name is Brother Christophe."

"Please, let me see him?"

"It is not possible."

Adelina, close to tears, tears of anger, said, "Is he allowed letters?"

"From you? No."

"You are a bastard, Abbot Jean, and I hope you roast in the hell of your own making!"

The old monk stood there, unperturbed by her outburst. He had been used to them for many years. "The news of the death has disturbed us all. Best that you go home now and I will see you tomorrow, here in the abbey."

"Please tell Geoffrey what has happened. Tell him that Gabriel of Lyon has now taken command of all affairs. Hell will reign now."

The abbot was not concerned in the least. "Face this new life with a brave heart and all will be well."

"That is easy for you to say. Easy for you, who locks himself away from life and pretends to obey the voice of God when the voice of God lies in the heart alone and one such as you has no heart!"

"Be careful what you say, Adelina de Polignac."

"I do not fear you, you old toad!" She turned her back and caught her grazing horse angrily. She mounted it and looked back. "You are here to help, not hinder!" She spat on the ground and cantered off.

Abbot Jean simply sighed and went back inside.

Geoffrey turned when he heard the knock on his thick door. The abbot came in. "Brother Christophe, Robert de Polignac is dead. His funeral service will be held here tomorrow."

Geoffrey's mouth dropped and for a moment his heart stilled. "My uncle is dead?" he asked as he stood and drew back his hood. His eyes implored the abbot for more information but there was none.

The abbot left the tiny room, the door clanged to a close. Geoffrey sat again, and stared unseeing at the huge book on the lectern. Then he turned his gaze to the crucifix above his cot but that, too, he did not see.

My uncle is dead?

Agnes suspended the bucket on the rope which Geoffrey had devised. He did not like seeing her struggling up the ladder with it, and he did not like carrying it up, either. It was a very ingenious device indeed but still it needed two people or the water would spill on the way up. "Christian!" she called in her sing-song voice. "Allez! Vite!"

There was no reply.

Surely he does not sleep, she wondered. It is far too hot.

"Christian? Please help me?"

Nothing.

The foreboding returned in a huge wave. Agnes, with heart in mouth or so it felt, clambered up the ladder. The bucket of fresh water soon toppled. "Christian?"

He was on his knees and very still. For a moment, she thought that perhaps he was praying like a Moor prayed. It was then that she saw the blood pooling on the floor.

Agnes scratched at her face, trying to stop her own denials but it was not possible. "No, no, it can't be," she whispered, hoarsely. She crouched beside him and touched. The touch, feather-light, was enough to topple him. Geoffrey's dagger was embedded to the hilt in his heart. And he had been crying when he died because his face was still stained with his tears. "Christian, no –" she whispered as she smoothed the hair from his face. Her denial soon became, "Why?" as she sat on the floor with him and rocked him, tightly.

It was Brother Andre who first saw the hermit-girl from the water-mill. She was struggling weakly up the grassy hill. As she drew closer Andre saw that she was bloodied and at first he thought that she was injured. Mortally. He ran to her, lifting his robe as he went, but she walked on past him, her eyes wide and glazed. She was whispering, "Geoffrey, Geoffrey?"

How popular is our Brother Christophe today, Andre thought.

# Chapter 22

"What ails you?" Gabriel asked that evening at the table. Adelina did not reply. Already he sat in her father's chair, by her mother's side. Marys was quiet, pretending of despair when her eyes held nothing but secret joy.

That afternoon, her father's body had been delivered to the abbey, and fresh air finally circulated around the great hall, but the smell of death still lingered. To Adelina, it seemed stronger than before.

"I asked what ails you." Gabriel had seen her toy with her food. She was far too silent and aggressive for his liking, but he did not believe for a moment that it was too late to teach this girl manners, show her the place where she truly belonged.

"If anything ails me, it would be no concern of yours, Gabriel of Lyon." She emphasised Lyon, with a hatefilled spark in her eye. "Since you asked, I shall tell you. My father is dead not yet buried, and you sit in his place, prouder than Philippe Augustus on his throne. Why should anything ail me?"

All's eyes were on him, except Marys's. She was too accustomed to her daughter's outbursts of disrespect. For the moment, Gabriel thought it wise to ignore it as best he could. "Henri Dupuy lives still?" he asked.

"Best if he died, too, though, yes? Then all control is yours. Or so you think. Where is this letter my father wrote? I want to see it, now."

"Adelina, have respect for those stronger," Marys said without glancing up.

"Stronger? Him?" She spat on the floor and glared at her mother. "This chateau and all its lands are mine, Mama. Mine."

"In name only, little girl," Gabriel said boredly and kept eating. "How is Geoffrey?"

She looked up, hate again in her eyes. "It seems from your smile that you already know."

"The love of your life has chosen celibacy, hair shirts and life of prayer. I would be angry, too."

"What is this?" Marys asked.

"Geoffrey. The little sparrow is now a monk."

"Robert would be pleased."

"Pleased?" Adelina cried. "The spirit of my father will never rest! You deluded him, you deluded us all!"

"Go to your chambers," Marys said.

"I am eating."

"Go to your chambers!" Gabriel bellowed.

Adelina glanced at Gabriel. He was giving her orders now? A half-smile appeared on her face and she ignored him as best she could until his third demand was ignored and he suddenly leapt from his seat, walked along the table, through the food, grabbed her by the hair and used her as leverage while he jumped to the floor. "Go or I will drag you!"

Adelina twisted in his grip and punched him on the nose. Her split knuckles screamed. He returned it, quickly, and she did not fly across the table for he still held her by the hair. Her nose bled profusely and agony lived again. She did not cry, although her eyes watered, but nor did she give in. Louis was on his feet at once to defend, as was Dedwyd.

"No! You will both sit!" she cried. "I need no man to defend me! No man, you hear!"

Gabriel let go and her knees buckled. He did not catch her as she fell. She struggled to her feet though, and took her seat again, grabbed the tablecloth to stem the blood. She glanced at her mother who did not know what to do and Adelina picked up the lamb joint, still with meat on it, and gnawed at it as if nothing had happened. But much had, and she shook fiercely.

"To your chambers."

"Why?" Adelina asked, looking up at her mother through her pained tears.

"Do as I say."

She laughed. "How are his kisses, Mama? Does he warm your naked body at night as he says he shall one day warm mine?"

"You speak nonsense!"

Adelina stared at her mother. "How could you, Mama? My father is barely cold!"

"Gabriel, what is she saying?"

He could take no more. "You wish to see your father's letter? Here!"

He threw it on to her trencher. Adelina still holding her bleeding nose, read it slowly. Words written in her father's flowing hand, words of truth, but all was a lie. She looked at Gabriel, then at her mother, who again knew not where to look, and Louis, Dedwyd. Tonight, the little archer was not smiling.

"I have decided that the wedding to Dupuy cannot wait until your birthday. You will be wed as soon as arrangements are made."

Then Baudoin will die, too, she thought. Adelina rose from the table. "Louis, escort me upstairs."

Louis hastily picked up a lump of meat and stuffed it into his mouth. He escorted his young mistress upstairs as ordered. "I wish you to be in service to me, Louis. Dedwyd, too. Perhaps you can stay with Michel until I am wed. When I am wed, you shall come to Allegre and serve me. You will be housed and fed and I shall sell my jewelery which will help costs of keeping you in service."

"The Dupuys already have their own retainers. I will not be welcome, Milady."

"Louis, you served my father faithfully, but I am now your master. That is, of course, unless you do not wish this to be so."

"I would follow you beyond the horizons, Milady. For your own sake, speak with Baudoin Dupuy first."

"This will be, Louis. It must. For my father's sake, I will not lose you."

Louis took a rag and tended her face with it for her nose was again oozing blood. "If he were not the master, I would have killed him for this."

"But he is the master or so he thinks. Perhaps it will be his way for a time, but not for eternity, Louis. My mother has become a dribbling idiot of late. Will she ever know what Gabriel of Lyon is? It seems that my father did not."

"You can never win against the likes of him, Milady. If you were a man, perhaps. But you are not. You must remember this. You must, for your own sake."

"You tell me I can never win? You say this to me?"

Louis smiled though there was not much humor associated with it. He knew her too well. He had known her all of her life; even as an infant she demanded her own way.

"Where is my girl?"

"In the kitchens."

"Summon her for me."

Louis stood back at Adelina's door. "Milady?" She regarded him curiously. "It has been an honor knowing you and serving you, and a privilege, but tomorrow after the funeral, I must go." His words were sincere and so very sad.

"Should I summon you, Louis? Should I send to the very ends of the earth, would you come?"

Louis nodded, took her hand and kissed it. Then he was away.

Jennet was not surprised to see her mistress cleaning her face of blood. Both she and Ella had heard the commotion but neither dared investigate, they stayed downstairs and imagined all kinds of hell. Jennet took the wet rag and dabbed at Adelina's face. Her top lip was swollen, her eyes held traces of darkness circling them.

"My mother says that a nose which bleeds takes away the bruising of the eyes."

"I do not care what your mother says. Where have you been all day?"

"I was summoned back yesterday but dismissed again when you did not come home. But here you are and that is all that matters now." Jennet lifted the tunic over Adelina's head and used fresh oiled water to clean her mistress's arms and neck and body. She had not washed for a long time and her smell was ripe. "You are thinner."

"Am I?"

"Oh, yes. Much."

"Jennet, my father is dead."

"Yes, Milady, I know," she said, voice soft, touch caressing.

"My father is dead and yet I cannot cry. Why is it that I cannot cry?"

"I do not know, Milady. There is no shame in tears. It is expected of us, perhaps that is why you cannot?"

"Because it is expected?"

Jennet shrugged. "I am very pleased you are home, safe. I have missed tending you."

As I have missed you, Adelina thought but did not say. She touched Jennet's hand instead and they both smiled. But too soon, Adelina's faded away. "Geoffrey is a monk now."

"Yes."

"Louis is dismissed and I am to wed earlier than my father wished. But I will not, Jennet. I cannot. For if I do wed, Baudoin Dupuy will surely die. Gabriel will make sure of this."

"But why?"

"Baudoin is the only heir, as I am, and all that is mine and his will then be mine should he die. It is Gabriel's plan that when all lands are mine, he will wed me so that all will be his."

"Remember some time ago, Milady, when I told you that it begins for you? That is what I meant."

"Do you know what it was I saw today?"

"Milady?"

"He and my mother were in my father's room. His private retreat. They were together as animals, Gabriel and my mother. He must have served her needs well, for now she looks upon him as a leper looked upon Christ."

"Perhaps she loves him."

"There is no such thing. Love was invented by men for their convenience and no other reason. This I know, now. Men look upon us as they do a favorite hound or a horse and at times our uses are even less. What are we except polite decorations which die in childbirth only to be replaced by another decoration?"

Jennet said nothing. She dared not. How she worried about the state of her lady's mind. To Etienne she would give sons and in turn he would give her food and clothing and shelter and if she was lucky, companionship without too many beatings. But he was only kind if she lay on her back and pleased him that way. Afterwards, he did not want to know her or so it seemed.

"Tomorrow will be the last time you shall see me in many years, Jennet."

"Milady?" she asked, alarmed, her voice little but a squeak.

"I am going to the Holy Land. We go to save Jerusalem."

Jennet was speechless as Adelina told her of Stephen of Cloyes, the shepherd boy, and what had been said to her at the gates of St. Denis Abbey. "That is my destiny, Jennet. To reclaim the Holy Land."

"Oh, Milady, you are so brave."

"None must know though, and I cannot join the others wearing the dress of a noble."

"Why is this?"

"I am too valuable as a ransom. Do this I ask, Jennet, and you will be free to marry Etienne. My father gave you his permission and such permission cannot be rescinded. Do it quickly, before Gabriel of Lyon decides you cannot. For he will recant this permission if he believes I will be hurt by it. He knows what it is I feel for you."

"And what is this you ask of me?"

"Give me your dress."

"But I have only one."

"You know many peasants, can you not steal one? This I ask you. I shall visit the Holy Land as a peasant and not a noble. Deliver the dress tomorrow to Agnes. I will leave for you one in which you can marry, and I shall write my permission so there will be no trouble."

"But, Milady, I dare not. My mother sews already the dress I will wear."

"You do not like my wedding dress?" Adelina asked and they both turned to the dress which was hanging on a hook over the screen.

"Milady, even if you wrote your permission I should be killed for wearing such a beautiful gown."

"Will you still leave a dress for me?"

"I would do whatever you ask of me, Milady. But I beg that you allow me to follow you to the Holy Land."

"You?"

"Please?"

"Jennet, the crusade is for children, for innocents. You are not a child."

"Would God turn me away because I am too old?"

Adelina looked into the eyes of her girl. "No one can ever know of this."

"No one will."

"Would Etienne wish you well on such a journey?"

"I dare not hope to discover. I wish to be with you. That is my place, Milady. With you."

"Then, the day after the funeral of my father, that is when we shall leave for Marseilles."

"Do you know the way?"

"No, but I will discover it."

"Surely God will lead us to Marseilles, Milady?"

"God or Louis." Adelina said no more, already the plan was forming in her mind.

And the plan would have worked had Baudoin Dupuy not been waiting under the shade of a huge tree when she arrived the next day for her father's funeral.

First, he met Marys solemnly and kissed her outstretched hand. People were plentiful and Gabriel could not order him away. Instead, Gabriel invited him back to the chateau for a conference afterwards. "On what matter?" Baudoin asked, half wondering if the wedding had been cancelled.

"The wedding," Gabriel said but offered no more and he led the grieving widow into the abbey.

Baudoin looked down at Adelina and wanted to tell her how lovely she looked this day but thought it not wise, nor appropriate. Adelina took his black-leathered arm tightly and as they walked in, to their places, it was as if this had happened before. However, this time it seemed that they were indeed friends. And this time there was no king, only the casket bearing inside it, her father's putrefying body.

Geoffrey watched from his place set high above the funeral crowd, his face hidden by the thick black hood, his tears hidden as well. Tears for many—for Christian, for Robert, for

Acelin. It seemed that anyone he dared love was certain to die. Perhaps it was fortunate then that the abbot had forbidden him to see Adelina, or speak with her. Such a demon could only corrupt the purity of his mind and body, it was said.

He had written her a letter though, and that would be as close as he dared venture this day.

He knew no other monks well enough yet to trust them with the simple message, so he would have to do it himself. Perhaps on the way to the crypt he would get close enough, perhaps.

And then tomorrow he would bury his own brother.

Did Adelina know? Did anyone here know?

Halfway through the long, long service which took forever, and would have bored her father senseless, Baudoin looked over and whispered to her but she did not hear his words. She was too busy studying Heracle, the uncle she had never met.

He sat directly opposite her mother and Gabriel on the other side of the abbey, at an equal distance from Robert's casket, the casket draped by the Polignac family arms. She could not see him clearly without drawing attention to herself but his profile was very like her father's The hair was the same, the beard worn in the same way, although Heracle had much more grey in his, and his nose was larger. If the brothers looked the same then Geoffrey's father would have been strong and handsome, too. Had the similarities been passed down to all the sons except for Geoffrey? She did not know, for none of Heracle's sons were there, nor his wife. He was alone but for one knight. It must be true, she thought, that only in physical similarities was the family connection strong, for in nature they were very different.

Geoffrey's father, Guillame, had been a man of letters, of kindness, a poet. Robert, a gruff but fair lord with money matters foremost always. Heracle? She did not know. Her father never spoke of him or to him and when the name was mentioned his eyes would close and speak he would not. Heracle was very rich. He lived in the fortress at Polignac as all of the first born sons had since time began and pilgrims still visited there to climb the tower and ask questions of the ancient Gods. The fortress was where the brothers had spent their childhoods and Adelina had once asked her father was it true that pilgrim's answers came from God himself? But her father had just smiled and said nothing.

Adelina noticed that occasionally the big man, Heracle, wiped at his eye. For many years he had not spoken to his brother. Why now was he here farewelling him from this life?

Hurry, she thought. Please hurry. I cannot bear this a moment longer. Baudoin, as if sensing her distress, squeezed her hand.

Not soon enough the service ended, the monks stopped singing their mournful hymn, and Adelina, walking with her mother, followed those carrying the casket. Each carefully placed their feet so as not to step in the ooze dripping from the box.

A hundred people followed them. So far, nothing was felt. Nothing. There was Gabriel and Michel, Louis and Dedwyd and Heracle with a monk, who carried the casket. Adelina could not see the monk's face. She kept her gaze lowered all the while but cry, she still could not.

Down into the bowels of the abbey they went until they came upon the crypt where lay the Polignacs of Lavoute and some not of Lavoute, too. Only the family, the abbot and the vassals carrying the casket were allowed entry.

It was a huge, dark place, musty and damp, and well below ground. High above, one alcove set into rock bore several skulls of times long ago. Robert de Polignac's casket was lowered into the sarcophagus and the monk whose face was still hidden stepped back first.

Heracle took from around his neck a chain and medallion and put it on the casket, then the large stone cover was manhandled into place.

The abbot said another prayer which Adelina never heard. She stood numbly, Baudoin beside her, the monk on the other side. Marys then let forth an ear piercing scream and flung herself on to the stone. But that was only expected and none really believed her emotion.

Gabriel guided her out and he was followed by the vassals.

"Leave me, Baudoin. I will farewell my father in solitude." Baudoin told her he would wait on the stairs.

The monk standing beside her caught her attention by tapping her and she turned. He lifted his face so that his eyes could be seen but they said to her, speak not. It was Geoffrey and he thrust two small parchment rolls into her hands and Adelina hid them in the folds of her dress. Then the monk was gone, following the abbot.

Two remained in the stinking crypt. Heracle de Polignac and Adelina. They were of the same blood but strangers. He stood proud and huge at the head of her father's sarcophagus while she stood at the foot. He was whispering in the dimness, whispered words to his dead brother who could not hear them. Adelina, her hand secure on Geoffrey's letters, said quietly "You are the uncle I was forbidden to meet. I am Adelina."

Heracle said nothing.

"He would have welcomed you, uncle, while he lived. I knew my father well, better than most. He would have welcomed you. He had made peace with most of his enemies before he died. It was as if he knew the future."

Heracle looked at the girl, his younger brother's daughter and he turned away and walked out without saying a word to her.

Adelina looked at her father's last resting place, just five pieces of stone, his name and the dates inscribed there. 1155-1212. One day, she thought, I shall lie here, too, with my father and my brother, for to her right lay the smallest sarcophagus she had ever seen. His name had been Michelet.

"Adelina?"

She turned to the soft call of her name. It was Baudoin.

"Soon," she said and sat on her grandfather's grave. She unrolled Geoffrey's parchment, for a note was secured to the other. But it was far too dark to read it in this light. It would have to wait. She pocketed the roll. Baudoin was impatient, and calling again. She went out of the crypt and took his offered hand and he led her back through the bowels of the abbey and out into the bright sunshine. She shielded her eyes from it. Most of the people had gone. In the distance her mother was being driven away. Michel, Louis and Dedwyd followed on horseback. Of Geoffrey she saw no sign. Her uncle was speaking to Abbot Jean. She shook free of Baudoin's hand and walked to them. "Abbot Jean, you delivered fine words of respect, all were lies though, and you, Heracle de Polignac, to you I have no words except these. Will you listen, even though I am a woman?"

Heracle arched his eyebrows in much the same way her father would, but proudly she stood. "I spit on you for tearing our family apart. Your pride has forbidden much. Mark my words, the Polignac name will shine again and it will shine though me. Not you or your useless sons." She stared at Heracle, hoping he would do something, but he said nothing. He turned back to the abbot and resumed his conversation as if she weren't there.

Baudoin led her away. "One day, you will burn."

"I would greet the flames with pride for in truth there is no agony."

"There is something wrong in your head."

"What is wrong is not in my head, Baudoin Dupuy. What is wrong surrounds me constantly."

"That is?"

"Men. I cannot abide them."

"So you would castrate me with your words?"

"You are an exception. I will visit Christian before I return to the chateau."

"Time does not permit."

"I give not a frog's fart for time, Baudoin Dupuy! I wish to be alone!"

"Then alone you shall be."

He walked off, found his horse, mounted it and without a glance left her to journey back to the chateau alone, on foot.

If he thought she would run after him and beg him to come back, he was wrong, for walking suited Adelina's needs well.

She walked down the hill to Agnes's house and there, under some straw, where she was told it would be, was the bundle—the wrapped dress and footwear of a peasant. She went upstairs to bid Christian goodbye. But there was nobody there. She stood calling for a long time. No one came. It was odd. It was strange. Perhaps Christian and Agnes were walking by the river? Or were gathering water? No. By the ladder was a pail, dry and on its side.

Adelina put the bundle down and climbed the ladder. She bent low and walked into the house. The chairs, the beds. The table. And on the floor, a huge stain. She walked closer and looked closely. She touched and put her finger to her nose. It was blood.

"Agnes?" she called to no answer.

She could not see Agnes's clothes anywhere. What had happened here? Adelina sat down and took from her pocket the parchments Geoffrey had given her. One was sealed and one was tied, so she chose the tied one. But it was not poetry she found here today.

Christian was dead, by his own hand and damned for all of time.

Adelina, who had just buried her father, sat very still in Geoffrey's house. The house he was ashamed of. She saw nothing. She felt less. Her heart had grown as cold and heavy as a stone. She was once again as she was when born. Alone.

Cateline, her friend and companion.

Raoul.

Acelin.

Her father.

And now Christian. She looked down at her hands, to Geoffrey's words, marks on parchment. He had cried when he had written this. He had cried.

And still, she could not.

She looked at the blood on the floor once again.

"The angels are absent now," she said to no one. "I am alone."

She stood, shaking, and had to find balance quickly or fall. In the far corner, Geoffrey's chest. Such things of the world he could not take with him on his journey to find God. Adelina opened it carefully—she was not a child now, not a curious little girl intent on stealing and hiding. Her fingers touched the billowing silk shirt and she held it to her face and breathed deeply of his scent. Then she saw a fastener of bronze and she took it, too. The silk shirt would be her nightdress for the rest of her years and the fastener she would always wear close to her heart.

It was all she had left to her now.

Baudoin was waiting on the roadway a short distance from the village. Her walk had not been the lengthy one she expected. He was sitting in the shade, waiting patiently and his horse grazed idly. The moment she looked into his dark eyes, this man she had to wed but could never love, the well overflowed. Baudoin was on his feet instantly, holding her, although it seemed that he did not know what

245

to do to ease her pain.

"Come," he said, "We are needed at the chateau."

Once home, Michel embraced her fondly and was surprised when she did not pull her face from his shoulder as she normally did. She clung instead, saying, "I shall never see you again, Michel."

"What nonsense is this?" he asked.

"It is not nonsense. I listened to your stories and you have taught me much. Your wisdom will have its uses in time and I shall always remember you fondly and with love."

"As I shall," he said, frowning and she then walked to Louis.

"Where is it you will go?"

"South, Milady."

"To?"

"Montpelier, perhaps Marseilles."

"Marseilles? How will you get there?"

"I shall travel south from Le Puy. I have not seen the ocean for many a year."

"Marseilles is at the end of the land then?"

"Oui."

"So there it is, at Marseilles, where I should find you?"

"I do not know where I will go, Milady."

"God be with you, Louis."

"Milady."

She found Dedwyd next. He still had little understanding of their language. He laughed too much to take note of her lessons and they had ended abruptly. "Do you go with Louis?" she asked. He shook his head. "Why not?"

"Gabriel has purchased him from me," Louis said.

"So he stays but you cannot?"

"Gabriel trusts him. He has no such trust in me."

"All is madness now," Adelina said and looked directly at Gabriel who was surrounded by people, including the abbot, much as her father used to be surrounded by people. All of this is mine, not his. Why do these people not surround me?

Adelina went to her room, her presence was not missed. She barred her door and took from her mourning dress Geoffrey's two rolls. Remember your promise made. She could not open it until she was wed. Adelina took out the silk shirt and lay the fastener on her table. Then she found a piece of broadcloth from the rags Jennet was still hiding under her bed, and in the broadcloth she wrapped shoes, hose, tunic and a dagger for eating, one for self protection, the blade of which was as long as her forearm; the jar of herbal ointment still in her room since the attack and a wad of rags for when she was cursed with the issue of blood. The dress would have to do as she could not take one of hers. She looked at her wedding gown but could not see it properly for tears were blinding. Poor Baudoin, she thought. Poor, poor Baudoin. He probably does like me enough to make a marriage not a hell.

Adelina reached for her quill and ink and below Geoffrey's letter, she wrote: "My love, my cousin who now has another name and another life, when next we meet we shall be old. It is destiny. I do now what my heart has always desired. I will journey far and take with me the only weapon I have truly had. My innocence. My love shall ever continue. Serve God well, but forget not your self. Adelina."

She summoned a page and put the parchment into his little hand. "Boy, deliver this to Brother Christophe tomorrow's eve. Let none know it is from me." The boy was very vacant so she told him three times and made him repeat the instructions until she was satisfied.

Then she was alone again.

Until sunset, she sat in her room by her window watching visitors come and go. She thought of Heloise Dupuy and knew that Heloise would die long before she got to the Holy City. She thought of her mother who would not worry at all of her absence, for if she never returned, then in time the estate would pass to her mother. And if that happened, Gabriel would no doubt marry her.

Adelina thought of Geoffrey, secluded away from the world of men, favoring a life of service to God now. She thought of her father in his grave, how his spirit was so close to her that she could smell him—a mixture of wine and horses and sweat but not offensive. Never offensive.

"Papa, if ever I needed you, it is now for what soon will be. This is what I was born to do, even if God saw it wise to make me woman. Papa, I will keep your name alive. I will be the son you wished me to be. I will be your Michelet."

She took the sharp knife from the broadcloth, not yet tied tight and she took her hair in hand and she began to saw through it, crying now, crying hard. Before long, her hair, the color of a roaring fire, was cropped and sawn well above her shoulders and tresses lay on the floor at her feet.

She put the dagger back in the broadcloth, wrapped her bundle tightly and used rope to secure a long strap to it so that she could put it on her back.

I cannot take a horse, she whispered, for it can be identified. I must walk. Walk to Marseilles where I shall join the crusade of children.

There was a banging on her door. Adelina ignored it until she heard, "It is I, Baudoin. We must speak. I have news."

"Leave me alone."

"Adelina, we must speak."

Adelina put on her cloak, covered her head with its hood and she opened the door. Baudoin stood there for a moment, wondering why she wore a cloak when it was so warm. She also looked different but he could not tell what the difference was.

"You said news?"

"We are to be married in one week."

There was happiness in his eyes. A lot of happiness. Tears filled hers.

"Do you not want this now?" he asked.

How could she say she had never wanted this?

"One week," she repeated softly and Baudoin reached out to touch her face but she pulled away quickly.

"I hoped this news would alleviate some of your pain."

"It does. It does."

"But you still wish to be alone," he said softly and sighed. "Do you wish me to stay for a short time?"

What was in his eyes? Hope?

"No. I wish nothing from you, Baudoin Dupuy. Nothing."

He looked at her strangely, before he nodded and walked off. The last she saw of him was his jet black hair falling to his shoulders, bouncing as he walked.

Adelina closed her door, and waited for night to fall.

# Chapter 23

She could not take her girl and nor had she intended to. It was very early of morning, far too early for even Ella to have begun her day's duty.

Adelina, in her silk-shirted nightdress, took up the broadcloth bundle, and with candle lighting her way, walked barefooted and silently down the stairs. The castle was as echoing as a tomb now. The great hall was a litter of discarded food and drink and she picked her way through the mess which remained for the charboys once the sun touched the sky again.

When it did, she would be long gone.

Down into the kitchens she went, stepping over somebody who had chosen the stairs as a bed. A knight she had never seen before lay there and how he snored. She looked closer. How ugly he was, too.

And how dark and still the night. There was no moon at all. And nor could she see a sentry on the gate. She dared not risk being seen. She went out by the courtyard gate and picked her way through the garden to the rope she had hidden amid the hedges.

Gabriel watched from the tower window. He sighed at what he saw in the darkness, silly girl to wear white. Did she know nothing? He turned and looked at Marys on the bed, sleeping soundly. A mourning widow indeed. Gabriel reached for his tunic. To bring Adelina back, he would need no armour. He put his boots on soundlessly.

It seemed to him that she was making her way to Lavoute by following the river. Shaking his head and biting back a smile, Gabriel went to the door of his mistress's bedchambers, sheathing his dagger as he walked.

"Gabriel?"

He looked back. "To sleep, my love." But Marys was stretched out upon the bed and almost purring, beckoning him back. Smiling and sleepy.

Gabriel walked to her and climbed upon the bed. He kissed her face.

"Already you leave me?"

"Leave you? Never. But there is something I must do before dawn, something important," he said, interrupting every second word with another kiss. "I will return. I will always return to you."

Marys touched the hair falling across his face and she whispered of her love for him. He said nothing. He kissed her forehead instead. Then he was gone.

Adelina's hands burnt from the rope. How often she would do this as a child, Geoffrey with her of course, on hand if needed to cushion her fall. He had always given her mail gloves. Mail gloves which became very hot the quicker she skimmed down the rope. Today though she had forgotten the gloves and halfway down the huge stone wall, her bare feet could find no traction and she slipped, burning her right hand more fiercely as she tried to halt the impending fall. She managed to grab the rope again and crashed hard into the stone battlement. Remaining soundless about this pain was nigh impossible.

Strength was fading fast. She looked down as she clung and then she looked up to the battlement. She was more than halfway down. Oh, yes a fine warrior. I would be dead already, she thought. If this were a battle, and archers rained arrows at me from below. Or above. I would be dead already. But a knight at arms would feel no such pain from a mere rope, so she continued down, even though her eyes stung and her hands screamed for it to end.

She let go at ten feet and rolled when she hit the ground, grabbing for something, anything, to break her plummet into the river. She mumbled, swearing again. This had been much easier when she was younger and carried less weight.

It was almost dawn. Already her plans were in disarray. She wanted to dress in the dark of the woods near the crossroads once she had found the clothing she had hidden there. She wanted to be in Le Puy as the sun caressed the hillsides.

Adelina tried to ignore her rope-burnt hands and picked up the broadcloth. It was a heavy burden, and she was barefoot as well, picking her way through the dense bush to the water's edge. By following the river, which she had done so often but always in daylight, and with Cateline as company, she would come to the bridge, and by the road she would go to the crossroads where her freedom surely awaited.

Already her feet were sore and tender. This is punishment for wearing shoes as a lady should, she thought. Geoffrey's silken shirt tangled in prickly bushes and snagged, bringing her to a tearing standstill many times which only fed her frustration and anger.

But ahead, finally, the bridge. Adelina sat and caressed her soft feet, already bleeding from sharp stones and burrs. The darkness around her was dissolving quicker than she had expected. She clambered up the steep slope and stood on the bridge for a moment, looking back at the chateau, what little she could see of it. It was not home now that Gabriel had declared himself Lord, with her father's blessing.

She had read that for herself, otherwise she'd never have believed it.

She limped on. Such a long way to the crossroads, each step forward in the fading darkness seemed to take her two steps backwards.

A very short distance from the crossroads she heard a horse snorting, and a man's voice soothing the animal.

Adelina had not thought she would meet any traveller at this early hour. She scrambled to the side of the road and waited for the rider to pass by. But the rider did not and the light was stronger now, her white shirt a beacon. She had to hide and crouched low, then lay on her belly. The rider came closer and to her horror she saw who it was.

Gabriel.

Her heart sank. She fought despair as she lay low and watched. How had he known? What sorcery did he employ? Did the demon never sleep?

His horse sensed her. His horse liked her. His horse expected an apple or a carrot whenever it saw her and when it saw her it would dance, its ears raise, its eyes flicker with life. It danced now, fought the bit until its mouth foamed and Gabriel upon its back turned his horse to the woods in the very direction she lay. A smile crossed Gabriel's face and he dismounted and set the animal free.

The horse seemed a better hound than her father's much cherished old snuffling thing. Hadn't Gabriel once commented on its love for her and her alone? The horse came straight to where she lay, its ears raised, snorting, wanting an apple. Adelina scrambled to her feet and forgot about her broadcloth. She was not as fast as she could have been because of her screaming feet and worse, the sound of the horse so close did nothing but remind her of Jean Pierre Dupuy. She bubbled with the same fear and was aware of nothing as she weaved in and out of the trees. Ahead, far ahead, the abbey. And close behind, Gabriel of Lyon, twice her size and strength. Gabriel, who knew her thoughts before she did.

Geoffrey's shirt sleeve snagged on a dead branch. It held her fast for a moment until she tore away and half of the sleeve remained on the wood. But that moment was all that Gabriel needed. An iron grip seized her wrist and the power of it was enough to almost tear her arm from her shoulder. She screamed in pain as she twisted in the grip. "No," she cried weakly, "No," and she dropped to her knees. Gabriel attempted to pull her upright again but she would not obey his silent command. His horse nuzzled at her back. She felt nothing. She prayed that Geoffrey would come as he had before. But no one came. No one

251

would.

"Running away, little one?" Gabriel asked.

"Freedom," she whispered, despairing.

"Running away from your duty, I think."

"Freedom," she said again and dared look up. He stood with feet apart and he was rubbing his face as he always did when thoughtful. "It is God's will I do this, Gabriel. It is God's will. I am on a mission."

Gabriel thought that amusing. "You, who thinks only of herself, on a mission? Interesting. Yes, a very interesting lie, Adelina. What is this mission so important that you choose to run, to neglect your dead father's wishes?"

She said nothing.

"You think I don't know of this childish plan? This, this Stephen of Cloyes and what he dreams of? This Children's Crusade?"

Adelina struggled to her feet, and as determined as ever when facing Gabriel, she turned and walked off, pushing aside his horse. It followed her.

"There will be no crusade for you."

"I walk to Marseilles. Goodbye."

"You will return to the chateau with me."

"I will never return to the chateau. I will never marry Baudoin Dupuy and you will never be my master. Your time is wasted here. It is better spent in the arms of my mother. Go to her. I am sure she waits feverishly for you. Again. If to do nothing but defile my father's memory."

"You shall come willingly, Adelina, or I shall take you by force. The choice is yours. I have no wish to harm you."

"I shall go nowhere with you except perhaps to hell."

His eyes glowed in anticipation as he stepped towards her and she retreated. To hell indeed, he thought. Her hair was shorn and did not detract from her wild beauty at all. The steady calm of cold eye was belied by the rapid throbbing in her throat. The fastener she wore on her breast was Geoffrey's. As was the shirt. Gabriel laughed and leaned against the tree which separated them.

"Tell me who you think you are, Adelina de Polignac."

His smirk angered her. She turned away and started walking again. Gabriel picked up her tied broadcloth bundle and one handed threw it at her. It hit her in the middle of the back and the horse shied as she fell.

But she could not rise. Gabriel's boot on her back kept her down. "You will come with me."

She spat on the ground.

"It is a long way to be dragged by what little remains of your hair, is it not?" Adelina punched at his leg, blindly, wildly. He barely felt it. Gabriel lifted her to her feet by what little hair he could grip and she screamed and fought wildly. Adelina sank her teeth into his hand, hard. She did not let go and the back of his other hand struck hard. Searing agony now but her teeth remained embedded and she kicked, too, wildly but could not find the target she wanted.

To release himself from her bite, Gabriel punched, hard. Very hard into her belly. She let go and fell heavily. She couldn't breathe. Adelina doubled in pain, unending agony with fires inside of a kind never felt before.

Gabriel kicked her to her back and his muddied boot went on her chest this time. She struggled it seemed for life itself. "You, my little wild cat, will marry Dupuy. You will take his lands when you are widowed and then you will marry me."

Adelina, barely able to draw breath, spat a bloodied, "Never! I would die first!"

He laughed. "Crusades indeed. This is an escape from your duties. It is no more and no less because God in his wisdom has abandoned you. God has seen fit to take from you all that you have ever loved. You are noble born, you fool, and noble blood fetches high prices. Crusade indeed. It would end with you sold into slavery. Is that what you want?"

"I am already sold into slavery!"

Gabriel mumbled to himself. "You go nowhere now except with me. On your feet."

Gabriel offered his hand. It dripped blood from her savage teeth but no pain showed in his eyes. Nothing showed in his eyes. Again, she thought of Jean-Pierre Dupuy. "I would rather die."

Gabriel tore the fastener from the silk and he pitched it far. Adelina saw it disappear but could only whisper her denials. "You are mine, Adelina, to do with what I please, when I please." His arm caught her across the throat and with his other hand he tore the hose from her body. She kicked, she fought, but the arm crushing her throat was pinning her to the hard ground. When she felt him come down on top of her, the muscles of her thighs locked tight, so tight that he struggled in vain, until he took from his belt his dagger and he held it to her throat.

"Prepare a bath," Gabriel barked as he came into the kitchens, Adelina over his shoulder.

Ella ceased stuffing her chicken. "Milady! What has happened!"

"I said, prepare a bath! Now, toad!"

Ella began calling for her mistress, but Gabriel, about to take the stairs, picked up a broom and struck Ella with it. The old woman shielded her face from the next strike. Charboys scattered and Jennet, carrying a pail of water, appeared from the great hall. "Milady!"

"A bath, now! Marys!" he called as he threw down the broom and proceeded up the stairs. "Marys!"

Adelina's mother appeared from her chambers, needlework in hand. She could barely believe what she saw.

"I found her at the crossroads, my love. This is what remains. She has been defiled. Spoiled."

"But…"

"She was running away. Running away to join that damned crusade of children."

Adelina's face was bruised, swelling, bleeding, and she lay heavy on Gabriel's shoulder, whimpering and broken.

Marys followed him into Adelina's chambers and he lay her on her bed. Her clothes—was that Geoffrey's shirt?—were muddied and torn and what showed of her body was bruised and welted. Adelina rolled to her side and curled tight.

Marys sat on the side of the bed and touched. She was cold, shaking, mumbling nonsensically. Again she wanted Geoffrey. Was there never a time when she did not? Charboys brought buckets of warmed water to the door and looked in, curious, but were soon chased by a glance from Gabriel.

"You say she has been defiled?"

"I am sure. I have seen this many times in my travels."

Marys's face paled. "Baudoin cannot know of this. But today he comes to visit. There are plans yet to make, wedding plans. It will go on, oui?" she asked, looking into Gabriel's eyes, silently pleading. "He must not know of this. Not before the wedding. He must not…"

"I will send word that she has taken ill. A contagion, perhaps?"

"Do that, yes. Good." Marys looked down at her daughter again. She did not know what to do, or what to say. "How many did this?" she asked.

"I don't know," Gabriel said. "I chased two when I heard the noise. Such pitiful screams. Terrible screams," he added softly.

"Send for Michel. Michel Dumont, yes, send for him and Geoffrey too. Quickly."

"Geoffrey cannot come."

"She needs prayers! She asks for him! Send for Geoffrey!"

"Whatever your wish, my love, but I fear he will be no help for today he buries his brother."

"What is this?" Marys asked.

"You do not know? Christian. He is dead by his own hand. Yesterday it seems he drove a dagger into his heart."

It was too much for Marys, far too much. Her tears came, she howled without control. Gabriel drew her close and held her face to his heart tightly. He looked down at Adelina as he whispered of love to her mother. And when the women came to tend Adelina, he took Marys upstairs and comforted her tenderly.

Ella and Jennet tended their lady, taking what remained of the clothing from her gently. They each had to lift her into the tub of oiled warm water. Jennet was crying, Ella, too, despairing so much that she vowed silently to kill whoever had done this, whoever had harmed this child of her heart. Who was so silent. So very, very silent.

Geoffrey was supposed to be praying, but prayers did little to ease the aching inside. He knelt for a long time, his skin sweating profusely under the coarse, black robe. It was clothing designed to remind him always of the flesh he wore, and somewhere—he had yet to find it –the spirit residing therein.

It had been a mistake coming here, saying to the abbot, I am here, I am ready now, when the knowing that he was not ready, and probably never would be, was reflected in the abbot's aged, cold eyes. But the abbot had said nothing. He had walked Geoffrey around the abbey and its grounds, talking all the while, but what words had he said? Geoffrey couldn't remember. As they had walked the grounds, had it been that moment when Christian had taken the dagger in his shaking hands? Had Geoffrey not felt a pain then? Had he not thought that this was a mistake?

With the study books and robe and small, dungeon-like cell came only a silent abandonment. No grace had been seen, heard or felt. Geoffrey had taken no vows as yet, and as he knelt on the damp, stone floor, with his head on his bed of straw, he wept.

He wept for all that could have been and was not. Most of all, he wept for himself. He had never been this alone in his life.

The day before, he could offer Adelina nothing. Nothing at all when his heart was filled with so much, his mind overpowered by quiet pain—her pain—which he felt in every part of his body as he stood so close to her. For only half a moment did the closeness last, and she did not know him then, his face hidden so. And talk he could not. Comfort her he could not, nor she him. Her father, his uncle, had been as a father to him when the other would not. It was the first time he had glimpsed his uncle's face that day, and he longed to say, I am Geoffrey. I am the one you did not want. I am your dead brother's son. The only one who lives now.

Oh, Agnes, he thought. Far better it was you who found him than me. Looking upon him, hearing Andre speak of everlasting peace while Geoffrey's own dagger it was he had used.

Geoffrey prayed for strength but felt less strong than ever before. He prayed for guidance, but still an empty void lay deep in his belly. He prayed for love to see him through, and saw Adelina's face instead. He prayed for wisdom and the void remained, so he crawled into his cot, fully realising that he could change nothing and do even less.

The loud banging on his door woke him with such a start that Geoffrey momentarily could not breathe. His heart beat savagely and bile rose immediately.

Andre came in. "Brother, are you awake? You have a visitor. Best you rise now, quickly."

Andre was one of a few who had not taken a vow of silence. Geoffrey thought he could not, for words to Andre were as necessary as breathing.

Geoffrey walked very fast indeed, faster than appropriate, to the abbey doors. His visitor was Gabriel of Lyon. Had he known it was Gabriel he would not have received him at all. Gabriel stood tall, proud, and he wore over his hauberk the Polignac surcoat. Geoffrey's hands, deep in the pockets of his robe, fisted and thoughts of blood spilling were strong.

"Keep away," was all Gabriel had to say.

"Again?" Geoffrey asked and leaned closer.

"I warn you, keep away from my chateau. For no reason will be the right one to herald your presence in my household."

"Your chateau?" Geoffrey asked. "What madness is this?"

"If you dare come on to my land, I will run you through. And you will die slowly. Very slowly. Man of God or not, I will gladly kill you myself."

Gabriel turned and walked away.

"I said, what madness is this!"

Gabriel stopped walking and studied his feet for a moment before he turned and said, "In case you do not yet know, I am now Lord of Lavoute Polignac."

"By what sorcery was this accomplished!"

Gabriel stared at Geoffrey until a smile crossed his lips. "You accuse me of sorcery now?" With a laugh, Gabriel turned and whistled for his horse.

Geoffrey watched Gabriel leave. He did not ride off to the chateau, he rode to the village instead, his mood alone enough to terrorize the serfs there. The serfs who now belonged to him, possessions to do with as he wished.

"Out of my way, Brother."

Geoffrey stood aside as two monks swept by—one was Andre. His only friend. "Brother? Am I needed?" Geoffrey called.

But Andre could say nothing. The abbot was within earshot.

Michel paced impatiently while he waited for the two monks to finish offering their prayers. He did not think that prayers could be as infinite in length, but finally, when the door was opened and the two appeared, he wasted not a moment longer.

Adelina was asleep when he came in and Jennet would not leave her side. Michel sat by the bed and pulled the covers down. He lay his hand on her heart. It was very quick. He touched her face and stroked her forehead until her eyes opened. Dull eyes. "Michel?"

"Yes, yes, say nothing, little one. I know what you have endured."

To that, Adelina closed her eyes and turned her face away. This was always how she cried, in silence. Michel looked to her girl. "When was her last bleed?" he asked.

Jennet had to think for they each bled at the same time, and her chore to take away the soiled rags. "Two weeks?" she offered.

Michel sighed.

'What has happened to her?" Jennet asked, tearfully.

Michel would not say. He was thinking and besides, the girl asked questions she already knew the answers to.

"I would but take her place to ease her pain, Milord."

"So she would then feel yours?" Michel asked and drew the covers back fully. He unlaced the nightgown. Bruises. His heart was breaking and he was filled with anger. From his pocket he took a sealed jar and he gave it to Jennet. "A small amount morning and night or when she cries," he said.

Michel's fingers touched Adelina's ribs and he watched her face intently until pain registered and his fingertips felt it too, the break of bones. Two bones. He scratched his head, deep in thought again. "She must stay unmoving. Should she not, she will cough blood until she drowns in it. Keep her thus at all times." he said and placed a cushion under her shoulder so that she was raised. "And should she speak of what happened, listen only. The memory will ease in time."

Their gazes met and Jennet knew he lied. What would he know of such things? He was but a man. "There is nothing more I can do here. God has blessed us that she is not dead. Will he bless us that she is not with child, too?"

"She will wish she was dead whether she is with child or not."

Michel looked at the girl curiously and needed no sorcery to read her mind. He rose tiredly and he put his hand on the girl's shoulder. Without another word, he left.

Jennet unsealed the jar and she wiped her face on her sleeve before she dipped her finger in. Within a moment, her finger was numb. She put a little onto her tongue. It too went numb very quickly. Oh, that I could rub this concoction into our hearts and minds, she thought as she began with the dark swollen bruise on her lady's face. Then we would feel nothing. For the next six days, Jennet did not leave her lady's side. She slept on the floor by the bed, her arm forever raised because Adelina would not let go of her hand, even in sleep.

# Chapter 24

"Adelina?" Baudoin asked, looking out from the rampart at the late afternoon view. Something was wrong. She seemed ill, yes, but it was an illness more of the mind. He had been sent word that she was not well and he had been busy these past few days, but he had brought her flowers and she had tried to smile at sight of them. He had tried to make jokes but she seemed hesitant in laughing. She'd never had trouble before with laughter. "Adelina, what is wrong? Has something happened?"

"What was that you said?" she asked vacantly.

"What is wrong? What has happened? What are the marks on your face?"

"I fell," she said softly. "I slipped on the stairs but I am much better now. Much better." She took his hand limply because it felt as if he would put his arm around her and she didn't want that. Not yet. Not for a long time. "Can I stay in your house at Allegre?" she asked.

"That is where we shall live."

"I mean now, Baudoin?"

"Now? Adelina, it would not be right."

"Please?" she asked.

"I cannot. It would be frowned upon."

"But I cannot stay here now that my father is dead."

"The wedding is only a week from tomorrow. A week is not a long time. Had you not fallen ill we would now be wed."

"Hear me. I cannot stay here a day longer," she whispered.

"The time will pass long before you have realised it. Come. I am hungry," he added with a smile.

Baudoin, sat between Gabriel and Adelina and studied Marys carefully as she chattered constantly of trivial things. Once, she had been beautiful, and she was tall for a woman, too, tall and thin and she moved with a subtle grace and dignity. But her eyes were very cold.

She was, he thought, his mother's age. Although illness had robbed his mother of beauty, some still lingered in her eyes even if it were a ghost from the past. Marys had no such beauty in hers. A cold woman indeed. How could Heloise and Marys have been friends? They were by far too unlike. Marys spoke to Gabriel as if he were her lover, so proud of him, so eagerly hanging upon his every word.

Adelina, beside Baudoin, ate slowly, in utter silence and once his foot mistakenly touched hers and she leapt high. She did not throw her wine into his lap this time.

"I should depart now, while there is light."

"Baudoin, you must stay," Marys said but did not mean it.

"I cannot, Milady. My parents are both ill. Very ill."

"Will they attend the wedding?"

"They both are eager to attend. But I do not know if they will." Baudoin excused himself and Adelina followed him to the courtyard. She walked slowly, though, as if further delaying his departure. He had spent most of the day with her and she was by his side always, so very silent the entire time.

His horse had been fed and watered and was ready. Baudoin took the reins, and almost mounted. Almost.

"I don't want you to go," she said softly.

He barely heard. "What was that?"

Adelina did not say it again. He looked into her eyes and thought he saw tears there. A very odd feeling overtook him.

"Baudoin, hear me. If I marry you, you will surely die," she said softly.

That he heard. "I have no fear of death. What I would fear is dying too soon, before I have truly known you."

"Your words are sweet and sincere but..."

Baudoin waited for more words. They never came.

"Promise me that you will take all cares, Baudoin Dupuy?"

"If you promise in turn to summon me should any ill befall you again."

Adelina looked into his eyes. What did he know? Or if not know, what did he suspect? "Take me with you and no ill shall befall me."

"I would very much like to, Addie, but I can't. Nothing has been readied for you yet."

She stood there, gazing at her bare feet and fighting back tears.

"It is only a week from tomorrow. I must go now while the light is with me. I know you want me to stay but I cannot."

Baudoin kissed the top of her head and mounted his horse, then he cantered over the drawbridge and did not look back.

Not yet wed and already she lied.

Adelina looked to the kitchen doors, to the man who waited there, watching her intently. How often of late had Gabriel tried to talk to her, and how expertly had she avoided him? She took most of her meals in her chambers, which she kept barred. She spoke to no one at all except Ella, Jennet and Dedwyd. Even Dedwyd regarded her strangely and offered her an occasional smile which she would not accept. He would perform miraculous gymnastic feats to no avail as well. And once he reached for her, if only to touch her face and force a smile from her but she retreated, very quickly.

It was very hard to look into any man's eyes now. Very hard.

She longed to see Geoffrey most of all, but even a letter was forbidden.

Gabriel took three steps toward her and the wolfhound at her feet growled a warning. Gabriel went back inside to Marys.

Adelina clasped her hands tight to stop them from shaking.

Charboys with a few moments spare played noisily and she heard them not. The dog nuzzled her hand and she caressed its head absently.

"You are my only friend," she said to it. Its huge brown eyes smiled at her. She knew what it wanted and she dug in her pocket for the piece of bread she had taken from her trencher. Once the morsel was gobbled, the dog loped off, saw the chickens and chased them.

Adelina went into the kitchens and sat upon the stool as she had so often when a little girl. Upstairs she could hear the voices of her mother and Gabriel. They were laughing.

"Is it true that you were handmaiden to my mother when she was young?" Adelina asked.

"Yes, Milady."

"And that you came with her as hand maiden when she married my father, yes?"

"Yes, Milady."

"Was she courted by all three brothers? She came from Arlempdes, yes, with a fine dowry to offer?"

"Milady, best you ask your mother of this."

"Yes or no, Ella?"

"Yes. It is all true but I should not be the one to tell you such things."

Adelina was thoughtful for a while. "She could not marry Heracle as he was already promised to another, is that not so?"

"Milady, how is it you know this?"

"He has had four wives, yes? Four wives and four sons and only one of the sons survives now?"

"Milady, where did you learn of this?"

"Where indeed. My future husband has told me more of my family than I know myself. I saw how they gazed upon each other at my father's funeral. I am not blind."

"Who gazed upon who, Milady?"

"My mother and Heracle. Something is being planned. I feel it but know not what it is."

"These are not your concerns, Milady."

"I wish to make them my concerns. It is said I am much as my father was in manner."

Ella smiled to herself and said nothing.

"All is like a spider web now and we are all caught fast in it." Gabriel has us trapped and waits patiently, enjoying our struggles, she thought.

"Milady?"

"What should happen if I died at this very moment?"

"Milady, no, you shall not die."

"What should happen, Ella? All that was my father's would then go to my mother, yes? Would Heracle marry her and increase his holdings yet again? Or would Gabriel marry her should I die? Of course I would not die now. I cannot die. God forbid me die until all Dupuy land is mine. Then it matters not what becomes of me." Her voice was sarcastic, bitter.

"Are you unwell again?"

"I am nothing, Ella. Nothing but a possession. A thing to be bartered and bought and sold at the whim of a man. Why am I so powerless? Why has God abandoned me?"

Ella wiped her hands of dough, and, as she had done so often before, took her in arms and held her. For a long time, Adelina savoured Ella's softness and warmth and quiet affection. She drew strength from the steady beat of the old woman's loyal heart.

"Baudoin Dupuy is a good, gentle man," Ella said and stroked the worried head. "He is strong and handsome and has good humour. Good humour is rare. He will not die until you are both aged, this I know. You will have a good life with him. I have seen you together, child, I have seen the way he gazes upon you. I know this will be."

"Do you think he could one day love me?"

"You ask will he love you as Geoffrey has loved you from the moment you were born?"

"Yes."

"All who know you can do nothing but love you, child. There are different kinds of love, that is all." Ella kissed her hair and went back to her work. There was a deep silence for quite a while. The charboys came in, noisy, rowdy and boisterous and Ella chased them with the broom.

"How long does it take to grow a baby?"

Ella almost dropped her broom. She should, after so long, have become used to Adelina's strange questions. "A baby is not like a flower, Milady."

"It begins with seed, does it not?"

"Well, yes, but..."

"How long does it take? How does one know?"

"Well, Milady, it takes almost a year. The bleeding stops, you are ill and not yourself. And of course, you get bigger. But you cannot know if it will live, Milady. Women I have known have suffered childbirth once a year for twenty years and have only three children to show for all of their agonies."

Adelina was quiet. "Should I have a son to Baudoin Dupuy, what is mine will then become my son's and not anyone else's, yes?"

"Well, yes. But more babies die than live."

"No, Ella. I will have a son. This I know. I will do what my father asked of me. I know now why he wished for a grandson. I know now. It is to stop the greed of others who would seize what is not theirs by birth."

Again, there was silence except for a burst of laughter from upstairs. Laughter from the one who would seize all he could if given barely half of an opportunity.

"Have you had babies?" Adelina asked.

"Yes, Milady."

"How is it done?"

Ella was sweating now, and wishing that the day could be over, because all she wanted was her bed. She whispered a quick prayer, crossed herself and asked, "How is what done, Milady?" She knew that this question was bound to come sooner or later.

It was late afternoon when the abbot called for Geoffrey, who at the time was with Andre in the apiary. Andre had no fear of bees and Geoffrey kept his distance, talking all the while to this young monk who had a smile for anyone at any time. His presence alone was healing and Geoffrey searched him out whenever possible. When he spoke of Adelina, Andre said nothing. He had never experienced such love and from an early age had devoted his life to God.

To God and bees this man devoted his life.

If Geoffrey had heard the story of the blessed bees once, he had heard it a thousand times. He was almost pleased of the escape when the abbot called him, impatient.

"Father?" he asked.

"You are to deliver a message to Heracle de Polignac. Now. A horse is being readied."

The abbot gave him a parchment and it was sealed.

Geoffrey sighed. Yes, he and Heracle had carried Robert's casket, but they had not spoken on the day of the funeral. Geoffrey remembered Christian once telling him so many years ago, that their ancestors were priests of Apollo. And then he had laughed that a Polignac would become a monk and all of their fathers fathers would turn in their respective graves... This was long before Robert made his wishes of Geoffrey's future known. But Geoffrey now felt uncomfortable in the Benedictine robes—it seemed that they were garments only, that in his heart he was a warrior, and his name was Polignac and always would be.

Were it not for the abbot's request, he would never have had the opportunity to speak with Heracle at all. The fortress he had often seen from afar, but he never dared approach for hell would have been kinder if such news ever reached Robert. But now he would visit the Polignac fortress, rising high above the village which bore the family name, and he would visit wearing his Benedictine robes.

It was mid morning when Geoffrey requested entry to the fortress, a huge imposing place, impenetrable. This fortress had never been taken and Geoffrey, as he stood before the huge gates, fully understood why. But still he could not imagine that his father, Guillame, had once lived here as a child.

The sentry regarded him coolly, questioning his presence without a word. "I am Geoffrey de Polignac, now known as Brother Christophe, nephew to your lord and master and I bring news to him. I travel alone and pose no threat. I come in peace as you can see."

The sentry stood on tiptoe it seemed to get a better view of this monk from his spy hole in the gate. An arrogant smile creased the furrowed face, then the little door slammed shut. Geoffrey stood, holding his horse's reins for a very long time and soon stepped out of the way when the gates opened. It was not to allow him access, though. Three knights, each fully armored and armed, cantered out and none attempted to avoid Geoffrey. His horse shied, took a sudden fright. Were it not for the knights leaving, Geoffrey knew he would have waited at the gate until sunset or eternity, whichever came first. So he darted in before the gates closed.

No one took any notice of the young bare-headed monk as he led his horse across the courtyard. Warriors were practising, washer women hanging sheets, charboys catching chickens and hounds fighting over a bitch in heat. This young servant of God was ignored by all but watched, too, for Geoffrey felt invisible eyes aware of his every move.

He looked up at the keep as he tethered his horse near a trough. Had my father been first born and not last born, this would be mine, he thought, forgetting for a moment, that he was a Servant of God now.

As none approached Geoffrey, he grabbed a charboy who ran by, holding a chicken by the neck. "Boy, where is your lord?" The boy pulled out of Geoffrey's grip and kept running towards the keep. He followed until a woman, perhaps as old as he, swept by. "Milady?"

She looked back, dark eyes shining. "Yes?"

"I am Geoffrey de Polignac. I have news for my uncle."

"You are who?"

"Geoffrey de Polignac. I am from Lavoute Polignac."

It meant nothing to her.

"I am the second born son of Guillame who died at Langeac many years ago. Show me to your Lord," he said, impatience rising.

"He is not my lord, he is my step-father."

"You are my half cousin, then."

"Do you carry arms?" she asked, bored.

"Milady?" Geoffrey asked, surprised.

"Assassination has been attempted before."

"But I am a servant of God."

"So I see", she said and led the way. Geoffrey followed her up the many flights of stairs, into the great hall where yet another four knights were sword fighting. "Wait here."

Geoffrey watched the knights as he waited, half hoping that he would be asked to join the play, then he realised how he was dressed. He regretted not showing himself bearing Robert's arms, proudly. The arms were indeed similar, although not identical. On the walls, reaching high, were remnants of ages past, of Apollean masks, of battle armours, and paintings of every Polignac since time began. Robert was there and Geoffrey was amazed, for he had certainly never seen what his uncle had looked like when young. Geoffrey studied the paintings as best he could, until one took his attention and did not release it. The eyes, so very bright and much like his own, transfixed him.

"1098."

At the sound of the voice, Geoffrey turned quickly, caught his toe on the hem of the robe and almost toppled.

"In 1098 he fell, Brother Christophe, at the walls of Antioch. Who you see up there is Heracle, the first Polignac to crusade but not the first to die in battle." This huge man was lumbering towards him, arms outstretched, finally catching him in a tight, breath-stopping embrace. "Geoffrey, Geoffrey, do not be alarmed. I have been expecting you. You have news from my friend the abbot. Is that not so?"

Yes, Milord. I have."

"If Robert taught you anything, he taught you manners. Good.

Come, sit with me. Some wine?"

Before Geoffrey could reply, Heracle had bellowed at his retainers to take their play elsewhere. And suddenly the great hall, four times the size of the hall at Lavoute, was very silent. Geoffrey did not know what to say until a huge tankard was placed before him at the long wide table.

"I hear that Adelina attempted to join Stephen of Cloyes. Is it so?"

Geoffrey did not know what Heracle was talking about. "I am not welcome at Lavoute now," Geoffrey said. "What happens there I know nothing of." It pained him to admit this truth. All he had received was a strange letter from Adelina, in which she spoke of being a warrior fighting with her innocence alone. Geoffrey had given it to Andre and he too did not know what it meant. They both decided it best to leave it be for if they scratched their heads in wonder for so long, Andre feared splinters.

"That you are no longer welcome, I have heard."

Heracle held his hand out and for a moment Geoffrey wondered what he wanted. He then remembered the parchment and took it from his robe. As his uncle read, Geoffrey again perused the huge hall. He sipped his wine—it was rich, dark and very heavy and not Auvergne made.

"Ah, yes. The wedding to Dupuy proceeds now that she is well again."

Geoffrey looked up, amazed. He did not know that Adelina was ill.

"On Saturday she weds and I am to offer her."

Geoffrey's heart, what was left of it, hit his feet. "But you do not know her."

"Know her? What has that to do with it?" Heracle asked. "The family's holdings will increase by this union, and that is all that matters." Heracle was silent momentarily, then he cleared his nose on the floor and two boys appeared from nowhere, or so it seemed, to take away the spoiled rushes.

"Best I leave, then. I have performed my duty," Geoffrey said.

"Stay."

"I have nothing to discuss, Milord."

"Geoffrey, sit. Listen to me."

Geoffrey, half risen, sat again when he heard: "It was your father, Guillame, who split the family. It was not me."

"Then someone lies."

"Both of my bothers could have remained here, but there was always much jealousy and vying for supremacy. When our cousin died, Robert took ownership of Lavoute. He also wedded the one I wanted the most but that is of no consequence now. Guillame, your father, who could not be, in his own words, useless and landless, took a holding at Langeac and built for himself a chateau there, all against our father's wishes. There he stayed in exile from the family until it was under siege and seized upon his death. My father was still alive then and would not agree to take you and your brother, Christian, in. He was stubborn, and would not be swayed. Your mother, Eloise, was not a noble but from this very village, and my father never once acknowledged her existence. It was your grandfather who turned your mother away, not I. It was not my decision. She had walked a long way with two small fatherless boys, only to be turned away at the gate. When my brother Robert heard of this, I, of course, was to blame. As I always had been."

Heracle stopped his tale long enough to fill his mouth with wine. Then he continued, and the light of the past still did not fade from his eyes.

"When my father met his death and caused death to that Dupuy from Allegre, it was too late then for me to take the sons of Guillame in. You were half grown, and Robert had already turned you and your brother against me."

"My uncle told me nothing of this, nothing of you."

"And still he aggravates me even though he is in his grave!" Heracle was laughing.

"How is this? How can a dead man aggravate you?"

"He has turned you into a Benedictine!"

"Milord, I have not yet taken any vows."

"Geoffrey, there is much you do not know. For two hundred years we have been at odds with the Bishops of Le Puy, and what is this before me now? A monk? I have lost three sons already. I have only two step-daughters and one son remaining. Should I lose him, please God, be that the case, who will be my heir? Only a Benedictine monk is left now for Christian is dead."

"I do not understand."

"Yes, you do. You understand."

"I did not know until today that you had sons, dead or alive. Who is this one who remains? I have a cousin I do not know?"

"Gervaise is in Paris and has been for many years now. My only remaining son thinks he is a woman. He dresses and acts so. He sings, he dances... he is not my son."

Geoffrey was very surprised at this and no words at all would come.

"I suspect this is yet another reason why Robert kept you from me. He knew I had no competent male heir. But that need be no longer. Yes, I have been expecting you, Geoffrey. Something good has come from the death of my brother."

Heracle's very large hand clamped on Geoffrey's and held tight.

"What say you?"

"Milord?" Geoffrey squeaked.

"You wish one day to be the Lord of Polignac, a Viscount in your own right? You wish for all of this to be yours?"

"I... All of this is so sudden."

"Then think on it. Think on what I have said."

Geoffrey could do nothing else but think for the next few days as he sat alone in his cell, and perused the word of God but was unable to concentrate on anything except the face of Heracle de Polignac, the one who had died, aged 23, at the walls of Antioch. Geoffrey seemed to know him, this long-dead ancestor, but could find no reason for such a revelation. Except perhaps in the forbidden writings of Origen who devoted his life to the preservation of the original gospels. The Contra Celsum fascinated Geoffrey as did De Principiis: "Every soul comes into this world strengthened by the victories or weakened by the defeats of its previous life. Its place in this world as a vessel appointed to honour or dishonour, is determined by its previous merits or demerits. Its work in this world determines its place in the world which is to follow."

That and more fascinated Geoffrey. Truths it seemed remained hidden but always appeared sooner or later. The great wheel had finally turned.

For one with nothing to one promised all.

Geoffrey did not know which way to turn. His wise heart was forsaking him, his thoughts not his own. This had been a dream, one he could only wake from, surely.

"As you can see," he had said to Adelina that day so long ago, "I have much of nothing."

For a moment, he wished it was true, for life with nothing was simple if not perhaps a life of avoidance. One which would possibly be lived again until responsibilities were faced with a brave heart.

The night before his life's love would become another's, he did not pray in the darkness of his tiny cell. He did not pray at all. He implored instead, what is it I should do?

And no answer came. Nothing came.

# Chapter 25

Jennet walked into her mistress's chambers and drew back the heavy leather curtains. Sunshine streamed in, but it alone was not enough to wake Adelina. Jennet approached the bed cautiously. "Milady? You must rise now," came the sweet, soft, sing-song voice.

Adelina opened one eye to see Jennet's huge smile and bright, sparkling eyes. Why is she so happy this day? What is this day? Adelina wondered. Realisation flooded. Today I wed Baudoin Dupuy.

Adelina put the cushions over her face and shooed her girl away.

"Come, Milady. We must set your hair in curls now or it shall never hold. Fortunately, there is no wind today. See? I have readied your beautiful dress... Come, Milady. Come. You have slept far too long already."

Jennet pulled the cushions from Adelina's face and grabbed at the others quickly, tossing them out of reach. Adelina rose on elbows—a sight indeed with her short hair askew and dark circles under her eyes. "Why is it everyone anticipates this day but me? Why are you so happy?"

"I anticipate a new life with you, Milady."

"And if I patted your head, would you sit and beg, too?"

Jennet for a moment let her hurt show. When she did that, her mistress was always touched by guilt. Today, she was not touched though. Adelina tossed the covers aside and lumbered towards the door. "Milady, no. People gather already in the great hall. Best you not frighten them so early this day."

Adelina turned and glared at her girl. Jennet smiled sweetly. In her hand a chamber-pot. Adelina spat a curse and grabbed the pot. "Already they gather? Dieu. There will be no peace. No peace at all. Already I tire of this day."

Grump, grump, grump, Jennet thought, studying the ceiling and the rope dangling from the crossbeam as her mistress used the pot. She said, "We never made your quintain, Milady. I have heard stories of your prowess as an archer. Perhaps when we live at Allegre, you would teach me?"

"Then paint the image of Gabriel of Lyon upon the quintain and we shall both have fun. What I plan will hurt him more than a crossbolt."

Adelina gave the pot to her girl who emptied it out of the window, looking first to see none walked unsuspecting below. "Soon you will be a bride, Milady. A married woman. I am overjoyed. I was up before dawn this day, helping Ella prepare the feast. I helped the Lady Marys cut the rose-buds, too, and they were still covered in dew. All was so beautiful. I cut the white, she the pink."

"Roses?" Adelina asked, already tiring of Jennet's stories of beauty and romance. All this talk was making her sick.

"For you to carry this day."

"Oh. Those roses. I suppose I shall be forced to bathe as well?"

"It is best to tend your hair while it is wet, Milady."

"I have bathed already this month. God! It is the revenge of my mother. Come. Let us get it over with."

To reach her mother's private chambers, where the tub lay, they did not have to pass the great hall, because the private chambers was high in the tower. Soon enough Adelina was enduring the preparations for her wedding.

"It reeks."

"Milady?"

"The soap. It reeks. All of this reeks."

Jennet sniffed at the soap. Ella had made it from Michel's recipe and to it, had added both lavender and rose oil. It was very pleasant indeed, it did not reek at all.

"Baudoin Dupuy goes to no such troubles this day. I know what it is he shall wear. He shall look the same, why can't I?"

"Oh, Milady. He knows that no eyes shall feast upon him. All eyes will be on you."

"God, why can it not be tomorrow!"

"We must endure today first, Milady. You will remember this day for the rest of your life."

"Being scrubbed raw with not one part of my body overlooked? I think that a bad memory it will make."

"You grumble."

"And you are insolent. Is Gabriel here?"

"I am sorry, Milady, but he has not died during the night. He came out from your mother's chamber this morning and seemed in good cheer. Is that not a good sign of the day to come?"

"The little archer?"

"He is here."

"And Geoffrey?"

Jennet shook her head.

"But it was my wish that he come."

"Perhaps he will yet. So many gather downstairs already, and many of them are strangers to me. Ella said that Lady and Lord Dupuy arrive soon."

Adelina was startled. "Lady Dupuy is well enough to come?"

"Yes, it seems so. I knew you would be pleased."

Jennet approached, armed with some thick goo on her fingers. "What is that?" Adelina squealed, recoiling further into the tub.

"It is some cream which will enhance your beauty. The mistress has ordered it. Now, keep still. Do you not want to be beautiful indeed for your new husband? Do you not anticipate the joys of this coming night?"

Baudoin helped his father into the carriage. The wound in his hip affected all of his movements and he was still wracked by fever of unknown origin. He may have been improving daily, however slightly, but Baudoin knew that the journey to Lavoute Polignac would most likely spell the end. Stubborn pride though had kept Henri Dupuy alive this long and no doubt one more day would not matter.

Baudoin turned back to collect his mother from the house and was startled by the sudden grip on his hand. "We gain much by this, Baudoin. Much."

"Yes, Father, I know."

Something appeared in Henri's eyes that Baudoin had never seen before. "God smiles upon us now," Henri said.

Baudoin nodded politely and turned back to the house.

Fortunately, his mother had full senses this day, but how long would it last, he did not know. She was dressed in deep red velvet, and Baudoin watched her come down the stairs. It seemed that she floated. "My son," she said and held out her hand. "You look very handsome today."

"And you are beautiful, Mother." Baudoin took her hand and walked her out to the carriage where Francois and Antoine waited.

"The room is ready for her? Are you sure?"

"Yes, Mother. Do not be concerned. I ask that you try to remember that her name is not Vianna. It is Adelina."

"Adelina. Yes. Adelina."

"Do you have your medicine for the pain?"

"You fuss too much."

"I do not like watching you suffer. Show me."

Heloise unwrapped the handkerchief clasped tight in her hand and there, hidden within a small, velvet drawstring bag, a bottle of her potion. It affected her senses but killed the pain. Pain already played within her eyes, though, but take the medicine she would not. Not yet, at least. Baudoin helped her into the carriage and told Francois to drive on.

He mounted his horse and looked back at the dull, ugly house and nervousness rising, much as it did before a battle, Baudoin rode out of the gates, thinking that he had forgotten something. But what? Halfway to the village he remembered, turned his horse about, and galloped back to the house.

He took the stairs three at a time, skidded into his chambers and took from his table a small gold box. Across the corridor he skidded again, and opened the door to the bedchambers.

His mother had struggled from her bed yesterday to oversee the cleaning and decorating. Always, though, she whispered, "Vianna will like this. Yes. Vianna will like this..."

From the high bed canopy, sheets of red silk billowed till tied to the bedposts by tasseled cord. Already, fresh flowers had been brought in from St. Paulien.

Baudoin looked at the tiny box in his hand, swallowed his fright, and put the box in the center of the bed. Then he was gone.

He rode out, knowing that he would not return here alone, or quite the same. Special chambers had been prepared for Adelina's girl, too, and all of the man servants were very excited about having a young, fair girl to work with, and no doubt, play games with. Baudoin had given his warning, but he knew it went unheeded, for men were men and could never be changed.

How he wished he could be as others were.

God, he prayed as he rode, help me? I am about to marry, and worse, she is a Polignac. He could not remember a thing that the abbot had told them, nor could he remember what exactly it was he was supposed to do, let alone be.

The wedding was set for early afternoon. It was not until lunch that Adelina finally appeared in the great hall, forced there by hunger alone. And she was neither yet dressed, nor halfways ready. Her mother sighed and turned the other way, quickly.

Adelina's short hair was stuck fast to her head in finger curls, another of her mother's creams was thick on her face and she wore one of her father's tunics. Her legs and feet were very bare.

All of the guests had departed for the abbey, all except Heracle de Polignac, who stood in his finery, chatting with Marys and Gabriel. Adelina came to a sudden stop on the stairs but too late, she had been seen. Adelina could have turned back then, but thought not. Soon she would be well away from all of them and time was not passing fast enough for her liking. She walked past without uttering a word, caring not if she shocked anyone, straight to the table overflowing with foods of every kind. And there she feasted, her hands filling as quickly as she was able.

"Adelina!"

"What now?" she said, not looking at her mother.

"Your uncle is here. Do you have any respect?"

"I am not blind. I know he is here. He offers me for marriage only and that is all he does. He is of no concern to me, now, or ever. Is that not so, Monsieur?" she asked, mouth half full of food, daring to glance into her uncle's eyes. Again, he said nothing, but this time, a smile lingered behind his eyes and almost touched his bearded face.

Up the stairs she went once again, back to Jennet who was eagerly waiting to dress her.

"She grieves still," Marys said.

"Grief? No. She is a spoiled child," Gabriel said and fisted his hand. "It is this she needs."

"No," came Heracle's forceful voice. "She is as her grandmother was. A fist only strengthens the resolve. She is as her grandmother was," he mused again. "The backbone of our family and from her, all gained their strengths." Heracle turned to Marys and said, for the fifth time that day, "You have grown a beautiful daughter, Marys."

And for the fifth time, Marys smiled sweetly while her hand was clenched on her goblet of wine.

"I have engaged an artist to commemorate this day."

"An artist? She will not sit still long enough for an artist..."

At first, Geoffrey ignored the knocking on his door. He knew who it was. Andre had a knock unlike any other's. "They arrive, Brother Christophe."

Geoffrey put his pen down. He looked sadly at the words now delivered to the parchment—words he had discovered lingering in his mind on awakening.

> *Stained glass embers*
> *tinted and flickering*
> *luminous, glimmering*
> *Are all I can sing of.*
> *Relinquished and vowed,*
> *dispersed from the flesh,*
> *all words have died now.*
> *Kindled in darkness*
> *touched only by silence*
> *memories weep long*
> *All, or Nothing at all.*

The knock came again, impatient. "Brother? They arrive. It is almost time. Do you sleep?"

Geoffrey rubbed at his eyes, and said, with anger in his voice, "No! I do not sleep! I am coming!"

The abbey was full and as yet there was no sign of the bride and her uncle. It was too airless for both Baudoin and Geoffrey, and they met in the fresh air by the rear door of the chapel. Baudoin looked up when he saw the monk approach. "Is it time? Does she come, Brother?"

Geoffrey drew the hood back.

"Oh, it is you."

Geoffrey breathed in the warm air. "Dupuy, tell me. Can you love one such as her? Can you love at all?"

"What would you know of such things? You care not for the world of men now. It is none of your affair. It has never been."

"Circumstance alone has given you this victory."

"Then it was you who birthed it. Had you not killed my brother, none of this would be at all."

"This cannot be happening. God could not be so unwise."

"You pain from jealousy when it is you to blame. Leave me in peace. Your despair is not mine."

"If you are so disturbed, perhaps you should cancel this wedding now and find some peace within yourself!"

Baudoin said nothing. He looked up at the sky instead.

"If this was not the wish of her father, my uncle and guardian and teacher, I would stand in your place!" There! Geoffrey had said it. But the pain lingered still.

"More is gained than lost. I cannot stop this. Move out of my way, Geoffrey. Can you not hear the village serfs overjoyed? Can you hear anything over your own whining miseries?"

"My whining miseries?"

"Move away, Geoffrey. I have no wish to grapple with one such as you."

"Why not? The clothing does not change who I am."

"Out of my way."

From afar the rowdy joy echoed up to the hilltop, but Geoffrey did not move aside. "Geoffrey, Brother Christophe, Sparrow, whoever you truly are, I will not harm her. I swear this on my life. Now, move aside now before I harm you. I am in no mood for this idiocy."

Geoffrey did not move-- one such as Baudoin Dupuy could never threaten him.

"She comes now. My wife arrives."

Their gazes met and Geoffrey finally stepped out of the way.

Despairing tears caught and entwined in a knot, a knot which choked him as he stood in his place at the rear of the chapel watching her walk towards another. The enemy. "Take me now, Lord," Geoffrey whispered. "Take me or give me strength to endure this."

Geoffrey, hiding his wet eyes beneath his hood, stared at the arches instead of the two kneeling at the altar. He prayed that time would pass quickly, but it did not. Always, always his gaze, however blurred, returned to her, an earthborne angel, glowing in white and pink, her head lowered in reverence, or was it fear and confusion?

She does not want this! his mind screamed, but was not heard by anyone.

I am dying, Geoffrey thought. This feeling can be nothing else.

His life and his love, as he watched, became another man's wife.

It was the first time in many years that music and gaiety flowed as quickly as the wine in the chateau's great hall. The mingling crowd was soon drunk in the joyous air, and four tankards of wine did nothing to fill the void—deep, bottomless. Nothing could dispel the misery which clung to Geoffrey's shoulders, heavier than a shroud. He sat alone, yet surrounded by people he thought he knew, and all the while only glancing from afar the angelic bride who today had forgotten of his existence.

She drinks too heavily, and she hides her nervousness behind her huge smile, he thought, as a page filled his tankard again and another passed a tray of foods in front of Geoffrey's eyes. Geoffrey studied the boy. He was Acelin's page and still here, possibly because he had nowhere else to go. This place, Geoffrey thought, is a holding pen for orphans and strays.

Perhaps it was the heady wine, but a thought strayed into his mind. If I go to Polignac, to serve my uncle, I shall take this boy as my page. Yes, that is what I would do. If I go. Geoffrey looked to the main table. Adelina sat with her new husband, their heads together. Each were laughing, hands clasped tight. Beside her, Marys. Heracle, then Gabriel. Henri and Heloise, with their knights, Francois and Antoine, were mostly silent. If any joy showed, it was hidden. Geoffrey himself had none at all to hide.

Two hours passed and the gluttony had no end. There was music and dancing, and as yet, no fights to heighten the entertainment. Louis was there, as out of place here now as I am, Geoffrey thought. Michel was in a deep conversation with Henri Dupuy and his wife, who to Geoffrey, looked very old and ill indeed. Did Robert wish this because he knew the Dupuy elders' time was close? Perhaps, he thought,

Robert was indeed as cunning and arrogant and obstinate as his elder brother had decreed. All of this is for greed, for the accumulation of wealth. There is no love. There never can be, or will be. Of that he was certain.

The moment Geoffrey had convinced himself of this unalterable fact, Baudoin Dupuy rose and with his new wife in hand, they left the great hall, again to cheers and laughter. They were leaving now, leaving, alone for Allegre and the long night which lay ahead.

Why can it not be me? he asked silently. It is I who know her, and only I who love her. Of all these gathered, only I... Geoffrey stood, hoping that she would see him, but the crowd followed the newly-weds to the courtyard. Perhaps she did glance at him and smile but that was all. Perhaps her smile lay only in his imagination.

And now it was over.

All of her pleadings to come, be by my side and give me the strength to go on, they were little but lies, for not once did she even search for him in the crowd. I am dying, Geoffrey thought as he leaned against the farrier's wall. I am dying.

It is all, or it is nothing at all.

He looked at the walls he once held dear but nothing remained now except cold stone. No pride, no joy remained. The death of one man had altered so much that the death of another to this world would not matter.

Geoffrey thought of Heracle's offer but saw no future in it.

It is all, or it is nothing at all.

Geoffrey went to the stables, collected his horse, and walked it across the drawbridge. He had decided to die to the world of the common man. He would return to the abbey and ensconce himself in his gloomy cell of meaningless prayer, and a vow of silence he would make and never break.

From this moment on, he thought, as he mounted his horse, I will choose nothing to all.

For all can be nothing without her.

# CHAPTER 26

"I did not see Geoffrey."

"He was there, hiding in his corner, sullen and sulking and drinking too much wine too quickly."

"He does that, sometimes."

The last person Baudoin wished to talk of was Geoffrey. "It went well, I think. Gabriel spared no expense."

"It was not his money, which is why no expense was spared. Do you think the remains of the feast will go to the serfs?"

"If that is your wish, I will see to it. Whose serfs, though?"

"Are they not all ours now?"

"Much lies ahead, Adelina. Much," Baudoin said with a smile.

"I did not have the chance to speak with your parents. How is your father now? And your mother?"

"Tomorrow they will be home and you shall see for yourself how they are."

"Your father smiled at me. I was shocked by it. He must be ill."

"Adelina, why is it so important that my father like you?"

"It is not important that he likes me. It is important that he sees I am as much a person as he is."

"It is more than that."

"If it is more then I know not what this 'more' is."

The ride continued in silence.

"We should reach Allegre by sunset."

"It seems so."

"The women in the village were busy gathering flowers for you when I left this morning."

"Flowers for me? Why? They do not know me."

"It seems that you are their angel, sent to deliver them."

"God, you jest, surely? I am no angel."

Baudoin glanced at her, smiled, and said nothing.

"Why would Geoffrey have hidden from me this day? Was he feeling miserable, I wonder?"

"Somewhat miserable, yes."

"But why? He said that this marriage was the best for all."

"Do you not know that he loves you above all others? Possibly even above God Himself?"

"Geoffrey? What nonsense. He is but a dreamer." Silence ruled for a short while. "I hope he does not take his vows. I want him to choose a girl and marry and raise many sons. He is all we Polignacs have left now. My uncle told me all this day. He cannot waste his life in solitude. It would be a terrible sin."

"Why do you tell me this?" Baudoin asked, already tired of Geoffrey, Geoffrey, Geoffrey.

"I would say it to him but he does not speak to me any more. It seems he does not want to know me. What have I done except grow older? And perhaps, wiser?"

"Adelina?"

"Yes?"

"I do not want you to speak of Geoffrey again. You are my wife now. Your duty lies with me. Did you not listen to what the abbot said this day of duty?"

"He hates me, that is why he said I must give my life to you."

"The abbot does not hate you."

"Ha! Our distrust goes back to when I was a little girl. He said then I was the child of Satan himself and that one day I would burn in hell for my sins."

"Why would the abbot say that of an innocent child?"

"I think that was the day I set fire to his leg."

"You what?"

"I was hiding under the table whilst he spoke to Papa, and I had a candle in my hand. He did not feel a thing till he smelled something strange. It was the hair on his leg burning. He had very hairy legs."

Baudoin laughed for a long time.

"It is not so amusing. I have done far worse. That day I was punished, but only after my father stopped laughing, much as you do now."

"Tell me no more. No more. Why do I not doubt that you would do that? I must admit the abbot did not look upon you with affection. But remember his words. You must love, honour and obey me."

"Love and honour, perhaps one day I may. But obey? Ha!" She kicked her horse into a canter, and then a gallop, laughing all the while. Today, she rode the horse Gabriel had given her as a gift. So hard he had tried to make amends. There was no other horse readied for her so this one she had to take. And she thought as she had first gazed upon such a beautiful creature, why must this animal be blamed? The horse was a fine one, of decent temper and fast, too. But so was Baudoin's and he soon caught her, and it soon became a race, and although she could have beaten him to St. Paulien, with much time to spare, she did not. She liked him too much to have him angry so soon. Not many men liked being beaten by a woman. That much she already knew.

"You ride well."

"I used to accompany my father. He was good, because when I fell off, he would not offer to help me up again. He would insist I do it immediately, myself. My father taught me much."

"Of riding horses?"

"Of life. If you fall, all you need do is stand up again. Tall and proud. He did, always."

They walked their horses through St. Paulien—it was never wise, her father used to say, to gallop through a village full of small children as they were too valuable as future workers, and there were many little ones here. Many indeed.

Adelina did not have to know which house was Eleanor's because Baudoin looked at it many times as they walked by. Adelina pulled her horse to a sudden stop. "What is it?" Baudoin asked.

"Speak to her. Speak with Eleanor. She is on your mind. I can tell."

"No. I cannot go there. It is impossible now."

"Do this I ask."

"Why?"

"I need to see her. I need to witness her beauty for myself. No one knows her except you. No one knows of this Eleanor at all."

"Come, quickly. It gets dark soon."

"Baudoin, I wish to see this woman, this one who has your heart!"

"No! Now, come! Make haste. Remember your vows!"

"But I am curious," she whined as she walked her horse onwards. "She has your heart."

"Adelina!"

From St. Paulien to Allegre, he would not be drawn into any conversation about Eleanor at all. "What is past is past. Today is our time. There is nothing but today."

"Even if today becomes tomorrow all too soon?"

"Why can you not be satisfied with wifely things and leave the philosophies of life to
others?"

"I think too much. I always have. Where is my girl?"

"She rides ahead with Francois."

Darkness was closing in as they entered the gates and gave up their horses to the stable boys.

Baudoin did not take her hand. Already, he was barking orders to all and sundry as she followed him across the courtyard, and there at the doors to the ugly house, were bunches of flowers in pots of water. So many pots that Adelina could not count them.

Adelina lifted her skirts high and picked her cautious way though. Many flowers were here but none were roses.

"I want to build a rose garden, Baudoin Dupuy. That is what I will do."

Baudoin rolled his eyes and led her inside the quiet, dark house. "My father will never allow it."

"Will you?"

"I have nothing against flowers. When I am Lord you shall have your garden, unless my father gives permission before then. Which I doubt he will."

"Ha! His permission indeed. A rose garden I shall have. He smiled at me, therefore he is almost accepting of me as his new daughter, and what I want, I have always had. One way or another."

"Your chatter of nonsense."

"To you it is nonsense. Not to me."

"Come," he said, taking her hand again and leading her up the stairs. "My mother has wished that we reside in the main bed-chambers. It is the one which she shared with my father."

He opened the door and Adelina saw immediately that her things were laid out, her dresses hanging behind a beautiful screen, her jewels, her combs... everything had been brought in from Lavoute, except for her bed. And for that she was pleased. There were billowing silks and fresh flowers everywhere she turned.

"It is beautiful, Baudoin. Is this your doing?" she asked, disbelieving that this was the room she had slept in once before. Gone now the gloom and dust.

"My doing?" He cackled. He thought that amusing indeed. "Here is my present to you. Think of me when you wear it."

Adelina sat on the beautifully made bed and picked up the small gold box. She opened it and Baudoin sat beside her but not too close.

He watched her beautiful green eyes study him after she saw what lay in the box, an emerald necklace.

"It was once worn by my great grandmother. A woman of great strength and beauty, I am told."

Adelina held it in her fingers, and the diamonds shone like stars. Truly, it seemed like a necklace of stars.

"How beautiful you are," he said softly.

"Am I as beautiful as Eleanor?" she asked.

Something crossed his eyes and he said, "I am wed to you, Addie."

"It matters little who is wed to who in these times. When the heart is missing it cannot be real."

"When I say you are beautiful, I do not lie."

Baudoin reached to touch her face but she pulled back and stood up, and moved about the room, trying to clasp the necklace blindly. A lot was on his mind but he said nothing. The wine he had requested was waiting and two pewter goblets as well. Baudoin uncorked the bottle and poured. Nervousness rising, he gulped his down and poured another while her back was turned. She did not hear, she stood by the window, looking down at the darkness, staring at nothing, and, he wondered, is she as nervous about this as I am? So he picked up the goblets and went to her. She was much shorter than he and he stood close behind her, very close, and put the goblet of wine into her hand. Her hair smelled sweet and he longed to bury his face in it, and remember the scent for all of eternity. He touched her arm gently and Adelina ducked away quickly. She would not meet his gaze.

Do I frighten her so much? he wondered. He prayed for strength to endure this night because he knew it would be very, very long indeed. It would be easier if she was not so young and frightened. Easier if she weren't as fair of face, as curved of breast and hip. He sipped at the wine and wished the bottle was not as far away. He felt as if he needed it all and more.

"Where is my girl?" she asked.

"Busy, I expect." Please God, he thought, I cannot do this if her girl comes to watch.

"She has had a terrible thing happen to her, you know. She does not trust men and here, this house is full of men. I have promised her that such a thing will not happen again because she wanted to die. And she is worth more to me alive than she is dead."

Baudoin frowned, what was she saying? Why was the goblet in her hand still unsipped and shaking? It was their very best wine and she would only hold it as tight as a rosary. Why? "Your girl will come to no harm here."

"And if she was with child from what happened to her, would you turn her from your house?"

"Adelina, what has happened?" he asked and stepped closer. Adelina again ducked away. A master of avoidance.

"I cannot say. I swore on my life never to say, not even to God who looked on as it happened." Tears were in her eyes, and she was rigid with fear. For her girl, a mere handmaiden? It did not make sense. Baudoin finished his wine and filled his goblet again. Any words he had were long gone. He simply wondered what he had done to frighten her so badly. She was not frightened when surrounded by people; she was not frightened as they journeyed here this eve, but only when they were finally alone. And how he had anticipated this night. For a long time now, ever since they'd sat in the abbey at St Denis holding hands, he had waited. And wondered much. So he lay upon the bed in his black leathers, boots and all, his back propped against a mountain of silken cushions, his feet crossed and jiggling.

Adelina could not look at him lying there, watching her intently. She felt his eyes searing into her, much as Gabriel of Lyon's had when he had torn open her clothing and feasted his horrible eyes upon her body, and took her so violently, and she knew that this was what Baudoin awaited, too. She saw it in every man's eyes of late. Except perhaps, for Geoffrey. And Michel. And Dedwyd.

"To worry so much, you must have great love for this girl of yours."

"Her name is Jennet."

"She will be safe here. And so will you."

Adelina turned to the window and drank her wine, forgetting for a moment that she was supposed to be a lady now. It was light wine and warm and it affected her senses almost immediately. She looked down into the moonlit darkness. How long would this night be?

While she stared from the window, her back to him, Baudoin tied a tight knot in the laces of his boot. "Adelina?"

She turned. He was trying to untie his boots and having great difficulty.

"Have you fingernails?" he asked.

"Some," she said. "Is it stuck?"

"Very," he replied.

Adelina put her wine down and sat on the bed. She looked at his face after first inspecting his boot and the size of the knot in the leather lacing. She picked at the knots and eventually used her teeth as well until it loosened. While there, she took the boot off. He spread his long toes on his very white and very soft foot.

Her feet were hardened, his were soft. And still he was waiting. Still he said nothing. "You lie there as if you are a king and I your servant."

"But I am king," he said. "King of my own world and you are my queen."

"Surely a king is able to take off his own boots?"

Baudoin unlaced his other boot, eased it off and threw it. She was amused by the light in his eyes. "You have fine feet," she said.

"Would I see yours?" he asked.

"Why do you want to see my feet?"

Because you will possibly let me see nothing else, he thought. "I would imagine that they are as beautiful as your hands," he said. He reached for her feet and Adelina lifted a leg on to the bed. She flinched when he touched. Her slippers were of pink satin and dirty from the ride to Allegre. "A lovely foot," he said and pulled the ribbon apart, slipped the light shoe off. He ran his fingers along her foot and looked into her eyes. But she looked away from what she saw there. He turned to his side and he kissed her toe.

Adelina curled her foot and tried to pull away but he had hold of her ankle. His touch was good but... "Please, not. Please, not." He sighed. He had longed to take his hand further up her leg, beyond her knee perhaps. The toes always made for a good beginning with Eleanor.

"Why do you fear me, Adelina? Is it something I have done to you?"

She lowered her head.

"Do you not know what is expected of us this night?"

"Yes," she whispered, voice shaking.

"Can it be that you do not want to lie with me?"

"I don't know. Your presence frightens me."

"Mine or any man's, Adelina?"

She looked at his dark searching gaze. What was it that he knew? What lay in his mind? What had Gabriel said to him this eve? Had he waited until after the vows to say, "Take your spoiled goods and get off my land?" No, she thought. No, they had both laughed, Gabriel's arm around her new husband's shoulders, tight. And she had known that they laughed about her. Even her mother was laughing. Everyone had been laughing.

Baudoin sat up and reached for her hands, clenched in her lap, tight. "You are frightened because you are so young."

"I do not feel young any more. I am a married woman now."

"And this you have never wanted to be."

"You know?"

"Oh, yes, I know,' he said, holding her hands in one of his and curling her short hair about his finger. "Did you think that by cutting your hair I would not take you as a wife?"

"I do not know why I cut it now. It was before I left to..."

"Yes?"

"I had planned on joining Stephen of Cloyes at Marseilles."

"The shepherd boy who leads all those children to their deaths?"

"He is on a mission."

"It will fail."

"I was found and brought home to face this marriage to you. You, who seems a friend, and one who seems very kind but is not. I know how black your heart is, Baudoin Dupuy."

He did not know what to say.

"You who takes serving girls and defiles and beats them for no reason."

Baudoin was taken aback. "What is this?"

"You had your way with my girl and you expect me to approach you with affection. I cannot. I cannot bear you near me because of what you did to my girl."

"Who told you these lies?"

"She does not lie."

"I would not do this you say to anyone, noble or servant."

"But your brother!"

"I am not my brother!" He was angry now and she flinched from him as he got off the bed, angry, pacing. "I had considered this night many times. I had hoped that by being a friend to you, you would come to trust me in time and perhaps even love me. Now you accuse me of violating your girl? When did this deed occur? Tell me, Adelina for I cannot remember!"

He had a very short temper. That was not good. It took much for Geoffrey to rage and he quietened, too, once he realised how angry he was. This frightened her. This reminded her of Gabriel. Of her father. Of Louis.

"When did I do this!" he yelled and stepped to her. Adelina scrambled across the bed to get away. She had no wish to feel the back of this one's hand. He was far too strong for that. "If you will not tell me, she will."

He went out, and left the door open. Adelina wanted to run away and she had never backed away from an argument in her life. Why was she so meek and afraid now? The silence was sticky until from far below, she heard Jennet's cries, "Milord! What have I done!"

Her feet found wings. One shoe on, she skidded down the long hallway, and lifting her skirts and train high, leapt down the stairs and into the kitchen.

Jennet was on her knees on the floor, the men servants watching curiously and Baudoin was ready to strike.

"If you beat her I will kill you!"

He turned to Adelina, his bride, and his hand lowered immediately.

"I am sorry, Milady, I am sorry, but had I said who defiled me Etienne would have died and my sisters and..."

"Who!" Baudoin demanded.

"Gabriel of Lyon," Jennet cried. Baudoin let go of her hair and Jennet put her face to the floor crying, until one of the servants, a young fair haired man, took her up and guided her away and out of the master's sight.

The news of who had defiled Jennet was too much for Adelina. For a moment she thought she would faint and so she sat on the stairs, quickly. Had he not threatened to kill Geoffrey if she spoke of what he had done to her? It had not been the knife at her throat but the vision of Geoffrey, dead, which forced her to yield.

"You feared me all of this time because of a servant's lies?" Baudoin asked, his anger gone and replaced by confusion. "Look at me, Adelina! Am I such a monster? Do you not halfways know me?"

She looked up from where she sat. "You are not a monster."

Baudoin rubbed at his face and bellowed at the servants to begone. Soon enough he and Adelina were alone. Baudoin took from his belt a dagger, and she flinched at sight of that too. He stabbed at an apple on the long table. He ate it from the knife and he watched her. "This is not a good beginning."

"It is not."

"You wish to go to her, now?"

"Yes."

"Then go. You know where I will be."

He walked past Adelina, still seated on the stairs.

For a long time she felt nothing except an aching numbness. Adelina swept the band of roses from her head and was almost about to weep uncontrollably into them when she heard, "Milady? I could do nothing else."

"I know, girl," Adelina said. Jennet crawled up the stairs and half lay near her lady's feet. Adelina put her hand in Jennet's hair and said, "He said he would kill everyone you had ever loved if you did not do as he wanted. And he told you what he would do to them. He said he would disfigure you so horribly that no man except a blind one would ever want you. And when he touched," she said, voice shaking and low, "and when he took you, there was laughter in his eyes as he fed from your fear. You don't have to tell me, Jennet. I know." Jennet put her face on her mistress feet and cried because it was all true. "I will kill him. I know this. One day, I will kill him for all that he has done. Revenge of many will be mine and mine alone."

"Milady, no, you cannot think such things. You would burn in hell for these things you think and say."

"I am already in hell," she said quietly. "My husband has sworn that you will come to no harm here. He is man of his word. This I know now." Adelina looked up and she saw the fair haired servant, almost hiding in the darkness. It seemed to her that Jennet's life would be good, here. Already she had one who cared whether she lived or died. "I have apologies to make now," she said quietly and struggled to her feet.

Baudoin was waiting, his leathers discarded because of the heat. He wore only his hose and Adelina could not look upon him for any length of time.

"Have you comforted all yet? Have you forgotten anyone? Because in your haste, you forget me," he said.

Adelina put her headband of roses down. "She had never lied to me before."

"That you know of. You trust the wrong people, Adelina Dupuy. She is a servant and will be treated as such."

"I am your wife, so it seems that I will be treated as your mother."

"You know nothing as yet. I had hoped, how I had hoped that this marriage would be as one in the eyes of God and not just in name. You shy like a skittish horse when I am close. This was not so in the past. In times past, we were almost friends. If it is me, I will try to make amends but you must tell me what it is I make amends for."

"Baudoin please, no more. It is not you. It is nothing you have done. It is not your family for I know your family now. I am frightened."

"Of?"

"I do not know!"

"What has happened to you? Where is the fearless warrior who lived in her dreams? Who has broken your spirit?"

Still she could not look at him and nor would she ever say. Was it true? Was her spirit

broken? No. It could never be. "My spirit is not broken."

"Is it not?" Baudoin walked to where she stood in the doorway and he lifted her face. Her eyes were brimming with tears, and were pleading with him, no, do not, no... Baudoin, on fire again from her presence alone, slid his fingers into her tightly curled hair and he drew her close.

At first she resisted until she heard him say softly, "I would rather your love than your hate. Come to me when you are ready, so that we will be one in God's eyes. I pray it will not take long, Adelina. Many sons I need." He kissed her hair and walked off, taking his bottle of wine with him. He disappeared into a room at the far end of the corridor.

Adelina sat and held her face in her hands for a long time.

Jennet had said that day as she curled her hair into endless circles, that the moon always sent forth a magic of its own when a man and a woman were together for the very first time.

But there was no magic in the early morning of the day all of her dreams were shattered. Gabriel had taken her very soul and had thrown it into the woods as easily as he had tossed away Geoffrey's fastener. For too long she thought she would never feel again anything but fear of men, of any man. She did not know what she felt now, though.

Adelina stared out at the darkness and touched the wedding ring on her hand. "Oh, Papa, what shall I do now? If you were me, what would you do now? Tell me, Papa. Somehow, tell me."

For a long time she stared into the night, and there were no thoughts to answer her despairing question. Then she was drawn back to the day before she departed for Paris when she'd sat in the tall grass with Geoffrey:

I have written a poem for you. During the times you feel alone ...

Adelina searched through her things quickly and finally found the parchment roll, next to her embroidery in the bottom drawer. Adelina stood by the candle-light and unpicked the wax seal with shaking fingers. It was certainly in Geoffrey's hand, she recognised it immediately.

*To share the cup*
*that binds*
*To bind the lives*
*that will be true*
*for all of time.*
*What will be hence*
*or was before -*
*Of no concern can be*
*for the two*
*who share*
*the cup that binds.*
*The cup will live*
*and live on long,*
*For both that share it*
*Live in One, Eternal Time.*

The abbot's words of duty and honour and love echoed through her mind as she put the parchment down but all she wanted was Geoffrey, because only Geoffrey would know what to do to ease her pain, because pain it was, so deep in her heart that a mace or a pole axe or even a sword could never match its intensity.

Baudoin Dupuy had never hurt her and nor, till tonight, had he frightened her, she who once thought she was invincible. Had she not clung to him and pleaded for him to take her, too? Please take me with you? I cannot stay here...

"My spirit is not broken," she whispered. On her foot, the remaining satin slipper. Adelina kicked it off and went up the hallway towards the only room where light shone from under the door. On it she knocked and soon it was opened by one who was hiding his eyes.

Heavens, she thought. He cries? Why? Is it because of me? She had never in all her life seen this happen. "What ails you?" she asked.

"Nothing ails me," he said and turned away quickly, wiping his face on his arm. He drained the wine until not a drop remained to be shaken out.

"If nothing ails you, then best we begin."

"Begin?" Baudoin asked.

Adelina took a deep breath and said, with head high, "What is the word, conse...conso"

"Consecrate?"

Baudoin looked away. From utter despair to joy. An icy determination lay in her eyes now, the look he recognised had returned. Adelina was back, the one he knew, the one of no fuss and all business had returned. What had he said to instigate this sudden change of heart?

"You are not too drunk to do whatever it is that must be done?"

"Addie, I would prefer that no 'musts' are needed tonight."

"But you said you needed many sons."

"Oh, Addie, come closer. I am not an animal. Time must be taken. Much time."

She came to him and he kissed her face, and her mouth and he tasted of wine. Baudoin was kind and funny and he did not struggle with the laces on her wedding gown while he kissed her, almost hurried now.

Adelina dared touch him, his shoulders were wide and strong and on his chest was much thick dark hair. His hand on her bare back was hot and the callouses on his hand scratched at her skin, giving her gooseflesh. And then his kiss, so long it was, stopped and he pushed the wedding dress from her shoulders. He stood back, holding her at arms length and she lowered her eyes as he looked at her. But then he surprised her by lifting her chin and saying, "You are exquisite." And so much lay in his eyes, too. So much.

"Do you really think so?' she asked softly. His fingers touched what his gaze had beheld and she closed her eyes. Baudoin took her hand and led her to the bed and on it she lay. His kisses began again, kisses following his fingers and all the while she wondered if this was bliss?

And then he was upon her and she squeezed her eyes shut because she had felt this before. Adelina held her breath and waited for the agony again. She was rigid and a dreaded heaviness filled her belly. It pained but only a little. The rigidity slowly faded. When when she opened her eyes again, Baudoin had stopped and he was gazing at her very strangely.

He knows, she thought. He knows I am spoiled. She turned her face away when he said, "You have been taken?" and she could not reply. Why did this have to happen? How could God be so cruel? And then he moved and he lowered his head and he kissed her mouth. It was a kiss as before. She knew then that he would not cast her out. Why? Did he love her?

It took so very long for him to finish this, and her mind was alive the entire time. But when his time came, he collapsed to the bed beside her and lay on his face, unmoving.

Adelina did not know what to do so she lay very still, staring at the wall ahead and seeing for the first time this dirty, dusty room, with its swords and crossbows and pole axes and shields and saddles... She wondered if any woman had ever been in this room. She thought not.

With a groan, Baudoin rolled to his side and his arm lay heavy across her stomach. He sighed and mumbled and still she did not know what to do. But the terror had faded and now she knew that she need not fear him ever again. But is this bliss? she wondered. It feels like nothing to me.

"Baudoin?" she asked softly.

He moved and mumbled a question.

"Were you weeping because you believed I had only hatred for you?"

He raised his head and looked at her strangely as if she had read his very thoughts.

"It is not true. It will never be true."

But she didn't say "I love you". Perhaps that would come in time.

He put his head on her shoulder and his breath on her skin was hot but she did not mind. She put her arm around him and there she slept.

Soundly.

All night long.

# CHAPTER 27

Heloise struggled valiantly to emerge from the carriage alone. Antoine was adamant that he aid her, and Heloise was too weak of body to protest. She wanted to do this on her own and could not. Little remained of her pride now. "Leave her, Antoine. Let her try for herself."

But Antoine shook his head. He dared not let his lady go.

"Do as I have asked you or I shall order it!" Adelina yelled.

Heloise managed to stand upright, alone, for a little while at least. Adelina walked to the carriage and took Heloise's weight against her shoulder. "Come, Milady. I will take you inside."

Again, the smell of rotting apples was very strong. It is death, Adelina thought, anguish rising and choking. Baudoin came to assist with his father who, too, could not walk without the aid of someone's shoulder.

"Vianna, Vianna..."

Baudoin said, "Mother! Remember that her name is Adelina."

"Baudoin please. Do not be angry," Adelina said as she helped Heloise inside.

"Vianna?"

"Milady, no. I am Adelina. You remember me. I am of this family now. I have married your son. I am Adelina."

"Adelina? Who?"

God, Adelina thought, Give me strength?

"I looked for you all night. I called for you but you did not come..."

"Give her the medicine, Adelina. She will sleep."

"Where is it?"

"In her hand. It is always in her hand."

Holding Heloise upright, Adelina took the velvet pouch from the clenched fist, and she uncorked the tiny bottle concealed therein.

There was precious little remaining and Heloise was very thirsty for it. Agony was torturing her face. She smelled dreadfully sour. "Come to bed, Milady, and my girl and I will tend you, freshen you." Adelina, not lacking in any physical strength, helped Heloise up the stairs and shooed Antoine who still hovered about, as useless and less pretty as a butterfly. What did she need of men? "No! I said, go away! We do not need you!"

Baudoin walked by carrying his father effortlessly up the many stairs. Halfway up, Heloise had to rest, for breathe she could not. "Oh, Milady, how long have you been so ill?" Adelina whispered, tears in her eyes. Her heart was breaking. How could God be so unkind as to make this woman, this beautiful woman, suffer so? What would Geoffrey say if he were here now? What profound nonsense would he tell her? Would he say that it is the Will of God and that the Will of God need have no reason? Why was it that when men fell short of an explanation, always, they turned to The Will of God?

Adelina called for Jennet, who appeared very quickly from the kitchens. Her cheeks were blooming with roses. It must be the fair haired one she loves now, Adelina thought.

"Help us, girl. Gather cloths and warm water. Find my oils, and then tell your Master that he must fetch up Michel Dumont immediately."

"No leeches, no leeches," Heloise cried, as Adelina settled her into her chair near the window of her private chambers.

"Michel Dumont needs no leeches. In him I trust completely. Will you?" She knelt at the woman's feet and looked into her ageing face. It was sickness alone which had harried her so.

"Please, I want no doctor, I want no more, no more of anything. Just let it end. Please, let it end."

Adelina, close to tears, fought them back bravely. The woman's gnarled fingers touched Adelina's hair and her face, feeling it as a blind man feels to see. "Vianna, you came."

Adelina sighed. "Yes, Milady. I came."

"Sing away my pain. Please, sing away my pain?"

"But my songs have died long ago, Milady."

"No, no. Never. Never. I have kept your lyre as I promised I would. There. It is there." Heloise pointed to the corner behind her screen. "Play for me."

Adelina rose to her feet and looked behind the screen. I cannot play a lyre, she thought, as she looked down upon the instrument. It was like a tiny harp and she counted six strings. She looked back at Heloise who was breathing hard from unheard agonies, her head to the side, sweat forming on her brow and lip. "Sing away my pain..." she whispered, voice breaking.

Adelina picked up the lyre and held it as she had seen a musician once hold such an instrument. It made barely a musical sound, though, when her fingers ran across the strings. She tried again, and used her fingernails to pick at the strings. It sounded somewhat better but it was certainly not like the music she often heard inside her head. She would need many idle days sitting in a solitary place where none could hear her, for yes, she could make music from this, given time. She could sit alone, and copy these music sounds from her head to her hands and then out for others' ears. But did Heloise Dupuy have such time to wait?

She put the lyre down gently, careful that it did not fall. Best for now that she copy the music in her head with an instrument she knew and loved to use, her voice. "Milady?"

Heloise opened her eyes but did not recognise the person standing there.

"Milady, it has been many a long year since I played. I cannot now, but I promise you that I will. Soon. For now, I will sing for you as I tend you."

Adelina sang, although there were no words to the music she heard in her mind, she hummed its haunting melody, one which had been her constant companion since she was but a tiny girl.

Heloise hummed it, too, and her eyes opened wide. "Vianna, I did not think I would ever hear that again."

As she sang on, it seemed that the room was filled with the voices of a hundred angels, and that Adelina's voice was but a croak in comparison. Still, the lady smiled for it seemed that the song stilled her pain.

Adelina took off the woman's shoes and they did not come easily away. Her poor feet were blistered and swollen. And yet there was a deep sigh when Adelina's hands touched them.

What is it that I do? she wondered. Is it just my touch?

Jennet came in with a brass bowl of warm water. In her pockets, her mistress's oils. "She is in pain," Adelina said quietly. "Be kind and gentle with her. She knows not what kind and gentle is. Of this I am sure." She looked to Heloise and said, "Milady, this is my girl, Jennet. She will tend us both, now. Do you not have a girl of your own?"

"She has had many, but none remain. It is too much for them," Baudoin said from the door.

"Leave us. This is woman's work. You should not be here."

"Should I not? Who do you think it is who has tended her these past two years?"

"It is no longer necessary that you do for I am here now. See to your father."

"He sleeps. The journey half killed him." Baudoin walked in and crouched by his mother's side. "Mother, do you need me?"

Heloise looked from Baudoin to Adelina and the pretty girl servant with her, and she said, as she touched his face, "No Jean-Pierre. Vianna is here now. Be good. Go and play. Mind you do not fall from the rampart again. Go. Play with your brother."

Adelina heard everything, and she studied her feet. She did not want to look at her husband as he rose unsteadily and kissed his mother's head. He took no offence at her words, and nor now, did Adelina. But of her he asked, "What can Michel Dumont do that the best doctors in all of Auvergne cannot?"

"Much, perhaps," Adelina replied. "How is it I am to know?" She walked with him to the door and closed it after telling Jennet to undress the mistress and lay her in bed. "Send for Michel now. If you say I lie ill, he will come immediately."

"I need not speak untruths."

"Do you want him to aid your mother? If so, tell him I am ill. He will not come for any other reason. He believes Dupuy is still the name of the enemy."

"I will send Antoine." Baudoin lifted her chin and kissed her lightly and he left her with a smile. Adelina turned back to her mother-in-law's chambers.

Jennet came to her immediately. Her face was very white and she seemed both frightened and confused. "Milady, I have not seen anything as this before."

"As what?"

Heloise, undressed and in her bed, was covered by bedsheet till Jennet drew it back. Heloise, not yet half a century in age, surely, was very thin and yet her belly was huge. Adelina touched. It was rock hard. She looked at Jennet, but Jennet knew nothing of the cause. "Closer, Milady. Look closer." Jennet pointed at Heloise's breasts, and looked away quickly. A discolored lump was so large in her armpit that the woman could not hold her arm close to her body at all, and from the woman's engorged nipple oozed a terrible, foul pus. The smell was sickening. "Give me the warm water and cloths, now. Do not stare." But what is it? Adelina wondered constantly. Was this the source of her agony?

Jennet was very hesitant to touch and Adelina could tell from her face that the smell and sight was making her ill. "Go then, away with you, but come if I call."

Heloise heard little and saw less. Her gaze was fixed on the ceiling. All she whispered was, Sing to me, Vianna, sing to me...

Adelina sang as best she could whilst she tended her husband's mother, even though her voice shook and she felt ill, too, for the more she attempted to gently wipe away the oozing pus the more appeared to take its place. Illness was rising steadily.

What is this? she asked, helplessly silent, as her voice hummed on sweetly. Her voice alone it seemed brought a smile to the woman's face. A smile that momentarily stilled the agony.

When Heloise was finally bathed and dressed and more of her medicine was found and taken, medicine to make her sleep for in sleep there was no pain, Adelina left the room. She did not know that she had been tending Baudoin's mother for all of the afternoon. She was not exhausted physically, but felt that no joy would ever live inside her again. This was confirmed when she heard footsteps on the stairs, and already she knew whose steps they were.

Baudoin appeared. He was dressed now, in tunic and hose and leather boots and he stopped immediately when he saw his wife. She rested her head against his mother's door and tears streamed down her face, silent tears.

"Adelina? Is she dead?"

"I wish she was, for there can be no agony in death."

Baudoin walked to her and sat beside her on the stairs. He hesitantly touched her hand, and with his finger, he wiped the tears from her cheeks with gentle touches. Whisper touches. "It is hard, yes? It is very hard. I am in debt to you for what it is you willingly do for my mother. She lets none near her. None. Until now."

"I do it not for you. I do not do it for your father. I do it for her. I have always been fond of her, whether she is in or out of her senses. And I don't care what name she calls me." Adelina was silent for a moment, then her thoughts found voice and she looked into Baudoin's face. "How can it be that I know a stranger so intimately? It feels I should have been born to her, your mother, and not to the one who claims that she is my mother."

"Adelina, such words."

"That is how it feels. I love your mother more than I do my own." Her true nature soon surfaced again. "I am hungry. When do you eat here? Early, late or not at all?"

"We have not eaten as a family for many months now. My parents eat in their chambers, alone, as I do sometimes. Mostly I eat when hungry. There is no set time or place."

"That must change."

"Must it, you say."

"Yes. When all eat separately there is no conversation."

"Oh. Conversation you want? In this family?"

"Where is it you go now, if I may ask?"

"I go to meet the Welsh archer who brings us the feast's remainders. I meet him..."

"In St. Paulien, yes?" she interrupted.

Baudoin said nothing but could not look into her eyes. He lies, she thought. He lies already, even in silence, he lies. He is wed to me one day and he goes to see the one who holds his heart in her hand the very next. "Then best you see to it that all women who are with child have the first pickings."

"Why is this?" he asked, a little confused.

"The village needs more healthy babies, not half starved ones."

Baudoin nodded and they each went their separate ways - he to his chambers to don his leather armour, and she to the kitchen, to find the cook. She was hungry.

Adelina had some tasteless soup, spoke a little to the old cook if only to see what nature he had and it was as she thought, he was wooden and had long since forgotten the meaning of a smile. This dark, gloomy place affects everyone sheltering under its roof, she thought, and decided she would take a walk, and speak to whoever was about. But these servants would not look her in the eye for fear of being beheaded, it seemed. The friendlier she was, the more fearful they became. How is it they are treated by nobility that makes them so fearful? she wondered.

In the stables, Francois was tending his horse's hooves and immediately ceased upon seeing his new mistress approach. The horse did not bite at her as she tickled its nose. Had Francois tried that he would be fingerless. Even the hounds followed her about. No doubt Henri's falcon would sit calmly on her arm as well. For a moment, he expected all flowers to bloom and birds to sing. That very morning, the villagers spoke of this woman-child as their angel as he handed out the Lavoute scraps, and they had begged him for her name.

He had told them her name and it was repeated with the reverence given to a saint. Unknown and yet loved dearly, how could that be? he wondered. And still, he wondered. "Milady?" he asked.

"When will Michel Dumont arrive?"

"Very soon, no doubt."

"He comes this way?" she asked and pointed to the gates.

"That is the only way in or out, Milady."

"Is it? At Lavoute there are numerous hidden ways in and out. If you know them."

"So I have heard."

"But failed to find, yes, when our families were not united as they are now? How is it you, as a man of war, feel about this union, Francois?"

Francois took a deep breath and leant upon the railing. "I am too old now to take up arms, so I would say, peace is better."

"I do not believe you. The warrior still lives in your eyes. You lie, as any old knight lies."

"At least I do not lie in the ground, Milady. At least the worms do not feast."

Adelina did not smile although she felt one very close. Best not to like this one too soon. She could not approach Antoine. His dark gaze passed through her, untrusting. "This animal has a name?" she asked.

"Many," Francois said. "And all are not for the ears of a fine lady such as you."

Adelina laughed. She had known all along that she would like Francois, very much. He was one who dared look her in the eye when he spoke.

"You had little time to feast yesterday, Francois."

"I had time enough, Milady," he said with a smile.

"How was the wedding, do you think?"

"I think it was a fine wedding."

He was like Michel in that she could not tell immediately whether he lied or not. Humour shone in his eyes, though. She liked that. This place needed much humour. "I am not the spoiled child that many think I am."

He said nothing for he had heard differently. Each time he bent to take up his horse's foot, she spoke again. And she swung about the post as if she floated on a cloud. He would like, very much, to see her dancing with ribbons in her hand.

"Do you still fight?"

"Milady?"

"You are not deaf, do not pretend to be. Have you a collection of arms to show me?"

"Yes, if that is your wish, but –"

"But nothing. What is your specialty?"

"Milady?"

"What is it you do best?"

Francois scratched his ear and said, "I wield sword and lance like no other for fifty miles."

"So you are not an archer then."

He pulled a face and admitted silently that he was not.

"I am a fair archer."

"I have heard this."

"Yes?"

"Oh, yes. A fine archer indeed."

"You think I jest? Dedwyd, who is in service to Gabriel of Lyon again, was teaching me how to use a longbow."

"A longbow?" Francois repeated. "You can use a longbow? Surely a longbow is taller than you, Milady."

"Yes, that is true. And using such a bow takes much practise. Dedwyd began when he was but eight years of age. Do you know that the arrows of a longbow pierce helmets from a good distance?"

"Milady, may I ask—"

"No, you may not. Where is your quintain?"

"Quintain?"

"Your dummy, fool."

"Is that what is used at Lavoute?" Francois asked, surprised.

"What else would be used?" she asked in reply.

"Here, Milady, it is tradition to use as quintains ones which bleed."

"But quintains cannot bleed."

"Ours do. Often. We use for practise those who have fallen foul of the master. You see, here we like to hear them beg for mercy."

"No," she said, stunned.

"Women and children, too, on occasion. This is the best way of quelling disputes that we have found."

Had he not said that, she would have believed him entirely. "Lies. I see by your eyes that you jest with me." Francois' face remained expressionless. "Surely you jest?"

"There is much you do not yet know about the Dupuys of Allegre."

"Now that I am here, I forbid such a barbaric tradition. You cannot kill those who till the soil and feed us. God. No wonder all go hungry here."

Francois then smiled for he could hold it back no longer.

"You did jest!"

"Come, Milady. I shall show you before you have my head." He led her through the

stables and into a store room of sorts where a lot of old weaponry lay. "It has been some time since a quintain was used. I would suggest, though, if I may, that you do not play your battle games in sight of Lady or Lord Dupuy. It would be frowned upon."

"It will not be in sight of any lord or lady. When does Baudoin go to St Paulien to visit his love?"

Francois for a moment was not sure if he should answer. Seemingly she knew, and was quite content about it. Stranger things he knew had happened before and would no doubt happen again. "He goes, two, perhaps, three times each week."

"In all weathers?"

"Unless the mistress is very ill. But now that you are his wife –"

"He will still go. I know him well enough."

"Yes, Milady."

"While he is away, you and I shall play. You shall teach me all that you know. Do it willingly, Francois, or I will order it of you."

"Milady, why do you wish to learn battle?"

"For the reason that if ever the war banners fly, I will be left to defend this holding alone. This is my holding, too, and you belong to me, therefore you will do as I say without question and without word of this to anyone. You will show me and I will attempt whatever it is you have shown me. That is the only way to learn. One must do."

"But you are a woman, fair and fragile. I cannot do this."

"Cannot? What is this word? Do you not know who I am? I am a Polignac and a Polignac does not know the meaning of cannot. Because of this the Polignacs own most lands south of St. Paulien. Yes?"

"Yes, but—"

"And nor do I like this word, but!"

"Yes, Milady," Francois said.

"It will be our secret, Francois. Your knowledge will one day save lives. Many lives. It is not just battle I wish to know. It is tactics. What to do if ever there is a siege and suchlike."

"And should war banners not fly?"

"They will. I myself looked into the eyes of Philippe Augustus, and saw many things hidden there. War banners will fly. I will be prepared for the days ahead."

"I do not want to harm you, Milady."

"You may be gentlemanly, Francois, and you may see me as a woman. I do not care how it is you see me. I tell you that bruises may pain but they also fade. Ignorance kills. When is it that we shall begin? There are woods nearby perhaps which are safe from prying eyes?"

"If this is your wish, then so be it."

Adelina took up a very old sword and it was heavy in her hand. She had once seen her mother attempt to pick up her father's broadsword. The most she could do was giggle and drop it immediately and Adelina, although small, was disgusted at what she had seen, and the way her father had laughed.

In her right hand, Adelina held this old sword, which was heavy and rusted, and she gripped its handle tightly, finding a balance quickly. She cut through the air effortlessly. Francois stepped back, surprised that all he had heard was indeed true. She played her games of esquire well.

"You see, Francois, I know much already. What I do not have is one to practise with, one with knowledge. I have chosen you as you see me as a person and speak to me as a person." She gave him the sword by throwing it, as Geoffrey had taught her. Francois caught it. "Clean it for me and bear it a razor's edge. I claim it as mine."

"Milady?"

"Yes?"

"Do you have hauberk and helmet, and perhaps, lance?"

She smiled and almost embraced him. "Dedwyd from Lavoute. He knows where my weapons and armours lie."

"But he speaks not the language."

"He has many fooled, Francois, but I am not among them. Tell him I have ordered that he is to bring it all to me."

Outside, Antoine was calling for her. Michel had arrived. Francois followed. Overhead, many storm clouds gathered and by the gate, one of the Polignac vassals, another too old to serve fully, Michel Dumont, was astride his horse. He dismounted as soon as Adelina appeared. She greeted him with open arms and Francois sighed. Does she not know her place, or he is?

"No," Michel said.

"No? You say no to me?"

"Yes, I say no to you. I will see to the master first."

"But his illness is of wound and fever and age. The lady is by far worse. I do not know what it is. You must see. You must help her."

"After I attend the master," Michel said, as patiently obstinate as ever. Adelina walked beside him into the house and as they climbed the stairs he glanced at her. "There is a sparkle I recognise in your eyes, little one. What is it you plan now?"

"Revenge."

"Already?"

"It is not what your evil mind conceives, Michel Dumont."

"My mind bears no evil. This you know."

"None can be wholly good. You lie. I have seen your temper."

"As I have seen yours many times over."

"Still you value the life of a man over that of a woman. Are we that unimportant?"

"Milady, be good and sit with Lady Dupuy now. I shall come by shortly."

Jennet sat by the bed, so deep in thought that she didn't hear her mistress enter. She looks so sad, Adelina thought. Her heart has been broken by Etienne. He no longer plans to marry her. She has been discarded, as one would discard a dress too small or worn. Jennet rose immediately but Adelina bade her sit and she stood behind her girl, close. "How goes she?"

"She cries in her sleep, Milady. She cries with pain all of the time. It is hard to bear."

"And worse for the lady. Misery has caused this. Misery alone."

"Then a slow death for us all, Milady, if that is the truth."

"I could have Etienne's head if that would make you at ease."

"No, it is not the fault of Etienne that he does not want to own what another has taken his pleasures from. But had you the power to take the head of Gabriel of Lyon, then that I would dearly love to see."

"I shall take his head," Adelina said.

"But Milady, you could not do such a thing. Not you."

"Then you do not know me, girl."

"I would be nothing without you, Milady. How I thank you for bringing me here and giving me a home. Without you, I am nothing."

"Ah. Nonsense. Even the smallest of ants, even a gnat has some measure of worth. You are much more than that girl, much more, even if it is only to me." Adelina looked down at Heloise, sleeping soundly. "My fear is becoming as the Lady Dupuy, unloved and miserable, and senseless and ill, and poor. That is what I am now, Jennet, I am poor."

"No, Milady, no."

"It is so. What once was mine for so short a time, now is not. It belongs to my husband and his family. Will there ever be a tomorrow when a woman can stand tall and proud and alone in this world of men, with full rights of the law to whatever it is that she owns? Or is? Or could be?"

"I would never wish for that. All I have ever wanted is a husband."

"And I see you making eyes at the servant boy. The one with fair hair and very blue eyes."

"My secret is out then," Jennet said.

Adelina laughed. "You cannot keep secrets. You cannot hide joy or misery."

"But you can."

"I have practised all of my life."

Michel finally came, and with him Antoine who was not eager to leave an enemy vassal with his mistress. But he was ordered out nonetheless.

"Will Henri Dupuy live, Michel?"

"He and God will decide. I cannot."

"Has he asked for me?"

"Not to my knowledge, no." Michel was studying Heloise from afar. Obviously he did not want to get close. Adelina took his arm and pulled him closer to the bed. "She has a swollen belly not with child and sores which weep foully from her breast. See? What is it?"

Michel did not have to look any closer to know what it was. "Nothing can be done," he said, quickly.

"But you have not looked yet."

"Nothing can be done."

"Surely you have a potion? An oil? An ointment?"

"No. I do not. The lord may live but the lady? No. No, her time is near. Hear how she draws breath? No. Her time is close."

"What is it that I can do?"

"You can pray that her agonies soon end. Where is your husband?"

"He has gone on business but returns this eve. It rains, Michel. Will you not stay?"

"I cannot stay. I am not welcome here."

"You are a treasured friend to me. Of course you are welcome."

Nothing she could do, or threaten him with, was enough to make him stay. Michel Dumont would rather ride alone to Lavoute, wet and in darkness, than stay breathing in the air of the enemy.

It was raining and almost dark when she stood in the courtyard holding on to his reins, tightly. "Why is it she suffers so, Michel? What reason would God have to do this?"

"I am not God to know. Just do as I have said. Remain by her side as much as you can but do not forget yourself. She is soon to die, but you, not you. You have far and long to go yet, little one. Far and long."

"She calls me Vianna," Adelina said, desperate for something to say so he would not leave her so quickly. "Did you know her?"

"No," Michel said quickly. "I was not at Lavoute then."

"You lie! You have been there from my earliest memory. Why will none tell me of Vianna?"

"It is not meant to be known. Forget, Adelina. Please, forget. I must go now. I must."

"Michel! Michel there is more I need to ask of you!"

But he did not hear her or if he did, he had no wish to stay a moment longer than necessary.

Baudoin was very wet when he arrived home. Wet and cold, too. It was late of hour, the house was dark and silent, and he hoped, how he hoped that Adelina would be asleep. But his hopes died quickly, killed before they arose for she sat in her night dress on the top of the stairs, waiting for him. She said nothing for no words were needed.

"How is my mother?" he asked.

"Michel could do nothing so I did as he asked and prayed that her end be painless."

"Pray? What good have prayers done? For two years now that is all I have done." Baudoin's leathers squeaked and his boots squashed water upon the stairs, a terrible squelching sound. "Do you sit in wait for me?"

"No. I simply sit. I wait for no one. You need not have come home in the rain, Baudoin Dupuy. You could have stayed in the arms of your love, in warmth and comfort. Do you think I do not know where it is you go?"

"I came home to you," he said.

"Why?"

"I need sons."

Could he not have said it differently? What had this Eleanor said to him today?

"Come," he said, offering his hand. "It is late, I am cold and tired. Much yet I have to do. Come." He wiggled his fingers impatiently and Adelina reached up and took his hand.

You shall have your son earlier than even you had expected, she thought. For already I am with child.

# Chapter 28

Adelina had neither seen nor heard from her mother since the day of her wedding to Baudoin, and she needed a woman to talk to—too many questions she kept to herself. Jennet was too busy at play with her new young man; Heloise was far too ill and out of her senses to remember what had happened so very long ago. Baudoin, her surviving son. was in his twenty-seventh year and twenty-seven years was a long time ago.

So Adelina had no choice but keep all of her questions locked inside. She would learn for herself about impending motherhood as and when it happened.

Of Baudoin she saw little except for the times he came to her bed. And always she knew that in his mind, it was not his wife in his arms, but his only love, Eleanor. It was late one autumn night when she finally said, "Baudoin, I am with child."

He was undressing at the time and turned to her quickly. "Yes?" he asked, and oh, how that voice was so full of hope.

"It seems so."

"When do you think it will come?" he asked.

She could only hope that what Ella had said was correct. Her baby would come in February, after the snows, and before the summer.

He seemed pleased, but for which reason? she wondered. To be free of the chore which brought him regularly to my bed or was he pleased because he would be a father? Perhaps, she thought as she watched his eyes fill with joy and relief, it is a mixture of both. He will be a father and free of me until another child is necessary. And it would all begin again.

Adelina did not have to wonder whose child it was. She had been taken by force barely two weeks before the marriage. She should have bled on her wedding night but did not and had not since. This child would be fair for Gabriel was fair. Adelina did not know how Baudoin would react if he saw the child and realised it was not of his blood.

Sometimes, on her worst days, she prayed, how she prayed, that the baby would die. If it did, Baudoin's attentions would return to her, not to Eleanor, and if she was one day with child again, then she would know whose flesh it was she carried inside her. She only thought of that during her loneliest moments though. Mostly, she felt that perhaps this child, who could not be blamed for its conception, would at least love her. Whatever, God's will was done. A child grew inside her.

Life droned on, and the months passed as slowly as the days. She was not ill as Ella had said all mothers were, although she had a belly very quickly, and her breasts were growing bigger by the day and were more in the way than ever before now.

Adelina's belly was huge and she was very uncomfortable, unable to sit or lie or stand for very long, and her temper, too, was ripening each day. The only person she could bear having near was Heloise. Heloise did not aggravate her. Baudoin no longer shared their bed. Perhaps he feared for his very life.

Her hair felt and looked like stable straw and her shoes did not fit. But she did not need shoes for she went nowhere, except to the village with Baudoin on occasion to help quell a dispute. It seemed that she was the one they listened to and she enjoyed being with the serfs. She learnt much from them.

Francois refused to allow her to sword-fight any longer, and he refused to practise archery, too. He feared she would be hurt and to hurt the mother would be to hurt the baby and this baby was the families' future.

Adelina was very much alone yet surrounded always by people. Had it not always been that way?

Baudoin had warned her not to tell his father until she knew, that there was no doubt of a grandchild in the coming.

It was late autumn when she knocked on Henri Dupuy's door, and did not wait for the voice to allow her entry. She walked in and regarded the old man cooly, in much the way he regarded her. She stood tall and proud, her hands behind her back.

"I did not call you," Henri said.

"You have never called me. You have never spoken to me. This must change. I have decided it will be so."

Henri Dupuy huffed, but he was too stricken to turn about and walk away for walk he could not. She knew she had a captive audience. "Henri Dupuy, I am with child. Or are you blind?"

"No, I am not blind. My son is the father?" he asked.

"Whose else would it be?" she asked, offended, her nose in the air now.

"With a Polignac woman, who can be certain which errant knight has spawned what?"

"Were you not so ill, and were I a man, I would hit you for insulting my name."

"You are insolent."

"Perhaps I am all these hateful things that show in your eyes whenever you look upon me. But I have the key to our future within me now and I feel it growing strong. Have some respect for what will be, bitter old man. You do not like me and I do not like you but I have no wish for my child to grow up as I did, unloved and unwanted and kicked aside until found of use. I tell you now, no, I warn you now. I am with child and he shall be loved. He shall be the first in this house to experience it."

"If it is a girl?" Henri asked.

"God would not be so unkind as to allow another woman to reside under this roof." Adelina turned and walked out. Henri was calling her back but she pretended she was deaf.

By the depths of winter, though, her attitude had changed considerably. It was bitterly cold, the snows were incessant and an illness was striking the villages. Many were dying, but the one she hoped each day would be released from pain, lived on. Barely. And Adelina often thought that Heloise clung to life for one reason only—to see the face of her grandchild before she died. Adelina was wrong.

When the day came that Heloise finally breathed her last, Adelina, who had been expecting it for so long, was taken unawares. The only joy she had, the only calm she could find of late was with the lyre and she could play it now—time she had much of.

Heloise, so ill that she could barely lift her finger, had not eaten in many days. Food could not be swallowed. Even soup trickled from her mouth. But on this cold, cold winter day, she asked to sit by the window.

It took both Jennet and Francois to help her from her bed, and there she sat, staring from her window, wrapped tightly in a blanket, listening, once the servants had gone, to Adelina play.

And she said, "Do not give this one away, too, Vianna. Do not, for a child given away is never loved. You should never have given your child away."

Adelina sighed. "I have not given a child away, Milady. I am Adelina and my child is not yet born. Give me your hand, feel."

Heloise's eyes brightened for a moment when she put her hand on the huge belly and felt the stirrings within. "Soon," Heloise said. "It will be born soon."

"But it is only January, Milady."

"This child is impatient," Heloise said and placed her hand in her lap. She regarded Adelina warmly. "Do not give this child away."

Adelina had no thoughts at all about this thing that grew inside her and made her miserable. She knew who had spawned it, Gabriel of Lyon. Gabriel, who visited sometimes, and spoke with Henri, and Baudoin, and regarded her very strangely indeed. Her hatred for him grew each day. And her mother had not bothered to visit, even though she knew that Adelina was with child.

She did not care at all. Had she ever?

"I will not see it born," Heloise said softly.

"Yes, you will. I know you will. How is your pain?"

But Heloise, wrapped in a blanket and in her favourite chair, took a deep breath and looked again at the view from her window. "Send for Henri," she said, softly.

For months now, Heloise was so wracked by unspeakable pain that her husband was barely thought of. Henri could not bear to be near her, it was obvious to Adelina that he had no love at all for his wife. Since autumn his health had improved and he was able to walk. But into his wife's chambers he never came. Again, Adelina had to lie. "Milady, he has taken to the woods with his falcons. I do not think he will be back until sunset."

"Jean-Pierre?"

Adelina closed her eyes. "He is with his father, Milady."

"Baudoin?" she asked, hopefully, her family now exhausted.

Baudoin was in St. Paulien for the day, perhaps two days and he would return only when he had to and not before. "Milady, best you lie in your bed. It is very cold today."

"No, I wish to sit here by my window. That is all I want." After a moment, she said, "Vianna, will you tell Henri that I have always loved him?"

Adelina did not like the feelings which flooded her. Heloise sat looking out into the cold distance, but what was it that she saw?

"Vianna?"

"I will tell him, Milady," Adelina said, eyes shining with stinging tears.

"Vianna, you have come."

But this time she was not speaking to Adelina. A small smile played on Heloise's lips and she brightened as if a glorious sight had passed before her eyes. Her hand reached out, too and the gnarled fingers closed around something which Adelina could not see. Had she been touched by an angel? And then Heloise sighed and slumped to the side. She breathed no more.

"No," Adelina said, voice shaking. "No. You cannot leave me, too. No!"

Francois heard the cry but he had known when he had touched his mistress that her end would come that very day.

Adelina could not be consoled. She is worse now, he thought, than she was when her father was killed by thieves.

"Brother Christophe? You have a letter."

Geoffrey took the parchment roll from Andre's hand and closed his door. He sat on his cot of straw and picked off the Dupuy seal. Drawing his candle closer, he lay upon his bed to read. At last, after so long, word from Adelina. He could not believe his fortune.

*My love Geoffrey,*

*Although that is not your name now, it is still your name in my heart. Each day I wonder why it is that a vow of silence could forbid you to write to me. For surely the written word is not spoken aloud? I also hope with each new day that you will visit but each day passes and you do not come.*

*On my last visit to Le Puy, I came to the abbey to see you but again, the abbot forbid me entrance. If it is a disease I carry, it is the disease of love alone, love for you. So it is that I must write, but my many letters always have gone unanswered. Does your vow of silence also stop you from putting your words to parchment? I hold you close to my heart in my prayers each night. Geoffrey, do you hold me, too?*

Geoffrey closed his eyes and bit his lip. He sat up, and turned the parchment face down. Anger was rising; such a deep well of it that he knew it would explode very soon. He fought it down as best he could and picked up the parchment again.

*I am soon to be a mother, Geoffrey, but woman life is still not for me. It seems that the wrong child died the day of my birth. I know of that, Geoffrey. My father told me long ago that I had a brother. I even know his name.*

*I am soon to give birth and yet I am full of fears. I will say, for if I do not, I shall rot within as Heloise Dupuy rotted. I will say that you are still my strength, Geoffrey; my heart, my existence. There is nothing within my heart now, and there has been nothing since we were separated so long ago. Of any joy or hope there is little. No one shall ever take your place.*

*Baudoin is a kind husband, but that is all he is. His heart lies with another and he is fortunate for his heart is warmed by her. I have none but you, so distant and you have your world now, a world I cannot be a part of.*

*Henri Dupuy nears death now. Each day the monks come from La Chaise Dieu to offer their prayers. Death is all that surrounds me, Geoffrey. Have I not seen enough of it?*

*My only wish is to see your face once again but it is impossible since circumstance and my husband forbid it. But each night I hold close your memory, for should my memory of your smile fail me, I know that I would die. If it is true that we live many times, then I shall pray now for God to smile upon me and allow me to be by your side, in another time and another place for it cannot be here and now. All of my previous sins were indeed great ones. Too great it seems. My love for you remains.*

She did not sign her name.

She did not have to.

Geoffrey immediately went in search of Andre and found him at the apiary where bees swarmed about his arms and hands. "Brother Christophe?"

Geoffrey spoke for the first time in many months. "Who gave this to you?"

"It was on the doorstep. Brother, your vow?"

"How many other letters have come for me?"

"A few, I believe."

Geoffrey fought down his anger as best he could for it was not Andre's fault. "They were not given to me, Andre! Why!"

"The abbot would not allow it."

Geoffrey spat. "Where is he?"

"Brother, do not face the abbot when you are angry. It can serve no purpose at all. It can only bring... Brother? Brother?" Andre could not chase, the bees were too thick on his hands and arms.

Adelina stepped into Henri's chambers. It was filled with people, with knights and praying monks and doctors who prayed, too for all else had failed them.

"She comes for me," Henri mumbled.

Adelina stood by the bedside and looked down upon the old man without any expression or emotion. *He is the one who has caused much suffering yet he suffers little. Where is the justice in that?* "You summoned me?" she asked, weakly, and wished that she could sit somewhere for she was almost in danger of falling. Her back ached so and she felt heavy all over.

Henri opened his eyes. Today they were a startling blue. He had no strength to lift his head from his pillows but turn his head, he could. He stared at her for a long time. *Adelina must, she knew, look old and tired but pride was alive in her eyes as she gazed down on the one who had never attempted to accept her, let alone know her. Make peace he would never.*

"Before all is gone," Henri croaked, "Go back to Lavoute."

Adelina looked about the room and said, "Everyone begone until you are summoned again. Everyone!"

Baudoin confirmed the order and soon enough the room was vacated.

"What did you mean, before all is gone?"

"Philippe Augustus sends his baillis."

"No. He gave his word to my father that while he rules, our lands are safely ours even though we pay him dues. You were there. You heard him."

"The king appoints baillis here!"

Adelina looked at Baudoin and said, "Is he out of his mind?"

"No," Baudoin said. "Why he wanted to tell you this himself I do not know."

She looked back at Henri. "And what then of the fate of Lavoute Polignac?"

"It is safe, of course." Baudoin said. "The king kept his word to your father but none other. Our lands are soon taken."

"I have no army," Henri managed. "If we do not surrender all it will be taken by force and many will die. Take the unborn child to Lavoute."

"I cannot. This is my home. Here is where I belong."

Henri grew very angry and Adelina was just as stubborn.

"This is my home, here I will stay. Here my child will be born."

"And kill it with your pride? You go to Lavoute. I order it."

Adelina looked at Baudoin and he nodded, silently. "I do not understand your madness."

"I am dying, Adelina." It was the first time the old man had ever said her name aloud. "I can wait no longer. Promise me that you will keep the child safe. That is all I ask of you."

"I am a Polignac and I keep my word. A promise made is never broken."

Henri lifted his hand. Adelina looked to Baudoin and he nodded. She stepped closer to the death bed, reached out and touched Henri's fingers. She had never touched him before and was surprised when his hand wrapped around hers and a smile appeared on his face. It seemed that he was not about to let go. Adelina pulled away first. "Go in peace, Henri Dupuy. We are no longer enemies." Their gazes met and Adelina turned away.

She walked from the room as quickly as she was able, her head down, past the monks and doctors. She could look at no one. Then she heard a sound she recognised from a distant past. It was Geoffrey's bird call, a very soft, sweet whistle, one she could never imitate. She turned back instantly and there he was, a solitary monk, with the rosary in his hands and heavy hood over his head, alone in the corridor now that all had returned to the death room and their prayers.

"Geoffrey?"

He turned and all she could see was his smile. He back tracked and swiped the hood from his head.

"Geoffrey!"

"Sh. Be quiet." Geoffrey looked back again to see if any had noticed his absence. It seemed not. "We must talk." He followed Adelina and thrust the rosary back into his pocket. He walked into a woman's private chambers, its billowed silks and roses sweetened the air. When the door was closed, the silence was loud. For a long time each stared at the other. What has life here done to you? he wanted to ask but all he could manage was, "It is good to see you again, my love."

"I see that you have taken your vows."

"Little else was left me."

"That is not true. Heracle told me of his offer to you."

"It was made in desperation only. This child—"

"Is a Dupuy, not a Polignac. There will never be a Polignac heir now and you are to blame."

"What would you have me do?"

"Go to Polignac, to the fortress, claim your right and take a bride. Our family depends upon you."

"If I cannot have you, I shall have no one."

Adelina turned away and she sat with a great deal of difficulty. She was huge, the poor girl. And Geoffrey hoped she would not start her birth now, because he had attended a birth once too often for his liking.

"You are ill." Geoffrey put his hand on her forehead. "You burn."

"It will pass." Adelina grabbed for Geoffrey's hand and held it to her face. "Geoffrey, I have missed you."

"And I you. I did not come here, God forgive me, because Henri Dupuy is dying. I came to see you. For too long now none would tell me news of you."

"I wrote to you many times."

"No letter reached me but one, smuggled to me by Andre. I have spoken to the abbot about this. He feigned ignorance."

"You expected honesty?" Adelina almost laughed. "It will do no good. None of this will. I am ill and I am with child and I fear I will die. I have dreamed it. I have dreamed my death. I cannot lie with the Dupuys, Geoffrey. I must lie with my father and my brother. I am Polignac of heart and Dupuy in name only. Should I die, you would see to this? You would see that I lie with my father and my brother?"

"You will not die."

"You do not hear me. I do not fear death, for I know what awaits me. It is the child, Geoffrey. I pledged to be a mother to this child in me. I have promised that I would give him what I never had. But I feel death looming all about me."

"It is the loss of Heloise Dupuy you feel and Henri will not last the night. That is all, my love. You are not going to die. I would not allow it."

How she wished she could believe him but she was a child no longer and he had no magic that she could now see or feel. He was just Geoffrey, disguised as a monk.

"Do you see my mother?"

"No."

"Does she think of me, I wonder?"

Geoffrey said nothing. The floor was hurting his knees. Should he not be used to it now? It seemed he spent half his time kneeling and for what? But he was kneeling now at his favourite altar, he knelt at Adelina's knee. And held her hands tightly.

"Does she miss me at all?"

"She knows that soon you give birth."

"Geoffrey, I have not seen her since my wedding. How can she know?"

"Many know, my love. Many."

"Geoffrey, what will I do? Baillis come from Paris to take this land. Henri has ordered that I return to Lavoute, to safety and have my child there. But I am not welcome. If you went to claim your rights and you lived at the fortress at Polignac, there I know I would be welcome and safe. Safe from all."

"And your husband?" Geoffrey asked. "Baudoin would not be welcome at Polignac. There he is still the enemy."

"The marriage was supposed to unite, not divide further."

Geoffrey touched her hair and held her close as best he could, breathing in his fill of her beautiful, sweet smelling hair. "What would Robert de Polignac do?" he asked.

"He would see the child safe for the children are the future."

"When is your baby to come?"

"This moment or so it feels. I pain and it goes. Then I pain again and it stays. I do not know what is happening inside me." She touched her breasts, swollen and tight, and she said, "Geoffrey, I pain all over. It is not right. It cannot be like this."

"Go to your mother, Adelina. Your husband is welcome there."

"Geoffrey?"

"My love?"

"Why have the angels abandoned me?"

Before he could reply, although he did not know what he would say, the door opened. It was Baudoin. He was surprised to see Geoffrey kneeling by his wife, but he saw her tears, too, so he said nothing except, "My father is dead."

Adelina covered her face with her hand.

"Brother Christophe, you are needed."

Their gazes met as Geoffrey walked by and Baudoin watched him continue up the corridor, taking his rosary from his pocket as he walked.

Baudoin looked back at his wife and stepped into her chambers. "Tell me I am not needed?" she begged softly.

"No. You are not."

"He made his peace with me, Baudoin. As much as he was able."

"Geoffrey?"

"No. Your father."

"Oh. Yes. Such as it was peace."

"You knew that Geoffrey came with the others and you allowed him into your house. Why? You forbade me to think of him."

"I know now that separation from a loved one pains more than a dagger to the heart."

"I have never kept you from your Eleanor."

"Which is why I bade Geoffrey come. He you will listen to and he alone has the courage to say things you do not wish to hear. You must go to Lavoute, to your mother."

"It is madness. This is my home now."

"You must go, Adelina. I report to the king's army in three weeks."

"He takes your land and you take up arms in his honour?"

"I have no choice."

"What good is this land to him?"

"He will not cease until all of France and England is royal domain. We can still live here when the baillis come providing we surrender without resistance. But I do not want you here alone when they come. I go to war, you must go to your mother."

"If a baillis is appointed this land will not be ours. I would rather die than give it away willingly."

"Tomorrow, I take you back to Lavoute. There you and the child will be safe until my return."

"But I have trained long and hard to be master of my own walls."

"So have I," Baudoin said.

"There is nothing left now. There will be nothing for our son."

Baudoin lay on the bed. "Lie with me, Addie."

"I am too ill."

"Lie with me. Just lie. That is all."

Adelina rose weakly and lay down beside him, his heart against her ear, the baby kicking violently. Baudoin put his hand on her belly and kept it there until the kicking stopped.

"Why I must report, I do not know, nor do I know for how long I will be gone. Or where the battles will be. There is talk of one or two years absence. I need to know though, whether you have yet come to love me. For I have you, very much."

"It is difficult not to love you."

"February, you say?"

"Yes."

"Geoffrey has promised, as much as he is able, to watch over you in my absence."

"Why do you do this?"

"He loves you, and he, too, would die for you," Baudoin said, honestly.

"I am sorry about your father," she said softly.

"I am not," he replied. She looked at his face and tears were in his eyes. Adelina squeezed his hand tightly. "All I ask is that you care for my son while I am gone."

"Need you tell me to do this?"

"No," he said. "No, I need not tell you anything. But I needed to say it."

As Baudoin rode across the drawbridge of the chateau Lavoute Polignac, Adelina knew that she would never see him alive again. She was cloaked in a sadness which would not lift. Adelina turned to her mother and she took a deep breath when Marys said, "Best you lie down. You are unwell."

"Come girl," Adelina said to Jennet. "There is much to be done."

She walked past Gabriel of Lyon without a word. She did not return his greeting but embraced Ella instead, for only Ella was here with welcome in her eyes. "We await this birth with much joy, Milady. It is a boy, this I know in my ancient bones."

"Be it a boy my mother will be happy." Adelina looked back at Marys who was chastising the washerwomen again. "For had I been born to piss whilst standing she may even have loved me, too."

"Milady!" Ella said, shocked.

"Ella, brace yourself for I have returned."

# Chapter 29

It has been such a long time, Adelina thought as she gazed from her window, as she used to in what seemed another's past. Jennet was busy unpacking. "Do you think Geoffrey knows that I am here?"

"I am sure he knows all which happens. He will visit soon, perhaps."

Adelina did not think so. "Only if the abbot allows it. It is sad, Jennet, to love another so much and there is nothing that can be done. Of all the time I have known him, all of my life, there was never a moment when I believed he would not be by my side." She paused for a moment. "But I was young then."

"Milady, you are still young."

"I am young at heart no more."

"Here, Milady. Lie down and rest. Sleep. That is what you need. It is only the miseries you have. Once the baby comes, all will be well again."

Adelina waited for Jennet to pull down the bedcovers. She lay down with a deep sigh. "I am here because I must be. It is not by choice."

Why is she so miserable? Jennet wondered. She could wonder all she liked, possibly until the snows came again. Her mistress rarely said aloud what lay in her heart and when she did, it seemed as if she spoke aloud to herself only.

"Rest, Milady. You have not rested or slept far too long now." Jennet left her mistress in peace.

Peace it was; the first quiet time Adelina had experienced in a year and she supped at it hungrily for the little while it lasted. When she woke, only then knowing that she had slept, her mother was standing at the foot of her bed. Adelina wanted to hide under the covers.

"You do not greet your mother."

"You did not see fit to visit me in all of the time I was away,"

Adelina said.

"Nor you I."

"Far easier it is for you to travel. Nothing holds you any longer. You need permission from none. You are your own person. But still you did not visit me."

"Allegre is a long way. I do not travel well."

"No. That is not it. You did not come to me because I lived in the same house with Heloise Dupuy."

"That is nonsense!"

"She died and you did not attend her funeral. You said you were once friends. Was that a lie, too?"

"I was not well," Marys said.

"You were not well? You don't know what sickness is."

"I know that Heloise suffered for many a year. There was nothing I could have done."

"Yes, there was. Always she asked of you, even when her senses were gone. Your memory remained in her heart. You and your sister. Yet you could not even spare her some words on parchment to ease her loneliness. Her pain. There was much that you could have done."

"She would not have known me had I gone to her. Michel told me of her disease. Even he was frightened by it."

Adelina's anger was rising with each excuse her mother uttered. "Which was a greater horror to you? Her disease of the body or the disease of her husband? Do not lie to me, Mama! She married a man you did not like and so you chopped off your friendship as if it were a chicken's head! I am a Dupuy and still you do not care enough to know my husband or even see for yourself where it was I lived."

"I would never have been welcome in your house, Adelina. That is why I did not visit you. Heloise was not the reason at all. You were."

Adelina said nothing. There were only a very few times when her mother would have been welcome, very few.

Marys did not continue. Already there had been enough pain. "I know that Henri was laid to rest this day."

"And still you did not come."

Marys took a deep breath and stepped to the window. "All is yours now whilst your husband is absent at war, yes?"

"Yes, all is mine but for a short time only. Again. The king takes it."

"There will be no baillis from Paris."

"What is this you say?"

"The officials will meet the fate of most wealthy travellers. Gabriel sees to it as we speak."

"But that will only anger the king! He will come next with

soldiers!"

"He is too busy preparing for war."

"Gabriel sees to this matter of the baillis, you say?"

"Yes."

"Could it be that he also had planned to make you a widow?"

Marys studied the horizon and there was no expression in her eyes at all. "That is foolishness. Gabriel served your father well and honoured him greatly."

"Gabriel honours those who serve his purpose and once the purpose is served, they are discarded. He will discard you, Mama. He will throw you away with the kitchen scraps."

"Love binds us."

"Love? You don't know what love is."

Marys turned. Her bright gaze caught her daughter's and did not allow escape. "For the first time in our lives, Adelina, we have something that we both may share."

"Tell me then, because I know not what it is."

"Our loved ones now fight a common enemy in the same war."

"Gabriel too, has been called to arms?"

"Yes. Tomorrow, he leaves."

She will miss him, Adelina thought. In her haste she had not lifted the veil which clouded the vision of her mother, the woman. She seemed young again, her hair was arranged differently, and grace and poise she had more of. Perhaps it is true that she does indeed love Gabriel even though he was a much younger man. And obviously she did not know of the evil that resided in him for there was a fire in her eyes now, a glow on her face, a certainty of purpose which Adelina had never noticed before.

"You have married him and did not tell me?"

"No. He is husband to me in spirit only, by law he serves me. And serves me well."

"Who remain as our protectors, then?"

"Only the archer, Dedwyd. He remains to protect us. Tell me what it is you know of serfs and villages and dues and disputes."

"I know only what I have learned from my father, my husband and the serfs themselves."

"Good, for I know very little of such matters."

"You have never wanted to learn. To you it was the domain of man alone, a place you forbade yourself to enter. When will you be your own person, Mama? Are you not a Polignac at heart yet?"

"Heracle said that his counsel is –"

"No! I shall only call upon Heracle if there be no other choice. If you cannot fend for yourself by now, Mama, you never will. I thank you for teaching me what it was I had to become."

"I have done all I could for you!"

"It was not enough."

"What did you expect from me!" It was only one more emotional outburst which Adelina had endured all her life. It did not affect her at all. "I expect what I received, Mama. Nothing. How could you teach me when it was nothing that you ever knew? You shame me because you did not want to know. You have done nothing for me yet you are still ashamed of me because I was not the one you wanted. The one you buried, Michelet, he is still most important to you. I am nothing."

"Adelina, your cruel words will be the death of me."

Adelina stared at her mother and thought of Heloise Dupuy, her quiet sufferings and

agonies and she said nothing. She knew that if words began, they would only become a hurtful waterfall without end. Marys was trying hard to make some peace, and this had never happened before.

"Do you not know how happy I am that you have returned? I have missed you so."

Adelina noticed that her mother seemed strangely sincere as she sat on the bed and took her hand, tightly. "I have never told you how precious you are, or how much I have always loved you. Such things are not to be spoken of. That is how I was raised. Girl, there were times I did not like you, yes, but never, never has my love for you faded."

"Why have I waited all of my life to hear you say those words, Mama?"

"Do not weep, now," Marys said, taking her handkerchief and blotting at her daughter's eyes. "A true lady does not weep. Tell me of Baudoin. Is he good to you?"

"In his way, yes."

"Is he kind?"

"Yes."

"A good father, you think?"

"I think so. He is gentle and calm most of the time."

"You are not the girl who once lived here. You have changed, daughter."

Adelina turned her face away and sighed. She was so tired—all she wanted was to sleep, and sleep, and sleep...

"Are you very ill?"

"It will pass."

"Then sleep," Marys said. "Sleep and I will fetch Michel."

The door closed and Adelina gazed up at the ceiling. There on the crossbeam, the dangling rope, covered now in spider webs. Adelina closed her eyes and the first pain gripped her hard. She let forth a scream to wake the dead. The birth had begun.

By midnight though, nothing had happened. Adelina was aware of nothing except the agony of it all. Relief came in moments only. Jennet knelt by her head all the while, holding her, whispering words never heard, feeling her mistress's pain as if it were her own.

And Marys was there waiting, too.

Ella had seen sent to fetch Michel but he was not there. Ella, with Dedwyd beside her, rode up to the abbey in the dead of the night, and pounded upon the doors, and screamed, and pounded and screamed until the door was answered by a very sleepy old monk. Valuable time was wasted while Brother Christophe was sent for.

Geoffrey appeared at the doors, sleepier than the old monk. Ella grabbed at his arm. "Come! Adelina is birthing! Nothing comes. I fear she will die!"

Geoffrey was halfway to the chateau before he realised he had forgotten his rosary and his shoes.

The past replayed in his mind; the nightmare revisited. He was but a boy again, his ear to the door, asking God to spare him from this, but spare him God had not then and spare him He would not now. Ella pulled him in and set guard at the door herself, for the stairs were blocked by curious men roused from their drunken sleeps. She looked into the eyes of Gabriel of Lyon who had asked, "He is allowed in and I am not?"

"Begone! All of you!"

"You bring the sparrow in? For what?" He demanded. "Is she dying?"

Ella, for the first time in many years, saw concern in his eyes. But she did not reply to his question, she slammed the door in his face instead.

"Milady?"

Marys, kneeling on the floor at the end of the bed, looked up when Geoffrey touched her head. "It happens again," she said, terror in her eyes.

Geoffrey looked at his hands, but they were not the hands of a small boy now. So he stepped back and took up the rosary hanging on the bed post and calmly, he leaned over Adelina. Geoffrey was praying for a miracle.

She did not know that he was there. Adelina's face was blue from repeated strain but she did not scream. Blood ran from her mouth where she had bitten through the piece of thick leather placed there for silence's sake. Jennet held her upright and mopped at her face when the agony passed for a short time, only to begin again very quickly.

Let them not die, Geoffrey repeated silently. "How long has this been?" he asked, voice shaking.

"Since morn," Marys said.

"Is it close yet?" he asked.

Marys shook her head.

He dropped to his knees and silently offered God his life in place of Adelina's.

In the darkness before dawn, Adelina, with barely enough strength left to breathe, looked at all those surrounding her bed. There was her father, Robert, standing next to Geoffrey. Cateline was by the window and smiling brightly and as shyly as ever before. By her mother was Heloise, and Heloise had her hand on her weeping friend's shoulder. But Marys felt nothing. So good it was to see them all again, so good. And yet there was a stranger in the midst of all these people she had loved dearly - a stranger she did not know. It was a woman, with hair the colour of her own, just like a roaring fire. She was tall and very beautiful and shimmered within a cocoon of wonderful light, light so bright that Adelina thought she was an angel. This woman, although she did not move her mouth, looked down at her and said, "Soon, you will know." She glanced at Marys, and then she faded away. Adelina looked back to her father but he had gone, too.

There was only Geoffrey, his hand clasped tight to hers.

And it all began again.

"It comes!" Marys cried, ecstatic. "I see it! It comes!"

"Again, Milady," Jennet coached, and held her upright for the final effort.

Adelina felt the tearing but there was no pain. She pushed again, obeying her mother and her body's demands. Tears sprang to Geoffrey's eyes, tears of pain because his fingers were being crushed by an incredible strength.

And then there was nothing.

Marys eased the baby out slowly by the feet and she turned it around and put it down on the bed under its mothers upturned legs. It was slippery and warm. "A boy!" Marys cried. "A boy! A huge boy!" Marys sawed through the cord that attached it still to his mother and Ella handed her the clean cloths in which his grandmother wrapped him tightly.

A huge boy, indeed, twelve or thirteen pounds of weight perhaps. And he did not cry at all, yet he breathed well. His eyes were open and calmly gazing upon his new world. Thrust from quiet darkness into this dim, noisy light; noise of voices crying and laughing at once.

The sun was rising and splinters of the new day's light seared into the room of the tower.

"Why does he not cry?" Adelina asked weakly.

"He finds no need," Marys replied, joy barely concealed in her voice.

"Let me see, Mama. Let me see."

Marys put the baby into the fouled bed and Adelina looked at his tiny face and he at hers. He was frowning and still quiet. His hair was very fair and his face and arms were very fat. This came from me? she wondered and sleepy, exhausted, looked at her mother, at Ella, at her girl, and then at Geoffrey who was standing well back now. Well back, and close to tears himself. Then he was away, quickly, without a word.

Ella and Jennet bathed Adelina, and changed the bedding from under their mistress as she slept. She would sleep for a very long time indeed.

Marys took the baby, her grandson, to show it off to the world.

None of the knights came near except Francois and Dedwyd. Gabriel, whose feet were on the table, did not even look when Marys thrust it under his nose. He turned his face away after a glance. To him the thing was a Dupuy. All night long he had prayed that the creature die. His prayers had not been answered.

"She lives?" he asked.

"Of course she lives."

"Good," was all Gabriel said. He rose tiredly and pushed past. All the screaming had kept him awake and in a few hours he had to leave.

He too, had been called to arms.

Adelina heard nothing of Baudoin, although each day she prayed that a letter would come. She had not realised how much she had missed him until he was not there and in a strange way, her heart was aching.

She named the boy Gervaise and he was a demanding infant and a spirited one. And each day he came to look more like his father although at times when he grinned at her, Adelina saw her own father reflected in the child's eyes.

Of the men, there was no news at all until one day in the early summer of 1214. Both she and her mother had awaited news anxiously for neither knew where in the world their loved ones were, or how they fared.

Neither expected Heracle de Polignac to visit that early summer's day. He was dressed for war and with him were seven knights, also dressed for war. He would not come inside though. He was journeying north and could not stay long.

He was surprised at sight of Adelina, so very thin. The boy he had only heard of, old enough to walk now, played in the courtyard with the daughter of a servant, and he did not look like a Polignac at all, nor, Heracle thought as he looked closer, did he seem a Dupuy.

"What news, Heracle? What news?" Marys asked, clinging to his reins as he sat on his horse.

"The king gathers his army to the north east while Louis gathers to the south west."

"Gabriel of Lyon? To which is he sworn? King or prince?"

"Of this I know nothing. I am wanted in Flanders."

"My husband, uncle?" Adelina asked.

"Aagain, I can tell you nothing."

"If you see him…"

"I will tell him that you are well and asking of him and that he has a fine son," Heracle said after casting a quick glance at the small child." Have you anything you wish to give him?"

Adelina took off the emerald ring which once belonged to the mother of her father, and she gave it to Heracle. He recognised it instantly, but said nothing.

Marys was not asked for a token because she was not wed.

"God go with you, uncle."

"Always," he said and was followed from the gate by his small army of loyal retainers.

Marys walked back into the chateau alone and Adelina called for the little boy who looked up at the sound of his name but did nothing. He returned to his play with his girl-friend, they were busy building a house of loose cobblestones. "Gervaise Dupuy!" He looked up again, and again, he ignored his mother. Adelina walked to him and lifted him by the arm and dragged him from his play mate. He screamed his objection, and he fought. "No! You do as I say!" He spat at her and Adelina smacked him, hard. To that, he cried, not from distress of pain or punishment, but from pure hatred, hatred which Adelina felt burrowing into her very core. The child liked only those who pandered to him and granted his every desire and any who dared cross him soon felt his hatred. He was still screaming and struggling for freedom when Adelina dragged him into the great hall and sat him upon his seat in the corner. Ella was bringing lunch to the table when the little boy shot off the seat, circled Ella's legs and galloped off down to the kitchen. Adelina was on her feet instantly and chased the boy who was halfway down the stairs before she reached him. His path was blocked though, by Geoffrey, who caught the boy under one arm and grinned widely at Adelina. "He escapes as you once did."

"As quickly?" she asked.

I remember so, yes."

"He exhausts me, Geoffrey."

"As you once gave, so it is given back."

320

"I do not find that amusing. Why are you here?"

"I was on my way to La Chaise Dieu and I noticed our uncle and his men. I am curious."

"There is war in Flanders."

"And you have only now heard?" Still with struggling toddler under his arm, Geoffrey went into the great hall and sat there with Marys and Dedwyd. He put the boy on the floor and even Marys was surprised when the boy climbed back onto Geoffrey's lap. There he fought to see what lay under the monk's robe.

Adelina ate sparsely and did not hear the conversation. Her thoughts floated above it. Her thoughts were of Baudoin. For too long she had not seen him. He had departed in the new year of 1213.

Each night for a week she had suffered the same dream. Her temper was short with worry.

"I shall take a walk," she said absently, heart heavy. Geoffrey watched her walk away but he could not follow. Marys held him fast with her chatter.

Adelina watched Ella at work for a little while but still her thoughts gave her no peace. She walked up into the servant's chambers and stopped at the end of the dark, hot hole of a corridor. Here it had been where she had played as a child with Cateline. Here, in the floor of stone, lay the covered entrance to a secret tunnel. The girls had both feared the dark but together were brave, especially when Adelina had stolen a candle, and aided by its light and the courage of a companion, the very bowels of the chateau were often explored. Eventually the narrow, cramped tunnel led out into a cave that kissed the very waterline of the Loire. There they would sit, Cateline and Adelina, at the mouth of the cave, the chateau looming high directly above them. Here they were both away from angry mothers until a few frantic calls were heard and the innocents would reappear in the kitchens, wide eyed, dirty and full of innocent wonder. Only her father knew where she would sometimes go and the most that he had said was, take care in the darkness. It was not a simple cave at the bottom of a cliff to him, either.

Here she sat again, alone, drawing her knees high as she did when a child. And if the weather was hot, as it was now, she would dip her bare feet into the water.

Even Geoffrey did not know of this place.

Her thoughts chased her here, too, thoughts of Geoffrey this time. Geoffrey, in the great hall entertaining her son.

I cannot bear to look upon him when he is clothed in God's black, when his hair is shorn so abominably that he looks like one of Ella's cookpots. I cannot bear to be near him. Why? she asked aloud. "Dieu, I beg you, tell me why?"

She sat there for a very long time and soon enough from behind came soft footsteps. Adelina knew the footsteps as well as her own. Will I find peace nowhere? she wondered.

Geoffrey sat down beside her and hugged his knees as he peered into the water. "I searched all over. Some talents you have not lost."

"I thought none knew of this place."

"You followed me here when you were this tall," he said and indicated with his hand the height of a child, no more than two years old.

"I do not remember. I do not remember being young at all."

"I reach for your hand, Adelina, but you refuse to take it."

"It will do no good to either of us if I do. Are you not supposed to be on your way to La Chaise Dieu?"

Geoffrey looked down into the water again. On the far bank, two village men were fishing. The fishermen waved and Geoffrey knew that the abbot would soon learn of this. But strangely, he cared not. "Do you not know that I am still Geoffrey at heart? Only my name has changed."

Adelina studied him in silence. She needed no words to confirm his lie. He had changed, yes, and so had she.

"Your mother searches for you."

"I care not."

"Your son cries for you."

"I care not."

"Still you blame me for all of your pain and misery."

Adelina turned to him, quickly. "I do not!"

"Always you have and always you will. What has come from this pain and misery, though?"

"More pain and misery."

"No. No, you are wrong. Strength has come. Much strength."

There was a very loud silence.

"The baillis did not come," she said to change the subject.

"And because of that, every three days you ride with Dedwyd and Michel to Allegre. Best for all if the baillis had come. You would have far less worry."

"Someone must oversee, Geoffrey. Antoine and Francois are at the war. The people of both villages need me."

"You cannot endure this any longer. You take no care of yourself. You are thin, and ill and tiring."

"Someone must oversee!"

"I have asked for a leave of absence and if it is granted, I will go to Allegre and take this duty from you."

Adelina reached for Geoffrey's hand and tears stung at her eyes when he gripped her fingers tightly. "You would do that for me?"

"Only for you."

The silence came again, the silence that each, for so many years, had shared in great comfort. How good it was that he sat with her now. How good.

"This remains when we are long gone," Geoffrey whispered. "Please God it happens not too quickly." Geoffrey raised her hand to his face and kissed her fingers. "Most of my prayers have been answered. Do you know why?"

"You know God, not I."

"My prayers were for you."

Again, he spoke of things lingering in his heart but when her turn came there was only silence. "If the abbot does not grant you your leave of absence I will... I will..."

"What?"

"Hang, draw, and quarter him."

"Alone?" Geoffrey asked.

"You may assist if you wish."

Their amusement faded quietly. "When you were small and you had dreamed or known of things to come, you would come to me, or you would sit alone and worry. I know this feeling well, Adelina. Tell me what troubles you."

"I have grown used to keeping secrets."

"Ah, secrets. Secrets that fester like boils and poison the heart? Very wise indeed."

She looked into Geoffrey's eyes and away again, to the water where it was safe. "When Baudoin rode out, so long ago, I knew I would never see him again. I knew then that what Gabriel of Lyon had told me a long time ago would certainly be."

"What was this he told you?"

"That when I am a Dupuy widow, he would take me for his wife. For many nights now, Geoffrey, I have seen the same battle. Nothing changes and so I know it is not a dream. There is much death and much dust rising. I have seen it, I have heard it and felt it, and each time I close my eyes the vision remains. I see my husband and he is dead. He lies under a large tree, dead."

Geoffrey's hand tightened on hers and she returned the gesture.

"He told me once that he did not fear death. That what he feared was meeting death before he had come to know me."

"Then he loves you and so that knowing you must always hold dear." As I do, he thought.

"You do not understand. I would not allow him to know me. He knew only the small part of me which I permitted him to see. No more than that. He was my friend, Geoffrey and now he is dead. My regrets are so many. He shall never see my face again and he shall never look upon Gervaise. Ever."

"You must have faith in life eternal."

"I do not have the faith or the knowing that you have, Geoffrey. I have tried and tried but I do not have this faith."

"You do. You do not recognise it."

"I have seen this place. This place of the battle, but I know not where it is. There is a monastery on a hill, and below, I see a harvest half finished. There are no serfs in the cornfields. All is abandoned and then I see why. Many soldiers gather. I see our king dozing under a tree and there is a call, and he runs into the monastery and there he prays, alone. He then leaps upon his horse and he goes off to begin the fight. It is so clear. It is as if I am there, watching. I see the Oriflamme and many men. So many men..."

# CHAPTER 30

"Ha! Otto runs like the dog he is!" Gabriel called and pointed out the emperor in his retreat.

Already he, Baudoin and countless others had driven the Germans away from Philippe's circle and there was now a break in the fighting. They all regained their breaths in preparation for the next onslaught.

Gabriel's eyes were sparkling. How he loved this. How he fed upon it. They soon came again, these fools with the sun in their eyes, and this time the German infantry was with them. The battle was fierce in the cornfields of Bouvines and much dust rose, dust from hooves and battling footmen, roaring, shouting, as equal faced equal. Footsoldiers fell, knights on horseback fell. Again, Gabriel lost Baudoin in the melee and it was not until Gabriel himself chose an enemy equal of rank to challenge, did he see from the corner of his eye, Baudoin struck to the ground. But Gabriel could not back away from his silent challenge and he hastened his kill for there was no time to lose.

He fought his way to where Baudoin Dupuy lay, not yet dead, and Gabriel pulled him by the leg out of the chaos, using his sword as he went, clearing space and felling several unfortunate enough to be in his way. Gabriel settled Baudoin beneath a large tree behind the king's circle. He was too badly wounded to know where on earth he was.

Fifteen yards away, the fierce battle continued. Time momentarily lost its meaning. For many months now they had travelled together, camped together, and talked for many a long night. It was Gabriel who took a piece of jewellery out. It had been given to him by Heracle, who still considered Dupuy the enemy. The ring slipped from Gabriel's gloved fingers to the grass by Baudoin's head. "This I had forgotten, friend," Gabriel said, picking it up and squeezing it into Baudoin's useless hand. "It is from Adelina. She gave it to me before I departed, the very day your son was born dead. Now that you die, best you know that indeed she once loved you. Once."

Baudoin, cut by axe deep into his shoulder, lay on his back staring up at Gabriel, begging him silently to end it. But end it Gabriel did not. He looked about, checking the battle in progress and noticed the red silk of the Oriflamme waving frantically above the dust clouds. He looked at Baudoin and ran back into the melee, to Philippe's aid. German and Flemish blood mixed on his sword, and again the enemy, too close to the king this time, were driven back. Gabriel and two others assisted the armoured king back to his feet, and on to his horse once more. Before Philippe plunged back into the fight again, he saw the face of the one who had helped save him from the German army. "You again," the king said. "I will remember this." Gabriel nodded, and he too, was swept back into the fight.

Victory was theirs, eventually. First the Germans, then the English and Flemish fell and when all was over, and prisoners taken, Gabriel searched the dead, looking for interesting souvenirs. Two of Heracle de Polignac's knights had fallen, but the old man himself had not. He was standing a distance away, looking down at Baudoin under the tree. Gabriel walked to him. "You fought well, my friend," Heracle said, he himself bloodied and tired.

"As always, Milord."

Gabriel looked down at Baudoin and saw the Polignac lance embedded in the belly and the dark eyes were open wide. Ants were already feasting.

"Now all will be mine again," Heracle said. "You, take the body back to the weeping wife. Console her in the manner we have already discussed."

Gabriel bent to one knee and from Baudoin's stiff fingers, he took back the ring.

Adelina sat by her window and stared beyond the courtyard to the rolling hillsides below, rolling lands for as far as the eye could see. It was hers now, all of it, hers. But there was no joy in the knowing.

Today she had lain her husband to rest beside his father and mother and brother. There was not a Dupuy left now save for Gervaise, the child Baudoin had never seen.

And for that she was pleased.

She had not cried. She had not cried when the casket was brought to Lavoute. Brought by her uncle, and with him, Gabriel of Lyon. The smell was abominable but it was not a new experience for she had once walked behind one such leaking casket before - her own father's. Adelina, who knew in her heart how her husband had died, demanded to see the remains. She could not bury him without knowing that this indeed was Baudoin.

But when the coffin was opened, she could not tell if it was the man she had married or not.

She had taken two steps back into Gabriel's arms and she had run.

She had then barred her door and let none in. She looked at the boy, asleep on her bed, for that was where he slept, curled into his mother.

He did not resemble Baudoin Dupuy at all. Nor did the child resemble her, except perhaps for the colour of her eyes.

She had known in her heart that he would not be like either of them. But the Dupuy name he would bear for what remained of his life. And she would be determined that he bore the name with pride.

She thought of the funeral, and how it had been, with all from Allegre there, again, to bury the last of the old masters. It was then, when it was over, that she saw the woman, alone, weeping quietly.

Adelina knew that this woman was Eleanor, the one who forever held fast to her husband's heart. And she felt nothing except sadness for this woman and could not understand why as it was she, Adelina, who was the grieving widow. She had approached her though, and she had said, "You are Eleanor?"

The most beautiful dark blue eyes that Adelina had ever seen turned to her. None of her beauty was hidden because of her despair. She was clothed in black and in black she would probably remain until her time was ended. "I am Eleanor."

But no words had come to Adelina. This is the woman whose arms he lay in, to whom all secrets were imparted and all love was given. And all he was to me, all he had ever been, was a friend. He had tried to love me, she thought, but he could not. Not as he had loved her.

"Should you ever need of anything, come to me." Adelina had wanted to touch her, perhaps feel where this woman's magic lay, but Eleanor clenched her handkerchief tightly. She had simply nodded before the quiet weeping began again because holding to Adelina's hand, was the little boy.

Adelina had turned away.

And still, she turned away. From the world. Voices from below still celebrated deep into the night: Gabriel of Lyon, Antoine, Francois, the three new retainers who had followed Gabriel home from the battle of Bouvines. That was the sole topic of talk, the battle. Much laughter from Gabriel, and very little sadness. She had not seen Francois or Antoine yet to speak to, and she knew in her heart that they would both be as silent as she. The king was building another abbey now, and he would call it Victory Abbey. The captured enemy's nobility were either ransomed or imprisoned in Paris. There had been a full week of celebration there, where torches turned the night into day, and now that Gabriel was home again, there would be a week more of drunkenness.

No tears remained. All had been shed too long ago. Nor was she fearful of what she knew would soon come—Gabriel, to her chambers. All that he had planned, all that he had wanted, had finally come to fruition. What was hers would become his or so the fool thought.

She would rather die than submit. She had her son now, and his name was Dupuy and it was he and he alone who would inherit all that her eyes could see. Still a baby though, not yet two years old, and sleeping soundly amid his child-like dreams.

For hours she waited for the hard knocking on her barred door and when it finally came, she did not acknowledge it because she knew who bade entry. She cared for nothing now.

"Milady?" Adelina looked to her girl but said nothing. She turned back to her window again when Jennet said, "He will break down the door."

"My husband is dead. Can none leave me in peace?" Adelina rose and walked to her bed. She sank down into it and sighed.

Still the pounding continued until she heard her mother's voice:

"Adelina? Your uncle is here and he wishes to speak with you."

"I am tired, I am ill."

But they would not go away. She looked at her girl and nodded. Jennet disbarred the door and Heracle, alone, swept in. He was not surprised to see her in her bed. Was she not taking this grief too far?

"My dear," he said and sat, without being asked, on the side of her bed.

"Uncle. Congratulations on your victory. For an old man it is said you fought well."

Heracle feigned deafness and reached for her hand. "Time is my enemy, this you know. What plan you now? Do you think of the future?"

"What is mine will soon become royal domain. Is there a future?"

"The king has reconsidered. All lands remain yours."

"Not mine but my son's."

He looked at the boy who was sleeping soundly under the covers, thumb in mouth. "You have done well during your time alone, Adelina. I am told that you alone oversaw large harvests in not one but three villages. I am proud of you and the respect you have generated for our name."

"Administration of affairs is a matter of common sense."

Heracle looked down at her as if he wanted to know more, so she said, "Treat them as valuable pets, with kindness and reward, and all is well. If I called them all to arms they would fight for me as I would fight for them. Do you know that the abbot offered to lend me three of his monks at dues time? I did not accept, of course."

"Why was this?"

"I did not know what he would expect in return."

"He is a man of God. He would expect nothing."

"Then you do not know him as I do. Is there any more news of the king?"

"The royal domain increases each month now."

"As do the treasury coffers, no doubt, at the expense of landholders such as we. I do not trust the king. Nor do I trust you and for this reason I wonder now what it is that brings you here. For something it is that you must want badly."

"I have heard you have been unwell a long time now."

Adelina turned her face away. Lie he could not, or did he expect her to have no sense? "I expect much trouble from Philippe Augustus," she said. "I care not for what you say. It is a knowing, uncle. It is as strong as it was when my husband rode away. I knew then I would never see him again. It was so. You will either tell me what it is you want, or you will leave me in peace."

So much like her father, he thought. Best then that he continue. "Why do you not marry and increase your holdings? I know of," he thought momentarily, "At least six eligible barons who would gladly vie for your hand."

"My husband is not yet cold in the ground. I will never marry again."

"A woman alone cannot –"

"I am not alone. I have Antoine and Francois at Allegre and soon they take retainers. I have Geoffrey and Michel, and Dedwyd, and I can call back Louis at any time. Thierry the Miller has now a valuable position in the village here and I trust him for he knows well that if he cheats me, he cheats himself. And I have your wisdom to call upon. But I have not yet needed to call upon you, have I."

The stubborn determination he had always seen shining from his younger brother's eyes now lay in this girl's. "Adelina, the intricacies of administration is for noble man not woman."

"And what of Eleanor of Aquitaine?" Adelina asked.

"That is different. She is of royal blood. You are not."

"She is woman, is she not? What matter is blood? Is it not all red when spilled? Uncle, I thank you for your concern, but what I do is perform these duties until my son is of age to take this duty from me. Until that time, the responsibility is mine and mine alone."

"You are silly little girl, Adelina de Polignac."

"Excuse me, uncle, but my name is Dupuy. Is that what irks you the most? Or is it the knowing that a woman can do as much as a man?"

"The only mistake by brother made was raising you as a son."

"My father raised me to find my own worth regardless of gender."

"There is a count from Toulouse who–"

"No. Only one holds my heart. Only one has ever held it. And it cannot be for he has chosen another life. So this life I will live alone."

"Your reign of this small kingdom will be short and fraught with disaster. I beg you marry now one already of wealth and power so that life can become as God decreed for you."

"I am not a queen, nor have I a kingdom. I have only inherited responsibilities. I do not wish to marry one of wealth and power, and I do not believe that God decrees what shall become of one man or woman. He grants us life but that life remains ours to make of it what we will. It is said that we take from life only what we have given it. Be that true, and if I sit, as you say God has decreed I should, as a lady of noble birth amid billowing silks all day, then I give nothing to any. That life is not for me. I cannot turn my back on my responsibilities now. I turn my back on nothing and no one, but if you persist in your nagging that I should marry, and not for love, but for wealth and gain, then I shall turn my back upon you, just as my father did. It is your choice."

"By the time you have seen the effect of your foolishness it will be too late."

"I see nothing but the glitter of gold shining from your eyes, uncle. I do not like it. You may now go."

"Oh, Milady," Jennet said once the door was barred again. "Dare you speak to Lord Polignac that way?"

"I fear no one."

Adelina held the little boy close and he did not in sleep squirm to get away.

The next day, whilst seated for lunch, Adelina noticed again the similarities between Gabriel of Lyon and the boy, Gervaise, who seemed to prefer sitting next to his grandmother at all times. Possibly because his grandmother fulfilled his every whim. The child even held his bone and chewed on it as Gabriel did. He looked at Gabriel and imitated his every movement, but Gabriel saw it not. Nor did he take any notice of the child, even when the boy offered him a chew on his bone and misjudged, the bone dripping with spit, plunging into his ear. He just moved away a little and wiped his ear and regarded the child as if it were a creature he had never seen before.

Gabriel had said not one word to her since his return. He had not spoken at the funeral, nor had he come to her the night before. Still her expectations were ripe. And today he seemed intent of gaze, as if working through his mind his plan. And knowing of course that she would never consent. When the child offered him the bone again, Gabriel swept it out of the child's hand and threw it across the room. The child cried, his heart and pride wounded.

*Have you not eyes! The boy is of your blood!* Adelina wanted to scream.

"Take it away! Its noise is too much!"

Jennet quickly swept Gervaise from his seat and he howled in anger all the way up the stairs.

"He is but a child. Have tolerance or leave."

Gabriel could not believe what he had heard. He turned to Adelina and said, "You would dare say that again?" It was not so much his words but the look on his face which angered her so, which built rage inside her.

Adelina said it again, so that this time he would hear and remember. She rose from her place at the table, picked up her eating dagger, scrambled across on her knees so that food and wine spilled, and she stabbed her knife into the wood very close to Gabriel's hand. She stared into his eyes and he into hers. "If you do not like what I have to say to you then you are free to leave this employ! Remember who it is you speak to!"

Gabriel looked down at the dagger, half a breath from his hand. "Do not anger me, child," he said looking directly into her eyes as she knelt on all fours upon the table before him. He was seething.

"What is it you do not like about my son, Gabriel? He inherits what you desire the most? I have only fulfilled my father's dying wish that I give him a grandson. What angers you?" Hate was alive in her eyes. "Could it be that you knew Baudoin would not be faithful to me? Or perhaps the chance of my becoming with child was not good? You did not want me as a virgin, no, no, you would wait until I was a wealthy widow, is that not true? Is that not what you said to me once?"

"Sit down," Gabriel said.

"I like it here. I see for myself the black, evil heart which shines from your eyes!"

"I said, sit down!" He did not like her so close.

"Adelina, this is foolishness," Marys said as she continued eating, unperturbed.

"Do you not know, Mama, what this thing is that sits in my father's seat?"

Gabriel had had quite enough. He leaned back, put his foot against her shoulder and pushed. Adelina landed on the floor. She was more than ready to battle him.

"It was he who violated me before my wedding, Mama! It was not some thieves in the night! It was he and what became of it? Do you not have eyes? Do you not see that the face of my son is but a mirror of this demon?"

Gabriel took a deep breath and continued eating as if nothing were wrong. Let the women fight it out, for that is all the girl wanted, a fight. He knew very well whose side Marys would take in this battle. She worshipped him.

"It is lies!" Marys cried.

"It is not lies. He did the same to my girl. He undermines all that I attempt to do and he will take what is not his and we shall be left with nothing if you allow this to continue! Mama, all of this is mine now, it is not his!" She turned to Gabriel. "I want you out of this employ! I demand that you begone!"

Gabriel put his feet on the table and laughed. "How pray will you accomplish this?"

"Do this I say or I will kill you myself!"

That amused him no end. He held up his tankard so that a charboy would fill it. "Sit down and eat. You aggravate me as a flea would."

Adelina let forth a scream and she ran in to attack but Gabriel's retainers simply held her fast.

"Send for a physician. I believe she has gone mad. Mad with grief perhaps? Or just mad. Take her away, send for someone. The poor little girl is ill."

Adelina fought and screamed all the way to her chambers.

"What she has become since she married Dupuy sickens me," Gabriel said.

Marys said nothing but her thoughts were loud.

"Is it true what she has said?" Marys asked.

"Of what?"

It was too distasteful to consider but still she was nagged endlessly. Had she not wondered herself, why the child did not resemble Baudoin Dupuy? Had it not been born early, too, and yet when it lay in her arms, she knew that it had come on time? Did he not sit as Gabriel sat, did he not study people as Gabriel did?

"You believe the ravings of that madwoman upstairs?"

"I know my daughter," was all Marys said. She did not add that she also saw how he gazed upon women, any woman.

"Do you think I am simple?" he asked.

"Excuse me?"

"She says I am her child's father. She accuses me of violating her. A child. Who is it you believe, Marys?"

Marys said nothing.

"Does it matter who has fathered it when it seems not to matter who has mothered it. I know, Marys."

"You know what?" she asked.

"Very few indeed know the truth of Adelina's parentage, but I am amongst that number."

"You speak idiocy now. You have drunk too much again."

"You know nothing of me, you stupid woman. Nothing."

"Gabriel!" He did not look back as he took the stairs quickly. "Gabriel!" Marys found her feet and ran after him, forgetting her grace and dignity.

"You wish that she knows who her true mother was?"

"Lies! You listen to lies!"

"You wish that she knows her mother was your sister who was poisoned by your beloved husband?"

"You could not be so cruel!"

"Then you do not know me at all."

"I do not understand!"

"No, how could you, Marys? Is there anything that you do understand? It is not you I want. It is Adelina. And I shall have her. Again. Have you not eyes, woman? Do you not see that the son she guards with her life is mine? Ask her and she will tell you who its father truly is! As her, and she will cry to you how it happened!"

Marys lifted her hand to strike but Gabriel caught it fiercely and tears of pain burst at her dark eyes as he twisted her arm and almost brought her to her knees. "I will marry your daughter and there is nothing you can do to stop me, woman. What is your wish, Marys? I tell your daughter now of her true parentage or do you follow me upstairs as you have always done, the obedient, faithful old dog that you are?"

Marys was frozen from the agony of betrayal. Her thoughts clouded, nonsensical. She had until now never understood the aversion most held for Gabriel of Lyon. To her, from his very first days at the chateau, he had been only kind and comforting and strong, and often humourous too, and he pleased her unlike any other she had ever taken to her bed. What was this he said now? What birthed this hatred in his eyes? How had he known of her secret?

"How did you know!" she pleaded.

"You idiot. Who was it that your husband confided his many sins to?"

"You lie! The abbot Jean is a man of God!"

"Strike me again? See where you are woman. I can say you were drunk and you slipped upon the stairs. I will have your daughter, it is your choice as to whether you shall be present at this wedding or whether you lie dead beside your faithless husband."

They stood halfway up the tower. Gabriel let go of her hand and Marys rose unsteadily. "Get out of my house! You are no longer in service to me!"

"I was never in service to you, cow. Follow me now or I shall take one of the servants as I have done many times over."

"Get out of my house or I shall have you thrown out!"

"Call upon a knight, Milady, and you will find that none challenge their master. This estate is mine to do with as I see fit. Soon it will be all mine, legally. Does that not please you as much as it pleases me?"

"Heracle will hear of this!"

"Heracle already knows! Who do you think I am allieged to! Was it by chance alone that I came to know your husband? Was it by chance alone that I saved his miserable life? There is nothing to be gained by mimicking a fish out of water. Close your mouth, Marys. It is not becoming of a lady."

Gabriel walked up the stairs alone and laughed to himself with each step he took.

Marys sat before she fell and rested her head against her daughter's door. The hound on the stairs, Robert's dog, nuzzled at her hand. Marys covered her face and wept. How she wept.

"What is that noise?" Adelina asked, listening closely.

"Your mother cries?" Jennet asked, stunned.

"See to it. Stop the noise, quickly. I cannot come." The boy was not yet half finished his slow feeding. Jennet opened the door and Adelina strained to see what was happening. "Lady Marys?"

Marys looked up at Jennet and grabbed the girl's legs tight, still wailing. "Come, Milady. Come." Jennet gathered her broken mistress up and guided her in to Adelina's chambers.

"Mama?" Adelina asked from her seat by the window. Gervaise pulled away the moment he saw his grandmother and he ran to her.

Marys took him in arms and said shakily, "All is lost. All is gone."

"Mama?"

Slowly the truth unfolded.

"I will kill him!"

"No!" Marys begged. "He is too strong, too good a warrior. You cannot. No one can."

"I would rather die than marry him. Heracle knows of this you say? I cannot believe it! I will not have him in this house a moment longer!"

"There is so much that you do not know, Adelina."

"Best then that I do know, Mama."

"It is painful. Painful for us both."

"You think I have never endured pain? Tell me this secret before it festers like a boil and poisons you more."

Marys took a cloth from her sleeve and wiped at her face but composure had long since departed. She was not a lady now, she was but a woman, pacing the chamber floor constantly, her grandson against her shoulder and she seemed not aware of his presence even though she held him tightly. "I am not your mother," she said.

Adelina at first thought it was something said in jest.

"All of the times we disagreed and spat hatred at each other, and you said you had no mother, how true it was."

"Mama, I spoke from anger. You know what I am like."

"You spoke of truths!" Marys sat and covered her face with her hand. "Your father married me because of the dowry I had. I had a sister, far more beautiful and younger, and Robert loved her always, yet he married me for my earthly worth alone. I could not bear him children. For many years we tried—"she paused, sighing. "But it was never me he loved. In the heat of passion he would call me by my sister's name. Vianna."

Adelina was not the only one stunned into a silence. Jennet's mouth gaped.

"She sang as you sing, with the voice of an angel. Her eyes were large and full of love for my husband. He needed an heir more than he needed to draw breath, and because I loved him dearly, I agreed that Vianna should come to live with us. She shared our bed and very quickly was with child. Robert could not divorce me and so it was arranged that I go nowhere at all for almost a year. It was rumoured that I was ill and had taken to my bed until the birth. Robert was away the day the babies were born. We did not know that there were two. The first, a boy, was dead."

"Michelet."

"Yes, Michelet. Had it not been for Geoffrey, you would both have died. Geoffrey attended your birth and he was the last to see Vianna alive."

"Geoffrey was there when I was born?"

"He was but a boy, with small hands. Useful hands. I thought you would die as Vianna died, in this very room, on this very bed. I could never speak of her. I could not bear to remember her death, so awful it was. I was mother to you in the only way I knew how, Adelina. I swear on my life that I have only wanted the best for you. But again, your father loved you more than he loved me, his wife. How was I to feel about you?"

Adelina reached for her mother's hand. "I have seen her, Mama. I have seen this woman, your sister."

"No, it is impossible. She is long dead now."

"During the birth, she came. She stood by your side, with Heloise. She said to me, that soon I would know. She looked at you, and she vanished. Papa was there, too, and Cateline..."

It is true, Marys thought. She is mad.

"You have reason now to hate me, Adelina."

"No. You are my mother for you are all I have ever known. Why did you not tell me?" Adelina asked.

"I had not the courage until now. Gabriel knows and would use this knowledge against me."

"Mama, what will we do? How can we be rid of him?"

"I do not know."

"I will never marry him. Never."

"Perhaps God will pity us and take him."

Both Adelina and Marys turned to Jennet who had spoken.

"Perhaps he will die, squealing like the pig that he is." Jennet spat upon the floor.

"Mama?"

Marys looked into her daughter's face. For the first time she did not see Vianna staring back at her.

"Mama, we shall stand together, you and I. This is ours, it is not his. It will never be his. Always it will be Polignac land."

Something shone from her mother's eyes, something Adelina had never seen before. Their hands clasped tightly.

Gabriel waited in the moments before dawn for Adelina to venture to the latrine as she always did upon awakening. He slipped into her chambers in the dim light, saw the child asleep—his own son.

The girl had taken to sharing Adelina's bed, why he did not know, and nor did he care. It slept between the two women, and now the girl's arm was around it tight as she slept deeply. Or so he thought, but as he approached, her eyes opened quickly and her scream was stilled by a hand over her mouth. "Remain quiet and you shall live."

Gabriel pulled the covers back and lifted the boy out by one foot. Gervaise screamed with fright, and then with laughter. Jennet attempted to grab the child but Gabriel hit her so hard that her head cracked against the bed post and she lay half in, half out of bed, whimpering and unable to move for the pain.

Gabriel, his hand clamped on the boy's arm now, walked out and down the stairs.

Adelina was still half asleep when she padded barefooted across the great hall only to hear her son's screams of pain.

She knew who was coming down the stairs. She saw her father's weapons, all of them under his coat of arms but how long would it take her to run across the huge room? Her feet found wings, her thoughts were savage but facing Gabriel unarmed she would never. Already she had felt the pain of his anger and he was a big man, and could easily break her with one hand. She tore down the crossbow and loaded it as quickly as she was able. Unfortunately she was not fast enough for she had barely drawn it back when she heard his laugh and looked up. He held her son by the arm and swung him from side to side, the stone wall closer with each swing of the screaming pendulum. He took his dagger from his belt, the same one he had once held to her throat. Now it was at her son's.

"You would kill me, my pretty bride?" he asked.

Those seven, calm words froze her entire being. The crossbow was loaded and pointed to the floor. She dared not raise it now for by the time she did and took aim, her son's blood would be spray over the stone wall.

"You have a choice, Adelina Dupuy. Consent to marry me now or your son dies."

Sickness rose, her hands shook. She tried not to hear her son's cries but they were so loud and piercing that she could not think.

"Consent to marry me or your son dies."

"May God forgive you," Adelina said. "It is your son!"

"You believe I care? Do you know how many sons I have? Five, Adelina, I have five. Illegitimate perhaps, and one more matters not. But it does matter to you, so I would suggest that you put the weapon down."

She did not know what to do. "I will, Adelina. I will. I have done it many times before."

Adelina dropped the crossbow. She had made her choice. "Give me my son," she said, taking a step towards him. But Gabriel's smile was huge and he did not move. Still he held the child fast and tight. "Please Gabriel! Please give him to me!"

"Marry me."

"Put the child down!"

Gabriel turned quickly at the sound of Marys's voice and he laughed at what he saw—the old cow in her nightdress, long hair loose and wild, a huge sword in her hand. A Dupuy sword, too. She barely had the strength to hold it, let alone use it. She would not know how.

"Put my grandson down!" she screamed again, a madwoman alive in her eyes.

Gabriel knew that if he stared at her long enough she would soon be defeated and probably cry. That was her greatest talent. Crying. "Put it down?"

"Now!" Adelina screamed.

He could not concentrate, one woman with sword in hand behind, one below in the great hall, lifting a cross-bow. Which posed the greater threat? Adelina, surely. Too late he heard the sound of the bolt, loosed.

It hit. Gabriel propped. The child fell from his hand, bounced against the stone floor and rolled, jelly-like to the bottom the stairs. There he screamed more and crawled to his mother.

Gabriel went down to one knee, gasping. The pain in his belly was intolerable. He grabbed the bolt and tried to pull it out but weakness flooded him. He sank to his other knee, hard, and turned his head as best he could. "Marys, have pity." But no pity lay in the old cow's eyes.

Gabriel lay wondering what would come next. He could not move. Beaten by a woman? It was almost amusing and a smile played on his lips.

"Finish what you have begun," Gabriel said weakly, feeling his life-force slowly ebbing, dripping on the stairs. "Finish it!"

But the women stared at him.

"You have not won," he said, spitting blood. And then he cursed them. How he cursed them both. His last sight was Marys, the Dupuy sword in both her hands. She raised it high above her head, a wild woman still alive in her eyes.

Courage at last, Gabriel thought.

# Epilogue

There was no aisle, save for the narrow track leading to the river's edge where people milled and talked in hushed tones on the white sand. For this celebration, inhabitants from all villages came, from the very young to the very old. There was room for everyone in this cathedral of God, with its invisible arches reaching high into the clear, blue heavens and beyond. It was here that Geoffrey felt closer to his God than in all his days and nights of silence and solitude. He looked down at the young woman beside him and squeezed her hand tightly.

Adelina de Polignac, glowing with happiness, beauty and youth, held fast to both the child in her arms and Geoffrey's hand. He shied from the attention, and she lapped at it because the attention came from many she knew and loved. Most of them were from the villages she now possessed. Some of the faces there he recognised, most not.

There was Andre, wonderful Andre, who had helped him choose the words, words which they hoped would be uttered forcefully and proudly to the abbot. But came the time to speak, Geoffrey had said, "I am leaving the order. My duty lies elsewhere now."

There was silence for a little too long. "As you will." And the abbot nodded, farewelling him with an impatient wave of the fingers.

Geoffrey had walked from the order, a free man. God's will was finally done. But God's will—or was it Adelina's?—was not yet fully realised. In a few minutes, he would be wed. The extended Polignac estate would remain Polignac now. Again he squeezed her hand as if hoping this were not a dream—or if it was, please God never let him wake.

"Why are you shaking so, Geoffrey? What is so terrible about this?"

Geoffrey tried, how he tried, to calm. Happiest of all about this union was Marys. There on her arm, Heracle with no doubt another plan at foot.

From one with nothing to one with all.

To Geoffrey, it seemed a dream still. Throughout the service, however short it was, however rushed, still he waited to wake. And once woken he knew he would be back in his abbey cell, his only company the Book upon the lectern.

It seemed an infinite dream and one which lasted well into the night. There was much feasting at Lavoute, much dancing and gaiety and plenty of wine flowing as easily as water from the deep, bottomless well.

Geoffrey sat in his uncle's chair, his bride beside him, her son running wild and free amid the guests, expertly taking wine when backs were turned. Geoffrey watched the antics of the stocky, solid boy. He knew whose son it was—eyes he had. And while the boy lived—and live he would for a warrior at heart he surely was—his name would remain Dupuy, and with the name came title, lands. All that the father had hoped for. The child reached for another goblet, caught Geoffrey's knowing gaze. But the boy did not put the wine down. A smile played on Geoffrey's lips and he looked away. Indeed the child was too much like his father.

Then Geoffrey looked to the stairs and to the year old stain still present. He had heard of course, how the head had rolled into the middle of the Great Hall, its eyes still open, surprise and a half smile etched there forever on the dead face... But surely that had been gossip. The tale was told so often that exaggeration alone imbued it with more power than was necessary. It was the way of mankind. Geoffrey knew that from the occasional text which was his job to duplicate. But there was no need to think of his old life now. How could one walk ahead in safety if attentions were in the past? But think of the present he could not, not while that stain remained on the stairs.

The boy, tired from too much running and stolen wine, lay his head upon Geoffrey's knee. It was instinct to touch and within moments the boy was asleep. Let him not suffer for his father's sins, Geoffrey thought. He is the only innocent left in this world. He took the child in arms and carried him up to his bed. The boy did not wake. He rolled to his side, and with thumb in mouth continued with his child's dream. His long fair hair curled on his forehead, long lashes rested on his cheek.

Should God give me a son, what will he look like? For that matter, he wondered who he himself looked like. Perhaps the Heracle who fell at Antioch? Geoffrey stepped back. Why couldn't this child resemble his mother? It would be easier for all if this were so. But it would never be. Gabriel, although dead a year, was still in the house.

I have become my uncle, he thought. I am caring for another man's child. I will be his protector, his guardian. His teacher. I have become my uncle.

Please God, let him not suffer the sins of his father.

"Here you are."

Geoffrey turned. Adelina, goblet in hand, bent low as she came in. She too looked down at her sleeping boy. "Geoffrey, there is so much you don't know,"

But Geoffrey touched her lips with his finger. Still he knew what was on her mind, unspoken. Such things as she wanted to say were best left unsaid.

"Do you love me?" she asked.

"Promises made," Geoffrey said softly and took the goblet from her hand. "Promises made, my love. Need I tell you? You are a child no longer. Come," he said.

"Back to the fray?"

"I think not."

# About the Author

Julie Harris is the Australian author of *The Longest Winter, No Exit, Fool's Gold, The Diamond Factory, Beyond Laughter: The Marie Corelli Story, Kizzy, A Tear of Blood, The Site, The Edge of Nowhere, One Act of Kindness*, and more. She has been published in Australia, USA, UK, Germany and France.

Julie lives with her husband in a small country town on the Darling Downs in Queensland, Australia.

For more information, visit her website: http://www.julieh.com.au

www.ingramcontent.com/pod-product-compliance
Lightning Source LLC
Chambersburg PA
CBHW022208010726
47493CB00002B/461